Vampire Vic[3]: Sacrifice

Vampire Vic Trilogy, Book 3

Harris Gray

Cover design by the Killion Group.
Editorial services provided by Adrienne Crezo.
ISBN 978-0988895799

This is a work of fiction. Names, characters, businesses, organizations, places, events and incidents either are the product of the authors' imagination or are used fictitiously. Any resemblance to actual persons, living or dead, events or locales is entirely coincidental.

Cover Design and Interior format by The Killion Group
http://thekilliongroupinc.com

BUCHAREST: MAY 7, 1586

The slayer ran down the narrow lane faster than the icy cobblestones suggested. He had received bad news at the Bucharest gate from the village drunk, a former slayer named Skender who had always shown a special fondness for young Trubadur Maistru.

Pickled Skender, as preserved as Granny Maistru's peppers, still wearing that ratty woolen toga and the skeptical face. As for Trubadur, he had been gone nine years, since his 16th birthday; and his face had recently been rearranged by the Morbius carrier. Yet he was instantly recognizable for Skender.

With his mother's complexion, Trubadur was often mistaken for a Turk. While the sultan in Constantinople had ordered the construction of these fortified walls, they were now manned by Wallachians to keep the Turks *out*. But the guards had stood aside as drunken Skender vociferously vouched for him.

"How did you know I was coming?" said Trubadur.

"No time." Skender pulled Trubadur by the front of his lucky shirt, tore it in fact, and pointed into the heart of the village. "The carrier is here. And he has made his choice."

"Halt." A burly guard lowered his halberd in front of Trubadur.

Of course it couldn't be that easy. Not in these troubled times.

"My name is Trubadur Maistru. The greatest vampire slayer of his generation. Son of Alexandru, descendant of Petrarch Vigilus, slayer—"

"Your hat, boy." The guard nodded at the tall badger fur cap. "I didn't hear a 'boyar' or 'prince' or even a 'duke' among the ancestral peasants you listed. No one to merit a hat of that height."

Trubadur tugged the cap tighter on his head. "You'll be eating those words, as soon as I finish my business here."

"You *have* no business here until you give me that hat."

Trubadur fumed. "If there comes a day when only I stand between you and a ravenous vampire, rest assured I will think twice."

"And if you were standing between me and your whore mother," said the guard, "I'd run you through with my cock without noticing, skinny peasant." His comrade got a big kick out of that one. "Now give it to me." The guard swiped at the hat.

Trubadur swatted away the attempt, entered the guards' quarters and set his hat on a shelf. His head felt small and cold. "I'll be back for this. Trust me, I'll know if it touched your greasy melon."

"It will never touch my melon, and that won't be grease, runt."

The guards' braying followed them into the village. Drunken Skender tried to keep up, but Tru's feet had wings. Over the past 15 days they had carried him from Târgu Mureş in Transylvania across the Carpathians and under the shadow of cursed Castle Bran, and finally into to his Wallachian homeland. He had likely traversed the same path taken weeks earlier by the vampire Mortimer Canterpark, the Morbius carrier, who had no doubt shape-shifted into a wolf to speed his journey.

His ran toward the residence Skender had seen Canterpark enter. Skender's directions were vague but he promised Trubadur would find it; and now as he flew past the tannery on the Uliţa Mare, he picked up a trail of red stones.

"Ho there, young man," Stefan Ionescu the tanner hailed from his shop doorway. "Time to be indoors!"

"Bolt your own doors, Domnul Ionescu." Trubadur slowed to a backward trot. "I am returned a slayer!"

"We have a few of those roaming the streets, too. All now with fangs."

Trubadur ran on. The red-splotched stones led him away from the guildsmen's street and down a cramped, twisting lane.

This neighborhood was familiar to him. For two years until

the day he left Bucharest, he had spent much of his time at the Rákóczi residence. Too much time—his love for the Rákóczis' daughter, Nadia, had distracted from his slayer training, necessitating the move to Târgu Mureş.

Trubadur didn't return under the illusion Nadia had saved herself for him. Nine years was a long time. He hadn't waited—his two children were eager to join him "as soon as father slayed the dragon." They couldn't know that this dragon could only be slain through mortal sacrifice.

Ugenosz and Stela would at least find comfort in the memory of their father's bravery, and the world's adulation for the name Maistru.

Boyar Bortalyu surely hadn't waited for Trubadur to clear the northern horizon before making his bid for Nadia's hand. But who knew; Bortalyu had been nicknamed "vampire fruit" for his rosy complexion. It was a good bet he had been turned. Trubadur imagined arriving just as vampire Bortalyu finally overcame Nadia's fierce resistance, to drive a stake through the bloodsucker's heart and carry his love to safety amidst the cheers of the crowd.

This fantasy had provided the resolve to continue when the never-ending Carpathian winter and a pack of starving chamois had nearly claimed him on the pass. To hold Nadia one more time in his arms, for one long, long night and maybe a goodly portion of the next day, that provided all the courage Trubadur needed to fulfill his destiny.

Even if she was married; a mission as saintly as his should absolve one discreet dalliance.

Now it appeared there would be no time for even one night with Nadia. Canterpark had chosen his Morbius. If Trubadur couldn't find him before he turned some poor innocent maiden into the most powerful vampire of all—and it had to be a woman, slayer lore made clear that the evil of Morbius could be carried by a man but only manifested in a woman—Trubadur wasn't sure he would be a match for her.

He had to destroy Canterpark before he passed the curse! In the past few years there had been an increase in the number of special, "greater" vampires who were nearly impossible to kill. If Morbius was reincarnated to lead them, slayers would be no match. Humanity would soon be no more.

Between the relentless agonizing cold that had moved in to stay some years ago, and the ever-growing packs of two-legged predators, most of Bucharest stayed behind doors. Now the setting sun drove the last intrepid few inside as Trubadur followed Skender's daubs of pig blood onto the Rákóczis' lane. Mortimer Canterpark stumbled out of a doorway 20 paces away.

Not nearly as dashing as Trubadur remembered, the vampire lurched over the cobblestones in his direction, passing under one stone arch and then the next, where the slayer waited in shadow. Trubadur stuck out his foot and down the vampire tumbled in a heap.

What good fortune—a drunken carrier. From his satchel, Trubadur pulled a double-pointed stake. A witch stick that the Târgu Mureș town fathers were certainly unhappy to lose, carved from an unearthed cherry log laced with iron. Wood that sank, except in the presence of evil. It had never failed to identify one of the witches responsible for Transylvania's otherwise inexplicable crop-and-livestock-destroying weather.

In Târgu Mureș, he had intended to lure Canterpark to the parapet of the town's going-to-ruins fortress and tackle him over the edge, a double-death sacrificial plunge. Instead, he had been beaten nearly to death and tossed solo into the former moat.

Upon waking from the ensuing coma, Trubadur had stolen the witch stick and whittled the ends to points. The potter had granted use of his kiln—God bless him, the potter at least understood gradations of evil, and where vampires and Morbius in particular ranked. After a series of firing and cooling that filled every cherry-wood pore with iron, the gleaming black stake was so weighty that it might not float in the presence of Lucifer himself. It was now made for sinking *into* evil.

Trubadur dragged the carrier vampire into the yellow light cast by a cross of candles doing a poor job of warding away evil from this lane. Through the timely tear in his shirt he jammed a point of the stake into his flesh and started the opposite point toward Canterpark's heart.

His own heart stopped. Blood stained the vampire's chin. And that scent on the vampire, it was … familiar.

Canterpark opened his eyes. Those eyes had haunted

Trubadur's fevered coma nightmares, orange-hot embers from Hell. But now that light was fading, chased deeper into oblivion by the candle's flame.

"You're too late, slayer. It is done."

"No!" Trubadur removed the stake from his own flesh and started it toward Canterpark's heart. "If you think that will save you—"

"Do your worst." Tears filled Canterpark's eyes, taking up the candlelight to create the illusion of liveliness. "But you must hurry." The air left his cheeks, and then the flesh began to abandon them as well. His last words whistled through a dissolving esophagus. "I'm dying, for some reason."

Trubadur leaped back as the vampire's handsome wool garments shrink-wrapped his ribs. A chill wind swept down the twisting lane and ruffled the corpse's blouse, briefly exposing mottled molten flesh. Trubadur ran for the residence Canterpark had exited. Pig's blood stained the door. He choked back a scream as he burst into the Rákóczi home.

No sign of Nadia's parents; only *her* smell lived there. That intoxicating scent she had possessed at age 16, that Canterpark had lately worn. A ladder led to her bedroom loft. As Trubadur climbed, he understood Nadia's presence here in her parents' home likely meant she had never married. How little that mattered now.

"Oh, Nadia."

She lay drawn up in a pathetic curl on the bed. By the light of the surrounding candles he saw dried tears on her face, and the mark of the beast on her throat. He wailed silently. Trubadur's body shook as he fitted the stake back into the pilot hole in his chest, the other end aimed at Nadia's perfect breast.

Now he *really* looked at her, and took in the air. This time there was no muting his cry.

"You *laid* with him!"

Nadia opened her eyes. "Trubadur? Is that you? My love—"

"Stop!" He gripped her throat and pressed the stake into her, fighting her attempt to slow its penetration. "How could you? How in the name of Heaven could you?"

"Please, Tru." Nadia's eyes went wide with terror. She struggled to speak through his strangulation. "It isn't as you think."

He clamped a hand over her mouth, unable to hear another word. "He was *Morbius*! He was the carrier, you stupid, stupid—" Trubadur used his body weight to force the stake down into them both, sobbing. "Don't you see, you fool? You're the one now, Nadia. You're *it*."

Nadia shook her head, wild-eyed, her hands slipping on the slick stake.

He peeled back Nadia's lip, revealing the hint of fangs already forming. His face contorted.

Nadia read it and went limp. The stake wedged between two of her ribs, forcing them apart.

He was horrified by her submission, and then overcome. He backed off the stake and gathered to hurl himself off the loft. Nadia caught him and they tumbled together against the bed.

She lay on top of him. "My love."

"Don't call me that." He twisted away but she held him tight, her blood mixing with his.

"You can't understand what I went through without you." She spoke quickly before his next attempt to flee or slay her. "After you left me, Father and Mother disappeared without a trace. My life became nothing."

"I didn't leave you. I had to train—"

"I know, my love. Trubadur, he—Mortimer, he loved me."

He bucked her off and again pinned her down. "He *used* you. He *chose* you because of what you mean to me. Because he thought I would be unable to slay you."

And was Canterpark right? Trubadur Maistru, heir to slayer royalty, descendant of Petrarch Vigilus who gave his life in a failed attempt to destroy the prior incarnation of Morbius, unwilling to fulfill his destiny and slay the vampire queen? Trubadur was devastated to know the answer was *yes*.

He slapped her, and again. He expected savage retaliation and instead saw his intoxicating Nadia staring back at him.

The Slavic curve and Roman intensity of her eyes, he had never forgotten them or the turbulence they brought to his insides. A fearful thrill gripped his body, like flying on the rope swing off the bank of the Dambovița River and into the void.

He worked up his last ounce of courage and saliva and spit in her face. “Vampire whore.”

This time she didn’t hold him; he half-climbed and fell down the ladder. He threw the stake into the hearth’s glowing embers and fled into the silent, freezing Bucharest night.

ATLANTIC CITY: MODERN DAY

When the vampires convened at the Boardwalk Hotel in Atlantic City, the air was filled with excitement, nervousness and anticipation. There was a storm brewing. The vampire community leadership was at their version of the G8 Summit. Lower-ranking (not to be confused with lower-order) vampires were welcome and encouraged to come to Atlantic City, but were not allowed in the meeting. Vampires leaders from Africa, the Middle East, the Far East, etc., played slots and craps while the select Group of 8 (which was really 11) met inside a plush conference room.

The table was big and round with placards assigning seats to these important vampires. It was five minutes ’til 11 p.m. The meeting was to start at 11 sharp. Important decisions were to be finalized tonight, followed by a feeding frenzy and orgy set up by the famous Australian party vampiress, Kelly Kale.

The agenda was set and the meeting was intended to move swiftly and without too much discussion. Details had been in the works for years, the wheels were in motion and there should be no turning back.

The current chairman of this council, the vampire Doyon, Joshua Linger, second-in-command at the U.S. National Security Agency, was accustomed to dealing with this kind of crowd: obstinate, loud, unruly, prone to getting off-track, and sometimes raunchy. On the other hand, the attendees knew what was at stake (vampires generally abhorred that figure of speech unless it referred to being all-in at the poker table), and the symbolism in the venue chosen for this meeting was not lost on them. They were taking a huge gamble.

Plus, Linger had emailed everyone a reminder of the severe consequences of going rogue off a council agenda. Robert's famous Rules of Order were in fact adapted from the original fifth century vampire meeting rules (Blasmigord's Council Conduct Code), shorn of the physical penalties. Those penalties had not been enforced in 77 years, but none were willing to take the chance.

Murmuring continued until 10:59. At 11 sharp, Joshua Linger moved quietly and quickly to his assigned seat at the "head" of the round table. Those who were still at the coffee pump pot got to their seats posthaste.

Linger cleared his throat. "Call to order and roll call."

There was palpable tension, nervousness, and tempered optimism in the room. Linger motioned the vampire to his left to proceed.

"Mao Fe Te from East Asia," Mao said with a toothy grin. His fangs had an inward curve which made his accent sound like a stereotype.

Since the Vampire Internecine War of 1936, all references to nationality were prohibited. They were only allowed to identify a broad region. The vampires were all very partial to their particular regions. "You can take the vampire out of the country," the saying went, "but not the country out of the vampire. Without a lot of torture."

Next vampire at the table stood and bowed. "Katanze Utz from Northeast Asia." Katanze and Mao could have been brothers. Except Katanze's fangs pushed outward like fishhooks.

They also got along like brothers—swimmingly one minute and *almost* at each other's throats the next.

Adamo Abele slowly rose. Smiled wide with perfect dentures. Pronounced his name as if talking to little children. "Aadddammmo Aaabbelle from the North-Central Mediterranean." He looked confidently around the room. Having taken his place at the table four centuries ago, Adamo was the second-oldest member of the 8.

(Which was actually 11, and which some wags had begun to call the V-8; this insult fell on deaf ears amongst this ancient group, who liked words beginning with *v* and so had embraced the term.)

The newest member of the V-8 (or 11) was the beautiful Kelly Kale. A permanent and perfect 27-year-old sun-bleached professional surfer, Kelly threw decadent parties, swaying and blackmailing dignitaries all over the world. Humans and vampires alike threw themselves at Kelly's feet, willfully giving in to their own demise. "South Oceana is in this house. I want to remind everyone—"

The Doyon Linger looked sternly at Kelly; she left unfinished her invite to the après party. Linger made a mental note to have a short refresher conversation with her.

A well-dressed, heavy-set vamp with a pencil moustache went next. "Placido Perez from Central America," he said softly. Always a good listener, Placido took in all conversations. Well-spoken with a golden voice and the gift of gab. He gave Kelly the *call me* sign as the next vampire stood up.

"Dikembe Mutombo, representing the great continent of Africa." Yes, that Dikembe. "I am very pleased—"

"Boris Dostonov," interrupted a vampire who looked like a seven-foot-tall angry Boris Yeltsin. "Central Asia." Dostonov epitomized the need for and challenge of moving to a One World Vampire Order. When Angry Boris growled, "Central Asia," everyone present formed a vivid mental picture of the borders of Mother Russia.

"Titathia Babas, Scandinavia, present." Titathia was the oldest of the group, veteran of six centuries of artful blood-taking and deception. A shrewd negotiator, Titathia was one of Linger's key allies. Always in a pure white dress with an aquamarine tiara, she stood just under five feet tall with flowing blond hair, the appearance of a nine-year old girl, and the strength of ten vampires.

Next was Moanmar Saladat. "Moanmar Saladat from the Mid-Eastern region of the Middle East, present."

Linger frowned. "The chair requests Mr. Saladat in the future be a little less specific identifying his region of representation."

The next delegate stood. "Ari Ben-Begin, just a little west of Mr. Saladat, present." Ari spoke rapidly, like a machine gun.

Last was the Doyon. "Joshua Linger, North America." Linger was a modernist, an idealist who believed vampires must abandon ancient ethnic, religious, and nationalist animosities.

"Blood, blood everywhere, and not a drop to drink," was his rallying cry. "Now please be seated. Before we start, let's all remember this is a private meeting. No public comment will be allowed and no loose lips to the media will be tolerated. Cone of silence. Thanks." He checked the agenda. "Will someone make a motion to approve the minutes from the previous board meeting? Any discussion or questions?"

Saladat spoke. "Everything looks fine, except there are several English spelling errors."

All eyes went to the human stenographer in the corner of the room. She grinned and shivered at the same time. The room's lights had been disabled, instead lit by hundreds of candles. Bright red carpet had been laid, accented with freshly black-painted walls to give the room a gothic vibe.

Linger raised his eyebrows. "Is there a motion?"

Titathia spoke. "I motion to approve the minutes with the caveat that the spelling is corrected."

Linger nodded. "Is there a second?"

Saladat smiled. "Second."

Linger looked around. "All in favor?" A round of ayes. "Any opposed?" No answer. "Let the minutes show that it was unanimous." He stood a little straighter. "First item of business. Only item of business. Our goal here, our goal as a species, is simple. No longer will we simply survive."

A number of the delegates pounded the table.

"For 400 years since the Romanian genocide we have assimilated into the human community while rebuilding our numbers, evolved and lesser vampires alike. Now over the past three decades we have assumed positions of power as befits our natural superiority."

Adamo Abele stood and spoke as if a teacher to his developmentally disabled students. "And so it is important we do not lose these hard-won positions."

Linger bared his fangs. "Did I open the floor to discussion?"

Abele sat.

Linger continued. "We have never been better positioned. And frankly the world has never needed our guidance more than it does today."

Abele jumped up. Linger bared his fangs. Abele raised his

hand. Linger steamed but recognized him.

"Our Doyon speaks of guidance. But what he actually means is domination."

"Of course," said Saladat. "We are vampires. It is our destiny."

"And give up everything we've gained?" said Abele. Adamo liked to play both sides of the fence. Most of all, he liked grafting. Grafting required humans (vampires were unreliable moneymakers), which required peace. "Humans *wait* for that excuse, to annihilate us. To send us the way of the Aboriginal Tasmanians, the Volga Bulgarians, the, the—"

"The dodo," said Kelly Kale.

Linger crossed his arms and scowled. "I guess the floor is open." He looked at Titathia Babas. "Do you have something to add, Tita?"

The little vampire girl crossed her ankles, feet swinging under her chair. "I was in Transylvania 400 years ago. I was *drawn* there. I was drawn to *her*. I barely escaped with my life. I've seen what happens when we are not united. And when we wait too long to strike."

"Come now." Abele looked around the table. "Are we going to listen to a little girl?"

Tita Babas shrieked and jumped onto her chair, restrained by Boris Dostonov as she started across the table.

"That was a joke," said Abele. "Of course I have all the respect in the world for our esteemed Scandinavian colleague. But neither was I born last century; none of us were. And we all know that every time we have tried to assert control, humans have nearly wiped us out. We are too few!"

"Unfortunately," said Linger, "we do not have the luxury of waiting. A small but well-organized network of slayers recognizes the danger we represent. And they have the Eye at their disposal."

"Morbius!" said Katanze Utz. "Victor Thetherson!"

"Morbius is not the Eye," said Ari Ben-Begin. "Morbius is the most fearsome vampire of all time. He is the Savior who will lead us to glory! And I have heard Victor Thetherson is a putz."

Little Tita climbed back down into her chair. "I'm afraid Morbius and the Eye are one and the same."

"That makes no sense," said Ben-Begin.

"I was there!" screamed Tita. "I saw it! They say Thetherson has the Eye, so he is Morbius! Although I am not drawn to him. Not at all."

"But Thetherson helps that slayer, what's-his-face," said Moanmar Saladat. "Come on please, does that make any sense?"

"That's the way it works!" screamed Babas.

"Order." Linger possessed a voice that triggered a warning in every vampire's ear. "There are two mistakes every vanquished people have made throughout history: Waiting for someone else to save them, and turning against each other instead of the real enemy. Morbius or no Morbius, the time is now for us to make our move. And it will only work if we are united."

"Please take no offense, Doyon," said Saladat. "But if we had listened to you in '36, we would have been huddled on the precipice in Spain." During the Internecine War, Linger—then José Linaré—had preached carving out southeast Spain as a refuge, their own Zion on the shores of the Mediterranean. "Easy for our enemies to push off the continent, off the map. Like the Yazidis."

"Or scattered to the four corners without a country," said angry Dostonov. "Like the Gypsies!"

Linger sighed. "I present to you"—he pointed at Dostonov—"the second trait of a vanquished people."

"And I present to you," Dostonov roared, "another 'man of the people' who only thinks of his own power!"

"My friends," said Abele, getting to his feet as every other vampire rose, fangs bared and eyes lit for battle. "I fear I have created this dissent. We cannot tear each other apart. We must remain united—on that I agree with our Doyon."

Linger stood with eyes closed and head bowed, ostensibly in his own thoughts but clearly tensed for action.

"And as the Doyon also said," Abele used his slow, soothing, teacher voice, "we have finally attained enviable positions. Why risk everything now?"

"I think," said Mao Fe Te, "the esteemed and very rich Adamo Abele is against revolution for a very personal reason."

Abele's face purpled. The slaying of Charles Valery a few months prior had unnerved him. Valery was the first; an alarming number of vampires enjoying lucrative, long-term symbioses with humans had now been slain. Eliminating conservatives was the first step toward revolution.

Abele knew who was behind it; he had been trying to find Cornelius W. Sanders (or whatever he was calling himself these days) before it was too late. Before revolution was on them.

He was here to separate conservatives like himself from the radicals who welcomed the next coming of Morbius. "And how did revolution treat the Chinese, Mao?"

"He does have a point there," said Katanze Utz.

"The revolution," Mao's voice rose, "treated us much better than the Japanese!"

"Please," said Saladat. "If Ari and I can get along after everything the Jews have done to the Arabs—"

"Of course you refer to reclaiming the ancient territory of our birthright," said Ben-Begin. "Which was sold to us by Arabs, who wrote the book on money-grubbing."

"I'm logging various procedural violations," said Linger, jotting notes. "We *will* have discipline."

Dostonov leaned back in his chair, satisfied by the dissent. He raised his hand in mocking request to be recognized. "Teacher? Is that a violation?" He pointed to Placido Perez and Kelly Kale walking hand in hand for the cloak room door.

All heads swiveled to the lovebirds, and then to a ruckus beyond the double-door meeting room entrance. On the casino floor, mayhem was unloading. As Linger motioned for the human stenographer to check the door, three slayers fell into the room. They had been crawling across the drop ceiling, à la *Aliens*.

"Right on time," said Doyon Linger.

An hour earlier, Slayer Sven stood in the back room of the Denny's off Atlantic City Parkway. There were 100 slayers in a room with a posted capacity of 55. Most stood, having many conversations all at once. Sven was the de facto leader, but really, leader in name only.

"Order. Order," Sven demanded. "Order!" A number of slayers stopped their talking. A few completely ignored him.

A big slayer dressed in Viking garb spoke loudly, "Everybody shut it!" He banged his Mjolnir on a small table. The table split in two.

Sven shook his head looking at the broken table. "Thanks, and you have to pay for zat." He surveyed the room. It looked more like a cosplay convention than a bunch of for-hire slayers. There were even a few furries toward the back of the room. He hoped some of those present were actually cosplayers who had lost their way. "First," Sven shouted, "I want to make sure zat all of you know zees ees a *slayer* meeting!"

No one left.

Sven shrugged. "I want to thank all zose who are here, and zee multitudes in zee parking lot across zee street."

A designated few in the Denny's banquet room streamed video so the slayers in the parking lot could follow along.

"Second, I want you to be sure you understand *why* you are here."

The room became a bit more silent. Then, a shout from a guy in the back dressed as Daredevil. "We are here to kill vampires!"

The crowd erupted, "Kill, kill! Kill!" Over and over. Finally, a man in uniform came over to Sven and whispered in his ear.

"Okay, okay!" Sven raised his hands. "Zee manager here at Denny's asks us to settle down. Let's get zees going, so zat we can get rid of some vermin!"

"Hear, hear," the Viking said.

Sven held up a piece of paper with notes scribbled on it. "Everybody should have gotten zee notes and agenda online. I hope you all memorized it. We have zee numbers, so we should overpower zee vamps pretty easily. My intel says zer are 40 to 50 vampires in, out and around zee main meeting room. Zee information we have gathered from our sources is true. Our infiltration of zee vampire nation is well established."

Sven knew they would lose some slayers, but they had numbers. Numbers always prevailed.

"I have a question," said an old man dressed as Dumbledore. "Where is Eugene? Our leader."

"Eugene, he could not make it. He is on a top secret mission. Even I don't know where he ees."

That was true; Sven did not know where Eugene was currently located. Mostly because he had stopped returning

Sven's calls. Eugene was not much for teaming up. He liked the accolades and the attention, but did not want to be part of a team. Unless it was Amway.

Dumbledore seemed to be okay with that answer. "What about the meeting room? The vamps in that room will be evolved. We need to know their Heels. Like that seer vampire, what's-his-name." More mumbling and talking throughout the meeting room.

Sven raised his hands again to quiet the crowd, less effectively this time. "We have zee numbers! Zer advanced bodies and tactics will not matter. Zer Heels won't matter, either. We are trained to keel, and keel we weel."

The crowd seemed to like that. They whisper-chanted, "Keel, keel, keel!"

A man all in black piped up. "Can we hit the slots before we start the slaying, or should we wait until after?"

Sven looked annoyed and disappointed. "We weel not be playing slots before or after. Some of you weel die. Thees is no joke. You need to get your minds right." Sven tapped his head. "Zees things out there aren't make-believe zombies. Zey are real. Real killers. Sure, zey are no match for us and our numbers. But keep your head on a sweevel."

A big burly man with a stovetop hat stepped forward. "I'm out. We are not prepared, and I don't want to die." Gasps and catcalls followed him out the door.

"Zees is your last chance to back out. Zer weel be no loss of face if you don't participate." Sven looked around the room. "Who am I keeding? If you walk away from zees, you will be branded a pussy and kicked out of zee slayer club. But seriously, some of you weel probably die. But dying for our cause is worth every drop of blood. Mostly zers. But some of ours weel speel, as well."

The crowd seemed split, some contemplating leaving, some upset that they drove all this way and could not gamble. Most talking and bragging about the carnage that was to ensue.

On the far side of the meeting room, a large woman dressed as Xena: Warrior Princess and a small woman dressed like Zelda made their presence known. They looked at each other and yelled, "They may take our lives, but they will never take OUR

FREEDOM!"

The crowd went wild. Cheering and yelling. The manager of Denny's be damned.

Sven let the crowd go nuts for about a minute, then spoke up. "Okay, let's go to zee rendezvous and take out zose vamps!" He led the charge out of the Denny's banquet room.

Joined by the overflow slayers from the parking lot, 300 motivated and misguided slayers ran into the Boardwalk Hotel screaming, not knowing who to kill or where the meeting room was. Sven was upset. He turned to the five slayers who had stuck close to him. "What's going on? Zees was not our plan. I explicitly communicated zat we were to infiltrate slowly, hanging around zee fringes, mostly outside, while *les trois mousquetaires* went through zee ceiling to zee main room. Zen we wait for zer sign. Zen, and only zen, were we supposed to go in 'guns a-blazin'."

A man in a wrestling singlet with a crossbow and shield looked at Sven. "A lot of people were having a hard time with your email. So it went around the web like a bad telephone call with spotty reception. No one seemed to know what to do or when to do it." The other four agreed with the crossbowed man.

Sven threw his hands wide. "What? No one could open my email? I used both EarthLink *and* Netscape." He clucked. "Good thing we have numbers. Because zees ees going to be a slaughter."

He was right, the carnage was swift and severe. Hotel security tried to do I.D. checks and were quickly overrun by the army of slayers, who the security personnel would later recall as "psychotic weirdos." The vampires enjoying the casino were caught off guard and still nearly wiped out the slayers in a matter of minutes. For every step forward, the vampires (and hotel security) killed a dozen slayers.

Sven and his merry men steered clear of the fray, hugging the walls and working their way to the meeting room. They could only watch the slaughter. Lots of angry vampires. The carnage was gruesome. Body parts all over. Some vamps feeding. Many slayers ran out of the casino once the fighting really started. Many vampires followed. They were not kind.

Sven was not surprised to see a lot of casualties. He was

surprised that the carnage was this brutal, unforgiving and immense. Screams rang out. Screams of anger and rage, but mostly it was screams of pain, misery and sorrow.

Sven pressed himself harder against the wall. He vacillated between running for his life and busting down the meeting room door. Meanwhile he noticed something odd and quite reasonable at the same time. Even though many of the gambling patrons ran for the exits, several still gambled. Cigarettes buttoned to their lips. Oxygen tanks doing their thing and their hands on the bandit or buttons. Sven surmised that death was coming fairly soon to these gamblers anyhow and a hot slot machine was not to be left alone.

The Viking grabbed Sven by the shoulders. He looked like he was going to cry. "We are all going to die."

"Yes, someday but not today." Sven recalled a line from one of his favorite movies. "We came here to chew gum and keek ass. And we are all out of zee gum."

The vamps guarding the meeting room couldn't help themselves, they left their post to join the fracas. Seizing the moment, Sven ran to the meeting room. One of his merry band ran away.

Three hideous vampires saw them and charged. The singlet-wearing man got off several shots with his repeating crossbow. Striking each of them. Slowing, but not killing any of the three vampires. Singlet Man held his crossbow up like a cross in an attempt to protect the slayers behind him while they attempted to gain access to the meeting room.

Sven tried to pick the lock with a Leatherman and a bobby pin. The three vampires tore at Singlet Man, screeching and yelling. The singlet man was no more. A piece of him here, a piece there.

His brutal death seemed to fire up Sven's remaining team. Twins in long black dusters and black cowboy hats protected his flank. They swung sawed-off shotguns from inside their coats and fired wildly. They both hit the first vampire square in the chest and he fell hard. The Viking swung his Thor hammer and sent the other two vamps tumbling to the floor, temporarily out of commission. The vamp with the two gaping chest wounds opened his eyes and made a motion to get up. Sven looked over his shoulder and pulled out a .44 magnum and split the vampire's head in two. "Zat's how eet's done."

He turned his attention back to the door. Then gave up, looked at the Viking, motioned to the door.

The Viking stood tall, put his hammer on his shoulder like a major league slugger and took a big swing.

On the inside, the meeting room was calm, collected and angry. The three misfit *mousquetaires* had crashed through the ceiling onto the big table. Two of the slayers were dispatched posthaste. They had run around wildly, right into Kelly Kale. She and Boris Dostonov tore them limb from limb. Gnashing their teeth and actually pulled their arms off. Tossed them to and fro around the room, bouncing off the walls like ping-pong balls. They were dead within seconds, but the annihilation of the two slayers continued.

The third slayer was put in a chair for interrogation. Titathia Babas worked him over with quick body blows. Placido Perez looked sternly at the terrified slayer. "Sir, let me tell you, you are going to die. This can come slowly. Hours will turn to days, days into months. The savagery that will come to you over and over again will be never-ending." Perez leaned in close. Calmly looked at the sobbing slayer. "Just tell us what we need to know. How did you know we were here? Why did you choose today and who is your leader?"

Babas walked behind the slayer. "You are mine; I will make this quick. If you talk to my friend here."

The other vampires were now re-convened around the table. Most were on their phones trying to figure out if they should join the fray outside or wait it out.

Linger too was on his phone. "Help, we are under attack at the Atlantic Boardwalk Hotel. Please send the authorities."

The slayer spilled his guts. Figuratively and literally. "We got direction from Sven. Sven the slayer. He—" He tried to collect himself. "He's our leader."

Perez looked dubious. "I doubt it. Tita, hit him again."

The slayer cringed. "It's true, he is leading us. He developed the plan." He swallowed hard. "We were hoping to get the great Eugene Foreman to help us, but he is nowhere to be found."

With a bang, the door of the meeting room split wide open.

There stood a big man dressed as a Viking, and an average-sized man dressed as a mime. The mime charged straight for Perez, firing his pistol, winging Perez in both his forearms. The mime's pistol clicked empty. With no time to reload, he hit Perez square in the throat with the butt of his gun. Perez's eyes widened. He grabbed for his throat. For an instant the room went eerily silent. Perez looked around in amazement. Before anyone could open their mouths, he hit the floor in a limp mass.

"Zee Heel," the mime whispered in awe.

Titathia Babas went crazy apeshit. She twisted and pulled off the captured slayer's head and used it to beat the mime's head over and over until both heads were mush. It was a bloody, unrecognizable mess.

Mao Fe Te and Katanze Utz each pulled an arm off the Viking man.

"Good," said Saladat while Mao and Utz took turns taking vicious bites out of the Viking's neck. "I hate Vikings. Present company excepted," he said to Babas.

"You think every Scandinavian was a nomadic plunderer?" Babas yelled at him. "You stereotyping offensive bastard! My ancestors were fishermen!"

Saladat apologized. The V-8 (now V-10) was spent. Delirious with anger and sadness. Outside the room, no slayer was left alive. Most of those who ran had been taken care of as well. Very few escaped. It was a total slaying debacle.

Joshua Linger greeted the arriving Atlantic County SWAT. He pointed at the meeting room, shaking his head mournfully, appearing to be in shock, needing to sit down.

"Look at him cozy up to the humans," said angry, blood-up Boris Dostonov, watching from the main room doorway. "We should tear these humans limb from limb and drink, drink, drink! Until they recognize our strength and bow to us!"

"No," said Adamo Abele. "The humans must never fear us. Respect, yes. Fear, no. We should tear *Linger* to pieces for putting us in this position."

"Shh, both of you," said Kelly Kale, standing between them, arm around Dostonov's, holding him in place, hand up Abele's silk shirt, scratching his back. "Our leader has a plan. He knows exactly what he is doing."

18,000 FEET ABOVE GILROY, CALIFORNIA

The Predator drone circled, biding its time. What a beautiful clear blue day. Great for hunting.

This Predator would be busy over the coming days. Today kicked off the killing spree. A targeted spree, if there is such a thing. The drone's targets had been selected—it was a long list. More anti-vampire leaders would be added to the list as time went on, until they changed their tune or were no more.

Down below in a coffeeshop in Gilroy, the garlic capital of the world, the targets were talking in library voices to one another as the Predator's pilots listened in.

"For all the ways you eavesdrop on everyone," said the first gentleman, "shouldn't you know how to stop everyone else from snooping on you?"

"Some of these vamps are top-level intelligence operatives," the second gentleman said. "They have tools you and I haven't dreamed of. I'm sure they knew the slayers were coming. Wouldn't have mattered. Short of bazooka-ing them, they're damn near invincible."

"A regular fucking Bay of Pigs, that's what that was."

"It's war, Mark."

The first gentleman—Mark—scowled. "Come on."

"Sorry. Z."

"Oh for Christ's sake."

These two gentlemen, heads of a large social networking company and a large federal department, had gone to great lengths to mask their identities. But they were so predictable that the vampires intent on vaporizing them had enjoyed plenty of lead time to put a microphone under their table. So predictable that the vampires even knew which table to bug.

Everyone is that predictable. That's the premise of the XFP software system. Collect enough data from computers, tablets and smart devices, traffic cameras, credit card readers, drones, etc., feed it into the same type of modeling software that predicts the weather and the stock markets (not nearly the creatures of habit that humans are), and an interested person can pinpoint someone's location at any time of the day or night with uncanny accuracy.

These two men may not have even realized that they had a proclivity to schedule private meetings in the garlic capital of the world. There is a subconscious appeal to such a place for folks who fear vampires. To reduce the chance of the vampires figuring them out, they consciously mixed up their meeting places, only going to the First Street Coffee Shop occasionally.

Every other time, to be exact. That is one of our habits, as a species. That's how we mix it up. That was an easy one for the XFP system.

"So now what?" This from Mark. Mark Z.

"What do you think? We need help."

"What the hell have you been doing? I give you every bit of data we have on them."

"That's passive collection. We need you to get active."

"I think this conversation is over."

"Don't act the saint, M-, uh, *man*. You manipulate your users all the time."

"Fuck you."

"Mm-hm."

"Okay. Why the hell not. It's Armageddon anyway. What do you want?"

"We need to know their Heels. Their weaknesses."

"I should start a survey? 'Hey, community, we're curious about your unique Achilles' heels. We promise not to sell it to any third-party marketers or slayers.'"

"Funny. No. These vamps, we're learning there are some ethnic consistencies in their Heels."

"Of course. It's evolution at its finest."

"That's right. Know the Heels of an Irish-Pashtun, a Scotch-

Indian, and a Brit whose great-great-great-grandmother was a scandalous fraternizer with the subjects of the Raj, and we're on to something. So you plant some faux advertising designed to appeal to folks with something to hide or protect—say, ads for steel nut cups."

"Real subtle."

"You're the marketing genius, you'll figure it out. You plant the ads and see who clicks. Couple that with all the data you already collect, their conversations, their 'likes' and what-not—mine the hell out of it, and the patterns will emerge."

"Sounds great, except for one thing."

"Yeah?"

"I don't trust you any more than I trust them."

"Fuck you, Mark. On behalf of every federal employee, I resent that."

"Fuck you, John Crittenden."

John Crittenden was the head of Homeland Security. But the name didn't seem to ring a bell for anyone in the coffeeshop. Nor did anyone recognize Mark Z. Just two hours south of the center of the tech universe, the garlic capital was in a completely different orbit.

One head overcame his animosity for the other and a deal was struck. As they walked out of the coffeeshop, the drone 18,000 feet up locked on the men and launched two Hellfire missiles.

The drone was actually locked on their cell phones. These major heads were of course intelligent enough not to use their own phones; they had each picked up a cheap prepaid phone for this meeting. However, the fact that they each felt compelled to *have* a phone was a security weakness that was exploited when each of them had made calls and sent texts. The Predator's pilots received information from a "dirtbox" that mimicked and overrode nearby cell towers, vacuuming up every bit of information from every phone in the vicinity. The heads' phones were easily identified.

Cheap phones with cheap GPS abilities—these phones couldn't locate themselves any more accurately than "somewhere within a 50-yard radius." And so neither could the Predator.

A rule of thumb in the U.S. government's targeted assassinations program was that a strike in the presence of 30 or more potentially impacted innocents required the president's sign-off. This implicitly suggested that fewer than 30 non-targeted casualties were acceptable. The Predator's vampire handlers were very much creatures of the federal intelligence network. By the dirtbox's reckoning, there were only 27 civilians within the 50-yard margin for error.

Hellfire missiles are supersonic, which means they arrived before their god-awful shriek. The first indication of the strike for either of the men was a horizontal hailstorm of bricks from the coffeeshop. The major heads (along with their minor bodies) were blasted to shreds.

Two hours later, Joshua Linger—high-ranking employee in the NSA, and a vampire—addressed the nation.

"Good afternoon. Earlier today the U.S. government authorized the first-ever drone strike on American soil. This precision strike was in response to an act of terrorism. Yesterday a group of terrorists attempted to assassinate various high-ranking officials of this government and governments from nations around the world. The terrorists managed to assassinate Placido Perez, chief of intelligence from Panama, before they were thankfully disabled.

"The National Security Agency and the Central Intelligence Agency with approval from the White House, authorized and coordinated the precision drone strike today. Killed were John Crittenden, the head of Homeland Security, along with the head of a major technology company. This will be a shock to many, as it was a shock to us to discover the identities of the men and women behind yesterday's terrorist assassination attempt.

"The timing and location of the precision strike was fully supported by weeks of multi-disciplinary and highly sophisticated intelligence gathering. A definitive count of other casualties in the strike has not yet been made. In the coming days the U.S. government will determine the extent to which any of these other individuals had terrorist connections.

"Before ordering today's precision strike, we obtained an opinion from the Office of the General Counsel. In the judgment of the OGC, the attacks from the so-called slayers were terrorist attacks from non-state actors. This puts them and anyone up their chain of command in the position of unlawful enemy combatants. Because of this designation, the preemptive strike today on Homeland soil was justified and necessary.

"Significant evidence tied the two men killed today to yesterday's assassination attempt. We are not at liberty at this time to release this information, because it involves ongoing plots against the U.S. government. Suffice it to say these two were not alone; a number of other prominent U.S. citizens, including high-ranking government officials, are members of this terrorist network looking to foment insurrection against the government and other law-abiding U.S. citizens.

"Let this be a warning to these individuals. Today's strikes were the first but will not be the last. We will continue to apprehend our adversaries or use lethal force as necessary until this terrorist organization is destroyed, root and branch.

"Vampires are citizens, public servants, and patriots. Whether you consider them hate crimes or terrorist acts, yesterday's attacks and the near-daily attacks of so-called slayers will not be tolerated. We have an obligation to act decisively, preemptively if necessary, to ensure the integrity of the U.S. government and the safety of all our citizens.

"Rest assured, we are up to the challenge."

BUCHAREST: JUNE 15, 1586

Five weeks of solid slaying was good for Trubadur's soul, and for the community. And the weather had warmed up, bringing an agreeable turnout at the market around the Curtea Veche, built in the prior century by Vlad Țepeș and improved by Mircea the Shepherd, both voivodes of Wallachia. Nowhere near the grandeur of the Holy Roman Emperor's Vienna or Prague accommodations—or even the Habsburg toady prince's castle at Alba Iulia in Transylvania—the modest palace and church were the pride and joy of Wallachia and Bucharest.

Marketgoers weren't browsing; they were stocking up. The black clouds boiling over the Carpathians to the north portended winter's cruel return, and slaying a hundred lesser vampires didn't change the bleak tide of the war. Most now believed vampires were God's punishment for mankind's sins.

"Those with an understanding of history, they believe differently," said Skender, reeking of the aniseed liqueur favored by Bucharest's small Greek population. "They say the vampire is Lucifer's revenge."

"One, please," Trubadur ordered a half-chicken from the roaster hawking his wares amidst tanners, armorers, haberdashers, potters, and a hundred other tradesman. "Lucifer should take his anger out on God."

Skender averted his eyes from the steaming chicken but drooled as he spoke. "By this version of the story, Lucifer gave us Light. Knowledge, to open our eyes to God's tyrannical, repressive rule. But rather than bless his Enlightenment, we curse that moment as the dawn of evil. And so we turned our backs on the one who took a tremendous risk for us." He grabbed

Trubadur by the arm as they started walking. "By the gods, will you not share your bounty with me?!"

"Of course," said Trubadur. "Breast?"

"I'm a leg man, if you don't mind."

They continued down the row of merchants. "And so Lucifer created the vampire to take his vengeance upon us?" said Trubadur.

"Those who *truly* understand history believe differently yet." Skender efficiently stripped the chicken leg to the bone. "They say vampires have always existed, even before Lucifer's banishment to Hades. His true vengeance is creating Morbius."

"Wing?"

Skender wiped the grease on his toga. "I couldn't live with myself. Your bones enjoy less shelter than mine, sadly enough. Miss one meal and you'll be no match for the next bloodsucker. Which makes me wonder again how you managed to slay Canterpark. Made from the mold of Achilles, he was."

Trubadur had perhaps exaggerated his role in Mortimer Canterpark's demise. "Like I told you, I caught him at a vulnerable moment."

As time had gone on with no sight of Nadia, Trubadur had begun to pray that something had gone wrong in the transmission. Had the monster's seduction of poor Nadia been mankind's savior—did their intercourse somehow terminate the Morbius bloodline? In his dreams, Nadia hadn't been turned into a vampire at all. Upon leaving the market he intended to proceed to the Rákóczi home, and peek through the windows.

Skender was surveying Trubadur's scrawny build. "Fully incapacitated, I should think."

Before he could take offense, Trubadur saw a commotion on the plaza in front of the palace. He shoved the chicken's remains into Skender's hands and ran toward the trouble.

"Vampire!" a Roma woman accused, circling a boyar, a man of privilege, land, and serfs. Judging by the length of his beard and the height of his hat—possibly the highest in Wallachia, even pulled down over his ears—a powerful boyar at that. He ignored the woman and made for the palace door.

One thing everyone could agree about the Romani: they had a sixth sense for evil. In front of the bust of Vlad Țepeș (aka Vlad

Dracula the Impaler; Wallachian hero or tormentor, the bust's graffiti took both sides of the debate), a strapping farrier laid hands upon the boyar. "Stay put, Domnul Nurkic!"

The boyar broke the farrier's formidable grip and threw him easily to the ground. He continued up the walk. The farrier picked himself up and made eye contact with an equally burly constable; together they attacked the boyar.

Black-eyed Boyar Nurkic was driven to the stones. The crowd gasped—vampire or not, to see a man of his standing accosted was shocking. The farrier and constable struggled to subdue the boyar; the crowd now recoiled in horror as Nurkic showed his fangs and inexorably won the battle. His face now more ursine than human, with one hand he held the constable at bay and with the other brought the farrier to him. His jagged fingernails gouged the poor man's eyes and his fangs sank into the doomed man's throat.

Ricocheting through the crowd, Trubadur shucked his cloak and unholstered a stake. Refusing to assume Nurkic was of the "greater" variety, he went for the heart and rammed the silver-tipped stake into the boyar's back.

Fused ribs pulped the stake tip. The boyar backhanded him. Trubadur flew against the iron picket fence. The boyar vampire returned to his meal.

"Hades spawn," Trubadur wheezed through ribs cracked first by Canterpark and now cracked again. "Back away from that man."

"Go for the crotch," Skender advised. He tossed a fresh stake to Trubadur and nibbled at dangling chicken skin. "I've heard Boyar Nurkic considers it his second greatest weapon."

Trubadur picked himself off the ground. "Ask him to kindly spread his legs and I'll take care of the rest." The lithe Roma woman shoved him toward the boyar and wished him Godspeed.

From the shadows of the recessed palace entrance a woman appeared, dressed head to toe in tight velvety leather.

"Master," said the vampire boyar Nurkic.

Trubadur's heart sank. "Nadia."

"Morbius, you mean," said Skender.

"Morbius?" The name was taken up by the Roma woman and then spread as panic through the onlookers. The constable flinched so hard he stumbled and sat back on the ground.

"We bless your arrival." Boyar Nurkic approached Nadia with reverence. "You will find a ready army, master. I have been ordered by Osman Pasha to escort you to Constantinople. We will leave behind a sufficient force to maintain order, and still have enough fang-power," his thick beard bobbed, the only visible indication he was speaking, "to surprise the Mohammedans in their lair."

Two slayers emerged from the crowd, a balding man and a ridiculously hairy one. Both reflected the sorry state of the slayer resistance: poor posture and poorly made stakes, poorly brandished. They looked to Trubadur for direction. He motioned them left and right in flanking attacks. A vampire sprang from the crowd and picked off the balding slayer, took him down and bit him. Trubadur picked up a hefty stone and charged the boyar.

At a dead run, he hurled the stone and pegged Nurkic in the back of the head. The vampire wheeled, hands to his skull. Trubadur slid on his knees and drove the stake into the boyar's second greatest weapon.

Such a wail Trubadur had heard many a time; it was the *mortis* arch he awaited, jaw dropped and chest thrust to the sky. Instead he received a double-fisted blow to the top of his head. The compaction crunched his vertebrae. Ears ringing and vision trebled, Trubadur stuck his foot in the boyar's gut and yanked out the stake. Even the greater vampires had been known to occasionally bleed out.

The boyar cuffed the stake from his hand and pummeled his face. Trubadur was somewhat conscious of being dragged up the palace steps.

Boyar Nurkic nodded deferentially to Nadia. "May I humbly offer my first sacrifice, master?" He turned to glare at a hesitant attack from the hairy slayer, who had been gaping in fascination at Nadia as he advanced. Now the slayer cocked the stake like a spear and flung it. The knotty pine whizzed between Nurkic and Nadia and floated off into the princely garden. The hairy slayer ran away and instead tackled the vampire feeding on his balding partner.

Grunting, in some pain, Nurkic hauled Trubadur to his feet. "Believe it or not, this one is probably the best of the lot."

"So he made good on a young boy's braggadocio," said Nadia.

Trubadur looked deep into Nadia's eyes. What did he see there? Regret? Love? Bloodlust?

"I would let you do the honor, master," said the boyar. "But I know that your circumstances preclude you from biting."

The crowd grew and pressed forward, humans alongside vampires. There was the impending spectacle, like the monthly impalings orchestrated by the Turks and their Wallachian lackeys. But it was also Nadia; vampire and human alike were captivated.

Among the crowd's vampires was Deacon Lupul. He had guided young Trubadur through his Orthodox studies. Now he hissed like a badger at his former pupil. "I never liked you! Neither did Jesus!"

"Boyar," said Nadia, "circumstances are also going to prevent *you* from biting."

"Master?"

"If you wore your hat properly, Domnul Nurkic," said Nadia, "maybe you could hear better." She pointed at the boyar's tall, bulbous hat. "Above the ears, please."

The boyar vampire bristled. "Of course, master." He lifted the hat higher on his head.

Nadia whistled at the size of the boyar's ear holes. "I see now you were simply trying to prevent pigeons from nesting in your skull."

The boyar's face flushed. He took his embarrassment out on Trubadur, cuffing him with a snarl. "Thank you, master. Now I can hear the blood rushing through this skinny slayer's veins. My appetite is whetted."

"Do it quickly," Nadia said as she stared at Trubadur. "Before one of these miserable slayers accidentally sticks a stake in your ear and does mortal damage."

Trubadur frowned, and slid a fresh stake from the loop at the small of his back.

"Drink him dry!" screamed Deacon Lupul.

Nurkic the bloodthirsty boyar dove at Trubadur's throat. The slayer grabbed a handful of thick black beard and wrenched the vampire's head back—a precursor to the coming *mortis* arch—

and slammed the stake through his ample ear hole.

The boyar turned to Nadia, reached for her, one last attempt to touch his long-anticipated master. Then he toppled back onto the stone stairs, the impact sending his hat bouncing and rolling to rest at Skender's feet.

"The ear was to be my next guess," said Skender.

The crowd recoiled. Then the humans came forward to witness the slain boyar, to puzzle over Nadia, to test the waters of insurrection.

Vampires bunched together before the plinth bearing the Impaler's bust. The Roma woman accosted them. A huge stonemason vampire lifted her off her feet and bit her savagely. This sobered the mob and created space for the vampires to make their escape toward the river.

The crowd now turned their attention to Nadia, their faces a mix of rage and rapture.

She was just as confused as she looked to Trubadur. "What is happening to me?"

He basked in the slayer's high. He wanted to slay her and kiss her all at once, and could only shake his head.

"My love," she whispered. "What am I?"

Someone in the crowd volunteered an answer. "The vampire queen!"

Nadia hurried through the palace door, which closed heavily behind her. Villagers buffeted Trubadur in their pursuit. Eventually they forced their way into the palace. Their disappointed yelling told Trubadur that Nadia had vanished.

Nadia's grandfather Grigor was the master mason for the rebuild of the Curtea Veche palace and church under Prince Mircea. He survived tripping one of Vlad Țepeș' forgotten booby-traps, and was rewarded with the discovery of a secret passage. One of the vampires on his crew was impaled ass-up by the devious mechanism, and so they named the passage Pucker.

Prince Mircea had worried about the allegiance of Grigor and a few of his fellow boyars. Grigor was reputedly on the payroll of the Holy Roman Emperor, who also loved secret passages. According to Nadia's father, the emperor eventually double-crossed the double-dealing Grigor, leading to Grigor taking a seat at a table of boyars massacred by the prince over plates of sarma.

Did that in turn lead to the ambush of the emperor's envoy as he returned to Vienna with the architectural drawings of the C.V.? Nadia's father left that call up to the impressionable young Trubadur; but he did possess graphic knowledge of the envoy's demise, and the secret tunnels. Trubadur imagined that knowledge in turn may have led to the disappearance of Nadia's parents. That, or vampires.

All in all, he expected to find Nadia safely back at the Rákóczi residence. He climbed the back trellis ignoring the fire from his broken ribs, crunching frost-burned ivy under hand and foot, and entered through the loft window.

In the main room below Nadia knelt at the hearth, staring into the flames. "So I am queen of the vampires." She nodded at the fire. "You can still salvage your sacrificial stake."

He climbed down the ladder. "The hotter the better. It will be a taste of what awaits you in Hell."

She fingered a gold chain that had previously hung around Boyar Nurkic's neck. "Haven't I proven myself?" Her hand trailed down her velvety speckled tan shirt. "How many of your enemies do I need to wear?"

Trubadur's eyes widened. It was chamois. "How did you know about my difficulties with the chamois?"

"Mortimer had vampire eyes everywhere. He knew you were coming."

He squeezed her jaw to force open her mouth. "You *asked* for this. Did you know he was the carrier? What did you expect would happen?" He squeezed harder.

Nadia showed him her fangs. "Your eyes are not right, my love. The boyar hurt you."

"Not nearly as badly as your *lover*."

"I understand your jealousy."

"But not my anger?" He tried unsuccessfully to menace her. "Not my *hatred*?" He reached into the fire and quickly withdrew, empty handed, silently cursing. "The stake was meant for him."

"And for you."

Trubadur's hand clenched in a fist as if it held the stake. "Because I do what is *right*."

"That is why I love you. But I have never been you." Nadia brought his fist to her lips. "And you loved me anyway."

"I misjudged you."

"That would be a first. I think you identified every potential vampire in Bucharest, nine years ago." She followed him as he stalked to the door. "Tru, tell me what happened at the palace."

"Vampires new and old from far and wide flocked to their queen."

"And?"

"And? How should I know?"

"You descend from the slayer who nearly ended the Morbius bloodline hundreds of years ago. You've told me the tales. You know all the lore and legend. Am I Morbius? Is this how it feels?"

"And how is that?"

"I *saw* it, Tru. I saw his weakness."

"His Achilles' heel."

Nadia's eyes blazed and her fangs glistened in the firelight. "Our Lord save me, I was one with the boyar and every vampire in that crowd. But I wanted you to *know*, I wanted you to *see*. I wanted you to drive that stake in one ear and out the other."

Trubadur gripped her, his body pressed to hers, Nadia submitting to the pain.

"I don't know what you are," he said.

"Then we find Mortimer. He will know what he did to me."

"That's impossible." Trubadur was about to describe what he had witnessed, but something stopped him. "He's gone. He fled, away from Bucharest. From Wallachia. To the west, never to return. I have my eyes, as well."

"Then we figure it out together."

"We'll do nothing together. I would be dead right now but for you."

"You are welcome."

He shook her. "I would be dead, Morbius would be dead, and the world would be *right*. Now, nothing is right."

"Then why have I never felt better? Maybe you don't know everything there is to know, slayer." Nadia put her forehead to his chest. "What if things aren't as black and white as we thought when we were young? Turks or Hungarians? Humans or vampires?"

"Hungarians and humans, every time."

"And if one is both human *and* vampire?"

"Then you'll be hated by all."

"But not by you. You can never hate me."

He yanked his collar back and forced her to his throat. "Bite me now, Morbius! Give me the curse, and I will drive a stake through my own heart and end the bloodline!"

Nadia kissed his flesh. A shudder ran through his body before he shoved her away.

"This is the last time we will see each other." He scaled the ladder into the loft. "Unless you force me to slay you. Which I am certain is our destiny." He ducked through the window and onto the trellis. The lattice snapped under his weight. Trubadur landed face-down in the cold mud.

SIGHT 'N' SLAY

The Astro at bat ripped a double into the corner and the crowd cheered. That just might plate a run. Everyone stood to see and yell encouragement to the runner going first to home. This gave Victor and Eugene the chance to give final instructions to Carmelita, the former-vampire mother of two former-vampire children.

"Jump over that railing, take off your shirt, and run as fast as you can across the field," Eugene instructed.

Victor grabbed her arm as she left her seat. "You are wearing a bra, *si*?"

This embarrassed Carmelita. After threatening her son not to leave his seat, she shoved her way down the row. The Honduran immigrant took every opportunity to express her gratitude for saving her and her children. Tripp was her true benefactor—first he had stopped Eugene from slaying them, and then he had cured them. But Carmelita reserved her deepest reverence for Victor.

And so she was all in for semi-streaking across the Houston Astros baseball field to create a diversion so Victor and Eugene could take down a prominent vampire.

An usher grabbed hold of Carmelita and she punched him in the gut. He made one more play for her as she climbed over the rail. Carmelita bit him in the hand, a vestigial act. The usher had her by the shirt, and then that's all he had, as Carmelita hit the field in bra and shorts and took off for center field.

Every security guard in the stadium converged upon her. This was according to plan, but Carmelita wasn't as fast as Victor had hoped. Security had her before she cleared the infield, leaving little time for Victor and Eugene to make their move.

Because Eugene insisted on wearing black, Victor had taken to wearing colors that had always appealed to him, greens and yellows. He had to work with Eugene, but he didn't want them to look like partners.

They leaped atop the dugout, swung over the lip, and dropped onto the top steps, striking an action pose.

The players were hardly surprised. "Look, it's runty Batman and super-sized Robin."

Their target liked to stand in the dugout at the entrance to the runway to the clubhouse, out of the television cameras' sight but able to see the field and talk to the team. He faced them now with that well-known knee-buckling glare.

Nolan Ryan had come out as a vampire only recently. In interviews he said he was pretty sure he had always been one, had been born as such. It gave him his edge, he believed; he would be surprised if Kobe Bryant wasn't one as well. He had become an instant vampire community leader.

He attributed his fangs' emergence to the reputed coming of Morbius. Known for his thorough preparation, it was no surprise he recognized Victor.

"Morbius! I'll be damned. Have you come for me?"

Victor cocked his head until Ryan's Heel came into focus. "I have."

Eugene drew a plastic crossbow from its back mount and thumbed the switch that unfolded the bow wings. "Divine comeuppance, Nolan. This time the high heat is for you." He turned to Victor with a glare Nolan Ryan could appreciate. Eugene hated asking for help. "Something you want to tell me?"

"Pec-delt junction."

Eugene held the crossbow at a relatively non-threatening hip height. His aim was phenomenal. Victor's jaw had dropped many a time the past three weeks as they slayed their way through an ever-increasing number of evolved vampires seemingly drawn to Houston, while they simultaneously searched for Amberly.

Eugene fired. Old Nolan Ryan was quick. He turned and took the bolt in the side of his shoulder. The dugout erupted in fury.

Eugene was imperturbable chambering another bolt. A strapping ballplayer charged; Eugene was going to shoot him—Victor slapped down the crossbow so that the weapon discharged in the dirt. He caught the ballplayer by the throat, took him off his feet and drove him onto and through the wood bench.

He turned to see a little fireplug of a player squaring up with his bat. Eugene's focus was good, too good. He was stalking the retreating Ryan and readying another bolt.

Dammit. Victor dove to protect the slayer.

Major league bats are wooden, not aluminum, yet the *clink* in Victor's head had a metallic note. In that split-ringing-second, he hoped he healed as quickly from concussions as he had from stab wounds.

He woke in his bed with Barbara at his side. His ex-wife put the softest kiss beside his lips, fuzzily sweet in his muddled mind.

"Welcome back, honey."

Victor smiled in spite of the throbbing pain. "How many times have you and I been reunited?"

"I've died a thousand times with you. I love it when we come back to life."

A battered Eugene paced with a limp behind her. He had taken a beating.

"Saved your stupid skull," said Victor.

Eugene mumbled through a fat lip. "I already expressed my appreciation to Mom." He ignored Victor's scowl. "But there were plenty more free-swinging morons where that one came from."

"Nolan Ryan?"

"Slain."

Victor tried to be pleased. He had loved watching him pitch for the Astros. That Ryan had turned out to have had an unfair advantage didn't detract from the thrill the ballplayer had given him.

Barbara's fingers stroked his cheek as she gazed into his eyes. A look of trust and love; how he had starved for that, for so many years. Now, with his concussed vision, he saw two Barbaras, two such looks, and he didn't want to blink it away.

"Publicola has been tweeting all day," she told him, referring to the anonymous blogger dedicated to convincing the world Victor was the evil Morbius. "He's telling everyone to watch his

YouTube channel at eight tonight. For a video message from Amberly."

Victor sat up. "What does that mean? Publicola? Why would he have a video from Amberly?"

Eugene's enraged snarl reopened his split lip. "He must be the Civil War Soldier." Tears welled in his eyes. "She better be in mint condition."

"Eugene, sweetie," said Barbara. "You know Amberly well enough to know she is taking very good care of herself."

"Obviously he doesn't," said Victor with great satisfaction. He squeezed Barbara's hand in appreciation for her strength and confidence in their daughter. Vampirism's reclamation of his mind amplified Victor's emotions. He burned red-hot while slaying the metro's bloodsuckers with Eugene, always certain that killing one more vampire would sway this CWS to release Amberly. Then he would come home and fall into a burned-out funk. It drove him crazy when Barbara didn't share his despair.

But of course she was right. He couldn't imagine anyone able to keep Amberly under wraps for long.

"We need to listen for clues," said Barbara. "Amber will guide us to her."

Eugene darkened. "I have all the respect in the world for the future Mrs. Foreman. She is brilliant. But the CWS won't allow that. He is the wisest person I have ever met. He has an understanding of the world—"

"Taught you everything you know," Victor mocked.

"He has been right about *everything*." Eugene jabbed his finger at Victor. "Including slaying you."

"Eugene," said Barbara. "Enough of that."

"No, no," said Victor. "Keep trying."

"Stop it, both of you. You are on the same team now."

"I am *never* teammates with a vamp."

"Good," said Victor. "Please give me a reason to suck you dry."

"Your evil bloodthirst, isn't that sufficient?"

"Boys."

Victor locked eyes with Eugene. "I really hate you." He turned to Barbara. "Any word from Tripp?"

"He's upstairs talking to a hacker friend, hoping he can trace back from Publicola's account to a physical location."

Tripp entered the room and frisbee'd his cowboy hat onto the ottoman under the window. "We live in a terrible time, my friends."

"Your friend couldn't help?" Barbara fretted. "What did he say?"

"He doesn't want any part of this. Hackers are flat-out afraid to hack. The drone strike changed the game."

"Wrong," said Eugene. "Vampires have always been a huge threat. People are just finally realizing it."

"That's the problem," said Tripp. "From what I've been reading online, and what Dr. Linciome hears from his anti-vamp associates who visit him at the rehab, people are rallying to the vampires' cause. The press conference from the NSA vamp had a huge effect. Suddenly slayers are the second coming of al Qaeda."

Thanks to Tripp's cure, Dr. Linciome was fang-free. But he was an inpatient at the Rice-associated rehabilitation facility, learning how to walk, talk and think again. The attack from X had done damage.

Eugene was in Tripp's face. "Are you completely nuts? *Vampires* are like al Qaeda! With fangs! There is no comparison!"

"I would say you're shooting the messenger, but I don't think you really got the message." Tripp checked his signaling phone. "Here we go. My friend just forwarded me a link to Amberly's video." He looked at the blank wall. "No TV?"

"The secret to a happy marriage, according to my parents," said Barbara. "No TV in the bedroom."

"We'll use my smartphone," said Eugene, displaying a screen that dwarfed Tripp's.

"An idiot with a smartphone is still an idiot," said Victor.

"And all vampires suck shit," said Eugene.

"Fuck you."

"Fuck you!" Eugene mimed his phone as a hammer driving a virtual stake in Victor's heart.

"There must be an app for repeatedly failing to slay me."

"Victor," Barbara appealed.

"All it takes is one, fatty!"

"Foremans are shitty slayers."

"Underestimate me some more, please!"

"That's *enough*," said Barbara. "Can we please watch the video?"

Eugene breathed loudly through his nose. "Send me the link. EugeneTVS1 at Gmail."

Victor stewed until the video loaded on Eugene's phone. Tripp knelt with it at Victor's bedside. Barbara sat beside Victor. Eugene resumed limp-pacing.

"How can your stupid phone reek of garlic?" Victor complained.

Barbara shushed him as their daughter's face filled the frame. "She's lost weight," she fretted.

Even in freeze-frame, Victor saw something in her eyes he didn't like.

Tripp clicked Play.

"Hello everyone. My name is Amberly. I have recently become a vampire."

Barbara gasped.

Eugene might have fainted. He toppled into the dresser, knocking Barbara's jewelry box and assorted personal effects to the floor.

"It must be that appraiser vampire's bite," said Tripp. "Not a worry," he soothed Victor and Barbara as he hauled the limp slayer onto the bed. "We'll cure her."

Victor and Barbara stared at the paused videoframe of their daughter showing a hint of fang. Neither could look away.

Eugene threw himself off the bed and dragged himself across the floor until he could just see the screen between Tripp and Barbara. Tripp touched Play.

"It was quite a shock," said Amberly. "I have remained separated from my loved ones during this period of transition and adjustment. I am in hiding, because I am afraid."

"Why doesn't she say she was kidnapped?" Barbara exclaimed.

"Stockholm syndrome," said Eugene.

Tripp hit Pause and took Barbara's hand, calming her. "I'm sure she's just being careful." He spoke with conviction but looked completely befuddled by what he was seeing.

"The CWS is using her to lure Victor to him," said Eugene.

"Oh," said Victor, "now your wise sensei on the mountaintop is planting video clues that only I can understand?"

"Do not underestimate him."

"I pray he *does* make the mistake of leading me to him."

"Shall we?" said Tripp.

Victor wanted to smash Eugene's face and instead slammed the bed with a roar. Eugene's phone popped in the air like off a trampoline. Barbara caught it and put her hand on Victor's bedded legs to calm him.

Tripp again touched Play.

"There is unfounded internet speculation," said Amberly, "of an evil vampire king who will lead vampires to take over the world. This wild rumor has led to unprovoked attacks against patriotic, law-abiding vampires. Attacks that are rooted in hatred for others and designed to create fear."

"What the hell is going on?" said Victor.

"That is the definition of terrorism," said Amberly. "Recently, a high-ranking Panamanian official was killed simply because he was a vampire. Placido Perez was his name. We must not stand for that. We are all Placido today."

"The CWS is messing with her head," said Tripp. "And ours."

Barbara saw Eugene's distress: lying on his back, gripping his head, and kicking his heels on the floor. She knelt beside him. "It's you he's working on. He's trying to turn you against Victor."

"No." Eugene stared at the ceiling. "She means what she says. Amberly is a vampire now."

Victor fought his way out from under the blankets. "If you even *think* about doing anything to our daughter, I'll rip your head off!"

Eugene turned his head like a spooky ventriloquist's dummy. "I'm not going to slay Amberly."

"I don't believe you." Victor in his rage wanted to toss aside Barbara and Tripp, break Eugene's neck and waste his blood on the carpet. "Out. Get out of my house."

Barbara pulled him down to sit with her on the bed. "Let's finish the video."

Tripp knelt before them, a safety barrier for Eugene, who lay still except for a twitch below his eye.

"It's time," Amberly continued, "for all of us to come together on the side of peace. It's time to stand together against those who would try to turn us against one another. The terrorists want us divided into tribes, classes, and religions. They want us separated by false borders and false differences. We must come together to stand for the one thing that matters: freedom."

Amberly paused to control the passion in her voice, staring at them through the camera, radiant, beautiful. "Rallies are springing up spontaneously throughout the world. I urge you to stand with us. This is not the time to be tricked into slaying each other. This is the time to slay the false borders the terrorists have tried to erect. This is the time to stake our claim to a brave, free new world.

"Thank you, everybody. I'm looking forward to working together."

Her face dissolved to a snazzy graphic of a woman's slender fist driving a stake into the heart of an oil-slick blob labeled *Terror*. Underneath the logo, *#StakeOurClaim*.

"What did we just watch?" said Tripp.

"I don't know," said Barbara. "Amberly was … compelling."

From over Tripp's shoulder Eugene plucked his phone, but not before Victor read a text message as it ghosted across the top of the screen. "I will run this video through my analyzer," said Eugene, "to see if we can determine anything about Amberly's location."

"Go to it, Batman," said Tripp with a grim grin.

"He's not Batman," Victor muttered. He looked at his pale yellow dress shirt and deep green slacks. "Where's my lighter fluid? I'm going to burn these clothes."

Tripp followed Eugene out the door. Victor was uneasy. He hadn't a clue what to say to Barbara in the wake of the video.

Vampirism had full hold on him now. The takeover was much quicker the second time around; the mental machinery activated by his curse hadn't been dismantled during Tripp's treatment, just idled. Once the treatment ended, once he was bailed out of jail and could resume biting, it had been a matter of greasing the gears and running through a few test cycles before throwing the lever that switched his mind from tentative to engaged.

It was the difference between seeing all sides and taking one. Victor's focus was monomaniacal: drink blood, save Amberly, kill the CWS. And Eugene with him, why not. All facets of the same treasured jewel.

At the same time he loved Barbara. She was constantly in mind, not as a distraction but as a motivator, a reward, a must-have. And it worried him that he was never ready to relate to her, to give her what she needed, to tell her what he was thinking.

(How could he? Deliberation no longer preceded his actions; his thoughts' only job now was to explain what he had just done.)

The earth beneath them was so unstable. Victor could fly over the shifting and quaking to accomplish his goal, only gently buffeted by the shockwaves. Barbara, though, was so grounded, unable and unwilling to move until Amberly came home. She was their rock. But each tremor in the earth shook her foundations. She needed him for support.

She stood in the kitchen, frozen trying to put together a meal. "What happened to her?" she asked.

"I don't know."

"I don't understand what he's doing. This CWS, why would he allow her to spout that vampire propaganda? How is that in his best interest? It's just feeding the perception that slayers are terrorists and vampires are the innocents."

"I know."

"You know, you don't know, you know." She raised her hands in frustration with him, the way his mother did—absolutely the only thing they had in common. "He wants Eugene to see that Amberly is a vampire, doesn't he? If Eugene couldn't believe his mentor would kill a human, now there should be no doubt. If he doesn't sacrifice himself to kill you, he knows the CWS will have no problem slaying Amberly."

In subdued fashion, Victor tried to lighten her burden. "I'm a little disturbed how well you can get in the mind of these insane slayers."

She slammed her fists on his chest, and again. "Tell me why he's obsessed with you! I don't understand—are you Morbius?"

"No."

"Are you lying to me?"

"No. Winnie said I'm not—"

"I *heard* him. Victor, it doesn't make sense. Nothing makes sense."

"I know."

She grimaced. "Please don't say that any more. It drives me nuts."

"I … won't." He took her shoulders and gave her a gentle shake. "I'm committed to finding her. But I don't have a clue. We can't find the diary. The only thing I know to do right now is continue taking out the high-level vampires and hope the CWS finally realizes I'm on his side."

"How could he not?" She spoke with her head against his chest. "Why isn't it apparent to him that you are the vampires' worst nightmare?"

Victor bit back an *I know*. "Maybe we just haven't done enough to convince him."

Barbara stared at him. "Then don't stop. If your instincts tell you to keep at it, then do it. I believe in you."

Victor fell all the deeper in love. "Can you take slaying lessons? I really, really hate my partner."

BUCHAREST: JUNE 22, 1586

For seven days Trubadur subsisted on dried meat from the horse that had met its end soon after the chamois ambush on the pass, and mead. Mead was introduced to him in Târgu Mureş by a traveling Northman who traded the fermented honey for slaying a lesser vampire duo that had been tracking him since Prague. The cask of mead may have contributed to the horse's lackluster showing in the chamois altercation.

He was holed up in the Curtea Veche stable, guest of the reluctant palace caretaker. Like his father before him, Trubadur's father held the caretaker position until he died. Trubadur had to assure Cătălin more than once that he was not there to claim his legacy.

That made no more sense to Cătălin than it had to Trubadur's father, Alexandru. Nothing about young Tru had made sense to Alexandru. The Church provided—why agitate? As Alexandru fell ill with pneumonia, the Church found Tru's mother a new husband, a widower sheep rancher near Câmpulung. Exhausted after surviving the Carpathians on the journey from Târgu Mureş, Trubadur had attempted to stay there and was driven off by his stepbrothers, suspicious he was there to lay claim to a share of the livestock. Why agitate? his father would have said.

He had heard two of the boys were vampires, that's why. His father hadn't understood that, either. No man could stand in place of God to judge another, whether Ottoman, Hungarian or vampire. Only God's judgment was legitimate, and that only came after.

Alexandru had been ecstatic when his young son asked to learn the Church's language, Latin. His joy was short-lived when he realized Trubadur's motivation was to read a document authored by Vlad Țepeș, discovered in a hidden room off the church's catacomb. And that the only Latin instructor in town was the former slayer, drunken Skender.

The document was Vlad's historical account of the nightmarish rise and fall of the vampire empire in the twelfth century. Vlad clearly believed he was divinely obligated to keep close watch on the surviving bloodsuckers (not to mention Hungarians, Turks and suspect Wallachians).

Vlad's tale cast Tru's ancestor, Vigilus, in the role of a Greek hero. The well-preserved vellum scroll described how Vigilus led the slayer army and personally made the sacrifice to end the terrible reign of Morbius. But unbeknownst to Vigilus, and to Vlad centuries later, before the hero leapt off the walls of Constantinople with the vampire queen in his arms, she had bitten her top general and transferred the bloodline. This Trubadur learned from Skender.

The royal Morbius bloodline had been carried for 400 years by that vampire general, who eventually adopted the name Mortimer Canterpark. In the meantime, perhaps twenty generations of Vigilus's descendants (most recently Trubadur's maternal grandfather) had chased the carrier across the known world and back, laying down their lives for humanity.

And here Trubadur sat tortured and paralyzed by uncertainty while greater vampires flocked to their queen.

Cătălin stuck his head in the stable. "Someone looking for you."

Trubadur chewed on sinewy horse. "Tell Skender I'm occupied."

"I'll be sure to tell the old drunk the next time I see him. It's Dragoș."

"How does Dragoș know I'm here?"

"It's no secret, boy."

"Only because you're telling everyone!"

"Our holy Father doesn't condone harboring secrets," said Cătălin as he left the stable.

"That's not a Commandment!"

After a swig and a swoosh of mead to wash the horse from between his teeth, Trubadur left the stable. He encountered

Dragoș in the courtyard, fronting a small crowd, slayers among them.

"What do you want, Dragoș?"

"A real slayer!" The tall bucktoothed slayer sidearmed a tomato that smacked sluggish Trubadur in the chest. Frozen, so its only mark was a bruise. "All we have is this imposter!" The men and women backing Dragoș laughed and mocked Trubadur.

He unholstered a stake. "Stand still and I'll prove my *bona fides*!"

Dragoș moved along the courtyard wall without straying too far from his supporters. He was a decent slayer, nimbler than he appeared with a tall man's levered strength and good reaction time. Trubadur had seen him take down a fearsome farmer vampire attempting to cart two intoxicated fair maidens back to his farm. They needed Dragoș in the war.

Of course with Morbius reborn, the war was already over.

"I thought you came here to slay Morbius," said Dragoș.

"So I did. And I will."

"Ah. You didn't have a clear shot in her bedroom?"

"I will strike no fatal blow until I am certain!"

"Most of us are satisfied by what our eyes tell us. For Trubadur, he can only be sure with his hands." Dragoș mimed a lover's embrace.

Two strapping women intercepted and restrained Trubadur.

"Careful, ladies," said Dragoș. "If he suspects you of being a vampire, he'll roll you about in the hay until you've had enough."

"Almost makes me wish for pointed teeth," said the woman with fewer chin hairs.

Trubadur fended her hand from his crotch. "Dragoș, you know the sacrifice necessary to slay Morbius. Help yourself."

"I would." Dragoș approached, stabbing his finger at Trubadur. "We all would. But you're the chosen one!"

"Said who? Said *me*! Now I choose *you*!"

"It doesn't work that way!"

"We'll only know that for certain after you make the attempt."

Dragoș colored. He loomed over Trubadur. "You wouldn't let me, would you? You would slay me to protect your vampire woman."

The crowd howled in rage. “Vampire lover!” The more bewhiskered of the two women punched Trubadur in the stomach.

“He would be protecting *you*, Dragoş, you fool.” Skender pushed through the budding lynch mob. “Morbius will take your soul and soil your bloodline. A few centuries tend to water down the story. The same way Gheorghe serves his wine.”

Gheorghe the tavern owner absorbed the hoots and the crowd’s agreement. He bowed. “I apologize for failing to get you even drunker, Skender.”

“Apology accepted.” Skender spoke to the crowd. “The last time Morbius appeared, 400 years ago, the world almost ended for humanity. If not for Trubadur’s ancestor, none of us would be here today.”

“We don’t need a drunk teaching us lessons,” said Dragoş. “We all know the problem with the vampires. And Morbius.”

“Perhaps I am the only one drunk enough to admit there is only one of us willing and able to do what it takes.”

The crowd stilled. The women released Trubadur.

“Fuck her to death?” said Dragoş.

Trubadur lunged and drove the stake for his heart.

Skender caught his arm. The old drunk had steel in his sinew. “I thought cunning Constantin on the Mureş taught you better. To quote: ‘Some lives are worth more than others, it is true. But every life is piss in the vampire’s face.’”

“That’s stupid,” said Trubadur.

“Constantin is renowned for his swordplay, not his aphorisms.” Skender linked arms with Trubadur. “Time for our stallion to leave the stable. I have something to show you.”

Trubadur traded glares with Dragoş as Skender guided him from the courtyard.

Skender stopped, pulled out an empty wineskin and pointed Trubadur back to the stable. “It’s quite a hike. Best bring some of that tainted honey I smell on your breath.”

Hearing “quite a hike” discouraged any followers as Skender led Trubadur out of town. The air was cold but calm and the sun was out, making their journey over the Wallachian plain pleasant enough.

They walked without a word between them for some miles. Skender sang Greek tavern songs while Trubadur sulked. Finally, the exertion dulled the sting of Dragoș's words.

"Hungry?" Trubadur offered a strip of horse.

Skender sniffed at the purplish salt-encrusted offering. "I was, thank you." He produced the wineskin from the folds of his toga. "Wine and its brethren have been my best distraction from hunger."

"Wonderful. More for me."

"I would encourage you to save it, to placate the creature we may encounter in the cave. Except I'm afraid that kind of offering will incense it all the more."

Trubadur rested his hand on his sword hilt and studied the desiccated old drunk. Slayer Constantin in Târgu Mureș had indeed taught him swordcraft—not for vampires but bandits, and as it turned out, chamois.

"The creature allowed me to pass," said Skender. "But I had the impression that decision was made case by case."

"Why don't you just tell me what is in this cave?"

"My memory is poor. This was many years ago when I was your age, and vampires and women competed fiercely for my attention."

They approached a rise of forested hills as the sun sank. "Then how will you find the cave again?"

"Some things you never forget. And I have a map."

"Sometimes you really anger me."

"With the scroll authored by Vlad Țepeș, there was a map, with some writing along the borders. Maddeningly vague, as writing from that time period tended to be."

"Last century?"

"Older." Skender used his staff to address the abruptly steep slope. "The map was not authored by Vlad Țepeș. It spoke of God and Lucifer: 'And so God bargained with him.' Or it read, 'And so God put one over on him.' I could not say for sure."

"Perhaps you should ask for some assistance with the translation."

"The fewer who know of this cave, the better. I thought what I would see there would explain everything. Instead it only confused me." Skender gave Trubadur a proud, envious look. "I have a feeling you will know what it means."

They struggled on slick pine needles over crumbled scree, rotting logs, and thorned bushes, each man breaking a chilled sweat. After a half hour of slow progress, Skender stopped at a pair of gnarled oaks.

"This one is new." He circled one of the bowed oaks. The earth gave way and Skender dropped—caught by Trubadur, saved from a long tumble over unforgiving ground.

This time Skender hugged the trees and worked his way up the slope until he was obscured by trunks and stunted limbs. "What he won't do to hide his tracks."

"Who?"

"The bringer of light. Up here, young slayer. The cave is here."

Trubadur climbed the wedge between the oaks to match Skender's vantage point. Indeed, there was a cleft in the earth, crisscrossed by knobby roots.

"That's it?"

"You expected a big round doorway with a rock to roll aside?"

"How did you get in?"

"I walked. The roots are new."

"This isn't a cave. It's a hole."

"It's what's inside that counts."

Trubadur drew his sword. "Then stand aside." He brought the steel snicking through the roots, severing enough to allow a forced entry.

The old drunken ex-slayer wasted no time. Feet first and eyes squinched against the probing root tips, he squeezed through the opening. "Just like I remember!" he called out.

Trubadur followed, sword unsheathed. "And how is that?"

"Dark."

Standing on what felt like a packed earth floor, Trubadur could sense more than see Skender, even in the light leaking through the rooted slit above them. "I feel as though I've placed more trust in you than I should have. How will we find our way?"

Skender breathed a little faster than Trubadur would have liked. "The light-bringer has thought of that." He was panting now. "Of course you should keep in mind we see only what he wants us to see."

"*Skender.* Your breathing is driving me crazy. Are you finally dying or just afraid?"

Trubadur's eyes adjusted enough that a faint red light became visible ahead. He shuffled forward, sword low and off hand high in protection. "What is this?"

"Give it time."

On the rippled cave wall, what had been a red blur slowly resolved. A painting, seemingly drawn in fire. The outlines of the figures flickered as if in flame.

"And now?" said Skender.

A deep red stag presented with its hoof an orange-red ball of fire to a nude woman cast in golden smoldering voluptuousness. "Knowledge," said Trubadur. "Lucifer offering Knowledge to the First Woman. Eve."

"You were a great student, when you sat still."

"You were a numbingly boring teacher."

"And why Eve and not Adam?" Skender quizzed. "Do you recall why Lucifer always chooses the woman?"

"Because women," Trubadur recited, "are the only true revolutionaries."

"I am proud."

"And wrong. *I* refuse to accept the vampires' rule. *I* will die to prevent it. What am I, if not a revolutionary?"

Skender's dry mouth crackled in a smile. "A passionate, committed follower. You follow your ancestor, Vigilus. And now you follow me."

"And what else could I do?" Trubadur's anger echoed off the close confines. "How else—*who* else, to destroy the bloodsuckers?"

"I am only repeating what is written."

"Boring, and maddening. A great teaching combination." Trubadur reached to touch the painting. "What is this substance?"

"I would not."

Trubadur hesitated. "What will happen?"

"I don't know," said Skender. "Seems dangerous, though."

Trubadur retreated a step. "So this is what you brought me all this way to see—and couldn't remember?"

"This is just the first one." Skender moved deeper into the cave. "And they're starting to come back to me now."

Trubadur caught a pinch of Skender's toga in the dark. He sheathed his sword and was towed forward.

Increasingly nocturnal eyes led them to the glow of the next painting. "God's punishment," Trubadur narrated the image of a bearded, crowned man hurling the red stag into pulsating, blackened flames.

"Indeed," said Skender. He seemed now to be barely breathing. "Lucifer banished to Hades. To an appreciative audience."

A row of yellow faces hovered over the scene, laughing. "Who are they?"

"You and me. Humanity." Skender's voice was a ragged whisper. "Cheering the eternal damnation of the one who brought us Fire. Who brought us Light. Who brought us Knowledge."

"But there's more to that story," Trubadur argued.

"And so there is." Skender continued deeper into the cave. Trubadur had not let go of his toga.

We're descending, he realized, the cave much colder than at the entrance. They had to shuffle farther this time. When they reached the next painting, gooseflesh stood up the hairs on his arms.

The colors were no different, hues of fire, but this one was lurid and shocking in its realism. The stag now seemed to be a costume worn by a human-like sculptor, molding a feminine figure from clay. The clay woman had fangs and wore a crown. Again there was a floating, leering, approving audience.

Now Trubadur had trouble drawing air. "This is disgusting."

"Satan's spawn," said Skender. "He is making Morbius."

"And how the vampires love it."

"Ah, there's the rub." Skender moved closer to the painting, which seemed to float unanchored to wall or ground. In the shifting blood-red light, Skender's wrinkles cast shadows that constantly changed his face. "You see what you expect. Now look closer."

Trubadur realized the audience had no fangs. "They are *human*?"

They heard a low growl. And a hiss. And some bleating.

"Give me room." Trubadur waited a beat, and drew his sword.

Skender's hand gripped his. "This is a fight we must not pick."

Into the painting's eerie light moved an awful creature. A monstrous lion, whose eyes were on a level with Skender and Trubadur's. For a tail he had a snake, long enough to flank the two men. Mid-back sprouted a goat, gagging on the fire licking from its chops.

The creature was mythical but its stench was real, of moldy fur, overused pastures, and death-decay. The smell put fear in Trubadur's heart.

"You faced it last time?"

"Only as long as it took to turn and run."

Skender clasped Trubadur's arm and together they bolted for the opening. The enjoined trio howled in deafening harmonics in pursuit. Trubadur had no idea whether they were running toward the entrance or a wall, and didn't care. They flew past the second painting. He was fumbling to unsheathe his sword when Skender gave him a mighty sideways shove.

He stumbled at high speed, flailing and falling headlong. The razor-rough floor cut him through his shirt and breeches, skinned his nose and filled his mouth with the flavor of ash. He gagged at the acrid taste, his constricted throat preventing a peal of enraged fear.

The creature continued after Skender. Trubadur rose to hands and knees, bloody knuckles purple in a cool blue light. He looked up to see another painting.

The style was completely different from the others. The artist must have worked on an overhanging section of the cave wall; Trubadur had to remain kneeling to take in the work. Instead of garish, smeared depictions, this scene was crisp and clear. Pale red Morbius lay on her back, her jagged crown ajar. The vampire queen had an inflamed crotch and x's for eyes. Standing in triumph above her was a man, human, etched in blue and sporting a red, recently-utilized member. The All-Seeing Eye sprouted from his forehead like a Hussar's plume.

What am I seeing?

Trubadur felt the weight of Mortimer Canterpark dying in his arms. He smelled the sex on Nadia, naked in her bed.

And he saw Nadia staring with revulsion at Boyar Nurkic's capacious earholes.

And so God put one over on him.

How long he knelt there, Trubadur couldn't say. A story played out in his mind, like the music of his mother's voice relating her day while she ground farro into flour, like his father's passionate descriptions of the history behind each palace chamber. As with those childhood evenings, the words caressed his ears without alighting, but the song settled in.

Tears ran down Trubadur's cheeks, and his brow unfurrowed. He was in His presence. He had no thought of leaving.

The beast snuffled past him, close enough to touch. Its wake was a chill that swept down Trubadur's collar and up his breeches. He waited a few heartbeats and then silent as a cat—and thankful the actual cat was handicapped by that goat—Trubadur crept out of the alcove and made for the entrance, brightly-enough lit to ruin his acquired night vision.

He struggled past the roots, Skender providing the final assistance. By moonlight they navigated the two oak trees and the rugged slope, saying nary a word until they exited the forest.

Perpetual winter had never felt so refreshing. Trubadur's knees shook as he sat on a grassy hillock. "You could have pushed me right into a wall."

"Trubadur my friend. I know that path. I've relived that journey a thousand times."

The young slayer rode a wave of exhilarated nausea. "The artist for the last painting—that was not the hand of Lucifer."

Skender looked south toward Bucharest. The skin of mead was empty and he appeared eager to get home. "I have to admit that the final painting is still fuzzy in my sodden memory. Did it make any sense to you?"

Trubadur took Skender's hand and used it to rise. "That was the picture of our salvation."

DETOUR

He could feel her out there. His daughter was close, Victor knew it. Her words from the video were codes that he decrypted as he walked Houston's downtown streets, head bowed so as not to see the sweet soft throats of the laughing, tipsy women moving from club to club on this pleasant, late night.

I need you, Daddy.

Amberly, where are you? Tell me, I will come to you, I will rescue you.

But I'm afraid you will slay me.

No. No. I won't let him.

Not Eugene. You.

"No!" He blurted it out, startled a couple necking against the wall. Ducked his head and walked faster down the sidewalk.

He checked his phone—still nothing from Eugene. God-damn the punk—if he later claimed to have been *incommunicado* in his Batcave, Victor would pummel him to death and take his chances with a new slaying partner.

"Excuse me." A beautiful young woman stopped him. Her blouse melted into her collarbone below a full, curved throat, silken flesh that he would enjoy as he buried his fangs, wavy hair that would caress his skull while he drank. "Aren't you Morbius?" Her two friends shrank against each other, thrilled at her audacity and goggle-eyed at where it would lead.

Just like that, slayers were out and vampires were back in.

"You must have me confused with someone else."

He hurried on ignoring offers to join them for a drink.

Victor was saving his bloodthirst. Who knew how many cops and staffers they would have to wade through to get to D.A.

Goodnight? The Houston district attorney believed he had Victor locked up for life after Raj Dajiv's fangs turned out to be falsies. Then Raj's blood test revealed vamp genes—he was in some sort of suspended transformation. So Victor had technically staked a vampire, and the judge ordered him freed.

But Goodnight was biding his time. He was quoted lamenting the depravity of this "vampire-on-vampire crime," and confident that vampires would "finally win their civil rights" and give him the chance to bring justice for Raj Dajiv.

Eugene had also heard slayer chatter that Goodnight had found the diary and had translators working around the clock, hoping to prove Victor was the evil Morbius.

They both agreed Goodnight was a high-profile target who needed to be captured, tortured, and slain. Now if only the stupid slayer would answer his texts!

He hustled along the viaduct to his old favorite parking place at the unlit end of the lot. He had decided to preoccupy himself behind the wheel and cruising Goodnight's neighborhood while awaiting the dipshit's response.

The Charger's rumbling purr encouraged the bloodlust that would fuel their attack on the D.A. Except the Charger didn't turn south toward Goodnight's house but instead continued northwest.

Only now did Victor recognize he had been fixated all night on the group text that had ghosted across Eugene's phone.

Parked in front of Jay Hansen's house, Victor anticipated the sigh of pleasure when Jay's wife realized she was finally liberated from her husband's abuse. He imagined token resistance before full submission—and then later, after Victor left her, as she and Jay readied for bed, as her pompous husband spouted his usual caustic bile while removing his over-starched shirt, the casual display of her bite mark.

For all the years Jay had baited and belittled him, Victor could only imagine how his wife had suffered.

The text on Eugene's phone was from "Project Well Done". Along with Victor's former employees, Larry and David, and what's-his-name the construction foreman, Jay was still contracting with Eugene to kill him. To *kill* him! That he himself had facilitated the slaying of 20 or so vampires in the past month was not a valid comparison. They were monsters—they thought differently, they were inhuman. Their slaying was impersonal. Victor possessed desires, dreams and fears, like any other man. He had the Sight. He was *Victor*. The attempted contract killing by these four idiots was personal. It infuriated him. He would put a stop to it.

He had been on leave from Bizco since his arrest. Emails from Darla were his only contact with the company. She sent prayers for Amberly and otherwise not a personal word, restricting her correspondence to occasional business updates: the accounting department deadlocked 50:50 on a motion by Tessa to erect a small black teepee monument to the slain vampire X; his XFP software was a smash hit and now installed on the computers and smartphones of everyone involved in the joint venture with Playco; she had declined the invitation to accompany Jay to Germany this week to meet with their Verrstagg superiors.

The gated entrance to Jay's Woodlands development was well-traveled even at this late hour. Driving in tucked behind a Jaguar didn't trigger any audible alarms. Jay and his wife Madeline lived off a wooded loop, a brick-and-stucco Tudor sitting at the back of a quarter-acre lot. It wasn't huge, Victor guessed 3,000 square feet, but very well appointed, based on the self-guided tour he took at the party the Hansens had hosted soon after relocating from Chicago. Victor had attended as his boss Don Chleber's surprise "date." The party had occurred after Tripp's first failed treatment and before his all-too-successful second attempt, in that very brief period when Victor was uncured and proud of it.

He had taken great pleasure intimidating Jay that night. Chleber was a facilitator, he had entertained the executives in attendance with tales of Victor's successes with their customers, interspersed with thirsty vampire jokes that grew bawdier as the night wore on. So Victor wasn't surprised at the initial adverse reaction from Jay's wife when she opened the door.

"What the fuck are you doing here?"

"Madeline. How are you tonight?"

"Same question."

Victor feigned expecting to see Jay over her shoulder. "Is your husband here?"

"I'm sure you know where to find him in the office."

"I'm on an extended leave of absence."

As Madeline prepared to close the door in his face, Victor stepped forward. She put her weight behind the heavy oak slab—the inertia she had to overcome was opportunity enough for him to push his way inside.

"What the hell are you doing? *Honey*," she called out, bluffing. The house was spacious but sound absorbent. "I didn't invite you in."

"That's a myth."

"I don't give a shit about who or what you think you are." Her voice spiked into the upper register, her whippet-slim body vibrated. "You're an intruder, nothing more or less. Now get the hell out of my house."

Victor strolled past the grand foyer's rough marble floor onto a thick opal rug that he was eager to ruin. "I will only stay long enough to leave a message for Jay."

"Get out!" Her eyes darted about in search of a weapon.

"We both know he's the real intruder. I wanted to do my job, that's all. He didn't need to *harass* me. He didn't need to come into my department and make my life miserable." Victor realized he was going back further than necessary. He took a breath and caught Madeline's arms as she tried to smash a lamp on his face. She was wiry but not strong; her arms bent and she dropped the lamp. "Now he's trying to kill me. No, it's even more disgusting than that. He's hiring someone to do it."

She cursed him and tried to jerk free, belatedly eyeing the alarm beside the door.

Victor had Madeline right where he wanted her. "I only want to convince him to stop. Words have been inadequate." Sentences like that tripped a hot wire that ran down his spine and enlisted every muscle in his body to envelop and bite her.

"You're fucking nuts! Jay is going to *kill* you!"

Victor's chuckle was a tortured growl from his chest. He squeezed her, too hard he knew, lifting her to him. She contorted so severely in his grasp that he felt and heard her shoulder crack. She screamed in agony and terror.

"You tell him!" Victor roared. "You show him this!"

Even with a broken shoulder she writhed and fought him. This was no contest. He had her in his mouth, he bit her hard as he bear-hugged her, squeezed life from her thin body like from a depleted tube of toothpaste.

Some automated master control switch sprang his lock jaw. Madeline collapsed into fetal position on the rug. Blood spotted the fine opal fibers. Victor spit out what was left in his mouth, adding to the stain.

The house's construction and circulation was so good, no violence hung in the air. Almost as if Jay was again refusing to acknowledge his abilities. Victor stood over Madeline to let his words drop and sink in. "If he keeps at me, I will come back."

He left the front door open. He wanted it agape, he wanted the neighborhood to see what had happened. Jay deserved it. *She* deserved it, for being with him. It sickened Victor, made him want to go back in the house and scream at her, made him hate her.

How can she be with that son of a bitch? As soon as he asked it, Victor tried to stop the answer from coming.

Because Jay had power.

The same reason Barbara loved him, now. Now, that he was unwilling to take no for an answer, when he no longer took anyone else's needs into consideration. Like Jay.

Victor stood on their flagstone walk and roared into the gated community's night. The air was as rich as the house, sanitizing his rage as it cleared his throat. The impotence, his inability to destroy their peace drove him to his knees.

I love the way Barbara loves me.

All those years of Jay's abuse; who was truly in the wrong? Jay, for expecting performance? Or Victor for repeatedly failing to deliver?

Maybe there was no question of right and wrong to be answered. Just an acceptance of the way the world worked.

Power wasn't a problem. To the contrary, it was a blessing. Madeline's error was picking the wrong man.

Still no word from Eugene. It was late and he was far too thirsty to go home to Barbara. The clock in the Charger told him there was still time to head back downtown.

BUCHAREST: JUNE 29, 1586

Trubadur's bung hole constricted and stayed that way as he journeyed down the secret passage under the Curtea Veche. He was bothered by the image of the impaled stonemason vampire, Pucker Passage's namesake, who occasionally appeared in his vivid dreams. Dreams, not nightmares, because a dead vampire was pleasant, no matter how gruesome the scene.

A bulge in the stone ceiling carved a groove along his scalp. Trubadur was almost glad his hat had been confiscated, the jagged rock might have torn a hole in the badger fur. Now he caught a whiff of Nadia's scent and relaxed.

He should have known she would scent him as well. Two steps past a darkened recess and she was on him, on his back, legs wrapped around his waist. Trubadur was not a large person. Neither was Nadia but her momentum and the crushing pressure from her legs drove him to his knees. Her nails dug into his throat. She hissed in his ear. "How did you find this place?"

"I finally realized 'Pucker' had another meaning. I found the lever hidden behind the painting of the sour-faced bishop." He struggled to breath. "Please, Nadia."

She released her grip and looked at the blood on her hand, fresh from his scalp.

He sat on the cold floor and stared up at her. "I have been looking for you."

Nadia ripped the crossbow from his hands. "How did you intend to get us both with one bolt? Or is Skender lurking around the corner?" She flung the weapon beyond the nearest sconce's illumination.

Morbius is taking over, Trubadur realized. She was more

vampire than before, skin nearly translucent and cheeks sunken. Her hair was bigger. "I'm here to kill vampires. With you."

The predator's intensity in her eyes flickered. "I don't know what you mean."

Trubadur rose. "The boyar's earhole. You saw it."

"Who couldn't? The wind whistled a tune through that cavern."

"You knew his Achilles' heel was there *before* you pulled up his hat." Trubadur took a step closer. "You said it yourself. Something is different about you."

"And that would be *Morbius*!" She maintained the buffer between them. "Are you saying I'm not? Then tell me why they are all *drawn* to me."

"I believe you are Morbius."

"And I see the disgust in your face."

One moment she was the dread vampire queen, and the next she was his Nadia. Back and forth, back and forth. The shape-shifting disoriented him.

"Canterpark's bite made you Morbius," he said. "But because you laid with him, you are something else, as well."

"Now suddenly you're certain?"

"I have seen it. An eternal oracle, you might call it." He moved so that the torchlight was on her face, as if he might glimpse the All-Seeing Eye. "You have been given a gift. You can see their Heels."

Nadia gravitated to him. "I don't know what I see. Or feel. Every night I have dreams. Nightmares, I suppose. I wake up exhausted. Exhilarated," she admitted. "Confused."

"It's the Eye. And Morbius. I do not believe they were meant to coexist."

She touched his cheek. "When you're here, the confusion goes away. Like it always has."

Trubadur cursed himself for allowing the hand of the vampire to soothe him. He backed away. "I'm here for a business partnership. To slay every God-damned vampire in Bucharest. Nothing more."

They heard someone approach. More than one. Nadia looked trapped.

"Our first opportunity," Trubadur whispered as he retrieved

the crossbow and slid further into the shadows.

Nadia's mouth opened but no words came out. Into the light walked two vampires.

"Master," said Trubadur's Orthodox studies instructor, Deacon Lupul. "We converted boyar Vedeanu. Croitoru was not receptive. And so, Ioan here is no longer thirsty." He referenced the hulking stonemason who had killed the poor Romani woman in the plaza.

Ioan sensed Trubadur hiding behind a stone outcropping. The stonemason was fast, on Trubadur before he could raise the crossbow. He lifted the slayer by throat and crotch and slammed him against the ceiling. "I am sated but I will still enjoy opening up this one. I don't have to drink from every fountain."

"I could take a sip," said the deacon. "Teaching you was less than gratifying, young Maistru. From everything I failed to instill *in* you as a favor to your poor father, I should get something *out* of you." He read Nadia's reaction. "What were *you* hoping to get out of your friend, master?"

Trubadur hit the ground at her feet. "We are not friends," he said, a foot in the crossbow stirrup, drawing the chamois sinew and pulling a bolt from his quiver. Ioan kicked the bolt out of his hand. Trubadur looked up at Nadia. "Heel?"

That part of her that was Morbius bared its fangs and howled. That which was Nadia sank her fingers under her lower left rib cage.

Ioan grabbed the crossbow in a stupid place. Trubadur hit the trigger and the chamois sinew cut the stonemason's wrist to the bone. While howling Ioan surveyed the damage, Trubadur unholstered a stake and drove it where Nadia had indicated. The polished wood entered the vampire stonemason as if through butter. Ioan stiffened like a statue and toppled.

"Holy Father have mercy," said Deacon Lupul, crossing himself.

"I'm afraid our good Lord did not accompany you when you crossed over." Trubadur cocked the crossbow.

"Traitorous harlot," Lupul spat at Nadia and dashed up the passage.

"Stop him," said Trubadur as he fitted a bolt. Nadia stood rooted staring at the stake protruding at a low angle from the dead vampire's gut. Tru took off in pursuit.

Had the deacon ever traveled this stretch of the passage? Did he know to duck?

Some distance ahead, Lupul bleated in pain and fear. Trubadur found him on his back, blood oozing from his bald pate.

"We'll give credit for this slaying to Vlad Țepeș and his shoddy construction." Trubadur put his knee on Lupul's chest and a bolt through his throat, fixing him to the floor. He touched his own bloody scalp and came away with red fingertips. "All this blood, and nothing for you to drink. It must be maddening."

The vampire deacon glared at him. "I cannot begin to tell you."

Nadia joined them, looking at neither. "His nose."

Trubadur triggered the weapon. A bolt disappeared up the vampire's nose. The deacon's deep-set eyes retreated further into his skull.

When he realized he was enjoying the moment alone, Trubadur left the slaying scene. He found Nadia at the entrance, leaning against the door. "That was incredible," he said.

She glared at him, hand trembling as she wiped away a tear. "Thank you for finding the right word."

Trubadur fought the urge to comfort her in his arms. "What you have is revolutionary, Nadia. Together we are going to turn the tide."

"Don't mock me with that name. You know who I am now."

"Who you are and the role you're playing was foretold. This was inevitable. Don't curse yourself."

"Mortimer already took care of that."

Trubadur patted his crossbow. "Shall we continue thinning the herd?"

Nadia grabbed his throat, fangs bared. He tried to resist and was easily held against the wall. "Do not speak of them that way, ever again." She yanked open the secret door and strode through the empty sanctuary, nave and vestibule, and out of the church.

Trubadur closed the passage door behind him and made sure the sour bishop was properly hung.

At the caretaker's quarters he opened the door without a knock. Cătălin looked up from the table, mouth full of mutton. "I saved you some leg."

"Thank you, good sir. But first we have some cleaning to do in the tunnel."

SUNKEN TREASURE

The Rice University rehabilitation center looked like a schizophrenic health club. Some patients worked out on high-end exercise machines while others labored with repurposed household items. Victor and Barbara found Dr. Winnie Linciome in that latter group, and sweaty.

"Oh thank God," said Winnie. He sank to his knees after pushing an office chair across the floor in an inclined plank position. "Dr. Mengele," he said to his physical therapist, "my friends are here. You'll want to pretend you're not torturing me."

His therapist was tall, boyishly handsome, wide-bellied. He laughed. "Isn't it amazing what you can get paid to do? Okay, you should probably take a break before Sharise gets her hands on you." He winked at Victor and Barbara and gave Winnie a congratulatory pat before moving on to another patient.

"Please don't hug me," Winnie protested. "I'm truly soaked." He received one anyway from Barbara. Victor was satisfied with a handshake. "I've never worked out this hard in my life." He led them to a table against the wall. "Actually, I've never worked out. But I've always been a stander rather than a sitter. I hear that pretty much guarantees a long, healthy life."

"Speaking of which," said Victor, nodding at Winnie's mouth. "How long do you plan on living?"

Winnie displayed rounded canines. "The cure works. Tripp is a genius. I'm eating a normal diet. No cravings." He rubbed his forehead with thin, trembling fingers. "Unfortunately there is no quick cure for recovering from a near-death beating and bloodletting."

Barbara squeezed his hand. "You're looking better every

time."

"Torture agrees with me, you're saying." His speech was a little slower than normal, his Austrian accent heavier. "Explains why I enjoyed working with Dr. Speer."

"Will you return to the Longevity Labs?" said Victor.

"Ironically enough, the Labs may have reached the end of its lifespan. Dr. Speer left and took his funding with him." Winnie gave them a sad smile. "Besides, we have a more acute longevity issue. It's no longer a question of how long our species will live, but whether."

"Victor and Eugene are doing their part."

"So I hear. It's not enough." Winnie couldn't stop his eyes from twinkling, but there was no happiness there. "Our slayer support organization is in trouble. Drone attacks, painting us as terrorists—it's working. Our side is scared, and vampires are ascendant. The hashtag 'stake our claim' is blowing up the Twitter-sphere."

Barbara got misty-eyed. "We don't understand what's happening with her."

It was Winnie's turn to provide a comforting squeeze. He scooted forward with wincing effort. "Mengele also had me clamshelling across the floor in that damn roller chair. My ass is burnt rubber." He chose his next words carefully. "Your daughter is going through a very challenging transition."

"She appeared well-adjusted," said Victor.

"We won't know for certain until we can talk to her," said Winnie.

"Morbius's diary," said Barbara. "We need to get that to this CWS, so we can get Amberly back and cure her."

Winnie frowned. "Of course that would be helpful," he said without conviction.

"We think the Houston D.A. has it," said Victor. "Eugene and I are going to find out."

"Listen." Winnie swallowed multiple times, struggling to master his brain or his vocal apparatus. "There is no guarantee this CWS will release her. No matter what he reads in the diary. We don't even know for certain she is still in his control." He looked back and forth at them, worry stitched across his tired face. "The best way to get Amberly back is to simply find her."

Barbara brought out her iPad, already on the Facebook page she had created for Amberly's return. "We keep hoping someone sees something and posts it, or reaches out to us." She checked the site constantly.

"I looked at your Find Amberly page," said Winnie. "Everyone blames the slayers for our predicament."

"Not everyone." Barbara scrolled down the page. "Fran Clark who I knew in high school just made a very anti-vampire post. A friend of hers was attacked in her own home. The vampire hurt her, broke her shoulder." She frowned as she read. "Madeline Hansen. That's her friend." She looked at Victor. "Isn't that Jay's wife?"

Victor's gaze rested unfocused on a deformed man hobbled by a rubber tube tied to his ankles and laboring across the floor with the therapist's encouragement. "I did not *break* her shoulder. It happened as she was struggling."

"What?" Barbara's voice quavered. "*You*, you attacked Madeline, in her house?"

He glared. "Jay is trying to kill me."

"Then bite *him*." She began to cry. "You bit his *wife*? I don't understand that."

"Barb, that's the only way I can get him to leave me alone. How can you not understand that?"

She shoved the little table against him. "Did you hit her?"

"*No.*"

"Did you *throw* her?"

"No. I only bit her, I had to hang on to her—"

She grabbed his chin. "I don't know that I believe you." Her hand shook and she let go. "We need to find our *daughter*. You can*not* do anything to jeopardize that. Do you understand me?"

Victor nodded, frowning. Barbara hurried from the exercise area and around the corner toward the exit.

Winnie rubbed his face, sighing and scratching his scalp. "I didn't know you were acquainted with Jay Hansen."

"You know him?"

"He was an investor in our longevity research. Schmoozing investors was Speer's job—I know, it's a wonder we received any funding—but I did meet most of them, including Hansen. And come to think of it, he was particularly interested in the research we were doing on *you.*"

"What did you tell him?"

"Nothing. I thought he was a prick." Winnie lowered his voice. "It turns out Hansen is also a contributor to the slayer cause. I just became privy to *that* donor list. A careful, limited disclosure was deemed necessary now that they are marked men and women. To allow us to try to protect them."

Victor sank in his chair, sullen. "Maybe you can protect Jay a little less."

The scientist rubbed at an uncharacteristic stain on his uncharacteristic sweat pants. "I will talk to him. I will make him understand what you mean to us."

"I can take care of myself." A vivid image of Barbara's disappointment brought a wave of angry embarrassment. "You and your slayer network will have to get by without me. All I care about is Amberly."

"We need your gift, Victor. It granted the world new life once before, long ago. Fortunately, saving Amberly will go a long way toward repeating the favor." At Victor's puzzled scowl, he leaned closer across the table. "Barbara is right. You cannot lose focus. That would give our enemies the opportunity they need."

"Who *isn't* my enemy? I am everyone's worst nightmare."

"All the more reason to remain focused. I can help. There is someone special I encountered, in Romania. It's time for you to meet her."

The deformed man stumbled in his rubber-band hobble and splayed out before them. Best he could with a hunchback, he looked up at Victor.

Victor grabbed him by the hair and wrenched his head against the hunchback's resistance. "You fucker."

"Whoa!" Winnie exclaimed. David Copperfield howled and scrambled backward, leaving Victor with a thin handful of hair. The wretch grappled with the rubber band, trying first to yank it off his feet and then to untie the now-tightly-cinched knot. He appealed to the physical therapist hurrying to his aid as Victor approached. "He's the one who hurt me!"

"I've never had a worthier victim."

Winnie pulled him back. The therapist bravely stood between David and Victor. "You should be prosecuted. David has severe impairments."

"I should be prosecuted for not killing him."

"Victor," said Winnie. "I'm going through exactly what this gentleman is suffering."

Victor turned on him. "Are the sufferings of a hero like you and a villain like him morally equivalent?"

Winnie gazed at him with something akin to pity. "When they're both caused by a vampire? I'm afraid so."

Eugene stepped on the band of police tape as a courtesy to the two elderly slayers. They didn't exactly shuffle their way along, but neither was there a hop in their step.

"Chop-chop," said Burton the Southwest U.S. district slayer commander, to Edna Campbell, pescetarian, former PETA member, humpback accentuated by her downcast demeanor. Burton's eye was on the sky. "For all we know they have this place under drone surveillance."

This was X's house. Eugene produced a key courtesy the realtor, who was also in Eugene's Amway network and eager to make an unearned leap up the pyramid-shaped multi-level marketing organization. "All the more reason to take our time and look like we belong." He held the door open.

Edna stopped on the stoop, overcome. "Go on without me."

Eugene took her hand and when she resisted, lifted and carried her over the threshold. "This will be cathartic."

"Sven, my beautiful Sven," she wailed. Eugene kicked the door shut before she alarmed the neighbors. "Dirty vampire bastards! He was better than the whole lot of them!" She crumpled blubbering to the floor.

"And he knew a lot of French words, hurrah for him." Eugene had no time for statements of the obvious. "Now let's find that diary."

No one believed in the power of Morbius's diary like Eugene. He was neither surprised the CWS would play hardball with Amberly's life, nor anything less than certain that the diary would clear things up. Either it would prove Victor right and result in Amberly's freedom, or prove Victor was indeed Morbius and inspire Eugene to one final, heroic, sacrificial act.

Slayer scuttlebutt said the vamp D.A. had the diary. But

Granny Foreman like Paul Newman playing Fast Eddie Felson had taught Eugene how to shoot pool like Tom Cruise playing Vincent Lauria. He smelled a hustle.

Now Burton was non-responsive. He stood in the doorway to X's office. "This place is still lived-in."

"They've been treating it as a crime scene," said Eugene. "The realtor just got the green light to start cleaning it up for sale. That's why we need to *hurry*."

Filing boxes were stacked against the walls. X's desk was messy with paperwork and knickknacks, and a *Sports Illustrated*. He had one of those bobbing pink flamingos. Beside the computer monitor was a mostly-empty bottle of Diet Dr Pepper.

"It's just so human-like," said Burton.

"That's how they style themselves," Eugene cautioned. "Don't fall for it."

Burton poked a finger at his nose. "Don't you pretend you can teach me a damn thing, punk. I've been slaying vampires since you were a spot of goo-goo your mama picked up from a truck stop toilet seat."

Eugene unshouldered his oversized equipment duffel. "Cap your colostomy bag, old man. I am going to beat every square inch of you."

"Put down your dukes." Burton sighed. "I guess it's just finally hitting me." He went to Edna and helped her up. "Why do *they* get to live forever? Doesn't it make you hate them all the more, babe?"

"Don't you 'babe' me," Edna mumbled. "My heart belongs to another." She gazed at the ceiling. "And he carried it with him through those pearly gates."

"Dammit." Burton's face melted in sorrow. "I've been staying so strong—so damn *strong*—until you reminded me how delicate is the thread by which we dangle. I didn't want to tell you. This morning I was diagnosed. I got the cancer." His shoulders shook. "Treasure your time on this earth, Miss Edna. And love the one you're with."

"Oh, you poor soul." Edna grunted from hugging him so hard.

Burton hugged her back passionately and moan-talked into her ear. "Those brave slayers were martyrs for our cause. Do not despair, Miss Edna. My last physical act on this little blue marble will be to avenge your French loved one's death."

Edna gazed up into his eyes. "If you survive it, it won't be your last physical act, sweet stuff."

"The diary!" Eugene was aggravated but also understood the allure of slayer women, of any age. He yanked open one desk drawer after another. "First the obvious places. Then we start searching for the hidden panels and passageways." He glared at the hugging, swaying slayers. "A little help here."

Burton gave him a disrespectful look. "So you can sit up all night in your slumber party jammies reading the diary with your big vampire buddy?"

"You're questioning *my* motives?" Eugene slammed a drawer and came around the desk. "I've been slaying vampires since you were a less-ancient man!"

"Listen Foreman—or should I call you Maistru?" The silver-haired slayer got in Eugene's face. "No one trusts you, alrighty? Your ancestor was a traitor, and you're a bad apple that fell right beside that same evil tree."

Eugene's long eyelashes butterfly-kissed Burton's long eyebrows. They both recoiled and rubbed madly at their faces. "Find the diary, old man!"

Burton threw an air punch at the back of Eugene's head for Edna's benefit. He started on the nearest filing cabinet.

Half an hour later he pushed away the last filing box. "Nothing but Metafist records," he referred to X's consulting company. Burton went from kneeling to sitting with a groan. "Are they publicly traded? Might be a stock worth looking at, people. They must have their software systems installed in a couple hundred companies and government departments."

Edna pulled a sledgehammer from Eugene's duffel. "Time to find the hidden passageway." She swung it against the paneled wall. The recoil staggered her, sent her reeling backward. She dropped the sledge and veered sideways out of the den. There came the sound of her crashing to the floor.

Eugene went to the dented wall. There had been a hollowness to the *thwock* of the sledge. He felt up and down, then retreated to the desk and ran his hands under the overhanging top until he found a switch. A section of the paneling swung open.

"Well I'll be," said Burton.

Eugene let him go in first. He had been at the receiving end of too many vamp booby traps.

Burton pulled the string from an overhanging bulb. It illuminated a nicely appointed man cave. Big screen television, leather recliner. Girly mags on an end table under a nearly-empty bottle of Old Granddad bourbon and a cigar stub in a ceramic ashtray.

Burton picked up a dog-eared book. *The Untold Story of Franco's Vampire Unit*. "History buff."

"*Vampire* history *vampire* buff," Eugene clarified. A big case of the creeps afflicted him, standing in this vamp sanctum. He yanked DVDs and books off the shelves, knifed the recliner's supple flesh and tore out stuffing, turned the chair upside-down and shone his laser-like flashlight beam into the crannies. Nothing.

After ten minutes he was sweating, cold and sticky stuff. He burst out of the vamp-cave to draw a deep breath of fresh air—in a vamp-den, that was barely better! He ran into the vamp foyer, nearly out of oxygen, eyes bulging and clawing at his collar, and then out of the vamp house. On the stoop with his head between his knees, the early summer Houston humidity had never tasted so sweet.

He couldn't bring himself to go back in. Evil permeated that house. Also because he was pretty sure Burton and Edna were screwing. Twenty minutes later they emerged. Burton leaned against a white pillar and Edna leaned against him, twining her fingers in his wiry white chest hair.

"Nothing to be found in there," Burton reported.

It was extremely rare that Eugene found a slayer he liked. Burton was no exception. "And you turned that place inside out, did you?" He softened; if they could find love in this insane world, a world on the brink of disaster, then God bless them. "It's fine. We have other clues to follow."

Burton crossed his arms. "You and your buddy the vampire king?"

"Why do you love this Morbius vamp so much?" said Edna, stroking the inside of Burton's thigh, strumming his corduroys like a rumble strip.

"I don't *love* him! Victor Thetherson is a vampire king who happens to have a special power we need! Why is that so hard to understand?!"

"Keep it down, sonny," said Burton.

Eugene put his hands to his ears, his misophonia in full sonic bloom. "Stop *rubbing* him!"

"Can't," said Edna.

Eugene jumped up and stalked across the yard.

Burton pursued him. "We're doing just fine without help from a damned bloodsucker."

Eugene wheeled on him. "How can you say that, after what happened in Atlantic City?"

"A bunch of bumblers."

Edna grabbed Burton's arm to steady herself so she could slap his face. "Don't you *ever* disrespect Sven."

"Sorry, hon." Burton asked for and received a make-up smack on the lips.

The sound was like teeth on a wooden spoon for Eugene. "I hate Victor more than you can imagine," he said. "Exactly how I hate every vampire, times ten. But unfortunately, Atlantic City was a representative sample of our slayer population. We don't have a prayer against evolved vamps without Victor. He is the only one who can find their soft spots."

"So you two are going to kill them one at a time." Burton shook his head with disappointment. "Meanwhile they wipe us out by the hundreds. And take over the world."

"People will see the light." Eugene unlocked the topper on his pickup so they could toss in the duffel with the sledge, flashlight, and gear that hadn't been needed—bandolier of stakes, five-gallon can of gasoline, rappelling equipment. "And in the meantime, yes. One vamp at a time."

"Make Morbius your next," said Burton.

"You can't trust a vamp," Edna crowed.

"He'll double-cross you, sonny boy." Burton slapped Edna where her ass used to be. "Why don't you go lock that door, sweet cheeks."

Edna cackled. "Maybe you should buy it and make it our love nest."

Burton watched her rickety sashay toward the house. "By the way," he said to Eugene. "I don't want you to worry. I don't really have the cancer. Just needed to snap that beautiful lady out of her funk."

Jay Hansen reached his wife's table a couple minutes ahead of Houston district attorney Goodnight. Jay didn't want to sit, he wanted to get his wife out of there, but neither did he want to make a scene, here where the Houston new-energy scene was made, the Refinery, a triple-decker restaurant and bar open-faced to the Woodlands waterway. Madeline had picked a table right on the riverwalk, the place to see and be seen.

The evening was calm, warm and not too sticky (Jay's sweat was not weather-related), and so the Refinery and riverwalk were busy. Jay nodded to the Robertsons, she the CFO at Anadarko just down the street, he a happy house husband who had been the first to invite Madeline into the neighborhood bunko club. Jay sat with his wife.

"What are you doing?" he asked with a water glass at his lips.

Madeline tapped the table to quell the shake in her hand. Arm in a sling and the pinch of her face behind oversized sunglasses suggested domestic abuse. The uncovered, weeping bite wound changed the picture. "Filing an assault report."

She said it at normal volume; to Jay, a scream at the top of her lungs. "Maddy. Please." He was a man who thought about his wife and strived to be romantic for her, a man who went beyond bringing home the bacon, dedicated to ensuring Madeline felt cared for. This was a public reveal of his inadequacy. "Please don't do this."

She glared at him. "I can't believe you're not standing up for me." This was at a near-whisper.

"Can I start you two off with something?" The server was aware of the tension, eager to take *no* for an answer.

Jay waved him away. "I *am* standing up for you," he hiss-whispered. "Come home with me and talk about it. Then we can take the next steps together."

"We're together now." Madeline nodded at the bronze-skinned man surfing between tables on a wave of *reaction*. The Woodlands was a plugged-in community. They knew what Houston's D.A. looked like, they knew he was a vampire, and they were fairly evenly and passionately split pro and con.

Woodlands people were naturally unencumbered by inhibition; the alcohol only made them louder.

"Take a bite out of crime, Goodnight," said one.

"You're a disgrace," said another.

"What's next, Houston police drone strikes?" said a third.

"This is the next civil rights struggle!"

Goodnight refused the last commentator's high-five, ignored accolade and barb alike. He took a seat with the Hansens. The server caught his eye, received a headshake, and crossed that table off his mental list.

"Mrs. Hansen?" he confirmed.

"Madeline."

"Why are we doing this in public?"

"That was my question," said Jay.

"No," said Madeline. "Your question was, why, period." She looked at the D.A. "Like I told you. It's this or a press conference."

Goodnight turned to Jay. "You are going to put this on me?"

"Because it's your job!" Madeline leaned into it. She had the full attention of everyone in the middle tier of the Refinery. "He broke my fucking shoulder! He assaulted me. And what about the fucking bite?" She yanked her shirt away from the mark. "Why is this okay?"

"I don't write the criminal code, Mrs. Hansen. Take it up with your local representative."

"Oh fuck you. Fuck *you*."

Goodnight only had eyes for Jay. "I thought we were clear."

"I *tried*." Jay's desperation was quiet and intense. "I am *trying*. This," he indicated his wife's situation, "is the result. He went too far—this is the legal justification you needed. For God's sake, *do your job*."

A cicada-like clicking emanated from the back of Goodnight's throat and Jay's guts loosened. "Unfortunately, our legal system is more unpredictable than ever," said the D.A.

"So you're not going to do anything?" Madeline continued to speak loudly enough to be heard at the surrounding tables.

"Of course I will." Goodnight clicked while he looked at Jay. "I will do what I promised."

Jay couldn't take his eyes off that twitching jaw.

"You fucking vampire." Madeline staggered away from the table. Jay rushed to her and she swung at him with her disabled arm, screaming in pain and collapsing to her knees. "Get away from me! How could you let him *do* this to me?" She clutched at her neck as if trying to tear away the skin Victor had touched.

The skin Victor had put his mouth on. Had sunk his teeth into.

Jay nearly went mad, on his knees and head to the floor to stop the heaving in his gut.

Goodnight crouched and spoke softly in his ear. "Maybe you're finally willing to sacrifice for what's right? For your beautiful wife?"

Yes. Madeline was Midwestern chic, that's how Jay thought of her. Humble, sensible, classy and sharp. Had been from the day he met her, when they were young, young, young. She was the best the world could create. Yes, Jay would sacrifice for her. Right now he wanted to throw himself into the waterway and let one of the water taxis run over him. But he wouldn't do that. He wouldn't leave Madeline alone. At least not with Victor Thetherson alive.

D.A. Goodnight rode a water taxi back to the Marriott where earlier he had hosted a national emergency conference on the very issue of prosecuting human-vampire altercations. Most of the discussion centered on whether vampires were covered by the Make My Day laws, allowing lethal retaliation for slayer attacks. Goodnight had made a compelling case in favor.

It was still a far cry from criminalizing the slaying acts themselves. Branding slayers as terrorists was a great start, but Goodnight was pessimistic humans would ever truly believe vampire lives mattered.

He was engrossed in editing notes he had taken on his e-pad. Vaguely he realized the water taxi pilot was talking on his radio, agitated. The *splashes* over the thrum of the taxi's motor snapped him to attention. Passengers bobbed in the taxi's bubbly wake, some in summer sportswear, some in evening finery, all in life preservers. Goodnight could not swim. He jumped to his feet.

A big middle-aged vampire sat him back down. "Sorry," said the vampire. "All out of life jackets."

The vampire was dressed in a light-blue polo shirt and khakis.

Accompanying him was a skinny young human all in black. An odd couple, but clearly simpatico in their loathing for him.

"Victor Thetherson," Goodnight recognized the vampire.

"You are really hating Judge Hobart right about now," Thetherson referred to the judge who had ordered him released.

"Just doing her job," said Goodnight.

"As are we," said the slayer Eugene Foreman.

Goodnight had an exceptionally inaccessible Heel. Heel*s*, plural. This evolved redundancy gave him confidence. On the other hand, he was convinced Thetherson possessed the Eye—it was the only way these two could have been able to slay so many highly-evolved vampires. So Goodnight carried a handgun. He was ready to test his own Make My Day legal theory.

"Time for you to die, vamp," said Foreman, drawing a slim stake from a bandolier inside his long overcoat.

Goodnight's blood pumped and his trigger finger itched. "Let's make a deal," he propositioned.

"Deals with vamps aren't legally enforceable," said Foreman. "One side is criminally insane." He looked to Thetherson. "Don't you have something to tell me?"

"Let me live," Goodnight offered, "and I'll give you something you will find very interesting. The Morbius diary."

Their eyes lit up. "Finally!" said Foreman. "Soft spot, Vic."

"We need the diary *first*, idiot," said Thetherson.

"If you mean to kill me *after*," said Goodnight, "why would I give it to you?"

"Nice negotiating, fatty," Foreman said to Thetherson. It was possible they hated each other more than they did Goodnight.

"What in the hell is that *sound*?" Foreman leaned toward Goodnight. "It's coming from you! Stop it!"

The fang-grinding in the back of Goodnight's throat was getting in the slayer's head. He kept it up. "Victor Thetherson, what kind of vampire are you? First you're Morbius, then you aren't, now you are? You help slayers, you assault women." He turned to Foreman. "And what kind of slayer are you? Did you help Victor attack his boss's wife?"

"What?"

"I'll bet you watched while he broke her shoulder and sucked her blood."

Foreman now appeared ready to plunge the stake into Thetherson.

"Honestly now," said Thetherson, "if you give me the diary, I won't tell dipshit here your Heel."

"Good vampire, bad vampire." Goodnight stared at him. "Either way, my boss wants you dead."

Foreman did something of a double-take. "The mayor is a vampire, too?"

Goodnight didn't like the mayor, so he said "Yes" and laughed, which gave them a glance at his rear fangs.

"Thanks," said Foreman. He rammed the stake into Goodnight's mouth, splitting the space between his palatine tonsils, breaking the tip against his spine.

Goodnight shot Foreman. He pulled out the stake and gagged on his blood as Foreman fell to the deck. Thetherson slugged him in the neck. The big vampire could hit; Goodnight felt one of his tonsils pop.

He had always dreaded this moment, and sure enough it was awful. His throat caught fire and his body went cold, for a moment, before a fever-fire swept over him head to toe, cellular civil warfare, brother vs. brother and parent vs. child.

Foreman sat up like Michael Myers in *Halloween.* The slayer wore a bulletproof vest. Now the redundancy in Goodnight's Heel brokered an internal truce, dropping his temperature back into his cool operating range. He brought the pistol to bear on Foreman's face.

That was the moment the water taxi pilot chose to abandon ship. The boat dove to a stop, lifting the stern and sending Goodnight's shot ricocheting off the metal roof. Thetherson kicked his pistol through the air and over the side, and put him in a chokehold. "His tonsils."

"I staked him there already!" said Foreman.

"You missed." Thetherson forced open Goodnight's readily-unhinged jaw. "Left of the epiglottis."

Foreman plunged a fresh stake in his mouth. It hit paydirt and pierced the other palatine tonsil, and Goodnight's body again flooded with self-destructing antibodies.

They let him lie on the deck, watching him die.

Goodnight weathered the immune storm. He tried to feign

death but when there was none of the oozing and structural collapse, the duo became suspicious.

Thetherson peered at him. “Back of the base of the tongue.”

The sonofabitch could truly *see* his Heel. Goodnight couldn’t get over it.

Foreman was unsure how to attack his lingual tonsil, allowing Goodnight to deflect his thrust, the stake gouging neck muscle. The D.A. howled with the pain. Foreman wedged a stake laterally between his teeth and shoved down on both ends. Goodnight’s jaw popped completely out of its socket and was torn mostly off his face.

“Oh good God,” Thetherson complained.

“Shut up!” said Foreman. He sat astride Goodnight’s writhing body and two-hand stabbed at his tongue. “What the hell is the ‘back of the base’?” He stabbed repeatedly until he nailed it. Goodnight’s body went rigid and then limp on the deck.

“This is absolutely awful,” said Thetherson.

Goodnight saw darkness and a beckoning pinpoint of light. And then he saw the boat’s corrugated metal roof.

“Come *on*,” said Foreman, looking green.

“Directly behind the nose,” said Thetherson, referring to his pharyngeal tonsil, or adenoid.

“Please God let this be the last one,” said Foreman, producing yet another stake and driving it home.

“You’ll never get her back,” Goodnight croaked his last words, his enunciation admirable under the circumstances.

“What?” said Victor.

“Are you talking about Amberly?” said Eugene.

Victor grabbed Goodnight by the shirtfront. The D.A.’s head lolled. Victor shook him and slapped him. “What do you know?”

Eugene elbowed him out of the way and punched Goodnight in the skull. “Tell me where she is!”

Victor shoved him aside and slammed Goodnight over and over to the deck. “Where is she? Where is Amberly?” Eugene tried to take over the interrogation and they wrestled over the body.

“Let me do it!”

“Get off me!” Victor threw Eugene into a row of seats.

Eugene jumped to his feet. “What did you do to your boss’s

wife?"

"None of your business." Victor took a swing but Eugene slipped inside and tackled him.

"Slaying vampires like you *is* my business!"

"I command you to stop looking for my daughter!"

Sirens reached them from shore. They realized they were wrestling atop the thoroughly destroyed vampire corpse, both of them spattered with blood and gore.

"We are in big trouble," said Victor, plopping into the pilot's seat. Full throttle he accelerated down the waterway. "This was the *worst*, the absolute *worst* fucking idea you've ever had."

"We sent a strong message to your vamp friends," said Eugene. "The return will be tenfold. Now slow down, you'll miss the landing."

Victor cut the throttle and looked down at the D.A.'s tortured head. "You really are a terrible slayer."

"You're like a bad Braille seer, groping your way blindly to the Heel."

Victor saw something in Goodnight's clenched hand. He stepped on the dead D.A's wrist, the fingers opened like a blooming flower, and there lay a memory stick.

"You're missing the dock!" said Eugene. "Reverse the throttle!"

Victor did so but they drifted past the landing, to the chagrin of the handful of people waiting for a ride. The stern came around until they were floating backward. Victor threw the throttle forward and the motor killed.

The sirens grew louder.

Eugene hopped on the prow and dove into the water. Victor grabbed the tie-off line and hurled it after him. Eugene ignored it and swam for the bank.

The boat was moving in the wrong direction. Victor clambered onto the bow, held the memory stick above his head, and launched. The boat swung and dumped him into a belly flop. He floundered to get the memory stick in his pocket while drinking the waterway and swimming for shore, would-be water taxi patrons carping at him all the while.

Victor sloshed across the parking lot and climbed into the passenger seat of Eugene's pickup.

"Are you going to get my seat wet?" said Eugene. He had changed into dry clothes.

"You brought a change of clothes?!"

"We were slaying on the *water*," said Eugene as he squealed out of the parking lot.

They crossed the waterway at the nearest bridge and headed south, no sirens in pursuit. Eugene avoided the interstate, doubling the travel time. Victor was shivering violently by the time they reached the Kroger where they had met. Eugene drove right on by.

"What are you doing?"

"We can't go home," said Eugene. "The cops will be waiting for us. We need to lay low. I got us a place." He looked over at Victor. "Stop that."

"What?"

"That clacking!"

"That is my teeth! I'm freezing!"

Eugene turned up the heat and drove on. After a few blocks he complained. "It's like a tomb in here."

"Sh-sh-shut up."

At a seedy motor inn on the edge of downtown, Victor and Eugene received catcalls from idlers congregated in the parking lot and hanging over the second-deck railing, as they entered a room together. Close to hypothermia, Victor made for the bathroom to shuck his wet clothes.

Eugene knocked on the door. "You can wear my skivvies. I'll freebird."

Grudgingly Victor opened the door a crack. Eugene offered his undies. Victor looked at them.

"Are those boys'?"

"I'm a slim, you fat ass!"

Muttering, Victor wrapped himself in a towel, threadbare and also too small, and hustled for one of the twin beds. Eugene reviewed the memory stick plugged into his laptop. "Tell me that's the diary," Victor chattered.

"It *was*," said Eugene. "I can only retrieve bits and pieces. It's ruined." He slapped the laptop closed and crossed his arms. "Because you got it wet."

Victor struggled to get warm under the thin covers. "Because you bailed out and left me stranded on a dead boat."

"Why didn't you gently lower yourself into the water and swim with one hand?" Eugene mimed one-armed swimming, holding his phone above his head.

"Shut up." Victor nodded at the phone. "They can trace those things, dummy. They'll drone strike us."

"It's unregistered, scrubbed, and layered with blackhat outbound masking encryption. Granted that kind of precaution is overkill when it comes to vamps. But that's one of my credos. Overkill."

"Okay, don't talk to me."

"You want to call Mom?"

"Don't call her that. No. She's never going to take my call again."

"Good. She deserves a whole lot better."

Victor put a pillow over his eyes and let the warmth relax away the shivers. He fell asleep.

Eugene stared at Victor's lips motorboating as he snored. Yes, he possessed the Sight, invaluable in the battle against the evolved vamps; but as the Foreman-Maistru slaying saying said, the only good vampire is a dead one. A motto like that left no room for exceptions.

Legend said there was only one way to kill Morbius. But Eugene wasn't prepared to sacrifice himself. Amberly needed him, he was certainly her only hope. She would have to be live-captured and brought in for the cure. No one else could be trusted to pull that off.

Eugene remembered the Arizona desert highway where Victor had disclosed a different way to kill him.

The same way Eugene's ancestor, Trubadur Maistru, had slain the prior Morbius.

Gay sex with a vampire—was this the terrible decision Trubadur had faced?

Eugene had to doubt the intelligence of his ancestor. There was a better way.

On his phone he accessed one of his favorite sites. This woman, Maria, was a bedtime whisperer. She made whispering and other sounds that ordinarily drove Eugene into fits of misophonia-induced insanity. But not when Maria made them. Sometimes her whispers and soft, repetitive sounds were the only way for him to fall asleep.

Some men found Maria's voice extremely attractive.

Eugene started one of her videos and knelt at Victor's bedside, setting the phone on the pillow covering Victor's eyes. He had to fight off slumber as he waited for Maria to work her way into Victor's dreams.

Victor no longer snored. His lips made crackly mumbling sounds. Eugene didn't like those sounds. Victor started to move, just a little, small readjustments in bed. Eugene's mouth was dry, his throat, his esophagus, his entire alimentary canal was dry with terror at what he needed to do. He was not Catholic but he crossed himself, and thanks to the thin blanket found the ridge just below the hump of Victor's stomach.

"Folding fresh towels can be so enjoyable," Maria whispered as Eugene gently stroked Victor.

Victor moaned. This was the absolute worst sound in Eugene's voluminous library of terrible sounds.

Eugene stroked. And stroked. The blanket's raised stitching rubbed his fingers dry. He hated that feeling. And his wrist was cramping. Carefully Eugene adjusted his position and switched hands.

"What is going on?" said Victor from under the pillow.

Eugene tried to finish him off. Victor lurched up and backhanded him. "What the hell are you *doing?!*"

"Killing you!"

Victor roared and started to go after him—looked down and thought better of it—and went to the bathroom and put his wet clothes back on. They felt *great*.

Without a word he plucked the memory stick from Eugene's laptop and left the room. He absorbed loiterers' derisive comments en route to the office. Victor rented his own room.

As he lay in bed, somewhat afraid to go back to sleep, he tried to figure out whose lovely voice he had been dreaming about.

TÂRGU MUREȘ: AUGUST 4, 1586

Nadia didn't eat on the journey to Transylvania. Ten days out of Bucharest she loped gracefully through deep Carpathian snow and brought down a goatherd—in no time she had the windburned, toothless young man hung upside down from a rock outcropping, ready for slash-drain-and-drink. Trubadur reached them in time to intervene.

They spent that night under a white cliff, sheltered from the bitter wind, their bed a soft beach of salt eroded from the mountain. Their finest accommodations yet, but Trubadur couldn't sleep as Nadia tossed and turned. She had slept little during their journey, which meant early starts and long days. Theirs might be the fastest Bucharest-to-Târgu Mureș winter transit in mankind's or even vampire-kind's history, and Trubadur was thankful for it, yearning to see his children. But he was exhausted.

They had left Bucharest in unprepared haste ahead of a mob bristling with pitchforks and fortified with Ottoman mercenaries on the payroll of one of the few powerful boyar vampires they hadn't yet slain. Bucharest's citizens were emboldened by the slaughter of their fanged masters and simultaneously intent on destroying their liberators. Nadia's role was unclear in their minds but Morbius's evil legend deeply rooted; and Tru showed no inclination to fulfill his destiny.

The secret tunnels radiating from the Curtea Veche had given them a headstart, although Tru wasted most of the advantage on a detour to the guard tower. As he strategized his assault from behind a meager pile of straw in the adjacent stable, Nadia finally convinced him the odds were too great, and they left Bucharest without his hat.

He was roused before dawn by Nadia's stomach growling, like a rooster's premature crowing. She was staring miserably at him. "I offered you the castellan at Castle Bran!" said Trubadur.

"He smelled like dung soup."

Trubadur angrily readied his pack for the day's march. "So did the goatherd!"

"The castellan died horribly," said Nadia. Trubadur had first hacked off his foot, misreading Nadia's indication of his Heel. The castellan stuffed Trubadur out a high window—his crossbow snagged on the castellan's belt buckle, giving Nadia time to come to the rescue—then led them on a chase through Bran Castle, that most imposing outpost of the Holy Roman Empire. For a portly one-footed man, the castellan had been nimble and fleet. Trubadur put 8 bolts in the vampire before resorting to slamming an iron door repeatedly on his head. "Do you see me for a carrion feeder?"

"I'll postpone slaying the next vampire until you've drank your fill."

For all the slaying they had done in Bucharest, Nadia had never been able to stomach drinking a vampire's blood. And so this was the famished state she was in when they crossed the Mureş River. They skirted the small village and walked below the fortress wall from which Trubadur had unsuccessfully attempted the suicide-slaying of Mortimer Canterpark, to reach their destination. Trubadur went first through the gate of a high, dense thatch fence, to keep a small pack of large sheep dogs at bay long enough for them to recognize him.

Gate and hounds protected a half-hectare homestead with sheepfold, haystacks (alarmingly depleted so that the central pole and pyramidal support braces were visible), stable, tannery, smithy, and the house, with its separate gate accessing a broad porch decorated with carved dowels that in warmer years encouraged grapevines and hops, and a steep thatched roof of the type otherwise only seen in the mountains. The home of his deceased wife's parents.

"You're really pretty," said Stela Maistru. The six-year-old hadn't let her father put her down or taken her eyes off Nadia in the five uncomfortable minutes with the Kárpátis.

"Your *mother*," said Etel Kárpáti, "was *beautiful*." She adjusted her granddaughter's scarf. It matched her own, which did nothing to enhance the old woman's plain features. "Our wonderful Zsuzsanna had an *inner* radiance."

"Trubadur speaks very highly of your daughter," said Nadia.

"A man 'speaks highly' of a dam for breeding!" János Kárpáti paced, away and back, each return trip like a bull's charge. "Not his wife!"

"I don't speak of Zsanna, period," said Tru. "I speak *to* her, in my dreams." He gave Stela's ear a tug and tried unsuccessfully to set her down, his knees trembling from the rigors and deprivations of their journey. "*Draga tatei*," he called her daddy's darling, and kissed her cheek as she squealed happily, tickled by his fuzzy whiskers. "Domnul Kárpáti," he used the formal honorific for his father-in-law. "I am grateful for all you have done for Ugenosz and Stela. And for me. If you could extend your generosity to allow us to break our fast, we will be on our way."

"But of course you will stay longer," Etel protested.

János pointed at Nadia. "The vampire will find no sustenance here."

"She does not drink blood," Tru bent the truth. "Nadia is different."

Nadia parted her lips to let her fangs show. "Actually I could use some blood."

Her mood was in flux, shifting like the battle line between well-matched foes. Cooperate or control? Embrace the vampires who were drawn to her, or slay them? Tru watched her desires swing to and fro, never settled. Conflict always.

"But I do not bite."

The Kárpátis' eyes bulged. Etel pulled Stela from Trubadur's arms and János hurled the accusation. "She is the Morbius! The tales from Wallachia are true. How dare you bring her to our village?"

"To our *house*," Etel spoke quietly, holding the squirming Stela. "How can you put us at risk?"

Tru opened his overcoat to reveal a belt of stakes and crossbow bolts slung shoulder to hip. "You were safer the moment I walked through your door."

"You were trouble the moment you set foot in Transylvania all those years ago," said János. "We should never have allowed you near our precious Zsuzsanna."

Stela slipped from her bunică's grasp and darted around the spinning wheel, a modern implement indicative of the Kárpátis' wealth and an obstacle for Etel as she tried to grab her granddaughter. Stela gazed up at Nadia. "Why don't you bite people?"

Nadia knelt so that they were eye to eye. "Why don't *you* bite people?"

Eyes on Nadia's fangs, Stela lifted her own lip to reveal a wide gummy gap. "I don't have any teeth."

"And just because I *have* teeth, doesn't mean I should bite people."

"This is enough talk of teeth and biting," said Etel. She meant to haul her granddaughter to safety, but faltered when her eye caught Nadia's.

Trubadur had seen it before. Vampires and humans alike, against their better judgment, both saw in Nadia their savior.

Queen of the Vampires, and Possessor of the Eye. Trubadur seemed to be the only one who recognized the conflict raging within her.

"I told you," said Tru. "Nadia is different."

"Morbius, you mean," said János.

Tru nodded. "I believe she is. She was chosen by Mortimer Canterpark."

The Kárpátis clutched the crucifixes hung from their necks. The carrier had brought misery to Transylvania. Vampires had suddenly emerged—some had been there all along, waiting, while others were freshly made. They occupied positions of power, in the village administration, in the armies of princes and voivodes, in the churches. They exacted tolls and tributes in coin and blood.

Transylvanians had always hosted the competitions of the world's empires. And the rich stew that was their language and culture was evidence of their willingness to pledge a new allegiance as conditions warranted. The Kárpátis and their fellow countrymen were in the process of accommodating this new world power.

"But you must understand," said Tru. "Nadia hasn't turned out the way Canterpark expected."

"Trubadur Maistru!" For János, the name was a lamentation. "What has become of the world?"

"Domnul Kárpáti," said Tru, "everything is turned upside-down."

"Die, bloodsucker!" From the high rafters—the Kárpáti roof had been an object of local ridicule when Trubadur helped János build it seven years prior—Ugenosz dropped, clutching a stake too thick for his young hand. Tru caught his juvenile slayer son and stayed the stake a hair's-breadth from Nadia's breast.

"*Apám*!" screamed little Ugenosz Maistru. The boy had his mother's cherub cheeks, his father's committed eyes, and his maternal grandparents' Hungarian tongue. "*Öljük meg ezt a vámpírt együtt!*"

Tru pried away the stake and knelt before his son with a wad of his blouse in hand. "Do you recall my final instruction, Ugenosz? I don't want you slaying anyone."

"Any *thing*, you mean!" Ugenosz moved easily to Romanian.

"We have to watch him all the time," said his grandfather.

"I have known Nadia my whole life," Tru told his son.

Ugenosz glared at her. "What does that matter?" He tried to rearm himself from the bandolier across his father's chest. "The only good vampire is a dead vampire."

"The family motto," said Nadia.

Tru held up the stake his son had wielded. Not much more than a boy himself, still 'chicken-boned' as Nadia's father had once described him, Tru's all-consuming passion for slaying made him ill-equipped to counsel moderation. "This is the stake I used to kill Ivan Mureşanu. He broke my arm in the struggle, so I had to pound it in with my forehead."

Stela touched the crescent scar on her father's forehead.

"Ivan's widow throws a tomato at me every time I see her at the market," said Etel. "She brings her own if they are out of season."

"Ivan was a lesser vampire," Tru told Ugenosz. "Stake in the heart. Now, there are vampires who are different. Greater. Their hearts are protected. But, there is always a weak spot."

"Like the heel of Achilles," said Ugenosz.

Trubadur beamed.

Etel pointed at curled paper, goose quill, ink and a small stack of books at a desk in the corner. "As you instructed, the boyar's scribe comes in every other day to instruct the children in your precious Latin."

"A waste of time," said János. "Thanks to the Reformed Church, we now have the Bible in Hungarian. If the Wallachians learn to read, there will even be a Bible in Romanian."

"My *Wallachian* father taught me that Latin will free you if you know it," said Nadia. "And enslave you if you do not."

"Did he teach you the same approach with vampires?" János fairly spat at her.

"*Apa*," Ugenosz addressed his father, "identify her Heel!"

"Nadia is the key to slaying these new vampires," Tru explained. "She *sees* their Heels. With Nadia—and *only* with her—we will win this war."

Ugenosz scowled. "We don't need her. They say each people have their own Heel. For Transylvanians, the throat. Wallachians take it in the buttocks."

János held up his hands, claiming innocence. "He received that information from Roma Skudza the Healer."

"In her wagon behind the market," said Ugenosz, "Roma Skudza feeds me auspicious food and essential wisdom."

"Does she now."

"We can't watch him all the time, unfortunately," said János.

"You *take* him to see the Roma woman," said Etel with a deep frown.

"And thank the Lord I listen to Skudza rather than spit on her," said János. "Otherwise our roof would regularly collapse under the snowfall with everyone else's."

Zsuzsanna's father made other Transylvanians look positively parochial. He employed Serbs, Moldavians and Austrians in his salt mining and trading business, and was open to wisdom from Catholic, Protestant or Orthodox alike. János earned his family a good living for his willingness to listen.

Even to the Roma. When Skudza the Healer had foretold a generation of winter and pointed out all the telltale signs, János had promptly built their steep, snow-tolerant roof.

"Repairing a roof is cheaper than repairing our reputation," said Etel.

"The more you repair your reputation," said János, "the weaker it becomes."

"Ugenosz," said Nadia. For Tru her voice was the complex harmony of the pan flute. He had found that everyone heard something different to love in that instrument, and so he insisted Ugenosz take lessons. "We too have noticed that each people has a similar Heel. But there are variations. And in Wallachia, the soft spot is generally up here." She tapped her head.

"The boy's confusion is understandable," said János. "To hit a Wallachian in the brain, one has to aim for the ass."

Wallachians were the one people János disparaged. Trubadur was fairly sure he was the reason for the exception.

"Parochialism has been a blessing in how it has divided the vampires." Tru lectured his father-in-law but spoke to his children. "But now parochialism prevents us from uniting against these vermin."

At the slur, Nadia *shifted.* The air around her became chilled, poisoned.

"Michael the Brave will unite Romania," said little Stela. "That's what my friend Maria says."

"They say this Mihai Bravu is quite dashing," said Etel.

"We cannot wait for the voivodes." Trubadur kept one eye on his children, the other reserved for Nadia. "Even the dashing ones. Voivodes unite us and divide us for their own ends. We must lead ourselves, against our true enemy. The vampire."

"That is why I am here," said Nadia, looking at no one. "To lead you to a better place."

The cold emanating from her reached the Kárpátis. They shivered.

Tru led Ugenosz and Stela to the pot hung over the low flames of the hearth. "I have missed your bunică's goulash." He collapsed into a dining chair. There was comfort being here; the Kárpáti house felt like home, deep in his bones. He was liable to fall asleep before he could fill his stomach. "Give your father a big helping."

János threw up his hands. "All right then. We will eat. Your *woman* can find her nourishment where she will."

"Did someone say goulash?" Through the door came a tall, stooped woman with a horse face accentuated by a messy mane of black hair hung to one side in stringy clumps. "Domnul Kárpáti," she scolded. "Do I need to hear from the Archduke's pompous messenger about the arrival of such an esteemed guest?" The vampire spoke a strange Romanian-Hungarian-Slavic mishmash, her accent indeterminate. "Not a fortnight ago you and I agreed to be more open with each other." She stood before Nadia and stared. Her face melted into spiritual bliss, displaying crooked fangs. "Mortimer, you chose wisely." Tears trickled from her wide-set eyes. "May He bless you."

"Doamna Maresi, you honor our home." Etel Kárpáti's words were hollow, bearing a curse. "If only you had sent your own messenger to alert us to your visit. We would have slaughtered our goat and saved you the entrails."

Stela ran wailing to her grandmother. "Don't feed the vampire our goat!"

"Don't worry." Ugenosz moved in front of his sister and grandmother, facing off with the vampire Maresi. "Bunică wouldn't give this monster the rats in our stable."

"Good!" cried Stela.

Trubadur coughed to get Nadia's attention and raised his eyebrows: *Where is her Heel?* But Nadia seemed in a trance, transfixed on the bent, menacing vampire.

Maresi wiped the tears from her cheeks. "Your grandmother would give me *you* to save her precious position, children."

Etel moaned. "That is a lie."

Maresi snorted. "Etel Novotná, I have known the women of your family for generations. As you climb, not a one of you has ever checked to see whose face supports her boot."

"And we all understand who you are, Maresi." János came to his wife's defense, shaking with anger and fear. "The Emperor's new bitch."

"Please," Etel tried to silence her husband. "Maresi is a guest in our home. I have enough goulash for everyone."

János stood up to Maresi, trembling with rage and the understanding of where his recklessness was taking him. "You claim to represent harmony for Transylvania." Trubadur was proud of his father-in-law, and disappointed that Maresi stood between him and his crossbow. "You ask me to bring Moldavian, Magyar and Saxon to the table to break bread. But it will be their necks. I will not stretch their necks for you."

Maresi bared her fangs. "Then you will serve your people's heads on a platter to the Mohammedan in Constantinople."

Trubadur realized Nadia's bloodlust was rising as she watched János's courage fail. He could wait no longer. "The moment the she-vampire walked in your house, János, her allegiance to the Holy Roman Empire ended." He stood dizzy-headed on legs begging for rest. "She has a new master now."

The vampire Maresi didn't argue. She might have dropped to the floor and kissed Nadia's feet, for the way she gazed at her. "Tell me my dear, what is it like to be Morbius?"

Nadia breathed in short bursts. "Wonderful." If Trubadur knew her, and he did, she imagined a bloodbath, Maresi burying her face in Etel's throat while she retrieved the butcher's knife from the yard and ran it across János's, creating a bubbling brook from which she could slake her thirst.

Stela began to cry.

"Father, there are two too many vampires in our house." Ugenosz armed himself with a distaff, long, flanged and pointed, made obsolete by the spinning wheel and now given new purpose. He spread his legs and nodded to Trubadur, as if they had pre-planned a coordinated attack.

Maresi batted the distaff from Ugenosz's hand and went at his throat. Trubadur rammed a stake through one horse-cheek and out the other, a bit that blocked her bite. Ugenosz spit in her eyes. Trubadur unholstered a bolt and screamed at Nadia, "Heel!" Maresi tore out the stake and shoved it between Tru's ribs, putting him on his knees. Etel thrust an iron fireplace poker into her husband's hands, then swept up Stela and grabbed Ugie by the scruff of the neck and hauled them toward the back door.

"I converted your teacher," Maresi told Tru, tongue poking out a cheek hole. "Constantin. He was twice the slayer you are. And now he's twice as happy." She spoke to Nadia as a compatriot. "It was a mystery to the Archduke why you are traveling with this slayer."

That slayer lay face-down and expiring, and Nadia was having a hard time remembering why indeed they were together.

Maresi was clearly of the ancient race, from the legendary time Nadia had been drawn to the moment she met Mortimer Canterpark. Maresi radiated power while simultaneously recognizing in Nadia, her Morbius, that there was something more, something much bigger and as-yet beyond her grasp.

Nadia shuddered with a longing to inspire this vampire to greater heights.

"News … didn't travel … " Trubadur's strained mutterings blew puffs of sawdust from between the floorboards. " … from Bucharest?"

"From *Bucharest*?" Maresi whinnied. "News only travels *in* to Wallachia."

Trubadur was right, Nadia realized. Whether human or vampire, parochialism was the chink in every would-be voivode's armor. Nadia couldn't explain why it enraged her so.

"That's the way we like it," Trubadur wheezed. He struggled to his knees, sweat-soaked, a stake in each hand and one stuck in his side.

Maresi wrenched the stakes from Tru's hands and threw them toward the hearth. "We?"

"Nadia and me."

Maresi sneered. "Do not smear Morbius with your Wallachian manure."

Suddenly Nadia could *hear* the vampire's soul, vibrating at the junction of hip and leg. An image formed for Nadia, of a little lumpy man nested beside Maresi's crotch, wearing a pointed hat and stroking his bushy beard. A lumpy, powerful little man.

"*We.*" Nadia was behind her, on tiptoes to whisper through the ratty mane into Maresi's ear, hand sliding across her stomach. Nadia felt the vampire move into her and she had to fight the urge to warn her. "Morbius sends her regrets." She pointed at the seat of the vampire's soul.

Trubadur wrenched the stake from his ribs and tossed it into the air. Maresi's eyes followed it. He buried the distaff halfway up the flange into her little lumpy man.

Little Ugenosz launched off the spinning wheel stool, plucked the bloody stake from the air and drove it through Maresi's nose. The dying vampire seemed to recognize the added insult, eyes crossed in horror at her wooden beak as she staggered into the wall, knocking a near-dozen of Etel's elaborate painted eggs off the shelf.

Nadia caught two of the eggs. She stared down at the expiring Maresi, mouth open and opening wider and wider until her jaw fell off. Always after Trubadur's assisted slaying and all the more so with this particular vampire, her emotions were mixed.

There was a tug at her blouse. Stela, her eyes darting to the destroyed vampire. Nadia shifted to block the girl's view.

"My father likes you, doesn't he?"

Trubadur lay on the floor bleeding. "*Draga tatei,*" he rasped, "go to your bunică. Ugenosz, fetch me the healer, Roma Skudza." The stake that had been in his ribs, now wedged in Maresi's skull, had only penetrated him a finger's-breadth. Maybe two fingers. He would survive.

"Your father," Nadia answered Stela. "He *needs* me."

Behind her the vampire audibly decomposed and exuded a meaty odor. Nadia gave Stela the beautiful eggs to hold and picked her up. "Let's go outside."

Stela tucked into Nadia and buried her face in her neck. "*I* like you, too."

Nadia ignored the Kárpátis' reaction as she carried Trubadur's daughter into the fresh air.

MORBIUS MAGNET

I cut the last tile for the kitchen floor and set it. It's a perfect fit in the corner where the cabinets meet. Like the other three corners, I mapped out the preceding tiles so that this last one was in the shape of a diamond. Carefully, I walk over the ungrouted tiles to the center of the kitchen.

I imagine energy from the world flowing here from all directions, focused through these four diamonds and converging where I stand. It's magical. I'm absorbing that energy, converting it, and sending a positive force for change back to the four corners of the world.

Now I need to replace those stained and peeling Formica countertops. And then the bathrooms—I'm ill just thinking about them, much less using them. I'm going to gut and redo those bathrooms.

"Aren't you little miss handywoman?"

Tall, crazy, mean-eyed Hilda talks a lot more these days. Not when Cornelius is present; then she sulks and keeps her distance.

She clomps across my tiles. I cringe but the thin-set holds. Hilda does something of a double-take. "Did you bring someone into this house to help you?"

"Well, thank you, Brunhilda. No, luv, it was all me."

Hilda shoots me a mean look and starts banging through the cupboards. "I told you. It's just Hilda." She opens and slams the last door. "Did you hide the squirrel cup, girl?"

"The chipmunk cup? I saw George with it coming out of the bathroom."

"It's a squirrel. I should know. It is my cup."

"I think he used it for his urinalysis."

"No! That dirty focker!"

"The boys are really into the measured life." The boys, that's George and Boris, Cornelius's middle-aged gay vampire henchmen. "They're trying to identify their perfect blood types."

Hilda's growl climbs to a roar. "That is my favorite cup! They know that! And this auto-washer does not get things fully clean!" She kicks the dishwasher and puts a diagonal crimp in the door. "This house smells of cat piss!" The dishwasher door sags open and Hilda stomps it, breaking the hinge. The broken door breaks two tiles. "Gaah!"

"Don't worry, they're easy to replace."

Hilda wrenches the door fully off the machine and raises it overhead. "How about all of them?"

"Hilda, my dear?" Cornelius strides into the house. He has taken to wearing stitched woolen blouses and baggy woolen trousers, no longer dressed or looking at all like a Civil War Soldier. He sports a tall felt hat that recently replaced his wide-brimmed Southern fedora. His blouse is splotted with blood. He goes out all the time, drinking blood like a lush. While I sit here waiting for him to bring home leftovers.

I'll bet he has lost twenty years. His hair has gone from straight, thin, and white to thick, tangled, and brown. He smiles a lot. Drinking blood agrees with Cornelius.

Hilda lowers the door. She looks at the dishwasher and its mangled hinges, then kicks open the screen door and throws the dishwasher door into the backyard. That yard was a weed-infested dump when we moved in, and it's worse now. Sometimes I yearn for Porkie Morkie to be here with me, but I couldn't take thinking of the little sweetie exploring that overgrown tetanus-laced minefield.

"The good news is, that probably won't depress our resale value," says Cornelius as he enters the kitchen and whistles at my tiling. "On the flipside, in this neighborhood I'm not sure there's a premium for new tile floors. But it looks great, honey."

"New tile works in *every* neighborhood," I say. We're in one of Houston's tougher areas, woods and hoods, Acres Homes. I only know this from George and Boris's discussions; I haven't been allowed to leave the house in the nearly two months since we relocated from the retirement home.

And for the first couple weeks that was fine. I was embarrassed by what I had become. Since my 17th birthday, vampirism had been slowly emerging—the result of being bitten by that appraiser vampire killed by Eugene, and the reason I had to break up with him. My vampirism accelerated with the bite from Cornelius. There is no hiding it. Even though Dad's a vampire—maybe *because* he is—I know how disappointed he and Mom would be.

Not to mention Eugene. He loves me, there is no doubt. With all his heart. And there is also no doubt he would slay me. That's my Eugene.

Lately I've started to feel differently. About my vampirism. About everything.

For the first time in my life, I have a cause (other than Eugene). It burns in me, more intensely every day.

And so I'm desperate to leave the house. The YouTube video was great. I know it's having an impact. I'm publishing another one tonight. But in my soul I know the videos need to be coupled with public appearances. Personal appearances. I need to speak to people! I need to let them *feel* my passion. That's the only way they are going to truly understand the revolutionary, world-changing opportunity that vampires have brought us. I need to be *seen.*

This is a point of contention with Cornelius. "You are turning our hideout into a home," he says.

"I had no idea I was so handy."

"You are here to make everything better, *draga tatei.*"

Hilda shrieks. "You and your Romanian cuddle words! I am so sick of them! You think of her as your, your—"

"My protégé." Cornelius puts his hand affectionately on my head. I remove it. "Amberly has a very special power and purpose—"

"Because you gave it to her!" Hilda stomps on a tile until it snaps. She stomps up the stairs and slams her bedroom door.

Cornelius sighs. "You have to admire her commitment to the cause."

"Brunhilda would like *me* committed." Cornelius's affection creeps me out as much as it does Hilda. "It would help if you refrained from treating me like your—"

"Protégé? But you are." Cornelius looks at my chest. "Have your bosoms grown again?"

Hilda screams from upstairs.

"Don't talk about my chest. Stop looking. And go change your shirt."

He looks at the blood stains and grins as he pulls a blood-filled vial from his pants pocket. "I brought you some. It's a blend, from a couple, three, or so, fine young donors."

After all the trouble my dad had, I'm amazed at how natural it feels for me to drink blood. It is yummy!

"I'm not a baby, you know. I'm perfectly capable of finding my own donors."

Cornelius scowls. "That's dangerous!" He reminds me five times a day that there can be no biting with my special form of vampirism. So I talk about biting all the time.

He takes my hand and guides me into the living room to sit. "Of *course* I am protective as if I were your guardian. So much is going to be asked of us. I need to ensure you are ready."

I maintain a nice buffer on the couch. "Eugene used to tell me you said the same thing to him."

Cornelius looks into his tall hat. "Indeed I did. You and Eugene have very different roles to play, but they serve the same purpose. To bring long-overdue change to the world."

"What do you see when you look into that hat?"

Cornelius smiles and sets the hat on the worn-out arm of the couch.

"Are you still using me to convince Eugene to kill my father?"

He runs his finger against the grain of the hat's felt, leaving a ruffled smudge. "Your father's destiny conflicts with ours. You'll see it soon enough, *draga tatei*. He has evil intent."

"I *know* my father. There isn't an evil bone in his body."

"I didn't say *he* was evil. Only his destiny. He will do anything he can to prevent you from uniting vampires and humans."

"My father loves me. He would never hurt me."

"Mm." The muscles in Cornelius's neck constrict, seem to be choking him. "Mm, you can't imagine, can you? That there could be forces more powerful than that bond." Tears fill his eyes.

Somewhat reluctantly I put my hand on his. Cornelius piles on with his other hand. "I chose you for this role," he says, "because I see something special in you. Are you happy I did?"

"Completely. For the first time, I understand my purpose in life. I finally understand why I'm here."

He squeezes my hand sandwich. "Stay true to that knowledge and that purpose, and everything will be right." He glances at his hat. "Although maybe we should decide on a different last name for you."

"For the past couple years I assumed it would be Foreman."

"Ha." He considers it. "Foreman. For-man. Funny. That works."

This makes me melancholy. Eugene and I can never be together. I will never wear his ring. I've come to terms with that. But I still feel our connection. It's there, nestled down in a corner of my mind. The best way I can describe that part of me, that corner? It's a place I wouldn't otherwise have found without Eugene. And I can never stay long; but for short visits, it feels like home.

Our bond is deeper than the vampirism that separates us. It's right to take Eugene's name.

"Every day I am more certain about my destiny. I need to be out there, touching people, teaching them, opening their minds and showing them the way forward. Biting them."

"Amberly!"

"I'm kidding about the biting."

This gives him another excuse to pat me. "There will be a time for you to mix and mingle. But not yet."

"I'm going crazy here!" I point upstairs with my eyes. "She wants me dead."

Cornelius smiles. "She couldn't if she tried."

"It's the thought of it! I can't take it."

"Patience, *draga tatei*. I'll speak to Hilda. Again. It's nothing against you personally. She is simply envious of your role. But she belongs to me. And so she belongs to you."

"So am I still a hostage?"

"Of course not."

"Then I can go *see* people?"

"It's too early for that."

I karate chop the end table and snap it down the middle. Sometimes I really enjoy breaking things.

Cornelius tries to soothe me. “You have enemies on both sides of the aisle, as they say. I still need to take a few of them into the cloak room. As they say.”

“Vampires? Why would they be opposed to what we’re going to do?”

“Change, my dear. Some folks just don’t appreciate change.” He stands. “Let’s go make another video, shall we?”

I allow him to take my hand and bring me to my feet. He’s in heaven when he’s next to me, that is obvious. Like a proud papa? I thank him for bringing home leftovers. “Now be a dear and have Boris or George put this in one of their bloody-good ’n’ bloody energy smoothies for me.” I do a great Cockney accent. Hilda hates it.

That evening, 50 million people watch the new YouTube video posted by the faceless Publicola. In the following days the video will receive another half-billion views. It opens with a young boy sitting on the edge of a concrete pad with his clothes torn, eye puffy and lip bleeding, schoolyard bullies walking away in the background. The camera looks down at a torn, creased piece of paper, strips of mounting tape on the edges, bearing a message in red marker, *Kick Me I’m a Vampire*. When the boy grimaces in pain and shame we see his fangs.

The youngster vampire looks up and there is a tall good-looking boy with an inscrutable expression. He shakes his head, and then holds out his hand and breaks into a big smile. Human. Hesitantly the vampire takes his hand, then relaxes in the warmth of the human’s kindness. They embrace, and it’s possible the vampire boy is going to bite the human as the image dissolves into a shot of the paper on the ground, now edited in bright blue to read “Stick with Me, I’m a Vampire.”

At the bottom of the screen a message appears: “Brought to you by the Ad Council.”

Dissolve to a beautiful young woman looking into the camera. “Hi everyone. I’m Amberly Foreman. I’m very pleased to speak to you again.”

The backdrop is freshly-applied “trains of the world”

wallpaper. It suggests a child's bedroom. And in Amberly's eyes there lives an imminent girlish giggle; but her lips finish every sentence in a husky purr. Experience and vampirism are sculpting away the roundness below her cheekbones, bringing her of age.

"We have grown up in a world of conflict. Our leaders have always promised to end these conflicts, which in fact *never* end. At an early age we realized there are no fixes, just pauses, achieved through terrible, permanent bloodshed. And so we become jaded, and accepting.

"The internet was supposed to bring us closer together. Instead it has only provided amplification for the loudest voices, the extremists who have always been among us. Now, they can reach each other across the globe and shout in each other's ears and believe they are making a difference."

In France, a 20-year-old dental student turns to her lover and says, "She is so right."

"And beautiful," says her lover, developing a deep fang envy.

"The so-called 'connections' being made," Amberly tells them, "are always *within* and never *between* tribes. For each tribe, political party, religion, nation, and ethnic group, the borders are sacrosanct, erected by history, eternal. New arguments for peace are made, and made louder all the time; the so-called problem solvers scream their messages while reinforcing those borders.

"Meanwhile, a phenomenon has occurred, gradually, and with no regard for borders. Vampires have evolved. We have grown into positions of authority and responsibility. Blessed with Biblical longevity—a gift we hope to share with humans—we have seen what works, and what doesn't. After centuries of patience and learning, we are ready to assume leadership roles all across this beautiful planet.

"*This* is a true tipping point. *This* is a moment for a revolutionary change in how we relate to each other. An opportunity to make decisions not as Sunnis or Shiites, Ukrainians or Russians, Democrats or Republicans—but as people."

In Bangladesh, a 45-year-old pharmacist whispers to her staff gathered around her iPad: "We are witnessing a historic moment, my friends."

"I would follow this woman to the ends of the earth," a young lab tech on her staff replies. "Even if that turns out to be in India."

"It sounds farfetched, doesn't it?" says Amberly. "That's a logical reaction—because until now, it *has* been farfetched. And it will continue to be so—*if* humans alone are running the governments, the religious institutions, the tribes. The change, the revolution I'm describing, is only possible under the guidance and partnership with evolved vampires.

"We have been living with you, peacefully, for centuries. The wars that have been fought have nothing to do with vampires, and everything to do with borders. Don't get me wrong; borders are often necessary, normal and right. But there is nothing *right* about killing each other. We have been killing each other in the name of borders and achieving *nothing*, other than the temporary enrichment of a privileged few."

"Oh my God, she is passionate," says a Nigerian oil services manager. "Because she knows the truth."

"Before we die," says his wife, "we must meet her."

According to the video's progress bar, Amberly is nearly done. "The revolution I'm talking about doesn't mean changing your party, or losing your religion, or renouncing your national citizenship. That 'Imagine' bullshit from John Lennon? Beautiful song, don't get me wrong."

Lennon's voice sings through the world's speakers: *No hell below us, above us only sky.*

"But it's a child's version of utopia," Amberly talks over him. "Religion, politics and nations are a part of human nature—and vampire nature. They are *good.* In the new world we're building, *nothing* changes in our ability to freely practice according to our beliefs and our nature.

"So what *does* change? There will be no more *war* over religion. No one religion will be allowed to attack any other religion. There will be no more killing in the name of borders. Why? We simply won't allow it.

"Vampires have learned the lessons of history. We are finally at the moment in time when we can share these lessons with you. We want to lead you. We want to take civilization to a level beyond what is currently possible.

"And sure, yes, we also want to drink your blood. Not too much," Amberly quickly adds, with great timing and a beautiful smile, displaying her even white teeth and small pointed canines. "As some of you can testify, it can be an enjoyable experience."

An immunology researcher at the National Institutes of Health experiences intoxicating joy. Young and recently emigrated from Romania, she is a high-ranking administrator at the NIH, thanks to a promotion that skipped a few levels, thanks in turn to her recent conversion to vampirism. Amberly Foreman's words touch her, inspire her; she decides she must meet this incredible young vampire woman, and pledge her fealty.

"Terrorists," Amberly concludes her message, "so-called slayers, are trying to stop us from achieving this historic revolution. Millions of you have been protesting against this murderous attempt to silence us. Thank you. Let's build on this energy, and stake our claim for a peaceful future."

The screen fades to black before the fist-and-stake logo and hashtag #StakeOurClaim materialize.

"Holy shit," says Eugene out loud to himself in his cheap motel room, stir-crazy on the tenth day of hiding from the Houston PD. "We are in a great deal of trouble."

Cornelius is acting like a regular vampire, staying out all night, sleeping all day. Maybe 10 minutes after he makes a small racket coming through the front door and climbing heavy-footed up the stairs to bed, Boris knocks on my door and slips inside.

He presses his back to the door as if something might be trying to get in. Boris was one of the founding members of the Bolshoi Ballet, which makes him a very graceful drama queen. "Are you a coffee drinker?"

"Not really."

"Time to grow up. Get dressed. Okay, you don't have to drink coffee. But you do have to come with us to the coffeeshop." He pauses to shush my gleeful exclamation, opens the door to peek into the hall, squeezes through the gap, and pokes his head back in. "Meet us *quietly* downstairs in 15."

We drive down a street of small homes, some better kept than ours, others much worse. "I'm so excited!" This is my first time outside in weeks, and it feels incredible. The street passes out of the ghetto and seemingly into the country, a sparse forest, here and there an unauthorized landfill. Even garbage looks good! "How did we get past Hilda?"

George drives his Lexus SUV with obvious pride, fine posture, two hands on the wheel, stiff in the neck. "Cornelius makes her cuddle him to sleep."

"Hilda swears she never gets good rest," says Boris. "And she claims to hate cuddling. But once she wraps her arms around the boss, it's lights out."

We've left the rural island of sorts, again in a neighborhood, shacks like ours squeezed between new three-story condos. Those shack-owners will enjoy very little sunlight. I know as a vampire I'm supposed to be opposed to the sun; and isn't that a perfect example of the stereotypes we're going to shatter?

"There's a cute little coffeeshop that just opened," says Boris. We drive through a gated entrance into an enclave of large new houses, each with their own wrought-iron gates, manicured lawns, surrounding a small retail center painted in muted pastels. It feels like a movie set. We park in front of the Homesy Coffee House and I wouldn't be surprised if the front is a façade for a few cheap tables seating mannequins.

George holds the Homesy door for me. "They're very welcoming to our kind here."

This makes me giggle. "Our kind?"

"Gay vampires!" Boris crows. This serves as an announcement of our entrance.

All heads turn in the busy shop. I'm blushing and laughing.

"I'm not gay," I tell a couple at the nearest table, and now most everyone in the shop is chuckling. George, as conservative as Boris is flamboyant, strides pinch-faced for the counter. A young woman jumps out of her chair in front of me.

"Amberly? Am I correct?"

She has a cute Eastern Europe accent, and she is a vampire. "Amberly Foreman," I introduce myself. She wants to hug me, decides to shake my hand, and then coos with delight when I embrace her.

"Amberly, this is Iulia." Boris pronounces it *Yoo*-lia. "Iulia wanted to meet you."

"I am such a fan of yours," Iulia gushes. She is maybe ten years older than I am and boyishly skinny. Iulia wears her hair in a swept-across helmet and has a plain face with warm, intelligent eyes. "I watch your YouTube videos many times."

"I'm flattered."

George walks up. "I ordered us all triple caramel macchiatos with a thick soy-foam cap." He casts a pained look at the barista. "He asked whether we wanted it speckled with cherry syrup."

"Yum!" Iulia and I exclaim.

"So Iulia is a big fan," says George.

"I'm just giving a voice to what a lot of people feel," I say. "I'm thankful the message is getting out."

"It's all anyone is talking about," says Iulia, super perky. She softens her voice. "I run an immunology research lab at the National of Institutes of Health. Usually the scientists discuss only antibodies. But lately you are the talk of the town."

George puts his hand on Iulia's. "'Talk of the town.' That's one of the precious aspects of welcoming non-native speakers to America. You keep the oldies but goodies alive."

"I learned to speak English at the home of my mentor, back in Romania. She was a great scientist. She loved old American movies."

The memory of her mentor is clearly painful. "Is she still with us?" I ask.

"Oh yes." The pain mixes with bitterness. "But I am dead to *her*. Since I became a vampire."

George still has Iulia's hand. Boris takes the other. "That's so wrong, honey," says Boris. "When people like that are confronted with something outside their comfort zone—*that's* when you see their true nature."

"Vampirism actually saved my life," says Iulia. "I was in a bad car accident in Bucharest. The emergency responders believed I was going to die at the scene. One of the paramedics bit me. My body began to recover immediately."

"Praise the Lord and the fang!" Boris flutters his hands in the air.

"My mentor visited me in the hospital, once. She said I would be better off dead."

George is outraged. "Someone needs to walk her over to the other side. What's her name?"

"Jaelle Skudza. She now performs research dedicated to destroying us."

"We had a Zumba instructor who was always making offensive comments about vampires," says Boris. "Finally we set up a private lesson with him and took turns—"

"Guys." A barrier is rising around our table, the solidarity of shared perspectives walling us off from the humans in the coffeeshop. "I know the pain is deep." I'm now talking to the whole shop. "But we can't create a new world if we're focused on the past."

Boris looks heavenward. "Amen, sister."

While we talk, a middle-aged vampire woman greets a young man entering the shop. They take the table next to ours and the woman brings their drinks from the pick-up bar. "What do I owe you?" the dour young man asks.

"I put it on my tab." The vampire woman winks. "One of the perks of being a vampire. So, you remember how unruly my class was?" The young man must be a former student of hers. "Pricks like Malcolm Schnittel? I now run a very well-behaved classroom."

"I am so amazed how my focus has benefitted from vampirism," says Iulia, our conversation running parallel with the next table's. "How much improved are my ideas."

George removes the lid on his drink and uses a stir stick to measure the depth of the soy foam, pleased at the result. "Iulia was just promoted in fact."

The young man pushes back from the next table and displays a stake holstered under his pullover. "Too bad your bloodsucking days end right here."

Boris sighs and prepares for a fight. He tries to stretch his shoulder but can't reach his elevated elbow with his other hand. George helps him bring hand and elbow together.

A man from a nearby table is alarmed. "Excuse me," he says to the slayer. "I apologize for eavesdropping. Do you intend to kill this lady?"

"*Vampire* lady," says the young man. "*Slay* her. Yes."

He reminds me so much of Eugene. His certainty and

commitment. Not his looks, Eugene is way more handsome.

Not his awareness, either. Eugene would have realized he had to contend with another tableful of vampires. He wouldn't have cared, of course. But he would have already had our measure.

The eavesdropper is perplexed. "You're her former student, right? Is this an old academic grudge?"

"Randolph did very well in my class," says the vampire teacher.

"I'm a slayer," says Randolph. For him, as for Eugene, this says it all.

"We thank you for your service," says the eavesdropper, well built, some Hispanic in him, wearing an EnerGreen jacket. "But we only expect you to slay the *bad* vampires."

The young man gives him a scornful glare. "Your false premise is that vampires can be anything other than evil." Clearly he has taken Eugene's online slayer course.

Everyone in the shop is listening to them. "Stereotypes," says Iulia. "My boyfriend is guilty, too. He thinks he knows the only two good vampires."

A plump woman knitting on one of the small couches joins the conversation. "I know a very respectful vampire at work. He only bites with permission."

The young man pulls out his smartphone. "Where do you work?"

"Son," says the EnerGreen employee. "It's inappropriate to go around indiscriminately slaying vampires. Just because they're a vampire doesn't make them evil."

"Sir, by definition, it does," says the young man.

"I know where you're coming from, Randy," says his former vampire teacher. "I went through the same debate before letting my neighbor bite me. First and foremost, I believe it's everyone's responsibility to be *good*. I can honestly say, I'm the same, *good* person. But now I'm the *best* me. My mind is quicker, and I'm more assertive." She winks at the plump knitter. "I'm dating an orthopedic surgeon now."

"Good for you, honey."

"They say we share 99.99% of our DNA," says the EnerGreen man.

Randy sips his drink, his other hand on the stake. "Time for last words, Ms. Nagel."

"I'd like to invite you to sit in on my classroom," says Ms. Nagel, "so you can see how normal it is. How *good* it is. I think you'll decide you were born five years too soon. You'll wish you could take algebra from me now."

"I'm so envious of women who *get* math," says the knitter.

The EnerGreen man flirts. "Your doctor boyfriend is a lucky guy. I've always pictured a vampire encounter being so violent. I'm curious about a more intimate relationship."

Ms. Nagel returns the flirt. "I can't promise it wouldn't hurt."

"I'm an architect by the way," says the EnerGreen man.

"I would love for you to bite him now," Randy tells Ms. Nagel, "so I could stake you both. But I have another appointment at the top of the hour." He draws a stake. "Let's finish you."

Ms. Nagel goes pale. "Randy, please. I'm the same Ms. Nagel who taught you to factor your polynomials."

"You are a vampire, and nothing more."

Customers scoot their chairs away from the scene, realizing Randy is intent on the slaying. George and Boris end their groan-inducing limbering and rise.

"Can you tell me one thing?" I remain seated and speak in a conversational tone. I have Randy's attention. "By slaying this vampire, have you done anything to make the world a better place?"

"Yes."

"Does this help the Middle East? Does it stop Putin? Does it end Islamic terrorism? Does it unite *this* country?"

"No!" the knitting woman calls out. "Republicans will still be at the Democrats' throats."

"If Democrats would quit sticking their necks where they don't belong," says Mr. EnerGreen, "we wouldn't have to keep stepping on them."

Ms. Nagel takes her eyes off Randy long enough to give Mr. EnerGreen a shut-down scowl. "And you wonder why you can't get any interesting women?"

Randy hasn't looked away from me. I stand now, aware that I'm in the clothes I was wearing when Cornelius abducted me. Stretched out, dull, the sweatshirt too big and the pants with giraffes, perfect for a protest sleep-out in front of the police station, not for wooing my most ardent enemies. Randy still likes what he sees.

"This is just one more false division," I tell him and everyone in the shop. "One more way to ensure constant warfare. If you choose to slay this woman—this vampire—then the strife and the killing will just continue, across the world and here in Houston." I move to stand before him. "I'm a vampire, Randy." I offer my hand. "Do you want to slay me?"

There is no struggle behind his eyes. What I said didn't really matter. He's in love with me.

He's squeezing my hand, pumping it. "I've never thought about it like that. I'm glad I met you. I'm Randolph Ivers."

"Nice to meet you, Randolph." Randy will not slay another vampire.

I rejoin the table and Boris and George sink back into their seats. They stare at me in awe. Randy doesn't go so far as to hug his former math teacher vampire, but he leaves the shop quietly. Mr. EnerGreen looks as incredulous as my vampire minders, and begins to clap, slow popping sounds. The rest of the coffeeshop joins him.

I wink at Iulia. "Maybe there's still hope for your mentor. And your boyfriend."

TÂRGU MUREȘ - CONSTANTINOPLE - BUCHAREST: 1586-1588

Nadia stood before the home of Dragoș, the former slayer, with clean hands.

For two years she had directed Trubadur's slaying. In Târgu Mureș, and then in Constantinople, they had spent every moment together and had turned the tide for humans living between the Carpathians and the Bosporus, from the Danube Gorge to the Black Sea.

A moon's cycle after János Kárpáti paraded Maresi's remains through the riverside marketplace, word had come of a contingent of the Empire's most powerful vampires en route to Târgu Mureș. Bishops, voivodes, generals, dukes.

"They journey to pay homage to Morbius," Nadia had said to Trubadur late one chilly night. She lay wrapped in a wool blanket on a bed hauled into the Kárpátis' stable.

"They come to co-opt you for the Habsburgs." Trubadur, as always, sat stiffly in a chair until sleep softened his spine. "You are every faction's tailor-made savior."

"János and Etel want you to take Ugie and Stela and flee. The vampires also come to punish you for Maresi's death."

"And after I slay them, we will receive guests from the Emperor's vampire enemies, looking to reward me. And I will slay them as well."

She propped herself on an elbow. "I? Is there no 'we' in this grim slaughter?"

"*I* call the slaughter joyful."

"And I feel joy that you find it such."

"And if I hadn't found you? If I had never awoken from the

fall I took with Mortimer?"

"Then I would be confused. And alone."

"How can you be confused?" He stood above her, fists clenched. "We are saving humanity."

She bristled. "Isn't it enough that I show you their Heels? That I am with you?"

"Do you care about your sister?"

"Of course."

"Do you care about your friends, your neighbors, your family?" Trubadur rushed on. "Do you care about my children?"

Nadia leapt from the bed. She bumped him and stayed in his face. "Do you see how your daughter clings to me? I love that! I love your son, even as he wants me dead. Like his father."

Trubadur had her by the arms. "I *need* you, I—"

"You what?"

Tru hardened his eyes and softened his grip. "I *understand*. Ugenosz is too young. His emotions rule him."

She laughed. "Unlike his father."

He pushed her away. "I have one emotion: hatred for the vampire plague."

"How long have I known you, Trubadur? Long enough to laugh when you demand I believe what you *say*, instead of what I *see*."

"And?"

"There are other emotions in your soul. Do you remember the promise we made to each other, before you left me?"

"To remain true to each other."

"You said you were a man of adventure. My girlfriends laughed—'Look at his skinny neck!' they told me. But I have never liked thick necks."

Trubadur scowled, self-conscious about his thin frame.

"You told me I needed to find a man to provide for me. Then in your next breath—"

"We promised to love each other."

Nadia's throat tightened. "No matter what."

"Neither of us could have imagined you would become *this*."

"Never did I believe your promises were anything but unconditional."

"There were no conditions. Just an assumption. That you

would remain *human*."

Nadia moved closer. "I am no less human. I am *more*." She placed her hand on his chest; his involuntary reaction was to move into her touch.

Trubadur gripped her wrist. "We are together for one thing only: to slay vampire vermin."

"Slaying sounds wonderful, my love." Billows of bloodlust covered her mind like the clouds on Bran Pass. She broke his grip and dug her nails into his skinny throat. "I'm in the mood to spill blood."

Trubadur knocked her hand away.

Nadia stayed close for a moment, drawn to the passion in his odd, beautiful face. "But whose blood?" She retreated to the little hut's door. "Man, or *vermin*? That depends on you."

She strode across the yard, scattering chickens and hounds. Trubadur's voice caught her at the gate.

"Man or vermin, you attract them all. I'll be there to decide who draws his last breath."

Transylvanians turn out for public spectacles. The arrival of the Holy Roman Emperor's delegation from Prague qualified. Men, women, and children lined Târgu Mureș' main avenue ten deep, from villages near and many days' journey away. Maybe it was the audience that brought out the best in slayers and vampires alike.

These vampires were a gruesome lot in their excesses. Their slaves slouched along chained to the coaches and filling garishly painted flagons with their own blood to slake their masters' thirst. Their ridiculously high hats and impractical robes were bedecked with crosses and the Emperor's iconography. Severed heads collected along the way were strapped like baubles around the necks of tethered chamois, keeping the beasts in constant moaning frenzy. Nadia was nearly as eager as Trubadur to see these vampires slain.

Walking at the rear of the procession was a cute vampire girl no more than 10 years old, long hair nearly as white as her dress, eyes bluer than her tiara's aquamarine jewels. Taken before she was able to understand the choice and her fate! Nadia's heart went out to her.

János Kárpáti stood reluctantly in the middle of the avenue, forcing the entourage to a halt. "Welcome to our humble village."

"Humble does not begin to measure the offensiveness of this pale cluster of wretchedness." This from a green-eyed Hungarian vampire general astride a massive warhorse. The horse wore a polished, spiked breastplate and poured steam from its flared nostrils. The Hungarian went bare-chested; his skin temperature was low enough for frost to coat his chest hair.

"Chain yourself to Prince Iglidore's carriage," he commanded János. "Bare your throat to one of his lackeys and fill his chalice as penance for allowing this atrocity to exist."

"Shouldn't you consider this village holy ground?" Nadia separated from the crowd and moved in front of János. "The place where the Emperor's favorite bloodsuckers declared their fealty to Morbius?"

The Hungarian's horse reared, threw its rider to the ground, and galloped away.

For Nadia, the Hungarian's spine glowed even through the mud caking his hairy back. His backbone sang to her, the song's vibrations filling her eyes and skull until she could smell his quivering weakness.

"Or maybe it will be accursed land." She knelt beside him and with her thumbnail dug a line from the base of his neck down to his wolfskin breeches. "The soil will be made barren by all this regal vampire blood."

Trubadur's sword had to fight through the taut muscle of the Hungarian's arched back to reach his spine. No problem—the vertebrae cracked like eggshell. White-hot energy traveled the vampire's length; like a lightning strike it burst the top of his head and blew out his fingertips. Face-down, the vampire sank into the earth, the first of many contributions to Nadia's prophecy.

Trubadur sheathed his sword and hefted his crossbow. A bishop atop a palanquin dropped his scepter and covered his mouth. Trubadur shot him through the hands and teeth, which rained down star-bright for Nadia, winking out as they hit the dirt. The bishop vampire slumped forward, viscous steaming fluid oozing from the bolt poking out the back of his head.

Nadia spoke to Trubadur as he fitted another projectile. "If they're going to be that obvious about it, I might as well go stand with Etel and Stela." She nodded to the eternally young prince who was barking useless orders at his alarmed retinue. A flutter of the royal heartbeat disturbed the sash running hip to shoulder. "His right breast."

Trubadur's aim was true. His bolt pierced that silk ribbon.

So many telltale signs, confirming what her Sight showed her. Hands covering Heels, overwrought trappings, contorted bearings. As they slayed together, Trubadur and Nadia had learned them all.

The vampires took hidden precautions. Some like the prince had lived for untold generations, plenty of time to design creative safeguards. He wore a patch of melted, annealed mail under his blouse, kept in place by leather cords fastened to the inside of his blouse, his pants, his stockings. All this became apparent when Trubadur's bolt splintered and the prince screamed and tore away sash, robe and blouse to confirm he was still alive. He laughed with the lilt of the insane.

Trubadur punched the vampire prince in the stomach, doubling him over, then rammed a stake in the upper right side of his back. Nadia marveled that a royal hadn't anticipated a back-stabbing. More tainted blood for the soil of Târgu Mureş.

Trubadur waded into the vampire delegation and slayed like a hero among mortals. Nadia imagined Achilles laying waste to the soldiers of Troy, which was an interesting comparison. She pointed out these Trojans' weak spots and her Achilles skewered them.

Internal armor shielded these vampires, granted them god-like invincibility but for the smallest gap of almost pathetic vulnerability. Trubadur might as well have been naked for his comparative lack of protection. And yet he charged them, raged at them, ended them.

Now it was every vampire for himself. Some reverted to instinctual bloodlust and attacked the crowd. To the Transylvanians' credit, the gory loss of a few unfortunate maids, men, children and elders didn't create a stampede. Most stood their ground, aiding each other and keeping the vampires occupied while Trubadur picked them off.

The little blond vampire girl had found a place to hide, among grazing sheep. She hugged a black-faced lamb with all her heart. Then she twisted off its head and hurled it at Trubadur, smacking him above the eye.

He looked at Nadia through the blood streaming down his face.

She sighed and touched herself above the left hip. "Here."

The little vampire howled in surprised rage. Trubadur unleashed a blizzard of bolts. The girl ran at high speed holding the headless lamb as a shield, the curly corpse taking one hit after another. In seconds she was out of crossbow range and heading into the northern hills.

They turned to the last vampire standing, a noblewoman with an insatiable look in her eye despite the caravan's ready food supply. She was dressed in the latest fashion, Bible-modern, simple robes well-designed to accentuate her curves and accented with gold leaf. Her hands shook as she stared at Nadia and tossed aside a plain arc of bronze holding back her hair. It chimed off the breastplate of a fallen vampire soldier. The noblewoman's bared temple pulsed for Nadia to see.

Her plight inspired a broad-faced old local vampire to chivalry. He stepped in front of her and bared his fangs.

"Trubadur Maistru. It seems I have taught you too well."

The young slayer was painted in blood diluted with sweat. "You're a better teacher than a man, Constantin. You should have slain yourself."

"I appreciate the morality lesson," Constantin mocked. "Can I assume you have already sainted yourself?"

"God knows I'm not perfect. But He does grant me a steady hand and a keen eye." The stake flew from Trubadur's hand, rotating so tightly on its lengthwise axis that it seemed to be self-propelled.

The vampire was shocked, first to see the stake in his left breast, and then to find himself still alive. "Ha! I *am* one of the chosen!"

Trubadur closed the gap between them and palm-struck the stake. "You were always more concerned with *who* you are than *why* you are."

Constantin bowed to this judgment, hinged at the heart,

folding in four sections and occupying a minimal amount of space at his slayer student's feet.

The noblewoman turned her head. Trubadur stepped over Constantin and rammed a stake in her temple.

Nadia felt a terrible pain in her side. She looked down to find a stake in her ribs and little Ugie preparing to hammer it home.

Trubadur caught his son's arm and took away his hammer. He bent down. "No!"

"She's a vampire!"

"Nadia is *different*."

"I hate her!"

Trubadur spoke quietly to his son. "Your mother is gone. That is no reason to hate Nadia."

"I hate her because she's a *vampire*!"

His grandfather hurried to them. János Kárpáti looked awestruck by Trubadur. And he seemed to have an inkling of Nadia's contribution to the mass slaying.

"You must trust your father," he instructed his grandson. When Ugenosz showed no inclination to do so, when he made a cross with his fingers to distract Nadia and aimed a kick at the embedded stake, János carried him off, thrashing and cursing.

Nadia groaned as she removed the stake. She handed the bloody thing to Trubadur and lamented the hole in her shirt. "I imagine you would have done the same at his age."

"I don't know what to do with him." He stabbed the stake in the earth to clean the blood.

She looked at the moldering corpses and the beginning of an impromptu celebration. "That was the most incredible thing I have ever seen."

"I had an apprentice traveling with them as a valet." Trubadur nodded to a squat young man fending off would-be revelers as he gouged holes in casks lashed to one of the wagons. "Last night he poisoned their blood-wine. Just enough to sap their strength and dull their senses. They would have killed me otherwise."

Nadia's perspective was unaltered. An image from the battle danced in her mind: Trubadur running low and launching himself at a fat hissing buck-fanged nobleman, suspended in mid-air with stake cocked. "God help me but I love to watch you slay."

He paused collecting and cleaning stakes to look at her. "God willing, you'll have many more opportunities."

She wanted to press her cheek to his and hear him breathe in her ear. "Today we crippled Vienna and Prague. It won't be long before we have routed them across the empire. What is next?"

He was forced to abandon a stake caught in the crossfire of two locals' gleeful, vengeful pissing upon the vampire prince's corpse. "Constantinople. Vamps from the eastern Ottoman empire have been called there to prepare for an invasion."

Nadia had *felt* that call—for her, it was a pull to *join* the gathering. She was excited and petrified to go. "Constantinople is many, many days' journey."

"We'll have plenty to do along the way." He grinned—this was not Trubadur's best look. "They will be waiting for us in Bucharest, so we will take a different route; east. On the Tauric peninsula we can find passage on a Tatar slaver ship. The arrival in Constantinople of a horde of freed slaves will be the diversion we need to do our work."

She marveled at his plan. "Stela thrills to hear the stories of Mihai Bravu defying Ottoman and Hungarian armies alike. She should know that her father is the most brilliant general of all."

He basked in the compliment, glancing at her while going through the bishop vampire's pockets. "Nadia!"

She was falling, hadn't realized it until the ground met her. Trubadur kicked dirt in her face in his haste to reach her. For the first time in ten years, she was in his arms.

She kept her eyes closed for a time.

"Nadia, my lo—" He checked the endearment. "Are you alright?"

Now she opened them. "It has been too long since I have eaten."

Trubadur ground his teeth and pulled her roughly to her feet. "Go find your meal."

Despite his disgust, he waited until she was stable before seeking out his family.

The Healer, the witch, the Romani woman Skudza, she had been in the crowd. Throughout the slaughter, Nadia had felt the Romani's eyes on her. Night had fallen when Nadia found her at the river, sitting cross-legged in the dirt in front of her wagon, drinking from the prince's tainted flagon. She wiped bloody-red wine from her mouth, and moaned.

"I expected you, vampire."

"Why?"

Skudza the Healer grunted a laugh. "Why does the vampire come?"

Nadia pointed at the light from fires that warmed the distant festivities and turned what was left of the vampires to ash. "You saw what I did."

Skudza drank again. "I see what you *are*."

Nadia advanced on her. The Romani's skin hung in wrinkled folds harboring a slurry of sweat, smoke and grime. Nadia thought only of the blood beneath. "You see too much. And know nothing."

The healer witch cackled. "Will you bite me? Will you make me the next Morbius?" The ridiculousness of it nearly capsized her. She lofted the flagon and received only dribbles. "Trubadur Maistru's potion has by now run its course. Drink from this poisoned well as you would."

Nadia produced a pick that János used to chip ice from the frozen Mureș. She took Roma Skudza by her wild gray hair and jabbed her in the wrinkled, creased throat. Blood oozed and ran along a fold. "I may fall ill, but I will recover." She jabbed her a second time, spaced like a pair of fangs. "I am Morbius after all."

She had found him on a bluff below the Ottoman sultan's palace walls, gazing at the sea. The end of the West was visible from this promontory, pinpointed by the Galata Tower on the other side of the Golden Horn estuary. On the far side of the Bosporus, the East began. South and west across the Sea of Marmara, the Red Islands fronted the channel leading to Greece. "I believe all the secrets of the world end up here."

Trubadur seemed lost in thought. "Was that the false promise that attracted the Eastern vampires?"

"Perhaps," said Nadia. "Now it appears your slaying has made it safe for the traders to return." A flotilla of merchant ships moved up the adjacent estuary and crowded into Constantinople's anchorage.

"We've also made it safe for the Persians to attack," said Tru.

"The city is about to draw the chain across the mouth of the harbor. No one wants to be caught on the other side." Which explained why the great Sea of Marmara was nearly empty.

"Does that mean the sultan won't be presenting us the keys to the city any time soon?"

A smile tugged at his mouth. He turned to look at her. Bolts of aquamarine rose from the bay in the setting sun and streaked his peculiar, perfect face. "The city—Istanbul, as the Mohammedans prefer it—is in a frenzy. We've emboldened the human population. Now they know where the Arab vampire usually conceals his Heel. From the scene I witnessed at the bazaar, woe to the Persian invaders. Istanbul has bloodlust to spend."

A fortnight ago they had docked the slave ship in this same harbor. Having slain the vampire crew the first day out of the Tauric port, they were fortunate to find able sailors among the slave "cargo." Ten more days sailing across the Black Sea and down the Bosporus had given the freed men and women ample time to work themselves into a lather. When the gangplanks dropped, 200 grudge-holding former slaves swept into the streets of Istanbul.

The Eastern vampires who had come together for their assault on the West were caught by surprise. Perhaps by their nature, rather than band together, they scattered. Over the succeeding days Trubadur with Nadia picked off the higher-order vampires one by one. It became a race to slay them before they destroyed themselves or managed to flee the city.

Nadia had been stunned to see how many lesser vampires, "stakeables" in Trubadur's vernacular, had followed their higher-order brethren to Istanbul, for the opportunity to be led by Morbius. Now they were leaderless and being slaughtered by the populace.

"This battle, I know it takes a lot out of you."

Trubadur shook his head. She had never seen him low like this. "The tide has turned. People are no longer sheep. A vampire confab was poisoned in Sofia. In Gura Humorului, the people set fire to a great hall full of them. Thanks to you, the war is nearly over."

"My first compliment."

He stared past the tall grass waving along the edge of the

bluff. "I wept for you every night after I left Bucharest. When I met my wife, Zsuzsanna, she helped ease my sorrow. She gave me Ugenosz and Stela."

"I'm sorry you lost her."

Trubadur's eyes watered. "When she would hold them, I couldn't help wonder what you would be like as a mother. With my children."

Nadia's chest was too tight to draw a breath. "I love your children. I would—"

"You lost that chance when you chose *him*."

She forced him to turn fully to her. "Look at me *now*. Do you think I can ever be with anyone else?"

The sadness in his face told her he had already decided. "I have only to look at your fangs to know the answer. The thought of you together haunts me every time I see you. Every time I think of you."

"I was lost without you! I had no future—not any future I wanted. I was a different person then."

"And everything would have been different *now* if you had resisted him."

"Yes. You would be gone. You would have sacrificed yourself to end Morbius, and I would be alone, betrothed to boyar Bortalyu. Do you remember boyar Bortalyu?"

Trubadur ground his teeth at the mention of the rosy-cheeked pig of a man who had regularly paid visits to the Rákóczi house, assessing Nadia's progress toward womanhood. "I would be gone, and you would be a boar's piglet-bearer. But the world would rejoice."

"You *are* the world, Trubadur. I don't care about anyone else. If you go, swear that you will take me with you."

"If I had the courage."

"But why does it have to be that way?"

He squeezed her so tightly. "Because I see your face every time we slay one of your bloodsucking vermin! I see it now! You're one of them."

"*No*," she whispered. "You know I'm different. You say it all the time."

"I lie."

"And Stela? Does she lie as well? She cried for us *both* when we left."

"It was a mistake taking you to Târgu Mureş."

"How can you say that?"

"You believe Stela loves *you*? Don't you understand why she is drawn to you? Why everyone is drawn to you? Because you are Morbius! That's your power, don't you see that?"

Her heart hurt. "Are you going to lie and tell me that's why you love me, too?"

"I don't. I don't love you."

"You *are* a liar."

"You're right. I lied. Your vampire lover, Mortimer Canterpark? I told you I didn't see him that night. But I did. I slayed him as he left your house."

Nadia could barely nod.

"There," said Tru. "I knew it. You loved him."

She let him see her tears. "Which bothers you more? That I could love a vampire, or that it wasn't you?"

"Why did you give in to him?!"

"Because I didn't believe you were ever coming back."

Trubadur stood apart from her, fists clenched. "I wish I had slain him in Târgu Mureş."

Nadia wiped away the tears. "I realize now I didn't love him."

"You are the liar."

"Because now I know what true love feels like."

He slapped her, and wanted to follow it up.

She stood before him, hands at her sides. "You and I are inevitable," she told him. "Don't you feel it?"

"Nothing is inevitable. Except that you are a vampire and I am a slayer."

"And how many have we slain together?"

"We?"

"*Yes*. You and I. *We* have decimated the vampires."

"Until you call the bloodsuckers 'them,' until you have their blood on your hands," said Trubadur, "there can be no 'we.' Now please excuse me." He practically ran up the hill. "I'm late to meet my beautiful, *human* children in Bucharest."

"I hate you!"

"Good." He left her on the cliff overlooking what was no longer a magical confluence.

She knocked on Dragoș's door, then kicked it in. A woman and two young girls looked up from their sewing in front of the hearth, as if this was a visitor's normal entrance. Their expressions quickly changed, to enthralled.

How incredible was the aura of Morbius. Did they see it in her eye? Did it precede her like the perfumes of Vienna? These vampires practically begged for her touch.

They had no sense of her transformation, ongoing for some time. Morbius had been in control in the early days, visions of vampire Heels bursting from her and falling like enchanted daggers into Trubadur's hands, against her will.

Over the past year the Sight had waged an ever-more effective war within her, allowing Trubadur to rout the vampires. She was dizzy always from the perpetual rush of overwhelming emotion. She died a thousand times, and felt the exhilaration of a thousand beginnings.

Each time she opened new eyes, she had seen Trubadur and Trubadur alone … until the day they left Târgu Mureș, to the wail of Stela's dismay, and Ugenosz's mournful tune on the pan flute.

Since that day, sip by sip she had weaned herself from blood.

Since that day, when Nadia watched the vampires fall, less and less did she feel self-loathing. More and more, she thought of Stela and Ugenosz.

Since that day, she yearned for a world where Trubadur's children could pursue love and happiness without the specter of a predator around every corner.

Dragoș, his wife and his daughters, all had been bitten and turned around the time she and Tru were sailing the Black Sea with a ship full of vengeful former slaves. Tru had taken the news hard, cursing Dragoș for his weakness, for his failure to fend off the vampire and safeguard his family. For not having a failsafe plan to ensure his family would never bring heartbreak to anyone else's.

At the threshold to Dragoș's humble abode, Nadia represented that failsafe.

When she crossed their threshold a second time, leaving, the screams from Dragoş's wife and daughters had attracted a crowd. Nadia was laughing and crying all at once, fangs bared and tears streaming down her cheeks. The crowd was drawn to her, man and woman, vampire and human alike, despite the blood on her hands.

AT THE COMITY CLUB

The party boat reversed throttle and eased up to the dock on the Ocean Star Offshore Drilling Rig and Museum. Galveston Channel's choppy water bucked the short gangplank, making for a tricky hop to the dock. Florence offered Larry her hand; he swatted at it and disembarked just fine on his own.

"Where do we buy our tickets?" Larry had been worrying about this since they bypassed a closed ticket booth on the Galveston pier.

"You dumb hick, I told you I already took care of it!"

The partygoers filed through a steel door labeled "Rig Personnel Only!" and descended stairs leading into the rig's belly. Larry stopped to watch a yacht pulling up to the rig as their party boat pulled away.

"They're coming from the Gulf," said Larry.

The yacht's deckhand controlled an automated gangplank that kept coming, nearly reaching Larry and Florence. The ship was big enough and the gangplank long enough to dampen the sea's energy, allowing the passengers to gracefully gain the rig deck. They passed through the steel door and down the stairs babbling excitedly in a smorgasbord of different languages.

"This must be a popular museum," said Larry.

"It's more of a social club now," said Florence.

Larry noticed how many of these foreign folks sported fangs. Likewise, there had been quite a few vampires on the party boat. He stared at the dark stairwell. "Maybe I'll stay up here."

"I thought you wanted to find Amberly."

He scowled and stepped through the narrow doorway. "When is the boat coming back for us?"

"Six," said Florence, following him down.

Larry pulled back his sleeve and brushed aside his arm hair to check his watch. "That doesn't make sense. It's almost seven now."

"A.M."

"Oh, sweet Jesus." Larry used his left hand for a clumsy sign of the cross, his right gripping the rail as the steel staircase corkscrewed turn after turn until he had no idea how far they had descended below the water line.

They bottomed out in a cramped circular chamber. A stylish man in a white dress shirt monogrammed with red and blue interlocking C's greeted them. "Welcome to the Comity Club. We're glad you're here." He held up two glow pens, red and blue. "Sir—giver or receiver?"

Larry's eyes widened. He looked at Florence.

"Neither," she said. She presented her wrist. "I'll be a taker."

The greeter winked at Larry and popped the top on the blue pen. "We have a two-pint max. It's an honor system, but we do have monitors—with itchy stake fingers!" He giggled and drew a blue *R* on her wrist. "Sir, in case your date didn't tell you—"

Florence grabbed his shirtfront. "Did I say he was my date, you ignorant shit?"

The man dipped his head in apology. "I only wanted to let you both know, this is a *safe* club. Our founder invented a prophylactic of sorts. Every vampire in attendance receives a safety shot. Other than losing a couple pints, a vampire bite tonight won't turn you." He winked at Larry. "In case you're curious."

Larry started back up the stairs; Florence grabbed his belt. "I have to get off this boat," he pleaded.

"It's an oil rig," the greeter corrected him. "Very safe."

"Were you blowing smoke up my ass?" said Florence. "Or do you want to find her?"

Larry stared at the door, through which classical string music lilted. "You think she's in there?"

"I know we have to go in there to find her."

Larry wiped his sweaty brow. "Why do we *both* have to go in there?"

"I thought you wanted to be a part of this." She opened the

door. "Unless you suddenly trust me to do the right thing?"

He retraced the sign of the cross and stepped across the threshold.

The room was small and the ceiling low, making Larry feel entombed with some indeterminate number of vampires among the 50 or so mingling attendees. Florence came alive. Her eyes flared and her breathing quickened as she visually separated the sheep from the wolves. A woman in nurse garb injected the prophylactic in her shoulder.

Florence fixed on a well-built man holding court for a small audience. "*Got*-damn, I hope he's a giver."

Three of his listeners were young women in revealing dresses. "Looks like you'll need to get in line."

"I budge." Florence got a glimpse of the man's wrist and gave a happy clap. "Hot damn."

A vampire whose bald swath glowed rust-gold in the yellowy lights cleared his throat and claimed the room's attention:

"My name is Ari. I come here from the Middle East." He spoke in clipped bursts. "By way of Atlantic City. Perhaps you heard of the trouble we encountered there?"

The crowd was instantly outraged. A human woman yelled, "The terrorists will not divide us!"

Ari awkwardly took the hand of a vampire in an expensive suit and held it aloft. "This is Moanmar. He is Arab. I am a Jew. If we can be united, so can you!"

Florence clapped along politely.

Larry could only think of fleeing.

"This Comity Club is a Godsend," said Ari. "The world needs many more of these clubs to build bridges between us. But, I have in important question for you."

The crowd hushed at his gravity.

"Does being united mean we need to be well-behaved? No! Let's get this party started!"

The clubbers cheered. Ari beckoned to a dark-haired beauty. A red *G* for "giver" glowed on her wrist. "This is Marina. She has volunteered two pints!" The crowd gave its approval. "In the spirit of unity, I give the first pint to my friend, Moanmar!"

The vampire Moanmar kissed Ari on each cheek, then opened his arms and bared his fangs to Marina. Trembling she stepped forward into his embrace.

Ari gazed on with great delight and anticipation. He clapped his hands. "Everyone, please! Don't make Moanmar drink alone!"

The assembled began pairing up. Florence made a beeline for well-built blood donor. Larry in a budding panic followed close behind, keeping his eyes down and his unmarked wrists visible.

A strapping blond stone-faced woman intercepted them. Florence tried to push past her and was driven into a corner.

"You better be a giver," Florence snarled.

"I work for the ultimate giver." The woman had a heavy German accent. Larry saw no fangs.

"You're the one who contacted me," Florence realized.

"You have Amberly?" Larry demanded.

"I know where she is," said the severe woman.

"She knows we're willing to help," Florence told Larry, "as Vic's friends." She gave him a look that said, *That's our story.*

The woman appraised Florence's frankly frightening form. "You do not look like you did on the television program."

Florence was stung and steamed. "Do you think they provide a makeup artist for life?"

"I can help make things better for you." The woman gave Larry the once-over. "For you too."

"I'm fine as-is," said Larry. In fact, he was miserable. After Darla fired him, he had been stuck in a series of temp accounting jobs, not enough to support him and his live-in mother. He blamed vampires, and Vic most of all. Larry felt old and washed up. He had aged ten years in the past two, physically and mentally. Vampires were getting the good jobs, they were making money, they were robust and always seen smiling.

Larry's motivation was revenge. That he could help rescue Amberly in the process made him feel almost heroic. But the gleam in Florence's eye gave him the willies. He challenged the tall stone-faced woman. "If you have information on Amberly, why not just contact Vic?"

Florence got in his face. "Vic is Morbius, you dipshit."

The woman interjected. "Of course you know that it is his daughter—"

"Shut it," Florence menaced her. She turned back to Larry.

"Do you trust Vic? Do you trust him to do the right thing, even with his daughter?" She stabbed her finger in his chest. "I thought you wanted to be the man? To be a man, period. I thought you wanted to humiliate Vic?"

So very much. "I just want to do the right thing," said Larry.

"Which is?"

"Save Amberly. Get her cured."

Florence jabbed him again. "And do you think Morbius wants vampires cured? No. So shut up, or I'll get the red pen and mark your forehead with a big juicy *g*."

Larry whispered so the woman could not hear him. "Why do you trust *her*?"

The cold-eyed woman heard him. "The man who has her is evil," she said. "He will do bad things to the girl."

Someone tapped him on the shoulder. Larry turned to a drunk woman sporting a red 'g' and a darker shade of red drying on a bite wound on her throat. "What's a girl have to do to make another donation?" She pushed up his lip and pouted.

Florence stroked the drunk woman's cheek as the music switched from Schubert to the *Beer Barrel Polka*. "You little blood slut, you're in luck. I'm a pint low."

Before the alarmed woman could get away, Florence had her by hair and hip and commenced to drinking.

Like a wallflower at the dance, Larry waited. He looked at the ceiling, the floor, the door. His bow legs trembled.

"So, uh, so then," he said to the severe woman, "how do we go about rescuing—"

She shoved him aside as the two Middle Eastern vampires approached, trailing an entourage. The vampire who had introduced himself as Ari folded his hands at his waist and addressed her.

"Hilda, isn't it? One of our associates recognized you. I believe you met some time ago in Athens."

A thin vampire behind Ari gave stone-faced Hilda the finger. She ignored him.

"Where is your master?" said Ari. "I wish he was here to receive a message. Maybe you could deliver one?" His hand was faster than Larry could track, seizing Hilda's throat. She grabbed his thumb and broke his grip and clapped him in the ear. The vampire Moanmar slammed Hilda against the wall, her head ringing the steel.

"Enough!" A short young vampire woman pushed through the entourage. "No more!" she squeezed between Hilda and Moanmar, forcing them apart. "What example are we setting?"

Even agitated, her Euro-accented voice was low and molasses-slow, mesmerizing. She also bared her fangs and dug her nails into Hilda and Moanmar's arms. "The future depends on recognition of our mutual long-term goal."

Ari pulled Moanmar back, clasping him as an ally, dipping his head to the young peacemaking vampire. "Out of respect for your establishment, no messages will be sent here."

"No. Not just here. *Everywhere.*" The music stopped so the young vampire woman could speak to the entire room. "A new movement has begun. Your ways"—she pointed at Ari and Moanmar—"are over."

"Our way is eternal," said Moanmar. He grabbed a nearby woman and bit her.

Ari moved in to Hilda. Larry had been jostled around but ended up close enough to hear. "Your master is of *no* time. Not the past, not the future. He exists for just a moment. We will not allow him to continue." Ari turned his back on her and called for the music and partying to resume. Hilda marched for the door, vampires and humans making way, Larry and Florence in her wake.

On the deck Larry breathed the sweet fresh sea air. Hilda went over the rail and descended a flimsy aluminum boarding ladder to a rubber dinghy tethered to the rig piling. Florence followed and reluctantly Larry did the same. His shaking made the ladder squeak.

"Hike up your skirt and get your ass down here," said Florence. She yanked him off a few rungs from the bottom.

He lay in the rubber dinghy staring up at the stars. "We need to get Amberly back, pronto."

Hilda pull-started the outboard motor. "It will be difficult to convince her to leave."

Florence settled cross-legged on the rubber floor next to Larry, licking the blood smeared about her lips. "I have just the bait."

BUCHAREST: MAY 12, 1588

Trubadur Maistru lit a candle and grabbed the bucket again to throw up. He knelt beside the bed where it would take place, shaking with fear and dehydration.

By slaying Dragoş's vampire family, Nadia had proven her commitment to humanity. Trubadur had been fighting his passion for her. Now with vampire blood on her hands, he was overwhelmed by his need for her.

But she was a vampire; she was Morbius. He wept, further draining himself of precious fluid.

He lit another candle. He remembered the candles surrounding this bed when he found Nadia after she laid with Mortimer Canterpark. It was almost dark, and a dark night coming at that; they needed to be able to see. But that was enough candles.

His hands shook as he laced the chamois jerkin tight around his neck.

The door opened below and Nadia entered. By the light of the hearth, she was beautiful. His heart tickled his chest and throat as it did every time he saw her. Her smile, the shape of her face, the way she moved, and the way she looked at him. To see her every day for the rest of his life, that was all Trubadur wanted.

Nadia was just as nervous. Her breath came in little puffs as she climbed the ladder to the loft. Her smile was so very beautiful as her eyes met his.

He gave her his hand and guided her off the ladder and into the loft. She wore a long unremarkable dress; with a single tug on a string she dropped it to the floor. She was naked before him; the candlelight caressed her body.

"I've waited for this moment for so, so long."

"Me, too," he could barely whisper.

"I love you, Trubadur."

He nodded and took her hands. "I love you, Nadia."

When he kissed her, he realized how foolish he had been to wonder if he could go through with it, if he could have sex with a vampire. This was Nadia, and he had wanted her forever.

"You're sweating," she said as he carried her onto the bed.

"It's hot in here."

She giggled as he kissed her. "You're dressed top to bottom in thick leather. Aren't you going to take it off?"

"I find the feel of animal skin very sensuous."

"Trubadur." She waited for him to pause and meet her eyes. "I'm not going to bite you."

"I know." He went back to kissing her, softly on the lips and elsewhere, and touching her, everywhere, sweating in his chamois leather, letting her untie his breeches.

Slow down. He needed this moment to go on forever, but no part of him was cooperating. Nadia breathed harder and moved underneath him in a wholly incredible way.

"Oh my God, I love you," he said. "Do you know that?"

What am I doing? I love her more than anything.

Her nails sliced the leather across his back. "I do. I do, Trubadur, my hero."

He was delirious in their ecstasy. "I want to be with you."

"Please, please. Oh, Tru, be inside me."

"Nadia, no, we shouldn't, we can't, this isn't right—"

"It's so right, my love."

They were connecting. "Please, Nadia, no … oh God …."

He was inside her, exploding inside her, and Nadia was screaming.

And she was dying, as he knew she would. As she must. As Morbius must.

Trubadur began to sob. Nadia bucked underneath him; she thrashed and twisted. And then she tore away his chamois jerkin and bit him.

Trubadur tried to scream but his throat was locked in her jaws.

Nadia died that way, in him as he was in her. Her muscles relaxed and he separated from her. Her mouth eased closed, and she looked the way he hoped to always remember her.

Trubadur had a panic attack. He leaped off the bed, lost vision, stumbled and pitched over the edge of the loft. He may have been unconscious before he hit the floor, but the corner of a sturdy bench made certain.

The angle of the light through the shutters suggested midday. Trubadur began to cry upon regaining consciousness. This went on for some time, waxing and waning as he labored to convince himself the nightmare couldn't be true.

The cave, he replayed every moment in the cave with Skender, the messages from the paintings vividly seared in memory. Looking for an ambiguity or caveat; the slimmest possibility would do. But there was none. Vampire legend, Maistru family knowledge, the cave paintings, they all confirmed his worst nightmare.

Trubadur couldn't accept what had happened in Nadia's bed. He was descended from a long line of slaying Maistrus, the greatest slayers in history. He had slain Morbius by having sex with her, and so claimed the most incredible, God-granted power any slayer had ever possessed:

The Sight.

But he had also been bitten.

Climbing the ladder took everything he had; he crawled onto the loft floor and briefly passed out. He finally rose and stumbled about in a daze, not looking at the bed, looking for nothing. He came across Nadia's diary.

Her parents were exceptional, teaching their daughter to read and write. And of course she wrote beautifully. Trubadur's heart broke over and over as he read the entries, dating back to the time before he left, when vampires were on the rise and threatening to wipe out humanity, and the two of them were thrilled to have found each other.

The house was cold when he reached her last entry, written the previous day. He had cried so much already, all he could do was ache as he read her final words.

Trubadur Maistru, to you I give my heart. And on this blessed night I finally give you my body. I cannot wait to wake tomorrow in your arms, finally fully yours, with the rest of our lives to be lived and made as we choose.

Trubadur took up her pen. It was his chance to say goodbye.

Yesterday did not go as planned. Nadia, as soon as we finished our beautiful love-making, before the welts began to rise on my flesh, you died. I know there is no need to describe it to you, as even good vampires surely do not go to Heaven, and Hell is closed to earthly prayers, but you went out with a production worthy of the greatest stage-performer and most creative story-teller. I am heartbroken.

And, it appears, a vampire. You promised not to bite me.

The other slayers are going to hate me.

The door caved in with a thunderclap and flying timber. Tall, bucktoothed Dragoș stood framed against the deep purple evening and the yellow lamplight from the merchants who had once again begun to stay open late.

Dragoș spied Trubadur in the loft. "You gutless worm." His buckteeth were as long as his fangs. He trembled with rage.

"Dragoș."

"Your Morbius bitch killed my family."

"I killed her. I slayed Nadia."

Dragoș scented the air and climbed into the loft. "What manner of perversion is this? Did you lay with her?"

"None of your business."

Dragoș howled.

"You are too late to take your vengeance," said Trubadur.

"*You* were too late, maggot! You were supposed to kill that bitch long ago!" The vampire threw Trubadur from the loft, jumped down on top of him and lifted him by his torn chamois jerkin. "But you didn't and my family is dead!"

"Your pain is nothing," said Trubadur.

"It's *everything*!"

Trubadur hung limp in his grip. "Nothing you can say compares to what I know to be true."

"I'm not here to *say* anything."

The leather shirt burst its last seams and Trubadur fell the floor.

Dragoş knelt over him. "I'm here to kill you."

As Dragoş plunged his buckteeth and fangs deep so terribly deep in his throat, Trubadur descended into a long nightmare of incomparable loss.

And then slowly he began to rise to the light, on a cloud of euphoric, unrestrained freedom.

TWISTED REVENGE

There was one question in particular Victor didn't want to hear when he walked into his house for the first time in 11 days. After Barbara slapped him and hugged him and slapped him again, and hugged Eugene and then slapped him, after she broke down crying in his arms and then sank into a dining room chair, she looked up and asked it.

"Why did she call herself Amberly Foreman?"

"Honestly Barbara. Who gives a shit?"

"*I* do!" She rose to challenge them both. "I need to understand what the hell is going on! Do you know?" she asked Victor. "Do you?" she asked Eugene.

"Uhm, no."

It was a first to hear something less than messianic certainty in Eugene's voice.

No, the first was when he had told Eugene they shared a common gay-for-Morbius slayer ancestor. True or not, the claim had served its purpose, and continued to give Victor pleasure every time he pictured Eugene's face.

"Then you better stop your God-damned bickering and figure it out!"

Barbara was close to a breakdown. Victor held her hands. "I agree." He would never stop bickering with Eugene. "I'm sorry I was gone for so long."

"One cryptic email, that's all I deserve?"

"I'm sorry. I was afraid the cops were monitoring our communications."

"I informed your ex-husband that my phone is secure," said Eugene.

Victor steered Barbara away from the idiot slayer. "I'm just happy to be home. We heard today the new D.A. is dropping the charges against me."

"And me," said Eugene. "My theory is—"

"I checked out of the motel immediately," Victor interrupted, having already heard Eugene's theory, having heard far more than enough of Eugene's voice. "I can't tell you how much I missed you." He wrapped Barbara in his arms and gave Eugene the vamoose sign.

"I've been going out of my mind," Barbara spoke into his chest. "Amberly has completely cut us out of her life." She broke into a sob.

"Has Tripp been around?"

"He's been in the lab, day and night."

Eugene pointed at the door to the garage. "Do you have a lathe? My tips are dull."

"Sure don't. Beat it now."

"By taking my name, Amberly obviously still loves me," said Eugene.

"Don't make matters worse," said Victor.

"Don't worry, Mrs. T., I'm going to get her back."

Victor turned on him. "You're an egomaniac descended from disgraced slayers, mentored by an evil S.O.B. You're not Amberly's savior. Or type."

"I will sacrifice everything to save her."

That pained Victor in the temples. The doorbell rang. It was Darla and her daughter Kimberly. Darla started to him, saw Barbara and stopped. "I'm sorry to intrude. We've been so worried. We wanted to just stop by."

Kimberly melted into tears. "I'm so sorry, Mr. and Mrs. Thetherson. I was there when she was kidnapped, I should have been watching. It happened so fast."

Victor beckoned them inside. "There was nothing you could do."

Barbara blocked their entrance. She glared at Darla. "Thank you for stopping by."

Darla put her arm around Kimberly. "The girls have been so close."

"I don't want you close," said Barbara. "Either of you."

"Barb." Victor squeezed her hand. "Kimberly has been working hard to find Amberly."

"I appreciate it."

"Please come in," said Victor, gently guiding Barbara backward. "Just for a minute."

Darla and Kimberly moved just far enough inside to allow Victor to close the door. "I'm online all the time," said Kimberly, drying her eyes. "Coordinating vigils for Amberly, promoting the 'stake our claim' movement—"

"The *what*?" said Eugene.

"I know you're a slayer and all," said Kimberly. "But you have to admit, there are bad vampires, like there are bad humans, but there are also—"

"There are no *good* vampires!" Eugene opened his longcoat to reveal a bulletproof vampire homicide vest bristling with stakes. "Unless they are decomposing on the ground with a stake in their soft spot!"

Kimberly stepped into Eugene's face. "Does that include Amberly?"

"We can safely assume," said Victor.

"Only if she can't be cured," said Eugene.

Barbara moaned.

"Why would you *say* that?" said Victor.

"Okay, bad ass," said Kimberly to Eugene. She pointed at Victor. "Why don't you slay him then?"

"Oh I am trying," said Eugene.

"Could have fooled me." Kimberly touched Victor on the arm. "I don't really want you to be slain, Mr. Thetherson. I just never understood what Amberly sees in him."

"She sent him a Dear John text," said Victor. "He's a slow reader."

Darla pulled Kimberly to the door. "I know how stressful things are for you right now," she told Barbara. "Please let us know if there is anything we can do."

"Fulfill your parental obligation and police your daughter's online activities, that would be a good start," said Eugene.

"Thank you for coming," said Victor. He hugged Darla.

She looked to Barbara. "I'm praying for Amberly."

Barbara nodded, arms crossed and lips tight.

Victor closed the door after them. Then he opened it again. "Out," he said to Eugene.

"I'm picking up buzz on the slayer sites," said Eugene on the threshold. "High-ranking vamps from around the world are in the area. Something's going down. We need to plan our next move."

"I'm planning to spend a long time away from you." Victor shoved him all the way out. "You're the man. Why don't you go try your luck with these high-rankers?"

"Why don't you—"

Victor shut the door but couldn't completely muffle Eugene's request.

"—go jerk off to a Maria video."

Barbara stared at him. "You've lost weight." She fluffed at his hair. "It's thicker. Your hairline is filling in again. You've been drinking a lot, haven't you?"

The Hi-Line Motel and the surrounding strip clubs, liquor stores and low-security apartment buildings were a magnet for slow-reacting people willing to experiment with new sensations. Victor had spent the better part of each day sleeping, after drinking himself into a blood stupor each and every night. "Some."

"Meanwhile I've been sitting here, worried sick."

He held her. "We're going to find her."

"I don't understand what's happening to her. Or you." Barbara retreated far enough to look at him. "You killed the district attorney, didn't you? How is that helping us get Amberly back?"

He didn't want to mention the diary, which would lead to admitting getting the memory stick wet. "It's one more evolved vampire eliminated, to show this Civil War Soldier I'm not Morbius."

Barbara worked to keep her emotions in check. "I think things are worse than we realize. Tripp is back to work on the cure. He won't admit it, but I'm pretty sure he doesn't think it's going to work on Amberly."

"Why?"

"I don't know! Do you? Why don't you?"

"I will go find out."

"And how are you going to do that?" She had him by the shirtfront and wouldn't let go. "Are you planning to go beat it out of Tripp?"

"No."

"Are you sure? Can you say that for sure?" She put her hand to his face; Victor was soothed, even though that was not her intent. "Your eyes aren't quite right. There's something *wild* in there."

Victor pressed her hand to his face. "That's what we *need*. The old Victor would be worrying. I'm *doing*."

Barbara kissed him. "I think we need something in between old and new. We need more *thinking*."

He moved away, irritated. "I am. That's all I'm doing, is thinking about Amberly."

"Thinking about her isn't the same as thinking about how to save her."

"I get that, Barb."

"Okay."

He took a deep breath that wouldn't fully release. "I'm going to work out for a while." He had the door to the garage open when Barbara's voice reached him.

"By the way, who's Maria?"

In a deep funk, Victor cut the workout short, which made him feel ashamed of himself. Seconds later he received a call from Dr. Linciome that, if he had only hung in there for one more set of lunges, would have been a great excuse to cut his workout short.

"Come to the Longer Labs," Winnie used the affectionate label for the Longevity Labs, sounding more like his old self. "There is someone I'd like you to meet."

"I'm not in the mood to meet anyone," Victor stewed, on the phone and then as he drove to the Rice University campus. "Unless it's the Civil War Soldier."

How was he supposed to get Amberly back? In the videos she didn't appear to be suffering or forced to speak against her will. No one had divined hidden messages in her delivery, no tip-offs to her location. She didn't seem eager to be found.

And she was a vampire. Victor was having a hard time with that. He felt betrayed by her, similar to how he had felt when Florence turned; *he* was their vampire, and they had gone behind his back. His jealousy was completely stupid but wouldn't go away.

The feeling of betrayal, the jealousy, and the resulting self-disgust, they were enough to make Victor want to chuck the whole thing and focus on taking care of himself.

Why is my life owned by everyone else?! As a human or as a vampire, I am under the constant pressure of obligation. *Everyone else takes care of themselves—Amberly does whatever she pleases, sees that idiot slayer against my wishes, and then it's* my *fault when she becomes a vampire?*

He had his own work to do. Vampires to kill. Yes, there was obligation in that too, but one Victor enjoyed. Vampires weren't going to slay themselves, and God knew that Eugene was incompetent on his own.

Constant thirst nagged him. The opportunities presented at the Hi-Line Motel had become the exception. Victims no longer lined up for his bite. "Dating" opportunities died with Nikki—and of course that was his fault too! Everyone *needed* him to be a vampire, everyone depended on his vampirism, from finding Amberly to stopping the evolved vampires' uprising. But only on *their* terms. Only when they said *yes*.

He was in the Longer Labs lot, but already starting to make the loop to return to the street—and there was Winnie on the berm having a smoke, waving him in.

Winnie had lost a lot of weight, failing to fill out his light pullover and slacks. He greeted Victor warmly. "Glad you could come, my friend."

Friends? Linciome hadn't recognized his existence until Victor became someone he needed. The manipulative endearment was a page from Tripp's playbook. "I understand Tripp is back in the lab."

Winnie followed Victor into the building. "That's how he earns his keep."

Victor ignored the receptionist's greeting and made for Tripp's lab. "You don't think the cure is going to work on Amberly. Why?"

Winnie took a while to answer. "As you are well aware, the curse is by no means monolithic. We can't assume the cure is universal."

Tripp loitered outside his lab door. "Using either of the 'c' words to describe vampirism isn't PC, Winnie. You're bucking for a drone strike from the thought police."

Winnie darkened. "They hit one of our leaders yesterday. An exec from British Petroleum."

"I'm sorry," said Tripp.

"He was working—completely behind the scenes, we thought—to create an embargo against any country that allows vampires to call the shots. His murder will likely end that effort. There is fear in our ranks. We're being so careful, encrypting everything, protecting our identities. But they're finding us."

Victor was interested in one topic. "Why won't the cure work on Amberly?"

"The treatment process is very complex," said Tripp. "Right now your primary focus should be getting Amberly back."

Victor bristled at the condescension in his voice and the patronizing look on his face. "As if I'm not trying?"

"I didn't say that, bud. Eugene says you found the diary."

"A copy. On a memory stick." Victor scowled. "It got wet."

"Bring it in," said Tripp. "I know a techie who will be able to recover at least some of it. Eugene says—"

"Eugene says this, Eugene says that."

"He is a talker," said Winnie. "As a matter of fact, he's talking right now to two of the people I want you to meet."

"Meaning there are more than two?"

"This place is crawling with them," said Tripp.

"These gentlemen are crucial to maintaining our funding," said Winnie, leading them down the hall. "They are also a microcosm of our challenge. They're on the same side, and see eye to eye on nothing."

Boisterous laughter came from the room.

Winnie raised an eyebrow. "Maybe we're making progress."

Eugene bristled to see Victor enter, but continued entertaining his audience. "So I pretended to trip and fall on my own stake. I said, 'I've fallen, and I can't get this stake out!'"

"You didn't!" said a man with limp hair atop a cherubic face and a mop-handle neck.

"You bet I did. Then when the she-vamp dove on top of me, I—"

"You staked her in the hip joint where I told you," said Victor.

"Is that a stake sticking *out* of you or *into* me?" said the other man, anticipating Eugene's punchline. He had Middle Eastern features and wore a finely tailored suit.

Eugene glared at Victor. "You only confirmed my *intuition*."

"Oh really? Next time we'll have you write down your 'intuition' before I tell you the Heel."

Eugene tapped his head. "It's all written down up here."

"Are you happy to see me, or is that a stake sticking into me?" the mop-haired man tried an alternate ending to the joke.

"Gentlemen," said Dr. Linciome. "I'm proud to present Victor Thetherson."

The men's eyes boggled. "This is unexpected," said the mop man.

"This is Greg Lindsleyberg," Winnie introduced him. "Greg works for the Bill and Melinda Gates Foundation."

"Being the spitting image of Bill or Melinda is a prerequisite to working at the foundation," said Tripp.

"That's the difference between laughing *with* me, and *at* me," Lindsleyberg told Tripp. "Please let me tell that one."

"And this is Mohammed Selim, from the Mohammed bin Rashid Al Maktoum Foundation."

Selim gave an abbreviated bow. "We too have a prerequisite. We all have to be named Mohammed."

"You just can't *look* like Mohammed," said Tripp.

Selim shook his head in disapproval. Eugene crossed himself.

"Glad to see you gentlemen getting along," said Winnie.

"Mohammed is having an unusually sensible day," said Lindsleyberg.

Selim drew a slow breath. "My senses are clear thanks to 10 consecutive hours without a press release describing how Microsoft's money has saved the world, again."

Lindsleyberg forced a belly laugh. "Of course when Mohammed reads that the world has been saved, he wonders why the Middle East is still a shithole."

They were now chest to chest. "Have you been to Dubai, my friend?!"

"Have you ever truly been *out* of Dubai?"

"Gentlemen," said Winnie, trying to separate them. "This is

why the vampires have a long, powerful leg up on us."

Lindsleyberg's cheeks reddened. "Because Mohammed and his crew think Allah wants vampires 3rd in the staking order, behind non-Muslims and the wrong Muslims!"

"Because Bill Gates and Ronald McDonald and all their Western atheist friends don't understand we can't beat vampires without God on our side!" said Selim.

"Holy Hannah," said Tripp, tall and loud enough to claim the floor. "Hannah the Holy knows we don't have to believe in God to *know* He's on our side. And I think we all agree with Hannah when she says, God helps those who help themselves."

"Amen," said Winnie. "We didn't bring Victor and Eugene here to put on a demonstration of human disharmony."

"And I am wondering," said Selim. "Why did you bring a vampire to our strategy session?"

"The worst vampire of them all, to boot," said Lindsleyberg.

"Look at that," said Tripp. "You two *can* find common ground."

"I am the great uniter," said Victor, sitting on the bed, as far as he could get from Eugene without leaving the room.

"He is the *real* Great Satan," said Eugene, pointing at Victor for Mohammed's benefit.

Winnie buried his hands in the pockets of his baggier-than-before pleated pants and strolled through the middle of the conflict zone. "Victor is nothing less than the answer to our prayers."

"Have you lost your mind?" said Lindsleyberg. "He's Morbius!"

Winnie wheeled on him. "Are you questioning me?!" The power in his voice took everyone by surprise, even with the slight slurring. "After everything I've done for us? The sacrifice I've made?"

Selim responded quietly. "Those who object to questioning have the most to answer to."

Winnie's fists unclenched. He nodded but it took him some time to respond. "Our time is truly short. You're going to have to place your trust in me."

Selim and Lindsleyberg looked at Victor, who shrugged.

Winnie pulled out his smartphone and called up an

application. “Let me show you something. As you both know, thanks largely to your funding, we’ve been working to identify and track every evolved vampire worldwide.”

“Meanwhile the vampires have been doing the same for the slayers,” said Tripp.

“Of course I wouldn’t call our slayers evolved,” said Lindsleyberg. He held up his hand in apology to Eugene. “Present company excepted.”

“This is a database snapshot from two months ago.” Winnie held out his smartphone for the foundationeers to see. He described a spreadsheet organized in columns labeled with broad occupations like Government, Law Enforcement, Industry, and Information Technology, and rows identifying various Houston metro districts. “We *had* a total of 58 evolved vamps.” He accessed another snapshot. “Now we have 20.”

Looking troubled, Tripp angled for a look. “Are they identified by name? Can we get a list?”

“I’ll email you,” said Winnie.

“Send it to me first,” said Eugene. “I’ll compare it to my database and send you corrections.”

“Just send it to all of us,” said Tripp, voice sharp.

Winnie called up more info for his audience. “This graph is a nice visual of what has occurred here in Houston over the past two months. You can see steep reductions in vampire counts.”

“These are great numbers!” Lindsleyberg enthused. “Do we know why we’ve seen such a precipitous decline?”

“We do indeed,” said Winnie. “Because Victor is slaying evolved.”

Selim exchanged a glance with Lindsleyberg. “So he—you, Victor—you slayed these vampires?”

“Of course not,” said Eugene. “Vampires don’t kill vampires. It’s against their code.”

Lindsleyberg’s eyebrows rose to star-struck heights gazing at Eugene. “But you do, don’t you?”

Eugene opened one side of his longcoat, displaying an official-looking piece of paper behind a clear plastic pocket. “I have a license to kill.”

Lindsleyberg did low-key jazz hands. “That’s why we’re here. We would like to partner with you.”

"Speak to me."

"Get this," said Lindsleyberg. "We want you to set up a slayer pyramid."

Eugene cocked his head. "A what?"

"A slayer pyramid," said Selim.

"A slayer *what-did-you-say*?"

"You know," said Lindsleyberg. "Where you have sales people under you, and they each have sales people under them, and—"

"Do you mean a Multi-Level Direct-to-Consumer Marketing Organization?"

"Yes," said Selim. "We want you to use your social media status to create a world-wide army of slayers. A pyramid-shaped army."

"That's crazy," said Tripp. "And maybe brilliant."

"Let's talk compensation," said Eugene. "Slay a vamp and take his assets? That's going to be an administrative and accounting nightmare to determine fair value and fulfill upstream obligations."

"No-no," said Lindsleyberg. "We don't touch their assets. *We* fund the pyramid—"

"Uh-uh-uh," Eugene warned.

"Sorry," said Lindsleyberg. "The multi-level marketing thing. Funding is where our foundations come in. You build the, uh, triangular thing, and we pay everyone. Extremely generously."

"There's nothing generous about slayer-based compensation," said Eugene. "They will be earning every penny."

"Undoubtedly," said Selim.

"This slayer MLMO," said Eugene. "I'm at the headwaters."

"Of course," said Lindsleyberg.

"Deal," said Eugene.

"Speaking of earning your money," said Winnie. "A formal, organized slayer network is an obvious target for the vampires."

"Rest assured we will work to protect identities," said Selim.

Lindsleyberg pointed to Winnie's smartphone. "With that database, we'll ID the vampires before the vampires ID our slayers."

"I would hope," said Tripp, tension in his voice, "you would prioritize the list to only focus on vampires who pose a threat."

"Only those with fangs," said Eugene.

Dr. Linciome's face was pinched. "An army of motivated slayers is great. But we're forgetting about the difficulty of slaying evolved vampires without knowing their Heels. Maybe 'impossibility' is a better word. We need Victor."

"It's in its early stages," said Selim. "But we have a method to use ethnic data analysis to identify their Heels."

"You'll never get the certainty we have with Victor."

"Doctor," said Lindsleyberg. "There's nothing certain about relying on a vampire."

"Understatement of the year," said Eugene. With smooth, practiced precision he unsheathed a stake and threw it on a tight spiral at Victor, who slapped it clattering across the floor. And then bared his fangs and charged.

"We can't trust a vamp," said Eugene, dancing out of reach as Tripp, Winnie and half-heartedly the foundationeers teamed up to restrain Victor. "This one least of all. Leave it to my slayer MLMO."

"An army of Eugenes." Victor made for the door. "Humanity is effed."

"Eff you!" Eugene screamed. Now he had to be restrained from charging after Victor. "Where is Amberly, you soulless bloodsucking coffin dweller? Where is your daughter?"

Victor stomped back into the room. "It's *your* fault! If you hadn't tricked her into thinking you cared about her, this wouldn't be happening!"

"It's happening because you won't get it over with and *kill* yourself!"

"You don't even *love* her!"

"Aaaggghhh!" Eugene fell to the floor, seemingly overcome with his love for Amberly.

Victor looked at the foundationeers. "You might want to consider finding a sharper point for your pyramid."

Dr. Linciome unhappily watched Victor walk out. He addressed Selim and Lindsleyberg over Eugene's moaning. "Not too long ago, the slayer army you envision would be our only option. But the winner in today's war takes advantage of technology. And airpower. Not boots on the ground."

Selim was interested. "Are you talking about—"

"Drones," said Linciome.

"Drones," Lindsleyberg purred. "I like it. Just like the vampires are doing."

"Drones commanded by my slayers," said Eugene, drying his eyes.

"Actually," said Linciome, "drones directed by Victor." He saw the foundationeers go sour. "We have a technology that will give us the ability to harness Victor's Sight. With your support we can accelerate the next step, the programming interface to the drones. We can be slaying vampires across the globe in six months."

Selim gave him a polite smile. "I like your visionary perspective. But I'm afraid my foundation will not support a vampire-based initiative."

"Ditto," said Lindsleyberg. "For God's sake." He gave Linciome a pleading look. "He's Morbius." He crouched and patted Eugene's shoulder. "We have the greatest slayer in the world. That's an asset we need to employ."

Linciome sighed. "Gentlemen. We all know what happened in Atlantic City."

"Because I wasn't there for them." Eugene retrieved his stake. "I have been dedicating my life to finding my beloved. Now I realize the only way to make this world worthy of Amberly's return is by eradicating the vampire menace."

"Bully!" Lindsleyberg clapped Eugene on the back, making him drop the stake he was holstering. "Come with us right now, young man. Let's get started designing your multi-level slaying structure!"

"The initiative must be top-secret," said Selim.

"A secret society dedicated to freedom," said Lindsleyberg as they escorted Eugene out of the room. "You know, like the Masons."

"I better not see a pyramid in our logo," Eugene warned.

As they left the building, Selim spoke to Dr. Linciome. "Our foundation is using new operations-management software that will greatly enhance the vampire tracking system you showed us. It is predictive modeling like you have never seen."

"The XFP?" said Lindsleyberg. "We're using it, too! Couldn't agree more."

Eugene's smartphone buzzed and his eyes went wide.

"I do have one question," said Selim to Tripp. "Who is this Saint Hannah?"

With Adrenaline-Powered Mother Strength, Eugene lifted Tripp and Linciome and carried them protesting across the lawn before wrenching his ankle and spilling them.

Tripp surveyed the grass stains on his tight-fitting Western-plaid shirt. "What the—?"

"I had laser lock," said Eugene.

A Hellfire missile came in low, narrowly missing two students making out under a mimosa tree, digging a trench and exploding into the Longevity Labs. Lindsleyberg and Selim were blasted and buried.

A deathly quiet pause preceded a chorus-alarm of cries. People rushed to the destruction to pull away debris. The Labs' receptionist emerged covered in dust, a trickle of blood from her scalp. Tripp guided her away from the rubble.

Linciome picked his way through the gaping hole that had been the Labs' front wall. He found Victor in an exam room lying under a fallen ceiling. He yanked plasterboard off the big vampire, who rose, debris falling off his back. Underneath him was a woman. She blinked and looked up at the men.

"I don't know how you found Jaelle," Winnie said to Victor. "But thank God you did."

"It will be a pleasure to teach this one," Jaelle said with a thick Romanian accent.

Pulling up to the recreation center at Bane Lake Park brought back shameful memories and put Jay Hansen's heart in an energy-sapping flutter. He tried to fire up his righteous, motivating hatred for Victor Thetherson. All his heart could summon was cold failure.

Florence's crooked form crossed the Audi's headlights. She dropped into the passenger seat and slammed the door, shivering. "Be a dear and turn on the heat." After doing it herself she looked at him and cackled. "You are just *loving* my choice of venue, aren't you? Fond memories?"

Could she *hear* his heartbeat? Jay hated everything about the world that had forced him yet again to enlist a vampire's support.

The shadows cast by his headlights on the recreation center door suggested the entrance to a crypt. Fitting, because the last time he walked out that door, Jay had thought his career was buried. "We needed a quiet place," he said. "This works."

"No thoughts of symbolic revenge?" Florence's voice sounded scarred and her face was a match, lines too deep to be natural and eyes the color of dried blood.

These days it was all about revenge. The money he contributed to the slayer organization? Jay wasn't thinking of the greater good; he wanted it to pay off personally, to produce the death of X (mission accomplished) and every other vampire who had used their fangs to bully him. Including Victor, of course.

The smell of tainted lunchmeat wafted to him with Florence's every shiver. "Let's wait outside."

"It's too freakin' cold," said Florence.

Jay abandoned the car and prayed she would follow him. He was afraid he would have to sell the Audi.

The fog of fear had lifted from Jay's mind when D.A. Goodnight was slain. Madeline was devastated that the acting D.A., a human, had declined to press charges against Victor for any of his "natural vampire activities." Jay was thankful, to have retribution left to his private hands.

He had contacted Florence. She was disappointed it was not a job offer, but overjoyed at the prospect of hurting Victor. She had a plan at the ready, telling him to meet her here that very night.

Florence was drawn from his Audi by a car entering the lot. A woman got out and they exchanged greetings. Barbara Thetherson was much better looking than Jay would have imagined.

"Where's Kimberly?" Barbara looked at Jay. "Are you Kimberly's father?"

"Who's Kimberly?" said Jay.

"That's the girl that's gonna help us get Amberly Thetherson," said Florence.

"Where is she?" said Barbara, on edge. "And who are you?"

He held out his hand and received Barbara's. "Jay Hansen."

She tried to pull her hand away. But he had her.

"I wish you nothing but the best getting your daughter back," said Jay, forcing her closer. "But that's not why I had Florence set this up."

"Let *go* of me."

"I can't. I'm sorry. I have to hurt Victor through you."

"What?"

"But you're not blameless, right? Your guilt is by association." Even the otherwise-deserted parking lot felt too public. He towed Barbara toward the darkness behind the rec center.

"Stop it!" She pummeled him and elbowed him and kneed him as Jay wrapped her up. "Florence!" she called for help. "Get your fucking hands *off* me! *Florence!*"

Florence pursued them. Her noises made Jay's skin crawl—there was a catch in her throat, quick breath hitching through a guttural clot. As Jay carried Barbara around the corner he caught a last lit look at Florence, hands flexing claws, mouth open and fangs glistening. Then they were in cooler darkness.

Barbara must have seen Florence too because now she focused everything on him. "I hated what he did to your wife. I didn't know he was going to do it, I would have done everything I could to stop it."

"Doesn't matter." Jay hugged Barbara from behind, hard, enough to make her cry out, her arms pinned to her sides. "This isn't about you, okay? I don't *care* about you." He meant to whisper and instead screamed in her ear. "What he did to Madeline, I want that done to you."

Florence was so God-damned eager. She slapped away Barbara's attempted kick—it was only a slap but Jay could feel how strong Florence was. Barbara struggled less.

"This is for Victor." He had gone from incredibly excited to about to cry. "He hurt my *wife*. He hurt her and if he thought I wouldn't protect her—I will do *anything* for her." Even *this*, even this act that was making his spine buck in revulsion, the worst most hateful torturous tickle, as Florence wormed in closer, overpowering Barbara, overpowering him, knocking them down into a jagged shrub. And still Florence pressed down, in a way that was too physical, too sexual, their three faces inches apart, Florence brimming with horrible lust.

"Call me Gale," Florence hissed into Barbara's ear and dropped to her throat.

Barbara screamed and Jay convulsed. He punched Florence in the temple, dumping Barbara as he tackled Florence, rolling with her in the landscaping chips, releasing all his hatred for vampires, screaming and sobbing and flailing.

Florence cuffed him mightily so that a ringing was all he knew. She was on top of him, grinding the back of his head on the sidewalk.

"I am going to fuck you up so bad," she said. All Jay saw was gaping mouth and fangs. She dug her nails into his face. "I'm going to tear you to shreds and eat—"

Barbara slammed a rock into Florence's neck. The vampire's eyes rolled up into her skull and she dropped into the woodchips. Jay screamed once more pushing her awful legs off of him. Barbara swung the rock at him but he was able to knock it out of her hands. He grabbed her by the wrist as she cried out in frustration.

They stared at each other, both of them sobbing, faces scratched and bleeding. With a primal grunt Jay shoved her stumbling into the landscaping, and ran for the parking lot. He had no more stomach for this.

His Audi, how Jay loved the feel of the seat and the look of the dashboard, the sounds of the closing door, the engine firing, the transmission engaging. He reversed at high speed, pumped brake and clutch to shift into first, and floored it, fishtailing, straightening out when he popped it into second. He hit the T-intersection going way too fast.

You have never been in a fight. You have imagined it, with certain women. Always the fantasy ends with you clawing out their eyes and smashing their faces. No, you don't fantasize like this often. But when you do, you kill these certain three women every time.

Florence wasn't on that list. But you are happy to discover that when do or die came, you did your best to cave in her skull.

Amberly, where are you?

Tonight you thought you were on the path to finding her. The call from Florence made your skin crawl, but she had a plan. That the plan involved Darla's daughter kickstarted your fantasy of caving in Darla's skull (she is at the top of your short list). But you would have hugged Florence and torn up that list, to have Amberly back.

Florence is unconscious and nightmare-moaning when you leave her. You want to pursue Jay but your legs barely work. You replay being at his mercy and drop to the grass at the corner of the building to dry heave, as his car squeals through the parking lot.

You have never been raped, but that felt like the beginning of it. The sensation of Jay breathing in your ear and touching you, with Florence pressing down and yearning to be *in* you, it sets you to screaming. You need to get moving, get home before breaking down.

At the T-intersection to leave the park you make a right and it's the smell of burned rubber that catches your attention, causes you to notice a car wheels-up in the field.

You back up to put your headlights on the wreck but the road is higher than the field and you only illuminate the wheels. You kill your lights.

The tire tracks indicate he hit the curb sideways and flipped. Maybe more than once, given how far away it landed. As you make your way to the accident, the lights of the distant development make it tough to see the littered pieces of the car, fractured metal and glass. The driver's side is nearest you. On your hands and knees—the car is empty. You look around and continue to the far side.

It's marshy, the grass is longer, the ground smells rank and squishes underfoot. You pause and hear him ahead. Your feet are getting wet.

Jay is on his stomach. His face rises from the muck and then settles back in. He moves his head side to side, coughing and choking, and lifts his face again. Again it drops.

You watch this repeat itself. When next he lifts his head you hold it up with your foot under his forehead.

"I don't know," he mumbles. "I think I had an accident."

"Jay, it's me. Victor's wife."

"Uhhhhng." He moans for a bit. "Need help, right?"

You consider this for some time. "No." You remove the support of your foot.

Jay's face moves weakly through the watery mud.

He lifts his head choking on the water. You hate this man for what he has done to Victor. But you want him *gone* for what he tried to do to you.

You use your foot again, this time on top of his head. When he tries to turn his face, you step down.

Walking past the wreck it now feels less likely that you will have a breakdown when you get home. Now you reconsider Florence. You find a piece of broken metal. You want this done. But the thought of approaching her in the dark behind the rec center is too much. You toss the would-be weapon, check your back seat, and drive off.

You weep on the way home. For Amberly. Florence lured you there with a promise to tap her vampire contacts and Kimberly's engaged, pro-vampire peers to find your daughter. You were desperate for the help.

"I'm the only one who can get you back," you whisper to her, gripping the steering wheel until it creaks.

INFLEXIBLE

"One … two … three," Victor counted. It was hard to count breaths out loud.

"Not out loud," said Jaelle Skudza, in her seventies, in a leotard and shorts, Romanian neuroscientist and mindfulness expert. They both sat cross-legged on yoga mats. "Let the numbers just float in and out of your breath."

One … two … three, Victor silently counted his breaths.

"Slower," Jaelle counseled. "And not through your nostrils. I see them flaring. Use your diaphragm."

"Should I open my mouth?"

"What matters is being *in* your breath. Not where."

"You seemed particular about the where."

"Close your eyes please. Fill your stomach with breath."

Victor didn't like to expand his stomach any further than it already was.

"Longer, slower," Jaelle counseled. "As thoughts arrive like little moths, it is okay to let them come in and then see them out."

"There is no way I can get a moth out without killing it."

"That's fine, Victor. Return to your breath."

"Counting?"

"Fine."

"Okay." He squeezed his eyes closed. "One …"

"Silently."

One … two …. Victor opened his eyes. "What's the goal here?"

"The practice of meditation is without a goal."

"What am I focusing on?"

"I told you." There was now an edge to Jaelle's voice. "Your breath."

"No I mean, what's my motivation? How does it help me slay vampires?"

"This is not slaying training."

Victor took a deep uncounted breath. "I mean will this skill you are teaching me allow me to find and slay the evolved vampires?"

"You are not here to accomplish anything."

"Winnie said that's what you're teaching me."

"Then he is *wrong*."

"Then why the hell am I here?"

"To learn how *not* to think! How *not* to have a goal!"

"That is the stupidest thing I have ever heard. I need to have a goal—I *have* a goal."

"No. If you have a goal that's where your thoughts will turn."

"No they won't. I will keep the goal in the back of my mind."

"It is impossible."

"No it's not—"

"Who is the teacher here?!" Jaelle's legs came out of lotus. "Why am I here? To learn from *you*? What do you have to teach me? Please I am all ears."

Victor straightened his legs with a groan. "Winnie!"

The yoga room door opened and Dr. Linciome slipped inside. "How goes the training?"

Victor nodded at Jaelle. "She says it's *not* training."

"Of a sort, right?" said Winnie to Jaelle.

"If he considers it training," Jaelle snapped at him, "he will grow frustrated when he doesn't see results."

"I am frustrated that this isn't training," said Victor.

Winnie crossed his arms and regarded Victor. "Did you have a bite to eat before you came? How's your blood sugar?"

"Fine." He had made eye contact with one of the studio's instructors on the way in, before Jaelle Skudza's arrival had put the staff and a handful of loitering students in a star-struck state. He would follow up with her when this session was over.

"Then this is easy. All you have to do is exactly what Jaelle tells you. How nice is that? Put yourself in her esteemed hands."

"As you constantly remind me, vampires are on the verge of

winning. We don't have time for this."

"You're eager to resume slaying one vampire at a time?" said Winnie. "We don't have time for *that*."

"Then plug me back into your machine and let's scale up."

"It's not that simple," said Winnie.

"Not for you, anyway," said Jaelle.

"Meaning?"

"Jaelle is the only person not to develop an aneurysm from the interface." Winnie was attempting low-key Warrior One. "That's only a slight exaggeration."

"I already passed your tests."

The drone strike prompted Winnie to relocate to the Mindfulness Longevity Tanning Yoga & Low-T Center. The Center's owners had maxed out on revenue diversification and still needed help making rent, and Winnie for the time being still had funding. Selim and Lindsleyberg had died in the Labs' rubble; their foundations, rather than condemn the attack, had disavowed support for slaying. But the anti-vampire coalition account remained open, and Winnie continued to tap it.

The tests had taken place in a repurposed tanning room: painted cinderblock walls with two gamer-style video stations tied to a satellite farm on the roof, a "pilot" before each screen; three programmers' chairs on a dais with a large shared screen and a mini-fridge, a poor-man's trendy startup incubation loft; and a dentist's chair outfitted with a virtual reality headset.

A standing ovation had greeted Victor when he walked in the room earlier that week. One bald, bearded programmer stood on tiptoes to kiss him on each cheek.

"Michael isn't European," one of the pilots had confided, bringing hoots from the rest of the room, Michael included.

"You are among friends," Winnie had assured him. "Everyone here understands that you are on humanity's side. And how badly we need you."

If asked, Victor wouldn't have identified with either side. But he had been thankful for a reason to leave the house. Barbara for the past week had not been herself. For hours at a time she sat in front of her easel and stared at the empty canvas. She said she was trying to find a vision of the way forward. It made Victor frustrated and angry, terribly aware of his failure to find

Amberly.

Jay Hansen was dead. A single-car rollover at Bane Lake Park, where Victor had come into his vampiric own at the Bizco company picnic, and where he had subsequently humiliated Jay in front of Darla and the Bizco accounting team. That park had it out for Jay. The cops were acting like it was a homicide. Victor's interrogation—one human cop, the other a vampire—had been unenjoyable for all. But they should have come away understanding he had no involvement.

They had also interviewed Florence, who reprised the interrogation for a television reporter.

"The cops saw I was the last number called on Jay's BlackBerry. We've been having an affair. We were going to meet at Bane Lake. Jay said this was going to be the night. He *wanted* me to bite him. But I couldn't go through with it. I didn't show. I'm assuming he was distraught."

Victor actually pitied Jay's wife.

Worse by far, Darla's daughter Kimberly had gone missing that same night. Victor's heart ached, but he hadn't gone to see Darla. He had only sent her a pathetic condolence text.

It all contributed to a growing sense of a fracturing civilization. It felt as though societally-enforced boundaries had dissolved, leaving each person to erect and defend their own. That there were no real authorities left to hold anyone accountable.

Victor knew he could thrive in such an ancient world.

"How could they not suspect Florence?" Barbara had fretted about Kimberly's disappearance. "She would see it as revenge on you both." Then she had returned to her near-catatonic state, and Victor had jumped at Winnie's invitation to his new command center.

That first test:

In the dentist's chair, a fighter pilot-esque VR headset and visor immersed Victor in a 360-degree panorama of a virtual roomful of NASA engineers, federal administration officials, private space entrepreneurs and reporters. This was a video of a Washington, D.C. press conference recorded earlier that day by one of Winnie's inside men.

"Find the vampire," said Winnie.

Victor tried to focus on the nearest person and his stomach reacted as if in a rollercoaster drop. "Weaahh."

"Hang in there, Big V."

"Oh, fu— for God's sake." He was *in* that room; he was walking through it even though he knew damn well he was reclining in a dentist's chair in a Houston Low-T clinic.

"What do you see?"

What did he see? A better question, what did he *feel*? Everything. Everything that everyone in that room was feeling, so it seemed. His stomach sank to his bowels.

"There, in front of me. The woman with the purple shirt and long skirt."

"You can see her fangs. She's unevolved. A reporter. Can you find the evolved vamp?"

"I, uh," Victor was sweating. "I don't see. I can't see."

"Sure you can."

"I'm *trying*."

He squinted and that made things worse, he zoomed in on a bushy-haired young man who was thinking about getting it on with the vampire reporter woman. That was obvious in the man's eyes, and of course Victor wasn't reading his thoughts but it *felt* that way as his brain corkscrewed into the man's desires.

He opened his eyes wide and sensations from 32 people flooded into his mind like through a suddenly unclogged drain.

Winnie put a hand on his shoulder. "Take your time big shooter."

Victor tore off the helmet and gripped his skull to stop his brain from bursting out. "That was awful. Virtual reality has a long way to go."

"Ha!" Jaelle looked ready to spit on the floor. "There is nothing virtual about my machine. It *is* reality."

"That helmet isn't off the shelf," said Winnie. "Jaelle customized it with an insert. A neuro-receptive, neuro-signaling material."

"It is an artificial mind, turned inside out," said Jaelle. "It creates a three-dimensional mapping to your neurons. The feeds from the remote cameras, they aren't only mapped to your *visual* cortex. They're feeding your mind *everywhere*."

"It's not enough to simply watch video," said Winnie. "This is the only way you're going to be able to see their Heels."

Jaelle crossed her arms and glared. "And speaking of which—"

"The crewcut astronaut guy talking to Elon Musk," said Victor.

"Bingo," said Winnie.

He belatedly realized he had seen it, a sunburst-haloed red glow on the backside of a man in a NASA-monogrammed blazer. Victor's body vibrated now with the memory. He wanted that vampire slain. "His Heel is his ass."

"Bonus points for identifying the rectum," said Winnie.

"Rectum?" said Michael the affectionate programmer. "It nearly killed him."

Jaelle scowled.

Winnie chortled. "We'll send a slayer to dispatch him."

"You have slayers ready to be dispatched?" said Victor.

That question was answered in the second test:

It was conducted two days later when Victor was able to get out of bed. The after-effects of the virtual reality session had felt like the flu. He had been too wiped out to rise and find his own meal; Tripp had been forced to reprise his old role and bring him a bag of expired blood.

Again in the chair and fitted with the VR helmet. But this time he was connected live to a slayer.

"Marcos Alioto here," said the slayer.

Victor frowned. He recognized that voice and maybe the name.

Marcos walked down a moderately busy sidewalk.

"Keep your head steady," Victor barked into his microphone. The head-mounted camera had a stabilizer, but Marcos had a bounce in his step.

Judging by the looks Marcos was receiving, he wasn't dressed to blend in. "You're Jasmine's dad," Victor realized.

Marcos stopped. "Who is this?"

"They didn't tell you?" Victor looked at Winnie, who shook his head. Victor growled. "Let's just get this done. Who are you looking for?"

"You tell him," said Winnie. "That's the test."

"Pietr Bisovich," Marcos answered. "I worked with him at

Heller Hellickson. I was always sure he was a vampire. He lunches at noon sharp. We'll catch him in the lobby."

"Don't point him out," Victor grumbled. "Wait for me to tell you. And stop swinging your head!"

Winnie nodded to one of the programmers at the large shared screen, partitioned for multiple camera shots. "We're going to give you another feed, from a traffic intersection camera. This should stabilize things for you."

Victor expected a split-screen but the (virtual) reality was stunningly different. He was simultaneously seeing the tops of people's heads and their faces. A man walking away from the traffic camera and approaching Marcos—Victor saw his partially-unzipped backpack and his eyes, which were giving Marcos a leery look. Somehow Jaelle's program was integrating people and objects from the different feeds.

Marcos turned to a knot of four teenagers. For Winnie and the programmers following along on two-dimensional video, the VR software seamlessly made the integrated transition. For Victor, the marginal readjustment in perspective unleashed a torrent of *feelings*, as if each body part on every person in view was shouting its story at him.

His hands froze to the chair arms. He couldn't remove the helmet and his mind was going to implode from the weight. Victor's eyes burrowed through the crowd looking for an escape. He was ready to scream when he found a peachy glow.

"Kill the traffic cam," Winnie ordered. "It's too much for—"

"To your right," Victor commanded Marcos. "The tall woman in shorts, with the green handbag tight under her arm."

Marcos pointed. He was nearly on top of her, and dubious. "Her?"

"Yes. That armpit, she's protecting it."

"Excuse me, ma'am, can I have—"

"Get lost," said the woman, dodging him.

Marcos pursued her. People stopped to watch. Victor closed his eyes and it made no difference, he was still anchored to the river bottom and drinking a stream of *thoughts*.

"Excuse me," said Marcos. "Ma'am, are you a vamp—"

The woman slapped his hand away. "Get away from me, you pervert!"

"Hey superstar," a beefy business casual man objected. "Leave the lady alone."

The woman's armpit throbbed putrid peach. Victor couldn't stand the *feel* of her. "Stake her."

"Stand back, sir," Marcos ordered. "This woman is a vampire."

"So's my brother-in-law," said the burly man. "So what?"

"So I'm a slayer," said Marcos right before he was tackled to the pavement. From the sounds and impacts, the beefy guy was joined by other like-minded citizens, piling on.

Winnie turned on his microphone. "Right armpit," he told someone at the other end.

Marcos's head and camera were turned toward the vampire woman, giving Victor a low-angle view of a stake impaling the slim gap between her handbag and shoulder. She sucked a last fanged mouthful of air and fell face-down on the sidewalk in extreme camera close-up.

"Holy shit," came the burly guy's voice. He and the others could be heard getting off Marcos who lay wheezing through what sounded like a rib-punctured lung.

The camera was removed from Marcos's head. Eugene's face filled Victor's senses. "Hey Robin," said Eugene, "you make a terrible sidekick." He looked down at Marcos. "Get up, hotshot. Your former coworker still needs slaying."

Victor tore off his helmet, which Winnie saved from being hurled against the wall.

After another wiped-out flu-ish day in bed, Victor had now returned to the yoga studio, where Jaelle was shaking her head in disdain.

"You failed my tests," she said. "Miserably."

"I found their Heels. Passed."

"I hate vampires," said Jaelle. She was under five feet tall, looking straight up into Victor's jowls. "You though, you only disappoint me."

Winnie followed as she left the yoga room and marched toward a sizeable crowd outside the locked studio doors. "Word is spreading that the mindfulness master is here," he worried to Victor.

The tiny old Romanian lady linked arms with the trainer

Victor thirsted for and poked her head outside to say something to her adoring fans.

"I'm not that impressed with her," said Victor.

"You're a terrible judge of character," said Winnie. "Jaelle found me when I was in the Balkans holding strategy sessions with our Old World allies. She introduced herself as the mental empress of the Gypsies. We crossed the Carpathians in the back of her horse-drawn wagon to Târgu Mureş in Transylvania. She said she catches flak from other Gypsies for calling a place home."

Victor didn't join Winnie's good chuckle, busy appreciating how the yoga instructor kept her hair tied back in a ponytail.

"She invited me into her very humble abode. And then showed me her neuroscience lab. Look, my jaw is dropping again just recalling it."

Victor gave him a courtesy glance.

"She did her post-doc at McGill. She is East meets West, my friend." Winnie put his hand on the wall to support legs that occasionally tremored. "She is also past meets present. She is the only one who understands your power, with the ability to harness it."

"Great." Victor was trying to give the ponytailed instructor a bloodthirsty look, but she was focused on dissuading Jaelle from inviting any more of the crowd inside. "Too bad she hates me."

"She appreciates you. Jaelle gave me the diary. She understands the true power of Morbius."

"Which is?"

"She is the false bringer of light," said Winnie. "Satan's revenge against us."

"She?"

Winnie looked haunted. Victor saw how much he had aged from X's attack. His skin had lost its fiber, his hair had thinned, his eyes had clouded. "Very soon we will have a tough conversation." His startled and pulled out his phone. Victor followed his gaze to the window—a vampire leering at Jaelle, face pressed to the glass while she flipped him off.

"I hated to bring her here," said Winnie. "But when she heard about you, there was no keeping her away. And these days there is no such thing as a secure site." Someone answered his call.

"We need a slayer outside the Low-T Center at Milam and McGowen." He checked with Victor. "Evolved?"

The vampire's Heel shone like a penlight flashlight beam, picking up spidery age lines in the window. "Left frontal lobe," said Victor. "Through the eye or maybe up the nose."

Winnie conveyed the slaying instructions and hung up as Jaelle came fuming toward them. She glared at Victor in passing. "Dirty disgusting vampire vermin." The little lady continued down the hall to Winnie's command center.

"Big V," said Winnie with a resigned grin, "what do you say we go make the mental empress's visit worthwhile?"

In the busy command center Jaelle impatiently beckoned Victor to a computer screen. "Let me show you what's wrong with you."

He turned to Winnie. "I don't need this."

"Please." Winnie steered him to the monitor. "Jaelle, Romanians are usually such a tactful people."

"I am Roma," she snapped at him. "Romania stole our name, but they do not own our soul."

"Victor," said Michael the programmer, "you can have my soul *and* my name."

"No thank you," said Victor.

Michael feigned offense. "I'm just saying I appreciate your service."

Jaelle pointed to a blizzard of graphed data points onscreen. "See this pollution? This is a time-lapse representation of your thoughts when we included the traffic camera feed. A well-organized mind will display a clear pattern. Look what happens when we try to discern your brain wave pattern." She hit the enter button, and nothing happened. "No wave, no pattern."

"I'd like to see you survive that, that, *onslaught*."

"Good word," Michael complimented.

Jaelle brought up another data-point graph. A sine wave pattern was obvious like a beginner's dot-to-dot puzzle. "This is *my* brain during the *onslaught*." She pressed <enter> and a smoothly rising and falling line traveled through the dots.

"I'll get better," said Victor.

"No," said Jaelle, regarding him with raw disdain. "This is how your mind will respond each and every time. Assuming you don't go *haywire* in the meantime. Haywire," she savored the word. "Such a perfect image of the weak and damaged mind."

"Jaelle, please," said Winnie.

She called up another graph. Again there was no doubt where the line would be drawn. The data points were bunched in a flat horizontal across the screen.

"This is how your mind responded when you saw the woman vampire with the soft armpit."

"That's called focus on the target," said Victor.

Jaelle slammed her fist on the desktop. "That is tunnel vision! That is the deer in the headlights! The rabbit paralyzed before the fox! The opossum—"

"I get it!" Victor roared. Michael backed away and work in the command center came to a halt. Victor's hands yearned to be around Jaelle's throat.

She leered at him. "There it is again. A red-rimmed hate-filled single-minded focus. Wonderful for the soldier. Not for the general."

Victor backed away seething. "It has served me well so far."

"By your own reckoning!" She left the chair and advanced on him. "You thrive on the *fear* you create—who wouldn't? My best student succumbed to the same auto-fallacy." The contortion of her face told the tale of a long-running tragedy. She seemed to be reliving the full story, from promise to misery, as her features went slack.

She retreated to the programmer's chair, looking old. "I have seen another part of your brain," Jaelle said in a quiet, accented rasp. "Operating in the background. The analogical connections between external stimuli and stored memories are something to behold. Truly I have never seen better."

Winnie exhaled in relief and squeezed Victor's arm. "Exactly!"

Jaelle clucked. "But here too there is a significant defect—an incredibly strong feedback loop. The most pronounced I have seen. 'Analysis paralysis.' A terrible self-destruction. I was frustrated just to witness it on the screen. It is no wonder it has been forced into the background by your vampirism."

Winnie rushed to preempt Victor's response. "That's *good* news. That's why we are blessed to have Victor—"

"No." She spoke to Winnie—Victor could see he had already been discounted, disrespected, dismissed. "Maybe I could work with his submerged self. That is a mind amenable to meditation. But not this, this, other." She sputtered with intensity. "I thought with the Sight that he might be different. But the vampire, *every* vampire, it *needs* something to grab onto. Something to cling to. This mind, it would take years to change." She waved at the door. "Tell him to leave."

"Jaelle, my dear," Winnie appealed, "we don't have any choice. And I can promise you that Victor—"

"No. I told you. I've seen his mind. It's time to find a Plan B."

"You don't know me," said Victor, even as he agreed with her. He knew exactly what his so-called curse had submerged—all the old hesitation and fear, the indecision and worry. Victor never wanted to feel any of it again.

Still, he knew damn well he was more than capable of using her machine. "We will make this work."

Jaelle swatted the air as if warding off an evil spirt. "Skudza women have been tracking the Sight for centuries, from one vampire to the next. Never has it truly *worked.* Deep down, I believe you do not want it to work. The vampire mind isn't capable. I should have known. Never will the vampire be our ally."

"I'm *telling* you." Victor struggled not to flip out. "I'll do whatever it takes."

"Victor," said Winnie, deflated, sad, and shrunken. "We don't have time to take you from street to street, building to building, searching for vampires. We need you to be the eye in the sky, surveying the landscape. You would need to work with video from the drones, from security cameras, from cop cams, traffic cams, activated smartphone cameras. All at once. The GoPro and the traffic cam? That was spoon feeding."

"Bring it."

"Big V, to win this thing, we need to put you front of a dam break."

The programmers and drone pilots couldn't bear to look at him. Their disappointment was awful, but Victor shrugged it off; it was nothing compared to years of disgusted looks from Barbara.

"Screw you all," said Victor. "This bullshit gets me no closer to the only thing I care about: finding Amberly." He contemplated dipping Michael and giving him something to dream about. Instead he made last eye contact with Jaelle. "I wish I had let the roof fall on you. Good luck with Plan B."

WIN-WIN

"I'm here to see Carl Yorbo."

"Victor Thetherson?" said the security guard. "Mr. Yorbo is expecting you. If you'll follow me."

She led him to an elevator separated from the rest of the bank. With a key she prompted the doors to open, stepped into the elevator with Victor, again used her key for activation, and stepped out.

"That will take you to Mr. Yorbo's floor."

The car rose smoothly for some time. EnerGreen leased a number of floors in this Houston tower, pending Bizco's completion of their suburban campus.

Also officing here was the private equity company that formerly employed Marcos the would-be slayer.

Walking onto what appeared to be a deserted floor only reinforced Victor's suspicion he was walking into a trap. Yorbo had invited him to listen to a proposal. The EnerGreen board chairman's voice on the phone had unearthed a memory, previously buried under the sensory overload from Jaelle's VR helmet. While hunting Marcos's former coworker, Victor had seen Yorbo enter this tower with a vampire who owned a glowing Heel. Victor *heard* more than *saw* this memory, as if the Heel sang to him.

His footfalls were soundless on padded carpet and against walls pockmarked with inset geometric baffling. The view out the far window suggested he was near the tower's top.

"Vampire Vic." Shiny-topped, fringe-haired Carl Yorbo appeared from a few doors down. "Isn't that what your fans call you now?"

"It was not always a term of endearment."

"You can call me Vic. You can call me Rick. You can even call me Buster. Just don't call me late for dinner." Yorbo tilted his head back and looked slightly cross-eyed down his nose, hoping for but receiving no smile. "Thank you for coming on such short notice. I know your time is consumed with finding your daughter, so you can cure her."

"Is that common knowledge?"

"I don't know how common it is, but I'm definitely on the know-ledge, and trying not to fall off." He paused and was disappointed again. "That one falls a little flat on the ear. It does work in print."

"What do you want?"

"I want to let you know I'm praying for your daughter. To any deities willing to heed an agnostic's prayers." Yorbo raised his eyebrows and chin. "You look leaner and meaner than the last time I saw you. When you find the fool who took your daughter, I pity him."

"Why did you call me here, Carl?"

"We want to help bring her back safe and sound."

"Who's we?"

A vampire stepped out of Yorbo's office, the one from Victor's virtual memory, he of the singing Heel. He was silent movie-era handsome with a thin mustache. "Salve," he said in greeting, dipping his head. "My name is Adamo Abele." He took the middle syllables for a long ride, along the way displaying a lack of visible fangs. "Victor Thetherson, I am here to make you the proverbial Sicilian offer. One you cannot refuse."

"Then let me start by saying no." This vampire like them all turned his stomach. Abele's Heel whined in his ear.

"Spoken like the true vampire bane. The vampire bane *vampire*." Hatred wafted from Abele. "You and I," he said to Yorbo, "we are citizens of our countries, of course. But we are also citizens of the world." He looked at Victor. "We are citizens of both, you see?"

"Not either-or, I get it," said Victor.

"Good, good." Abele spoke slowly and condescendingly as Victor boiled. "But it is even worse for you, Victor. You are citizen of nothing."

Yorbo hesitated before putting a hand on each vampire's shoulder. "Let's talk about what we *like* about each other. Signor Abele here tells me you are endowed with the ability to see the chink in a vampire's armor." His went into deadpan. "That's why I'm not a politician. There's no way I'm giving up the right to say 'chink.'"

"And why do you like that?" Victor asked Abele.

"We don't. But we hate Morbius more."

"You know I'm not Morbius?"

"Of course," said Abele.

"Tell that to the Civil War Soldier."

"Cornelius?" Abele laughed. "I don't believe he will listen to me."

"Morbius is your vampire savior," said Victor. "Why do you want to kill him?"

Abele seemed to find this amusing. "We are not all convinced Morbius is our savior. Some of us realize there is much more to lose than to gain. Not every vampire is a revolutionary."

"I can attest to that," said Yorbo. "Compared to EnerGreen's climate change adversaries, Adamo and his friends are card-carrying conservatives. They provide us the opportunity to keep the world from turning upside down."

"How do you propose to kill Morbius?" said Victor.

"Sacrifice," said Abele. "The Morbius bloodline is true evil. And to stop evil, certainly we can agree, we must *all* make sacrifices."

The elevator door opened and out came Eugene.

"Agreed," said Victor. He wore a homing beacon linked to Eugene's smartphone. Now he tossed the little beacon-disk to the floor and ground it under his heel, lest he forget when they were done here. "We'll start with you."

The vampire turned malevolent eyes on Yorbo.

The EnerGreen chairman paled. "I'm going to make a motion to hire a new security firm at the next board meeting."

Crossbow leveled, Eugene rapidly closed the gap. "Slayer Investments was the deal runner on the REIT that owns this tower." He flicked off the crossbow's safety. "We hired the security firm." He moved the weapon from Abele to Yorbo. "Both of them?" he asked Victor.

Yorbo's eyes bulged. "I don't partake of the red stuff. Not counting merlot."

Victor was getting high on Abele's fear. "Just this one."

Abele regarded Eugene. "You are the one who helped Cornelius murder Charles Valery."

Eugene clicked his heels. "Eugene Foreman. Vampire slayer. At your service and deathbed." He peered at the vampire. "And I know you. From Sven's mission dossier. You're one of the bloodsuckers that slaughtered our freedom force."

"Freedom force?" said Abele. Victor watched him perhaps subconsciously keep his Heel turned away from Eugene's crossbow. "History's master propagandists would be proud of that euphemism. You dirty terrorist."

Eugene circled. "And I'm sure Capone considered Eliot Ness a terrorist."

"As a society we're really grappling with our perspective on vampires, aren't we?" Yorbo tried to promote discussion over menacing. "Victor, the videos from your daughter have really inspired people to recognize the benefits of tolerance."

"Zip it, baldy," said Eugene. "Vamps inspire no one."

"Amberly is inspirational in any form," said Victor.

"Would you just tell me where to shoot this vamp?"

"Gladly," said Victor. He was nearing his word limit for the day and needed to save a few to woo his next blood donor.

Abele ran for the elevator. The weighted ends of Eugene's bolo orbited around the vampire's knees and took him down with an *oof*. Eugene closed on him, Victor and Yorbo close behind. The vampire pleaded with Victor. "How long have humans and vampires lived in peace? That does not need to change. I am here to offer you a deal to end the conflict."

"I've become a fan of conflict," said Victor.

Despite his predicament, Abele radiated confident malevolence. "Without this deal, you *and* your family are marked."

"Heel," Eugene requested.

Victor held up his hand. "What's the offer?"

Abele wiped sweat from his thin brows. "We kill Morbius. And hand over the revolutionaries to be dispatched via your Sight. Then you leave us alone and we go back—"

Eugene shot him in the gut. "No deal." He missed the vampire's hot spot by an inch. The slayer had an intuition for the Heel.

In a fetal position Abele groaned and bled on the carpet.

"Please don't," said Yorbo. "Adamo's associates are going to assume I set him up."

"Your bad, baldy." Eugene reloaded. "Heel, Victor."

Victor shoved him away and crouched to claim Abele's full attention. "How are you going to kill Morbius?"

The vampire groaned and grunted. "Suicide bomber."

"How do I know you won't do the same to me?"

"Unfortunately, we cannot offer a martyr's ticket to an afterlife paradise. For a vampire, this world is everything." He managed a pained smirk. "If we had *two* willing bombers, then yes, you would be next on the list."

"Not good enough."

"*Il mio nome è* Adamo Abele." The vampire gave him a very sincere look. "By giving you my word, I give you my blood."

Victor nodded. He trusted this vampire in a way he would never trust Eugene and his true-believer slayer ilk.

Eugene pointed his crossbow at Abele's face. "I'll guess eyeball."

Victor slugged the base of Eugene's skull, dropped him like a sack of potatoes. The vampire collapsed onto his back in relief. "We have a deal," said Victor. "On one condition. When you kill Morbius, you announce it to the world."

"Agreed." Abele grabbed weakly at the bolt in his abdomen. "Will you give me a hand?"

The bolt was buried to the wire feathers and covered in blood. Victor tugged but couldn't get more than a slippery pinch-hold. He grabbed a handful of the vampire's shirt and lifted him off the floor—

"*Basta, basta*!"

—and punched the butt of the bolt, driving it farther into Abele's gut.

"*Per amor di Dio*," the vampire moaned.

"Like removing a headless nail," said Yorbo, impressed.

Victor put the vampire on his stomach. The tip protruded from his back but Victor still had too little to work with. "Nope. Can't get it."

Abele did a shuddering girl push-up. Victor stalked to the far end of the floor, unable to be near the vampire another moment without finishing what Eugene started. Yorbo helped the vampire to his feet. "Victor, we've reached the moment in our meeting when you state for the record that this was not a set-up."

Victor brooded at the window. "Carl didn't know I was bringing Eugene."

"The Sighted vampire paired with Eugene Foreman," Abele wheezed. "Eugene *Maistru*. When one has lived as long as I have, these entanglements should no longer be a surprise. By now I should be able to anticipate them."

Yorbo warmed to the topic. "You've hit upon the fallacy of predictive modeling. The idea that to predict the future, all you need is history, every data point from the past. And a powerful computer." He distanced himself physically from Abele even as he engaged him. "But our brains are non-linear. People and vampires, we will never be predictable."

"*Al contrario*," said Abele. "We are very predictable. It is God who steps in to ruin your predictions."

"Fascinating," said Yorbo. "Deus ex machina. The ghost in the machine, the hand of God, reaching down at that crucial moment to set things right."

"That is an error a vampire never makes." Abele's posture improved. His strength was returning despite the bolt inside him. "To assume God has your best interest at heart." He turned to Victor and nodded at Eugene. "Would you mind?"

Victor's lip curled in disgust, for the vampire, for Eugene, for the whole situation.

But the deal they had struck was a good one. Liberating. The loss of the diary was now moot. These conservative vampires would take care of Morbius and make it known to the Civil War Soldier, who would no longer need Amberly as his pawn. She could be cured and move on to the next stage. Eugene-free.

"Be my guest."

And Victor could get on with his life. With Abele's assistance they would kill enough evolved vamps to destroy the threat. Barbara would be overjoyed to have Amberly back, and overjoyed with him. This was perfect proof that he was finally ready to live up to the heroic man she yearned for.

Abele knelt beside Eugene, head bowed. “Charles Valery, this is for you.” He popped the top couple buttons of Eugene’s high-collared jacket to expose his throat.

“Could I get you to pause for just a second,” said Yorbo, “so I can get a drop cloth?”

“Quiet.” Abele tied a rubber tube tight around Eugene’s throat, damming his carotid. He took a big pinch of Eugene’s skin, flicked and rubbed it like a druggie prepping an injection site, anticipating a dam-break blood hit when he buried his fangs and released the tubing.

Yorbo fretted and fumbled at his own buttons. “Don’t mind me, I’ll just slip my shirt under his head and catch the worst of it.”

“Touch us and I will tear out your tongue,” the vampire rasped. Breathing rapidly, he spat out his falsies, revealing a terrible mouthful of jagged fangs.

“Aw shit,” said Victor. He caught Abele by the forehead. “No.”

The vampire snarled and grabbed Victor’s wrist. “Back away!”

“I can’t let you.”

“You will not *let* me?” He struggled to get free of Victor. “You have no say!”

Every time Abele twisted away from one hand, Victor placed another upon him. Now they were grappling over Eugene.

“I won’t grieve his passing,” said Victor through the effort. “But not by you. Not like this.”

The vampire’s face purpled, jaws snapping. “I may not be able to kill you, but I will enjoy trying.”

Victor stomped the falsies. Aghast, Abele bent to retrieve them and Victor wrapped him in a bear hug.

It was like having his phone on vibrate, the feeling of Abele’s Heel against his abdomen.

The vampire unleashed a string of Italian expletives, finishing in English:

“I will strap a suicide vest to your daughter and—”

Victor dug his thumb into the vampire’s appendix. Abele babbled and wailed.

"Victor, please don't," Yorbo lobbied.

"Convince me you'll uphold your end of our deal," said Victor. "Or die."

"I promise you," said Abele. "*Il mio nome—*"

Victor shoved him away. "I don't need to hear your name again." He shuddered with relief to separate from the vampire, violently frustrated not to have finished the job. "I *see* you now. I can *find* you. Keep your promise."

He grabbed purple-faced Eugene by the jacket-front and dragged him to the elevator.

"Wonderful," said Yorbo. His knees gave out, leaving him sitting in the middle of the floor. "I'm glad I was able to broker a win-win deal."

SALVAGED DIARY

15 May 1588

[...] starving. Stela and I intended to steal from the market. Instead, when they learned Trubadur Maistru is our father, we were given all the food we could carry. He saved Bucharest, Wallachia, Transylvania, the whole world from the vampires. Father is a hero! They apologized for driving him away and wanted to celebrate his return. I told them he is deathly ill but that come what may, I would protect them. That prompted laughter from a hideous fool who could be justifiably mistaken for a vampire. Lucky for him Stela was there. She is the only one who can calm me.

We found a double-pointed stake in the fireplace, I do not understand the purpose [...]

[...] old drunk named Skender. His milky eyes unclouded for a moment when Stela told him about all the ash she had to wash out of the bedsheets. [...] bite marks on Father. His face went as white as Father's. I told Skender he was a foolish drunk. Father will never be turned; we are descended from the greatest slayers who ever lived. He tried to convince us to leave with him. I cannot imagine what sort of hovel he calls home. I am perfectly capable of taking care of Stela.

[...] terrible nightmares, eyes open, but we cannot wake him up. This morning we pulled back his lip and saw that his teeth are becoming fangs! I am afraid [...]

17 May 1588

This morning I awoke to find Skender poised over Father with the double-pointed stake. I watched silently from above. He could not do it. He fell over Father weeping. The sound was awful, a repetitive hiccupping that drove me crazy. "He is Morbius without the gift!" cried Skender. Stela wept and I chased Skender out.

Father's fangs [...] eyes opened briefly and through his cracked lips he whispered, "I bring the light," before falling back into slumber.

18 May 1588

From a neighbor's workshop I borrowed the biggest hammer I could lift. I told the neighbor I was cracking Hungarian nuts. He thought that was funny. He told me there is talk that Father was bitten and is it true? I said no but that it could be the plague and so he should not visit.

I cried like a child as I knelt beside Father with hammer and stake. Stela threw herself on his chest and screamed at me that Father will be a good vampire like Nadia. I am ashamed to admit I am glad she stopped me. I pray she is right.

[...] Father is waking up. Stela will not leave his side and so I bring her food and play my pan flute for [...]

[...] a strange light in his eyes. Stela does not seem to see it. She hugs him and reads him her fanciful tales on the writing materials we found in a desk. Father barely notices. His mind is elsewhere. I wish he had not awakened.

I found pages of writing in a woman's hand. I believe it belonged to Nadia. Father grabbed the papers and cursed at me and hid them.

Skender visited. He was very nervous to find Father awake. He asked [...] Father finally said she did. [...] Can you see, he kept asking Father. Can you see? Father said he could see everything he needed to. It became a terrible argument. Skender left and Father followed him and I followed them both. At Skender's mean hovel by the river I watched in horror [...]Father killed him but he did not bite him.

21 May 1588

I saved Skender's books and papers before they demolished his shack. I hid them from Father. One of the books is about vampires. It says the Morbius can only be a woman. But that a man can carry the curse. And give it to someone else by biting them. The Morbius can only be killed by sacrifice. Now I understand the double-pointed stake.

[...] slayers know Father is a vampire. They say he committed the ultimate sin, a slayer who laid with a vampire. They are afraid of him. At the gate he killed a guardsman with his sword and drank his spilled blood and stole his tall fur hat.

25 May 1588

Father talks to himself. Sometimes he forgets I'm there, or that I am a slayer. He talks to his tall fur hat; he tells his hat that he wants to lead the vampires. That he needs to find his Morbius.

Father only has eyes for that hat. And Stela.

Tonight [...]

Stela would not flee with me. Her protests woke Father. He struck me. I am afraid what he would have done to me if Stela had not intervened. She wants us all to get along. Father told her she is special. He asked her if she wanted vampires and humans to get along. Stela loves that idea.

[...] tonight. How do I get her out? She won't leave with me. She loves Father and cannot see what he has become. No one will help me. Everyone is afraid of Father. I would sacrifice myself to kill Father, but he won't let me. He would kill me. Then I could not save Stela. [...]

10 February 1600

On this day 21 years ago I was born. To the greatest line of vampire killers.

My father and I have laid waste to that line. The Maistru name is now reviled. We are slayers who lie with vampires. We are slayers who slay humans.

I killed her. Twelve years ago, I killed my sister. I put a stake in Stela's heart to save her from my Father. To save her from becoming Morbius.

The townspeople burned the house down. They would have impaled the creature who was my father, driven the post from stern to stem. He fled. In the 12 years since then I have heard reports of sightings, and that recently he sought berth [...]

[...] pity. Cătălin allowed me to live in the palace stable and

assist with his duties. The vampire menace faded along with memories of Father, but no one forgot I killed my sister. So I returned to Târgu Mureș. I provide for my bunică as bunic Kárpáti is in his final days.

I have Skender's map. I have been to the cave. I have seen the paintings and the Hellspawn that guards them. And the cryptic message, "Munus studiose tuenda." It led me to Dragoș living in the forest outside Sighișoara. He did not understand or seem to possess the ability to see vampires' Achilles' heels. Of course there are no longer any such "greater" vampires, and the lowly ones that reveal themselves are easily staked.

Dragoș bore the scars of many slaying attempts. He said he was invincible. Yet today I heard from the Roma Skudza that he died lying with a Saxon woman. Roma Skudza is curious, will the Saxon woman be able to See?

This is the last I will talk or write about our sins. I would burn this record and hope to reduce all memory to ashes, like those in Father's bed so many years ago. But Roma Skudza wants it. She wants me to read it to her so that she can commit it to memory. She will need to find some other scribe for that.

[translated from Latin]

BARBARA

Other than to protect Porkie the Morkie in the backyard from the evening owl, you haven't been outside in a week. It's midday and Winnie Linciome wants to see you. The heat feels good for a minute as you walk from the nearest parking spot four blocks from the Mindfulness Longevity Tanning Yoga & Low-T Center. Now the air feels like it's tarring your skin, blistering it.

At least a hundred people wait unsheltered in front of the center, the source of the parking problem. You approach a young man at the end of the queue. "This is quite the crowd."

He removes his ballcap and sweat trickles down his forehead. "The yoga Gypsy is giving individual lessons. Or readings."

"They make you wait outside?"

"They figure it keeps out the riff-raff." The young man winces at what he has said, as loudly as he said it. He lowers his voice. "Vampires. Too sunny for them. They want her dead."

"I was told there's a separate entrance for the Low-T Center."

He spreads his arms in mock offense. "You think I look like someone who would know where the special Low-T center entrance is?"

You smile. "I don't even know what 'Low-T' is."

"It's for men low on manly juice. And yes I know where it is, but only by coincidence, because I just heard a significantly less manly gentleman talking about going there."

You are able to enjoy him, even if there is no laughter in you now.

"It's right around that corner." The young man acts resigned to being outed. "Low-T men like to come in through the alley." He comically deflates further. "The password is three quick knocks and then the mournful cry of the evening dove."

You give him a nice pat on the arm. "More men should be as considerate as you."

"Unfortunately," he says as you walk away, "that's another hallmark of low T!"

He wasn't far off about the need for a secret knock. There is no signage and the door is locked, and when you knock a wary voice comes over the intercom. "Yes?"

You contemplate hooting like a dove. "Barbara Thetherson for Dr. Linciome."

A brief pause and the door unlocks. Winnie waits for you down a short hall.

"Barbara. It is so good to see you. Welcome to the vampire resistance command center." He doesn't seem to have recovered much since the last time you saw him. He might have regressed, the way his dress shirt and pleated pants droop on him. His color isn't good. "We're expecting a drone strike any day now." It's his nature to joke. But clearly he's worried. "So now you are *very* excited you came."

You hug. "I needed to get out and see a friendly face. Even if it's the last one I see." Neither of you are eager to end the hug, the physical support. "And to talk to someone who is actually doing something."

Winnie holds your hands. "How is Victor?"

"I wouldn't know. No, I take that back. Thirsty. That's his primary occupation. Finding someone to bite. He says he's looking for Amberly."

He gives you a squeeze. "He's having a difficult time."

"I don't have any time or sympathy for excuses." Simultaneous with the tough talk comes an intense swell of love for Victor. It makes your voice quaver until you can steel yourself. "He had a 'work meeting' this morning, that he swore was necessary. I don't care if we go broke and have to sell our house. The only thing that matters is finding Amberly."

"You got my message, that we posted the diary on the Publicola site?"

"I saw it. When I went back to reread it, it was gone."

"He took it down. But we have it on our site now, too. The word is out. The vampires are working hard to corrupt our site—

our techies are seeing attacks from every direction. But it's too late. The diary will be reposted to a thousand sites by tonight." He squeezes your hand. "Thanks to Victor getting his hands on the memory stick. He *is* helping."

"He found the diary? He didn't tell me. He doesn't tell me anything."

Winnie tries a smile. "Communication is not the vampire's strong suit."

You shake your head vehemently. "I'm tired of that excuse. Supposedly he needed to be a vampire to 'be himself.' He can't have it both ways."

That's not quite true; he can have it as many ways as he wants. But your expectations remain the same.

"The diary was incredible to read, even if it was fragmented," you say.

"Water damage, unfortunately." Winnie leads you into a little office and closes the door. "The memory stick contained copies of both the original diary and a relatively poor translation. Our tech did a marvelous job restoring as much as he did. And we were fortunate to receive assistance in the translation from the same magical Romanian lady who translated the original diary for me."

"So Morbius must be a woman, right?"

"Correct. The carrier can be a man—Mortimer Canterpark long ago, and then Eugene's ancestor, Trubadur Maistru. But Morbius must be female."

"Everyone should finally understand it's not Victor. That's wonderful."

Winnie looks ill. "Would you mind if we sit? Too many late nights, and I've been skipping therapy. I'm regressing from the concussion."

You're too agitated to sit, but you do it for him, facing each other on squeaky wooden roller chairs. The room is so small your knees touch.

"Tell me what's wrong."

"The diary," says Winnie, "demonstrates that Victor's ability to see evolved vampires' Achilles' heels has been separate from the Morbius bloodline for centuries."

"So it proves the Civil War Soldier or Publicola or whatever he calls himself, he was wrong about Victor. Now he can let Amberly go."

Winnie's face is clouded. "He also goes by 'Cornelius W. Sanders.' He hasn't been 'wrong' about Victor—he has been *lying*. He knows Victor isn't Morbius. But he needs him dead. That's why he was so desperate to keep this diary from coming to light, and why he's so distressed to see it on the internet." Winnie waves his hand over his debilitated condition. "That's why he sent X after me."

"I don't understand. X was a vampire. How could they be working together?"

Winnie stands and tries to pace, even though his legs aren't working well, and there's really no room. "Not an hour after I posted the diary, I received a phone call from a woman who runs the Robert Louis Stevenson society."

"The *Treasure Island* author? He has a society?"

"Very devoted, as it turns out. She has in her possession a diary, as well. Relatively recently discovered in Charleston. Quite a find, she tells me; no one knew the famous author had traveled to the States as a young man. Right as the Civil War was breaking out."

You wait.

"When she saw the name 'Morbius' in our diary, she made the connection to hers."

"Robert Louis Stevenson knew Morbius?"

"Of a sort." He refreshes his computer screen and has you slide into his seat. "You need to read this."

Blog post on NewSucks.com

This diary was only recently discovered in a Charleston, South Carolina attic and turned over to the Robert Louis Stevenson Historical Society. The three-story house served boarders up until the end of the Civil War. Experts concur the diary is authentic, opening a window into an undocumented moment in RLS's young life. He was only 10 years old, but already displaying a keen observant eye and a knack for a good tale.

The Lost Diary of Robert Louis Stevenson
January 11, 1861

So the "rebs" as they like to be called—and why must everything in the States be abbreviated? Everything but the work-day, which is interminable, and not just for the Negro; men and women alike move from task to task as if it's a race. Two days ago the "rebs" fired upon a federal troop ship attempting to fortify Fort Sumter here in the harbor.

This act of war is an "inflection point" for tobacco in the Amsterdam exchange. I don't know what that means but I believe I have reproduced it faithfully as spoken by the vampire referred to as Valery.

Against the wishes of my mother and her outspoken family, I have accompanied my father and uncle Alan to the States. Father and U.A. are designing a series of lighthouses for the Carolina coast. My mother was vehemently against this journey, period, and my accompaniment in particular because of the impending hostilities between the southern slave states and the remainder of the nation. When we get home I will try to mollify her by suggesting she make a "tobacco play"! (Again courtesy the vampire Valery.) Except now there is talk of a blockade and we fear we are trapped here.

It is not only the rebs we should be concerned with. Vampires are everywhere here. I had never before laid eyes on one; last night I encountered a gathering. I hesitate to tell father, because of the danger I put myself in. He is perpetually tense already because of the tongue lashing he's due to receive from my mother upon our return; his lash will be literal upon my bare backside if he learns of my escapade.

Last evening I walked the pier, itself a poor choice given the harbor hostilities, but too alluring to forgo. Facing east into the sea seems to make all the difference for my chest and breathing, although I know there is no common sense in that position.

While gazing with fascination at a whaler low in the water with a bellyful of oil and presumably en route to Nantucket, I noticed in passing a thin man with the most intense visage. Although he was garbed as a soldier, a reb officer with sword and stiff bearing, he did not fit in. And it was not only the exceedingly tall, sparsely-furred chapeau. He did not open his mouth, yet instantly I knew him for a vampire.

Fascinated, I followed him for some blocks along the quay. Followed him into a warehouse. (How would I offer a rational reason for <u>that</u> *decision to Father?) At which point I lost him amidst the high racks and stacked pallets of cotton and, yes, tobacco. I wandered about the warehouse, now in thrall to the immense quantity of goods. Enough to supply Scotland and the lesser Isles for a year! Eventually I heard voices that pricked the hairs on my neck and sent me scurrying into a small, cold room.*

The voices drew nearer. And then a scream—a woman, mortally terrified. In a panic I looked for a hiding place; as I mentioned, the room was small! And without salient features. Now near soiling my britches, I prised open a barrel and climbed inside. It was half full of pickles in brine. I replaced the lid above me.

The barrel was gouged, perhaps damaged in transit and likely accounting for the available space for me. After brushing away splinters, the hole gave my eye a view of the scene.

Perhaps ten vampires entered that cramped room, boisterous, variously boasting of and denigrating each other's bloodsucking prowess. I imagine a band of pirates behaving so. They hauled in with them the woman.

"So do you find Charleston to your liking, sir?" This from a burly vamp with a local drawl.

"I do," said my fur-capped soldier. His words were measured, accent-free, with an undercurrent of restrained malevolence.

"And our women? How do you find them?" At this point the woman unleashed another spine-striking wail. When there was no (other) answer, the burly local pressed. "Willing, and able? I wager they are. I can personally say I've presented five such eligible women to you. Martha here, she is a belle of the South. And a radical."

A rooster-voiced vampire let out a reb yell of affirmation.

"Committed to her core," the burly vampire continued, "to upsetting the imbalance perpetrated by the moneyed interests the world over. Including the smug bankers and their industrial lackeys to our north."

"Gentleman," said a French-accented vampire I would soon

learn was named Valery, "why must parochialism enter this search for the perfect Morbius? The vampire, he is a man of the world, not of factions. Our Morbius must represent us all, North and South, East and West. Although we can probably all agree to common cause against the English vampires."

"Sir," the burly local had waited impatiently for Valery to finish. "You will not take this woman for the Morbius?"

"Correct," said my soldier vampire.

The woman screamed her last. The rooster-voiced vampire crowed again and leapt upon her. There was an awful, <u>awful</u> frenzy. I shrank, tried to submerge in the brine to stifle my sobs. The feeding ended with hard feelings, a couple of the vampires alleging to have been cheated of a fair share of the poor maiden's blood.

One of them, a slight, curly-headed youngster, paced back and forth, fuming right in front of my barrel. "We ne'er get to eat any-lore!" He was overly endowed, fangs too long to bring his lips together, contracted words bubbling through a mouthful of slobber.

The others mocked his impediment as schoolyard children do. "Ah-ee, ah-ee, I uh so thirsty 'or the 'lood!"

"Shut your 'outh!" (Between his Southern accent and the impediment, my translation doesn't do justice to his utterly unique patois.)

The burly local vampire had not lost his focus on my soldier. "Do you see the result of your dereliction of duty, sir?"

Through the hole I caught only a glimpse of movement—maybe that's all anyone saw. The Confederate soldier made contact with the burly local and I heard that vampire hit the floor.

"Do you compare this whore's death to the sacrifice I made?"

The floored local groaned. "I wasn't comparing nuthin'."

"I am sure he meant no disrespect," said the French vampire Valery.

My soldier vampire didn't hear him. "I gave my daughter's life to Morbius. Do you understand that?"

"I don't understand a God-damned thing about you," the local muttered.

"My son, my son!" The soldier vampire's voice went hoarse,

guttural, horrible. "My son thought he had to protect his sister. I cannot blame him for that, I could not blame him, could not punish him. Can you imagine finding your son, standing over your daughter ...."

His voice cracked; I sensed more than saw motion and heard the bone-cracking thud of his boot heel breaking the breastbone of the burly local.

"Your daughter is dead," the soldier vampire continued to re-live the memory, "and it is at the hand of your son. And he did it," the words were torn from his breast, "he did it, you understand, he thought he had to kill his sister, to save her from you."

I felt at the time the soldier vampire had to refer to himself in the second person to avoid going insane from the memory. As the confrontation continued I realized, at least by the standards of civilized man-kind, his sanity was long gone.

For the moment all I could hear was breathing. My ears made up for the deficit of my limited vision. I could pick out the unique cadences, the huffs and nasal whistles from four or five vampires, including the seething from my soldier and the airy wheeze from the broken local. If not for my increasingly violent shivering from soaking in the cold brine, I fancy I could have separately identified everyone present.

"No," said my vampire, his breathing intensifying, "you can't imagine that. None of you can. That is my cross to bear. As they say." He tried to laugh at his own joke and managing only a sharp bark.

"Trubadur, mon ami." Valery made to soothe the soldier vampire. "There are no bad vampires. Only the uninformed. We need to educate the colonial vampire. A heavy burden, to be sure."

Trubadur, my vampire, backed him off with a growl. "They call me Cornelius Sanders here."

"Cornelius W. Sanders," said a vampire with a deep twang.

"Mustn't forget the double-u," said Trubadur, Cornelius W. Sanders, the soldier vampire. "Americans have a special love for the middle name," he explained to Valery. "My predilection is for demonstration. I have always found it to be worth a thousand words." He unsheathed his sword. "This would be a more

elegant slaying, but I'm afraid I did not inherit the All-Seeing Eye from my beloved."

He ran the burly local vampire through. The sword was visible sticking out his back. He was unhappy with the state of affairs but clearly not dying.

Cornelius the furry-hatted soldier put a foot to the vampire's chest and extracted his blade. "See? Still, I will not butcher the job. Fortunately, I have done quite a bit of slaying. I seem to have a sense for the right spot. As my mentor long ago referred to it, the Heel."

Schnip-schnick! With a quick one-two of the blade, the local vampire lost his feet. Maybe it was only the brine sloshed by my reaction but I swear I heard his life flooding out his stumps.

The other vampires turned away as their compatriot expired. Deflated, really, until he was two-dimensional lying on the floor, not much thicker than the rough clothes he wore.

A vampire with a whisper in his breath finally spoke. "Begging your pardon, Cornelius sir. While most of us here are partial to asking the Morbius to first lead us in wiping out the Northerners, I think we have all rapidly adjusted to thinking a little more broadly."

"No." Cornelius drew a flask from his gray woolen coat. He took pleasure removing the cap and putting the opening to his lips. After a sip: "I have been waiting too long now, to rush her appearance." He smacked his lips, a compliment to the distiller. "No. I have traveled north and south in these formerly-united states, so I can say with authority that we are not ready. We have not yet sufficiently ... Valery, what is the term that is all the rage? Evolved."

The French vampire took the flask and raised it in toast. "Patience is a virtue, mon ami."

Cornelius stoppered and pocketed the flask. "It can also be a vice, my friend."

"I know when to act, Trubadur. Pardon. Cornelius." Valery made a sweeping bow in the manner of a musketeer before his liege. "For instance, my delegate in Amsterdam is buying every bale of tobacco at market and in transit. In every gambit, one waits and watches for the inflection point. That's when we make our play."

The whisper-breather stepped forward. Vampires seem to be naturally bold, easily reaching foolhardiness. "You say you've seen the North. And yet you dress as a Southerner. Clearly you've taken a side."

"Not at all," said Cornelius. "I just like the look."

"Well then," said the whisper-breather, "with absolutely no disrespect intended, the boys and I took up a collection, and got you this." He produced a hat, wide-brimmed and cream-white to deflect the southern sun.

The vampire Cornelius was drawn to it. He paused long enough to doff his moldering mange-y chapeau and tuck it under his arm before taking the gift. He looked inside the hat as if looking for something, gazed deeper than I would have imagined the hat had capacity for exploration.

He nodded as if the answer had been found. "Thank you." Cornelius put the hat on. It did complete the outfit.

"Now," he said, "who is hungry for a pickle?"

That last line is my own poor joke, dear reader. The vampires did not treat themselves to a pickle but instead followed Cornelius and Valery out of the room. I wanted to follow them—there was something alluring about this soldier vampire, this Trubadur or Cornelius, the vampire who would choose their "Morbius." But as I rose my knees seemed to have abandoned me. I toppled forward and so did the barrel, spilling pickles and brine across the floor. The liquid flowed under, in and around the drained, deflated corpses, their life and essence too far gone to preserve.

R.L.S.

"Am I reading this right?" you ask Winnie. "This Civil War Soldier, this Cornelius, is ancient? And he's not a slayer—he's a *vampire*?" Saying the word pushes you to the brink. "He's the carrier of the Morbius curse? Trubadur Maistru? Am I reading this right?!"

His nod is the warden's, to the executioner.

"Then how can Amberly be with him?! What are you *saying*? Are you saying it *wasn't* that fucking appraiser vampire that turned her? Are you—what are you *saying*?!"

You have him against the door.

"Are you saying Cornelius fucking *bit* her? He *bit* Amberly?! *Don't!*"

You are screaming in his face.

"Don't *say* that! Get out of my way!"

Winnie has enough strength to keep the door closed and you in the room. "Barbara, please. This isn't the end of the world."

"It is."

"No. No. We need to figure this out—"

"Take it down." You pick up his laptop, you want to smash it against the wall to demolish that diary. "Did you tell them to take it down?"

He's shaking his head. "It's too late. They had a thousand hits within minutes of our post. Everyone was searching on 'Morbius.'"

"So? Take it down!"

"Barbara, it doesn't work that way. This diary entry has been copied and posted to hundreds of sites already. It's all anyone is talking about."

You have to sit or you'll collapse. Winnie guides you into a chair. "What do people know?" you ask. "How many people know who this Cornelius is? How many people can make the connection to Amberly?"

"Enough."

"Did Eugene know? Did he know his fucking *sensei* was a vampire?"

"I am sure Eugene was duped. It was obviously in Trubadur's best interest to sell himself as a slayer. He needed Eugene to sacrifice himself to slay Victor."

It dawns on you. "*You* knew, didn't you? You knew who this Cornelius is—and what he did to Amberly. That's why you don't think the cure will work on her."

"I suspected." He looks absolutely miserable, his color more sickly by the second.

"So why are you here? Why aren't you with Tripp, finding a better cure?"

He shakes his head. "With the concussion, I'm no help in the lab. I have been trying to help train Victor—"

"I don't care about that! Tell me about Amberly—what does

this mean? What does being Morbius *mean*?"

"I think it will mean different things to different people. Because the diary was fragmented. Because of all the different motivations."

"What do *you* think?"

"From what I've read, and heard, Morbius is meant to lead the vampires. Just not the way that vampires and humans alike will understand. She leads by seducing humans."

You start to cry before you realize why. "Amberly doesn't want to come home, does she?"

You turn to Winnie's computer at a *message received* chime. A notification floats onscreen:

New search hits on parameters 'vampalooza' 'Amberly' 'Morbius'

You click on the link and are taken to a message board for a "vampalooza" happening in Cancun in two days. "What is this?"

"Some kind of vampire gathering, I guess."

"Don't 'I guess' me. You had your computer set to send you updates." You're scanning as you talk. "It looks like it's a rally for vampire-human harmony."

"That's correct."

"And they're saying that Amberly is going to be there?"

"That appears to be the rumor. Trubadur made a tactical mistake painting Morbius as evil in order to turn everyone against Victor. Maybe this is his attempt to rehabilitate Morbius's reputation."

You open the door. "Don't start any rumors, but I'll be there, too."

Standing in the hall is a short olive-skinned woman, hair swept up and back, a shrunken wild-eyed Sophia Loren.

"Jaelle, this is Barbara Thetherson. Victor's wife."

"I couldn't help but overhear." The little wild-eyed woman, Jaelle, takes your hand and studies it, rubs it. "You want to rescue your daughter. Which is fine, it is all you can do. But she is turned now."

"Who the hell are you?"

"Jaelle is a neuroscientist," says Winnie. "And empress of the Gypsies."

"Instead of palms, I read minds."

You take your hand back. "I don't care who you are. I don't need you pretending to know anything about my daughter."

"Your husband is also gone to you."

You give Winnie a look, blaming him for what you're about to do to this woman. "Where do you get off telling me this?"

Jaelle cackles. "I come from the birthplace of these curses."

"Go back there. Or at least get out of my way." You are ready to shove her aside, but she sees the future and moves aside.

"I have read your vampire husband's mind."

Halfway down the hall, you turn around. "I guarantee you don't know Victor's mind. You have no idea what he's capable of."

"Capable? What kind of word is that? I see what the brain *does*. Your husband, he does like the wolf."

"There is another side to him. An amazing side. Victor's mind works like no one else I've ever met."

"I've seen that side, too. The wolf has sealed it in a cave. Never to emerge."

"You're wrong." A screaming meltdown is coming as you argue with this smug Gypsy know-it-all while Winnie stands there useless. "*I've* seen it. Victor has brought those two sides together before. He'll do it again."

She shakes her head. "Even with years of training, it's not possible."

You leave the building screaming. In the alley you hear the door open behind you, Winnie trying to catch you. He's winded and shaky when he does. "I apologize," he says. You keep walking as Winnie's gait becomes more ungainly. "Jaelle is more fatalistic than we're accustomed to."

"I don't have any more time for any of you. All I know is Amberly needs me. Whether she knows it or not."

"Please, Barbara. Don't go down there. It's no place for you."

You slam him up against the side of a building. "It's the only place for me. The *only* place." Right now he's standing in for Eugene, Tripp, Victor. He represents every man who has let Amberly down, and you want to scrape his face along the stucco. "I'm coming back with Amberly. You better have that fucking cure *fixed*."

"You cannot believe the day I had."

That out of Victor's mouth, at the door to the walk-in closet where you are packing.

"That business meeting I told you about? I knew that the EnerGreen director would bring a vampire. So I—"

"I don't really care."

"What are you doing?"

"Packing."

"Why?"

You are not going to tell him. It occurred to you as you drove home, that it has always come down to you. High school projects, college projects, Wal-Mart projects, any time you were part of a so-called team, the only way things got done, right, was when you took it upon yourself.

"I'm leaving you."

"What? *What?* Why?"

You are face to face inside the closet. "What were you doing today?" you ask.

"I, I told you, just now. I tried to tell you—"

"You had a business meeting. Meanwhile, where is Amberly?"

"Barbara, come on. That's why I was there."

"Bull. You were there for yourself."

"Just the opposite—I thought it was a trap. But I was willing to take the chance, to help us find Amberly."

"How?"

"How? By, because, the vampires …." He struggles to get his thoughts in order. "Because it's all *connected*. Everyone thinks I'm Morbius—but it turns out *this* vampire understands I'm not."

"Everyone knows you're not, Victor." You go back to packing, and it drives you nuts that your stupid brain wants to pack a swimsuit. You grab your black sleeveless blouse, black slacks and black shorts.

"No, no they don't. That's the *issue*. That's the *problem*, Barb—you *know* that. But now I have a deal."

You push past him to gather cosmetics. "I don't care."

"They know who Morbius is," he says, and your body

temperature drops. "These vampires know who it really is. If I promise to lay off them, they'll kill Morbius."

"*What?* What are you talking about?" You're about to go insane for the second time in a couple hours, and your body can't handle it.

"All I have to do is promise not to hunt them down."

"*Victor!*" This is a shriek, you are shrieking in his face. "Your daughter is Morbius! Amberly is Morbius! Everyone fucking knows it but you!"

"No."

"Because all you care about is your*self*!" You try to claw out his eyes but he holds you off. "You made a deal with the devil! How could you not *see* that?"

"No-no-no, that is ridiculous. Barbara, that's *wrong*."

You abandon the cosmetics, it's too much to figure out what's an allowable size. You can buy it new at the airport or go without.

"Wait. Barbara, *wait*. Don't leave." He's trying to hold you back as you head for the garage. "Please don't leave. Tell me what's happening."

You curse him knowing that he's causing you to surely forget something you'll need. "If you don't want me to leave you," you open the garage door and throw your suitcase in the car, "then you better be moved out when I get back. Go fake-fuck your girlfriend Darla."

Your last image of Victor is with his mouth hanging open, with no clue what to do.

MAKING THE ROUNDS

Belatedly, Victor decided he should follow Barbara. That was approximately five minutes after the garage door closed, as he stood unmoored in the kitchen and wondering why she had packed a suitcase.

Where was she going? A hotel? Did she have a lead on Amberly?

He called her—at best she would answer to tell him to go to hell, and like a fictional spy he would glean her location from ambient sounds. Her phone was turned off.

He called Amberly's number, but it went straight to voicemail, as it had since she disappeared. The mailbox was full. Victor texted her.

Amberly please come home. I don't care what's going on. We just want you home.

He could feel the message evaporate as soon as he hit send.

What was he supposed to do? For the first time since his vampirism had kicked in and brought back that beautiful *certainty*, Victor was aimless.

Amberly was Morbius? That made absolutely no sense. After stalking around the house, ranting to Porkie as the Morkie glumly watched from the arm of the couch, Victor forced himself to sit at Barbara's computer in the dining room's recessed nook desk. He searched on Morbius. There were 268,000 hits. The top spot belonged to a site called "New Sucks", which touted itself as *Debunking the myths and objectively assessing these legendary times.*

As you may have heard, a diary containing contributions from three sixteenth-century Romanians with varying ties to Morbius was recently discovered. It was originally posted anonymously to the Publicola site. Publicola immediately took it down, claiming it was spurious.

'Publicola' is now widely believed to be Cornelius W. Sanders. The diary (when read in tandem with, believe it or not, the recently discovered diary of a young Robert Louis Stevenson, linked here) makes a compelling case that Mr. Sanders is actually the 400-year-old Morbius carrier, Trubadur Maistru. So we might prudently view Publicola's assertion with some suspicion.

"What?!" Victor smacked the desk. Porkie jumped off the couch and hopped into his lap. Scratching him helped keep Victor in the chair, kept him from punching the monitor.

"I was supposed to know *that*?" he demanded of Porkie, keeping his volume below a shout. "If Trubadur Maistru is Eugene's ancestor, and Trubadur supposedly killed Morbius, and this Publicola is the Civil War Soldier, Eugene's dumb-ass slayer sensei, and the Civil War Soldier is Trubadur, and Trubadur is the Morbius carrier … "

He was talking himself in circles, this was obvious in Porkie's wet, bulgy eyes.

" … and if and only if all that is true, then Amberly is supposedly Morbius? So suddenly everyone believes everything that gets anonymously posted on the internet? And I'm supposed to be spending my time surfing the web, instead of being out in the real world, looking for her?"

Porkie listened, hoping to hear *walk*.

This was all just a different version of what X had been selling Eugene. And what Eugene's 'sensei' had blown up his ass. "At least the whole world can agree that Eugene is an idiot." He kept reading.

The sixteenth-century diary follows below. As there are gaps, and as we know you busy surfers have a full plate of best-of lists and Facebook updates to finish, we summarize it here:

Trubadur Maistru was hunting the Morbius carrier, Mortimer Canterpark. Mortimer was looking for the right girl to bite and turn into Morbius. Mortimer found her in Trubadur's girlfriend, Nadia Rákóczi. Mortimer bit Nadia—while having sex with her. Mortimer died, and Nadia became the vampire Morbius.

Nadia finds she also has a brand new power, the ability to see vampires' Achilles' heels. With Trubadur's assistance, they slay beaucoup de vampires, seriously reducing the population. But Nadia and Trubadur can't resist each other, and soon we have our second vampire-human sex-and-a-bite session. Nadia dies [one can imagine a subsequent Carpathian public service campaign, warning vampires of bee-sting sex-death], and Trubadur is now the Morbius carrier, sans Heel-Sight.

Like a good carrier should, Trubadur looks for the next Morbius. And decides, 'Why should I search far and wide, when I have a perfectly good candidate right here at home?' In the vein of a Greek tragedy, Trubadur's young son prevents his father from turning his little sister Stela into the vampire queen, by killing her.

This behavior crosses the line even for slaughter-jaded Romanians, and Trubadur Maistru flees before a thousand pitchforks.

We're able to pick this story back up in 1861, thanks to the diary of a very young Robert Louis Stevenson, recounting his harrowing time in a Charleston warehouse, hiding in a pickle barrel. [Sorry for all you would-be best-selling authors who 'just have to work harder than the next writer;' real talent is obviously God-granted.]

In a Civil War nutshell:

Trubadur now dresses like a Confederate soldier and goes by the name Cornelius W. Sanders. He's under a lot of pressure from Charleston Confederate vampires to select his Morbius from the local girls. But Cornelius isn't ready to pull the trigger. This decision is endorsed by his French vampire friend Valery.

[What did young RLS see from the pickle barrel? A unique and violent breed, greedy to be led by a map of sorts, Trubadur Maistru, to their treasured Morbius. A re-read of Treasure Island might be predictive as to how the current re-play of that initiative will turn out.]

Final editor's note: An old-money vampire named Charles Valery was recently slain by one Eugene Foreman, he of slaying and multi-level marketing fame. Rumor has it—and no we didn't start this one, and yes we can reliably confirm it—Eugene is the protégé of Cornelius W. Sanders a.k.a. Publicola a.k.a. Trubadur Maistru. Our most famous slayer, trained by history's most infamous vampire? File that head-spinner in 'Takes one to know one.'

Okay, in the tradition of one of our favorites, the P.S.S., one final-final editor's note: Eugene Foreman has been romantically connected to Amberly Thetherson, the 'everything goes better when ruled by a vampire' YouTube sensation and daughter of Victor Thetherson, a portly vampire who appears to have inherited Nadia Rákóczi's ability to see evolved vampires' Achilles' heels. Rumor now abounds that Trubadur Maistru did finally choose and bite his Morbius: none other than Amberly Thetherson. Who now goes by 'Amberly Foreman.'

Oh and did we mention Eugene Foreman is the direct descendant of Trubadur Maistru?

We have no idea where to file any of that.

"Get down, Porkie."

Victor shut off the computer and called Dr. Linciome. A woman answered. "I'm looking for Winnie."

"I'm sorry, he's indisposed at the moment."

"This is Victor Thetherson. Get him on the phone."

"Umm, Dr. Linciome has had a relapse. They're taking him to the hospital. Would you like to speak to Jaelle?"

Victor hung up. He could only imagine the abuse he would suffer from the yoga neuro-Gypsy for having Morbius as a daughter.

He was surrounded by disappointment. Everyone had lost faith in him.

Barbara, why would she make that comment about Darla? As if he was thinking about Darla, when he was with her.

Of course now he *had* been thinking about Darla. Because she was the only one who trusted him, who had faith in him, who loved him no matter what. How could he not think about her, after the way Barbara had treated him?

He was so thirsty. These days, finding blood took time, planning, patience. Victor had sacrificed this primal need to focus on doing everything everyone asked of him. But no one cared about his sacrifices.

Even so, going out for blood under the circumstances felt indefensible. He could hear the criticism. So for a night and a day Victor paced the house, started and shut down the computer, started and canceled texts to Barbara, worked out, and even took Porkie for a walk, pretending it wasn't a scheme to get blood.

Not too long ago, walking Porkie was a guaranteed thirst-quencher. Women of the neighborhood would "happen" to come outside to water their plants or check the mail just as Victor and his dog passed by.

Now, everyone was on edge and everything had changed. Many women didn't like to get bit more than a couple times. Amateur slayers were popping up left and right. Porkie wasn't as cute as he had been as a puppy.

It was enough to drive a vampire back to the blood bank.

Yet visiting Tripp really had nothing to do with his thirst. Victor just needed a friendly face.

The former entrance to the Longevity Labs was now chewed-up dirt bisected by a temporary sidewalk running between construction equipment and dump bins. The new entrance was set back another ten yards and draped in thick translucent plastic. It was just after six p.m. and the construction workers were packing their tools. As a vampire Victor believed he could walk past a bank's teller line and into the safe without being challenged. So he expected and received no questions as he strode through the dusty work zone and into the Labs' undamaged back half.

He found Tripp bent over his computer.

"I hear you're looking for a *new* cure."

Tripp straightened his back for a moment before it bent again. "And now you know why."

"You knew Amberly was Morbius?"

"Vic, I'm not up for a big confrontational blow-out."

Victor tried to soften his tone. "I just want to know what's going on. So I can help her."

"Okay. Sorry." Tripp still looked defensive. "Me too. I've been working at this non-stop for two weeks, since Winnie came to me. All he really told me was that Amberly wasn't a standard vampire. I took that to mean 'evolved.' Now I understand what he meant."

"Why wouldn't the cure work on an evolved vampire? It worked on me."

"The way Winnie described it, your strain is 'eager' for the cure. And it seems to be unique among the evolved set."

"How do you know?"

"That's an awful story, actually." Tripp groaned and rubbed his temples. "HPD was providing us blood samples from every vamp they took into custody. Maybe a month ago we received a sample that didn't react like any other. Its immune cells turned on our treatment—they were ferocious. This was our first look at blood from an evolved vamp. The cops don't arrest many of them."

"Maybe that changes with the new, human D.A."

Tripp shook his head. "That's not the end of the story. Testing a blood sample is one thing; we wanted to test the cure. The new D.A. was assistant D.A. at the time. We had her on our side, and we convinced our HPD liaison—also human, not coincidentally—to allow us to attempt to cure this evolved vamp. Involuntarily, it probably goes without saying."

Victor had a visceral response to involuntary treatments but said nothing.

"This evolved vamp, he called himself Claudius. Thick, bad-ass accent. Scary dude. We performed the procedure at the jail in a back room. It didn't work. After pretending to be debilitated, this Claudius killed an officer and a nurse we brought in."

"Not Marcella?"

"Someone else, thank God." Tripp looked ill. "I'll burn in hell for that."

"You already had a spit reserved."

"Really? And here I thought I was basically a good man." Tripp's laugh was a dry spasm. "I honestly feel like we've all lost the ability to tell right from wrong. Like vampires have broken our moral compass. The needle just spins."

"Bully for you that life used to be so simple."

Tripp didn't take the bait. "Unfortunately that wasn't the bitter end. Claudius got a lawyer who threatened to sue the HPD for civil rights violations. He claimed his vampire client killed our people because the treatment made him temporarily insane. They threatened to bring it all to light, the involuntary blood sampling, the inhumane treatment at the jail, the involuntary, botched cure. With vampires now seen as victims of intolerance and terrorism, with all the troubles police departments have had with civil rights issues in general, everyone was nervous. Meanwhile you and Eugene off the vamp D.A. and the assistant D.A. moves into the top spot. She wanted everything to go away. So they declined to press murder charges on Claudius, ended our blood sampling program, and moved the vamps out of that big holding cell."

"The vamp pit."

"Now they have to treat them just like human detainees. Letting you off the hook for slaying Goodnight might have been the new D.A.'s way of thumbing her nose at the vamps and their lawyers."

Victor looked at the research papers strewn about the desk. "You're not afraid of another drone strike here?"

Tripp appeared numb to the threat. "I'm trying to keep a low profile. It's possible they were targeting Lindsleyberg and Selim. Or they might have known Jaelle was here." A strange smile grew on his face. "And now I have something of a seal of approval. I want to introduce you to my girlfriend."

"I don't have time to go running around town."

"We don't have to go that far." Tripp led down the hall to Dr. Speer's former office. "This is more agonizing than introducing girlfriends to my grandpa back in high school. I'm nervous you won't like her."

"Why wouldn't I?"

A small, cute young woman with magnetic eyes jumped up from behind the desk. "Iulia," said Tripp. "I want to introduce you to my best bud, Victor."

Best bud? Victor didn't know Tripp thought of him that way. It brought a small flush of shame for not living up to that honor.

"Pleased to meet you, Victor." Iulia gave him a sparkling, fanged smile. It stopped him in his tracks; at the same moment she seemed to hit a forcefield around him. Their hands hovered inches apart before sagging to their sides.

"Is that the secret vampire greeting?" said Tripp, tense.

"You're dating a *vampire*?" said Victor. "Are you nuts?"

Iulia retreated to the edge of the desk. "Your daughter is the best person I have ever met. How could she have been raised by *you*?"

"You saw Amberly? You know her?"

"I wish I could call myself a friend. Our meeting was brief. But wonderful. Unlike this."

"Where is she?"

Iulia flicked her cap of thick brown hair away from her radiant eyes. "I will not tell you."

"Vic hasn't seen his daughter since she was kidnapped weeks ago," Tripp protested on Victor's behalf. "You need to help him."

She glared at Victor as she spoke to Tripp. "I don't trust him."

Victor returned the glare. "Tell me where Amberly is. Then I won't tell Eugene that your Heel is up your ass."

"Out!" Iulia unleashed a scream. "Get *out*!"

Tripp propelled Victor from the office and closed the door behind him. "You are a jerk."

"She's a vampire. What did you expect?"

"Kindness, I guess."

Victor now saw "best bud" as just another manipulation. "Why in the hell are you dating a vampire?"

Tripp ushered Victor down the hall. "I've been hot for Iulia since grad school. Rice was the first time she had been outside Romania, and yet she was top of our class. She's brilliant. I tried but couldn't make it happen with her, and then she left to work in the immunology lab at the Institutes of Health in Atlanta." They reached the plastic construction wall. "She moved back to Houston a couple months ago, recently a vampire. Becoming a vampire saved her life, actually. It's an amazing story." He decided Victor wasn't in the mood. "All I know is she's just as wonderful as ever."

"She has no problem with you inventing a cure?"

"Big trouble. Iulia truly believes in a harmonious vampire-human future. She's leaving for some human-vampire confab today. Her goal in our relationship is to convince me that vampirism is not a disease to be cured."

"And that doesn't make you suspect her motivation?"

Tripp grinned. "She dug me then and she digs me now."

Victor studied him. "But you *are* still committed to an improved cure for Amberly?"

"One hundred percent." Stress creased Tripp's forehead. "But I'm flying blind. I tried to convince Speer to stay. Wasn't happening. I need Winnie's help but he just doesn't have the capacity."

"I understand he's back in the hospital."

"I talked to him," Tripp confirmed. "A very one-sided conversation. He is flat-out depleted." The bend crept into his back. "They're saying he might never really recover from the concussion." As Victor pushed aside the plastic flap to leave, Tripp took his arm. "I know Iulia is on the list. I need you to promise me you won't target her."

"I can't speak for numbnuts. Or his slayer pyramid."

"She's special to me." Tripp reluctantly let it stand at that. "How's Barb holding up?"

"She's dealing with it best she can."

"I'm glad you're there for her. She has to be feeling helpless."

"Actually she just left—"

"You need to take special care of that lady."

Victor was about to unburden himself and tell Tripp what they were going through. Now he hardened. "I don't need marital advice."

"I'm just feeling bad I haven't been a good friend."

"No," said Victor, "you're playing big brother, setting me straight. Like you always do."

Tripp started to retort before pausing. He forced a smile. "And now we can part on our normal, strained note." He was rubbing his temple again. "Just let Barbara know I'm doing the best I can here, would you?"

More frustrated than before, Victor drove for home searching for an excuse not to go back to that quiet house. He was crazy thirsty, but it was too early to hit the clubs.

I should go see Darla, just to make sure she knows I'm thinking of her and Kimberly.

The thought was honest but he could feel an ulterior motive, a tickle at the thought of seeing Darla, that had nothing to do with comforting her.

He kept the car pointed home, committed to thinking about anything but Darla, and recalled a strange comment Barbara had made about Kimberly's disappearance. He put the Charger through a tight U-turn at the next intersection.

At Florence's house, no one answered his knocking. Victor could tell someone was inside, in the gloom that trickled through dingy lace curtains. He banged on the door. Someone shuffled toward the back of the house. He decided the circumstances were such—a missing girl in a throwback world—to justify forced entry.

The doorframe was old and soft, the deadbolt plowed through the jam. Someone hurried to the basement. Victor first verified that the 2nd-story and the main floor were empty, before heading down.

The stink prepared him for the sight of Florence's husband, Buddy, cowering in the corner of a terrible excuse for a man cave. The television set was a 19-inch black and white with rabbit ears. The poster on the wall was Florence and Buddy giving each other rabbit ears in front of the Dollyworld sign. The basement was unfinished.

Buddy's arms, face and neck had bruises that ran together. He was hooked up to an oxygen tank, the tube taped over bruises and stuck up his nose, which ran with the same off-color stuff leaking from his eyes. Victor thought about the things Florence had told him, about what Buddy had done to her. Before she was turned. It helped him stomach this sight. "Where's Florence?"

Buddy shrugged.

Victor nudged aside beer cans. He wanted a closer study of Buddy's reactions. "What do you know about Kimberly Kieler?"

From his shirt pocket Buddy fumbled out a smoldering Swisher Sweet and a lighter. "Nothing."

Victor believed him. Buddy appeared devoid of emotion or motives. He had run from Victor's arrival not out of fear but more like a creature uncomfortable in the light. His hands shook from real physical problems.

"Kimberly is Darla's daughter. Florence's boss—"

"I know who Darla is. Didn't know she had a daughter."

"Mm. Are you curious why I ask?"

Buddy looked like he should be hooked up to life support. "Not particularly."

Victor wanted to hurt him. "So I hear Florence was fucking Jay Hansen."

"Heh." Buddy got a chuckle out of that, the sound lost to a hole in his esophagus. "That would be quite the coup. But no." He took a drag. "She wasn't fucking Jay, I can tell you that." He used a big amorphous ceramic ashtray atop the television set to carefully snuff his Sweet, and pocketed it. "She was fucking Larry, though."

It was after sundown when Victor rang Larry's doorbell. Larry was prompt answering. And even quicker to try to close the door. Victor blocked it open with his foot. The short bandy-legged accountant made a game effort keeping him out, before cursing and retreating. "You've got no right to come into my house uninvited."

"New rules," said Victor. "Maybe they're old ones. My rules, for sure." Fear poured off his former employee. It made Victor thirsty. "I just came from Florence's house."

"You trying to get the band back together?" Larry's attempted cool humor fell flat as he backpedaled.

"I'm trying to find Kimberly Kieler."

Larry physically stumbled. "God-damned loose board." He stomped on his hardwood floor.

"More cockroaches?" said his mother Gail, gliding regally into the front room.

"Mrs. Cocachello," said Victor. "I was just asking your son

what he knows about Darla's missing daughter. Since I'm pretty sure Florence is involved." The more he let it sink in, the more sense it made. And the more he was afraid for Kimberly. "And Larry is screwing her."

"Ha!" Gail Cocachello threaded her arm through Larry's. The contrast was striking: bright purple pantsuit against Larry's faded flannel and jeans, Gail's erect posture against Larry's bow-back, Larry with eyebrows to spare and Gail relegated to penciling them in. Sweating—they had that in common. Victor saw it, heard it, smelled it like yellow raindrops running across a windshield. "I heard you were the one always mooning after Florence," said Gail.

"You love to hear all the rumors, don't you?" said Victor "I know that's why you owned the café. To listen and to poison."

Poison. He hadn't consciously chosen that word. Gail recognized the connection before he did. "Your father was a poor goof," she referred to his death by botulism-tainted duck served in the Cocachello restaurant. "But at least he wasn't a cheater like you."

The past fought to enter on a surging, oily wave. It broke against the fortifications vampirism had built to protect him. He advanced on mother and son. "How can you cheat, Gail, if there are no rules?"

"*God* has rules."

"Yes. But you don't understand them." Victor separated mother from son and lifted Gail Cocachello into his arms. Things got weird.

Gail's eyes fluttered. She was actually looking forward to this.

Victor got excited despite Gail's pantsuit and her loose neck. He smelled fear in three distinct images: Gail's, ruby-red and pumping like a Valentine's heart; Larry's, a melted stick of Mitchum deodorant; and from another, sprinkling down on his forehead and tickling his eyes, like … owl feathers?

Gail was easily breached. Victor sucked for all he was worth, like from a washrag. Drank a pint while Larry pounded on his back.

He laid Gail gently on the hardwood and parted a neck fold to display the bite mark. She moaned and ran her hands along her hips.

Larry dropped to his knees. "Ma!" Tears trickled down his cheeks. "Ma! Open your eyes!"

They fluttered open and stared at the ceiling. "The vampire. He took me, son."

Victor stood over Larry. "Where is she?"

"I will kill you for this," Larry sobbed through gritted teeth.

He put Larry on his back and snarled in his face. "Where is she?"

Larry's features seemed to implode. "Attic." He pursued Victor as he took the stairs. "I'm *protecting* her from Florence. She said she'd kill her if I didn't—or drink enough she wished she was dead. We did it to get your daughter back!"

At this Victor clubbed him and Larry tumbled down the stairs. Victor heard her now, heard and smelled and sensed, Kimberly's fear was the owl feathers, he *saw* her as he twisted and pulled the handle to the attic hatch and released the short suspended staircase. She came down facing forward, stumbled, and Victor caught her and hugged her to him as she wept.

Larry pleaded as Victor carried Kimberly down the stairs. "I didn't know what Florence was going to do. I just wanted to help find Amberly!"

Kimberly spoke into his shoulder. "My phone."

Victor snapped his fingers. "Phone."

Larry hustled upstairs and retrieved it. Now his tone changed as Victor carried Kimberly and her phone out the door. "Your daughter doesn't want to come back to you, do you know that? She's a vampire through and through! And it's your fault!"

A small crowd of neighbors brought Larry to a halt on his stoop. He hissed his parting shot. "They say she's this Morbilus, or whatever. Congratulations, you sonofabitch."

Kimberly curled up in the passenger seat, facing the door, quietly sobbing. Victor tried to engage her before letting her be.

At Darla's he came around the Charger to help Kimberly but she was already running for the front door. Darla came out holding her phone and Victor understood they had been texting each other.

Darla hugged her daughter hard enough to hurt and ushered her to the house while reaching back for Victor. He had been about to leave, but instead took her hand and followed them into the house.

Darla tried to see and touch her daughter everywhere. "Are you okay? Are you starving?"

"They fed me."

"Who's they? Kimberly, what happened?"

"Mr. T saved me." This brought a fresh release of tears. Darla let her cry. Kimberly exhaled a shuddering breath that relaxed her shoulders. "I was at Larry's house. He said it was the only way to get Amberly back. He tried to pretend that I wasn't really kidnapped—"

"*Who?*" Darla broke in. "Larry? *Larry* kidnapped you?"

"It was Florence. She said we were going to meet with her vampire contacts. She said they wanted to work behind the scenes with the StakeOurClaim movement, and in return they would help get Amberly back. We met at Pappadeaux. I think she drugged my crab queso. I woke up in Larry's attic." She made a face. "He's a hoarder."

Darla looked bug-eyed at Victor. "She was at Larry's *house*? How did you know?"

"Florence's husband told me."

"Larry was good to me," said Kimberly. "He and his mother. She's kind of a bitch, but she wasn't going to let Florence hurt me. Florence wanted to bite me. She was fucking scary."

"Kimberly."

"There's no other way to say it. She told Larry she'd turn me if he didn't keep his mouth shut and keep me prisoner." Kimberly shuddered and sobbed. "He was just as scared of Florence."

"I don't care." Darla held up her phone and looked to Victor. "Did you already call the police?" At his head shake she dialed nine-one-one.

Kimberly disconnected it. "I'm afraid what would happen—"

"I don't give a *shit* about Larry."

"To Amberly. By Florence."

Darla wasn't convinced. "We need to tell them you're safe."

"Just don't call nine-one-one for God's sake."

Darla searched for a general HPD number. "*You* need to start calling everyone, to let them know you're safe."

"I need to *sleep*, Mom. I'll post something later."

"Sleep later. Your grandparents don't Facebook. At least not well. Call them," she ordered as Kimberly headed upstairs. "Hi, this is Darla Kieler. I reported my daughter Kimberly missing. Kimberly Kieler. K-i-e-l-e-r. She's back. She's fine. I don't know what we're going to do—yes, that's right. I don't know if you need to—okay. Well, I guess just let me know if you'd like us to come down. Okay." She scowled and put her phone on the counter. "They were *so* relieved."

That made Victor chuckle. Darla laughed and began crying and moved into him for a hug. "What am I going to do? What if Florence tries again?"

"I am going to tell her I will kill her if she comes near either of you."

Darla relaxed in his arms. "Thank you," she said. "You're my hero."

That affected Victor. "It's nice to hear something positive."

She pulled back and dried her tears. "I shouldn't be leaning on you."

"I don't mind."

"I don't have that right." Darla looked as if she might collapse. Victor guided her to a chair in the living room and took a knee beside her. "I have been so unbelievably shaken up. I'm sorry, I guess I don't have to tell you. How are you holding up? You and Barbara. I'm so sorry about what's happening with Amberly."

"I have no idea what's going on."

"There are a lot of rumors out there. Please don't let it get to you. Like me." Her face showed the stress. "She'll figure things out and be alright. I know it." Darla tried to smile encouragement. "Thank you, Victor. I meant what I said. You saved me. I've missed you, but I understand. Sorry. You should go, I'm sure."

He shrugged. "Nowhere to go at the moment."

She raised her eyebrows. "Home, I would say."

"Barbara asked me to move out."

Darla took his hands. "Then you need to fight back and tell her *no*. That's how it works. You can't keep making up and breaking up."

"This is hardly a normal situation. Or relationship."

"Everyone feels that way. Everyone has unique situations. But everyone shares one constant. You have to work at staying in love."

"Mm. And *you* would have to work at it, with me?"

Darla started to answer, twice, reconsidering each time. "This isn't about you and me. You've made that painfully clear."

Victor paced to the dining room and back. "All I know right now is I'm tired of Barbara criticizing everything I do. Or don't do. It used to be that I wasn't decisive enough. Now I'm a selfish idiot who never thinks about what he's doing."

She stood and held him in place. "Clearly you're thinking of others. You just saved my daughter. It's not right that Barbara only loves you if you do exactly what she wants." She lowered her eyes. "It's not for me to say that. I know she's coming from a very stressful place."

"It's not just Barbara," said Victor. "No one approves of what I'm doing. I'm tired of it. I can't please anyone, anytime." He put his hands on the nape of her neck, his fingers under her hair. "Except you. Always and every time."

"Victor. Please don't."

"I want you to know what it means to me."

Darla shook her head, too slowly to convince him she wanted to break free. "I'm too beaten down to say the things I should." She pressed her cheek to the inside of his wrist. "To say no to you."

Victor kissed her cheek, as chastely as he could. "I won't make you say it. I'm very glad Kimberly is safe. Now I need to find my daughter."

"How?"

"I'm not sure. But I think I need to get to her before Eugene does."

VAMPALOOZA

The Avett Brothers. I cannot believe I have a backstage pass to see the Avett Brothers! They are singing right now, to a crowd that Bono guesses is at least 10,000 people. And if anyone should be able to measure the size of a crowd …

It's Bono! And I think he's in love with me. He won't leave me alone. It's getting a little creepy. Maybe because he's older than I thought. Still sexy though, for an older guy.

Bono is one more thing for Hilda to be jealous about. She's standing in a fold in the stage curtain, lurking really, glaring. I'm used to it, of course, but for crying out loud, she's the one who brought me here!

It was two o'clock this morning when she slipped into my room. I was so sure it was go time. She couldn't wear an *I'm-on-your-side* expression to save her life.

Turns out, she's my ally. "There is a gathering in Cancun tonight," she told me. "The Vampalooza. A communal gathering of vampires and humans. Everyone hopes you will appear. If you want that, you must come with me now."

I leaped out of bed and yanked open my dresser. "Do you have a suitcase?" I asked.

"There is no time to pack." Hilda held up a Wal-Mart shopping bag. "I purchased some appropriate clothing for you."

I'm not a snob. Mom worked there for years and she isn't one to pass up a good family discount. But I should have been a little more concerned about Hilda's taste.

Of course all I was thinking about was leaving that house. For Cancun! Friends at McNulty prep were here last year and had an absolute blow-out. They made it sound so exotic.

And they were right. The air when we stepped off the plane—I didn't think it would be much different than Houston. But the smell, it's wonderfully ancient; makes me think the United States has scrubbed that smell away. And the color, it's stupid to call it vivid and washed out all at the same time, but that's the truth. I'm in love.

And that's while wearing a thick lavender sun hat like a canvas sombrero. It's not easy to fall in love in a Wal-Mart canvas sombrero, one that I had to wear on the plane as a disguise to keep Hilda happy and haven't been able to take off until Bono frowned and gently removed it from my head and put a match to it and threw the burning hat into the sand behind the stage. Unfortunately, I'm still wearing a roomy floral pullover and culottes.

And still in love with Cancun.

And still the love of Bono's life, as far as I can tell.

"I subscribe to your YouTube channel, Amberly. Your vids inspire me!"

"Oh, Bono."

"No, I'm not kiddin', you know? Truly revolutionary. I've dropped all the other malarkey I've been peddling and signed up full-time for your cause!"

"Bono, I'm blushing." Bono is wooing me while we are serenaded by the Avett Brothers!

"Luv, this is where it's at." He points at the huge Vampalooza crowd, the epitome of the brotherhood of vampires and humans. "This *has* to be our future, you know? We'll tear each other apart, if we can't come together."

"God that's good. I'm going to use that one."

"Really? You don't have to say that."

"No, I mean it. It gave me goose bumps."

Bono nods. "That's what we shoot for, love. The bumps."

"She has what it takes, doesn't she?" Cornelius had tiptoed up and scares the crap out of Bono. Scares me more, the way he's staring at me. I glance at the curtain; Hilda is gone.

"Bono, this is my, uh, well my friend, I guess."

"Practically her father."

"Cornelius."

"Trubadur," he corrects, turns it into his introduction.

"Trubadur Maistru. From Bucharest."

So the rumors are true. I guess that explains his Romanian cuddle words.

"Romania," says Bono, cocking his head, neatly recovered from the shock. "I don't hear it."

"I lost the accent a long time ago," says Trubadur. "But I'm working to get it back." He doesn't waste time getting his hands on me. "I can tell you're smitten with our Amberly."

"The planet is smitten, my friend." Bono is very intuitive; he senses my discomfort. "Can I inquire as to the exact nature of your interest in our Amberly—"

"Can I trust my eyes?" Seth Avett interrupts. He does it in style, at the microphone in front of the cameras—the media is here—and 10,000 humans and vampires. He has just spotted me. "The rumors were true! Ladies and gentleman, the pointed and the rounded, I am bowled over to own the very distinct pleasure to introduce—"

"Whoa-whoa," shouts Bono. The stage is huge, he has a long way to run, giving Seth Avett the cut sign all the way. Bono is the emcee after all.

"The peace-bringer," Seth says. "The next Nobel Peace Prize winner! The great Uniter!"

Bono stops halfway across the stage, admitting defeat and absolutely crestfallen.

"And may I say, the sexiest little vampire on the planet!" This brings the crowd to a fever pitch. And me in a floral pullover and culottes. "Amberly Foreman!"

I turn to Trubadur. "You do *not* bite Bono." In passing I whisper to Bono to be careful, and join Seth Avett at the mic.

"Hi, Seth."

"Hello Amberly. Or," he says to the crowd. "should we call you *Morbius?*"

He might as well have punched me in the stomach. I can't draw breath enough to speak.

Half the crowd seems to have been punched, too. The human half. Immediately prior, you couldn't tell human from vampire in the seamless gathering.

Now there is separation, like oil from water.

It's the vampires. Hearing *Morbius* seemed to trigger a

preprogrammed set of actions. Bare fangs and scream at the moon. Band together with other vampires. Start chanting, *Morbius, Morbius*.

Humans are picking up the chant, *Morbius*, *Morbius*, seeking harmonious solidarity. But their eager voices are dissonant with the vampires' lustiness. They coalesce into packs while the humans look like weak wildebeest separated from the herd.

It starts to my right, maybe twenty yards from the stage. Vampires have a man and a woman trapped in front of a Bonfils blood donation booth. One vampire feints an attack to draw their attention and the others jump on the poor couple's backs and bring them down.

Their screams are terrible, merged with the feedback squeal of the fallen microphone and now one with the screech of an incoming missile. One of the Vampalooza's many rented booths disappears in a geyser of sand, body parts and flyers.

"Drone strike!" a reporter screams. I see the machine glowing high overhead in the setting sun. The smell of hot sand and blood wafts across the beach.

Vampires lose their minds, entering frenzy. The sweet young vampire woman I met in the Acres Homes coffeeshop leaps to the counter of her Comity Club booth and screams with bloodlust. Humans piss themselves—for hunters the perfect olfactory complement to blood. Biting begins. The security personnel guarding the stage wade into the fray, but not all of them are trying to stop the violence. The Asian Avett Brother dips Brother Scott and bites his throat.

I yell at everyone to stop, a worthless attempt. There is a grunt and a snarl to my left—a skinny old hag runs at me. Two men burst from the opposite backstage wing—George and Boris! They high-low the hag and crash into the Avett Brothers' upright bass. George and Boris are slow to rise—there was already something wrong with them, George half-blind and crippled, Boris clutching his stomach and neck. The hag is quick—she headbutts George and twists his head with a *snap*. He falls face-up, which now means on his stomach.

Boris howls mournfully. The saddest sound, cut off by a string from the upright bass, a garrote that decapitates him.

"You bitch!"

The hag is a vampire, clearly not evolved, in a Western-cut shirt, unbuttoned far too far down her front, bolo tie hanging between her saggy boobs, huge Lone Star belt buckle.

It's Florence. I remember her from the Xtreme ReVamp television show. "You evil, disgusting demon."

"You're not cut out for this role, sweetie," says Florence. "Morbius is wasted on you." She wrestles me to the stage floor. "Do you want to see your friend again? I have Kimberly," she breathes hard, foul fumes in my face, "in a safe location. But it won't be safe if I leave here without your bite."

I received a text from Kimberly a few hours ago. My dad rescued her.

"Bite me or your friend dies!"

"Why would I *bite* you?" I ask.

Florence yanks her collar from her throat. "You know damn well why."

"Sorry. I don't negotiate with terrorists." I knee her between the legs, punch her in the throat, and kick her in the chest with both feet, launching her over the lip of the stage. She's strong but lightweight.

A vampire separates from the melee and runs at the stage, screaming, "*Morbius!* She who would rule us all!"

The ugly drooling vampire leaps seven feet off the loose sand onto the stage. He tears off his shirt to reveal a suicide vest and picks up the microphone. "*Sic semper tyrannis!* Thus always to tyrants!" He drops the mic and comes at me with the detonator held high.

Fifteen minutes earlier, a solemn-eyed Mexican with long drooping mustaches stood at Eugene's Melaleuca booth. "I'm interested in joining your pyramid scheme."

Eugene glared. "Don't ever use that term again. It's multi-level marketing." The booth was a front to gain access to the Vampalooza, but he had already sold $5,000 in merchandise and filled gaps in his various downstream distribution channels that should grow his worldwide revenue by two percent. "And Melaleuca is excited to welcome you aboard. You'll find these products nothing short of revolutionary."

"I mean your *other* pyr—" The mustachioed gent caught

himself; made a triangle with his fingers.

"I have a number of MLMOs actively seeking LatAm network leaders," said Eugene.

The man leaned in. "You know the one I mean." His eyes slid to the left and to the right. "I want to deal in *stakes*."

Eugene gave him the *come here* finger and the man joined him inside the booth. "I want you to pick out every vamp that passes by."

"That will be good training, thank you."

Eugene put a paintball gun on the counter. "And then shoot them."

The man solemnly assessed Eugene's seriousness or sanity. "Won't that make them angry?"

On the beach, vamps and humans laughed together, here a cornhole game, there a hacky sack circle. They sang along to the Avett Brothers, humans drowned out by the vamps' more powerful and frankly more beautiful voices. The inter-species fraternity made Eugene sick. "Slayers can't hide. Slayers can't blend in." He put the gun to his shoulder and shot a Frisbee-playing vamp on its fresh weeping Vampire Che Guevara neck tattoo.

The vamp howled and grabbed its neck, coming away with a smear of yellow and red. It turned and charged; then stopped when Eugene unbuttoned his summer-weight overcoat to display a bandolier of stakes. The vamp roared and flung the Frisbee into the ocean, daring his fellows to complain.

"I'll be back in fifteen," said Eugene to the prospective slayer, leaving him to man the booth with the paintball gun, three stakes, and a stack of Melaleuca brochures. He walked along the ocean on his way to the stage, waves crashing, mind reeling.

The Civil War Soldier was his vamp ancestor, Trubadur Maistru. Amberly was Morbius. He was their fool. Eugene stomped a sand sculpture of Disney's or Dracula's castle.

"What the hell do you think you're doing?" one of the sculpture's creators accosted him in German, one of Eugene's seven fluent languages.

Eugene veered at the band of teen Euro-dressed vamps and humans, a stake in each hand. Snarling and scolding the teens backed off and Eugene continued along the beach.

The stage was full-size rock'n'roll, completely plugging the beach, forcing him to dodge the surf to skirt the ocean-side wing, on thick pilings ten feet above the sand. He climbed a ladder on the back side and entered an off-stage area cluttered with sound equipment and roadies, sub-divided by the retracted stage curtain. The Avett Brothers played 20 yards away, loud even behind the speakers.

A sound tech in headphones held up the *stop* sign and yelled, "You can't be back here." Eugene ignored him, searching for Amberly.

An older-than-average vamp in tailored cabana clothes stepped in his way. "Trubadur said you would show up."

"He tells a lot of lies," said Eugene. "But he got this one right." He flung a weighted throwing stake, ineffective against the vamp's reflexes but buying time to raise his crossbow. The old natty vamp was on the move, dodging amongst the equipment. Eugene's first teak-tipped titanium bolt pinged off the housing of a floodlight, scattering roadies.

He loved the sound of a chambering bolt. The next shot was high and wide, but right where Eugene wanted it, spot-on a hanging light, shattering and spattering the vamp with bulb bits, forcing the creature to its seersucker knees and clawing at its eyes. Eugene sighted the hollow of the senior citizen vamp's throat and squeezed the trigger, which jammed.

"I'm fingering you," said another wrinkle-faced vamp, its finger between the crossbow's trigger and guard. The vamp kneed Eugene in the nuts, took away his crossbow and dragged him across the floor by his hair. Eugene didn't fret it, he had deep roots. He was tossed to the feet of the wounded retiree vamp. "The first sip is all yours, my dear."

The blinded vamp held his linen shirt to his bloody eyes. "Boris, I can't see, much less drink."

Boris dropped a knee on Eugene's throat. "Feeeel your waaay," he sang with an annoying vibrato. "Blood speeds the healing."

The wounded vamp blinked rapidly. "Is he B negative?"

"George." Boris was exasperated. "The blood type diet is meant to *optimize*, not *limit* us."

Windpipe crimped, Eugene operated in a black buzzing cloud.

He rammed a stake into the middle of that cloud and received instant relief.

Boris rolled on the floor with a stake in the stomach, howling in a perfect third to the Avett Brothers' harmony. George was so prim picking up a mic stand that Eugene was slow to react and took a blow to the solar plexus. Dented nuts, neck and gut, he had lost the capacity to draw a breath.

"Aww." Boris extracted the stake from the flared nostrils of the Vampire Che Guevara face silk-screened on his shirtfront. "My Che."

"Your fang shooee chee is way out of whack, vamp," Eugene wheezed. "Another hole should put you right with the universe."

"How sad," said George, eyes squinted as he fought to reach Eugene's throat while keeping him from drawing another stake. "You brag about your endless love for beautiful Amberly. But obviously you are ruled by hate."

The vamp was a steel spring with a giraffe neck; every time Eugene pushed the geezer away, its mouth ratcheted closer. "My sacrifice will save the world," said Eugene, one hand on the vamp and the other seeking a stake.

Boris pinned his arm to the floor. "You are here to take Amberly's life. We give ours to protect her. Who is more noble?"

"The crowd would love this," said the hovering sound tech. "Maybe you should bite this guy on-stage."

"Good idea," said George, frustrated by Eugene's bucking and chin-tucking. "This is killing my knees!"

"Amberly Foreman!" an Avett Brother introduced her to the crowd, eliciting a deafening cheer.

Boris hauled Eugene up by the lapels of his summer-weight long coat. Eugene used the momentum and his impressive flexibility to run up the vamp's chest into a backflip. He landed out of his coat, a stake in each hand.

"Hurray for you," said Boris. "You can beat two old gay vampires." He sprang into the air and spun like an ice dancer. Halfway through the second revolution his foot whipped out and smacked Eugene in the face.

He crashed into a guitar rack, scattering the next band's instruments. George attacked and Eugene used a bass guitar like a pike, catching the vamp in the gut.

"*Morbius*?" said the Avett Brother to the crowd. Vampires roared, raising the golden downy hair that covered most of Eugene's body. Amberly was at the mic. And in the opposite wing gazing love-struck at her was the CWS, looking younger and dressed funny.

Boris attacked. Eugene blocked his bite attempt by staking his throat. Boris threw him against the back wall, the impact popping open the door.

George charged, cursing him over Boris's strangled moaning. "You hateful sonofabitch!"

Eugene waited motionless until he could smell its old man coffee-breath and then staked the vamp above the knee. George buckled and Eugene reared back with his last stake.

Hilda grabbed his wrist. "Too much backswing."

She kicked him in the head, once-twice, and threw him out the door.

He hit the beach and scrambled to his feet. Hilda landed on him, feet first.

She was a load. Bones cracked in Eugene's back and neck.

He was relieved to be able to wiggle fingers and toes as Hilda dragged him into the water and held him under. A wave knocked her sideways into a ragged rock, freeing him to take a breath.

They both turned at a din of human screams. Vamps were turning on the humans.

"Gets your blood up doesn't it," said Eugene.

"I am not a vampire," said Hilda.

"Collaborator," Eugene accused. "Vampire Vichy."

"I hate the French," said Hilda. "And Romanians." She punched him, as quick as any vamp, and slashed his chest with a broken conch shell.

An explosion rocked the Vampalooza crowd, followed by panicked cries: "Drone!"

A monster wave broke and slammed them onto the packed sand. Eugene labored to his feet in time for the outbound undertow to dump him for another big drink. By the time he reached shore, Hilda was climbing the backstage ladder.

Amidst all the rage and terror filling the air and the water filling his ears, a woman's scream stood out. He knew that voice.

Near the collapsed sand castle, four vampires had his once-future mother-in-law surrounded. Eugene snatched up a croquet mallet at a full run, unscrewed the shaft and ran one of the vamps through. Mallet head to vamp head and now there were only two.

"Eugene," said Barbara Thetherson. Eugene thanked God she was unharmed. "It's good to see you, sweetie."

"Eugene, the slayer?" One of the vamps was intimidated. "Who sold you a ticket?"

Eugene stood in front of Barbara and put up his dukes. "Please don't run away."

The two vamps ran, at him, tackled him. His neck felt like broken spaghetti. His head thudded against the sand. Barbara was thrown down beside him, a greasy blond vamp atop her, at her throat. Eugene threw a deathblow kick that missed the vamp's temple but broke its nose.

The greasy blondie screamed at the vamps pinning Eugene. "Can't two of you control one human?" In the next instant the vamp was rendered inert by the rap of a cane—to the temple!—wielded by a tall thin-shouldered vamp.

The cane-wielder surveyed the remaining vamps with extreme distaste. "Knuckle-draggers." He jabbed one in the eye with the chiseled point of his cane, followed by a jab to the chest, exploding its heart.

Eugene was impressed. He kicked his other attacker in the chest and the cane-wielder finished it off with a similar one-two combo strike.

Barbara had been watching in awe. Now her breath caught. A mother's premonition. She turned to the stage and a bomb went off. The shockwave swept across the crowd and they ducked against a wet scorching wind.

"Amberly," Barbara moaned, blinded by sand and stumbling toward the smoke-shrouded stage.

Chaos resumed from its momentary pause. Humans called for help for the injured. Vamps also went to the fallen, and helped themselves.

With Eugene a few steps slow, the cane-wielding vamp caught Barbara and held her as she fought to reach the stage. "You are Amberly's mother, yes?" This and his karate chop to a thirsty vamp's throat gained Barbara's attention. "Trust she is fine."

They saw stirrings on stage, Amberly on her feet. "I was sent to help you connect with her."

Eugene yanked her away. He had to talk with his head cocked to the side and a hand bracing his back. "The lady goes nowhere with you, bloodsucker."

The vamp put thumb and finger to his mouth and whistled. A plump pair, man and woman, hurried to him, each holding a turkey leg and a 22-oz mug of beer, throats and arms sporting fang tracks. "You refer to the knuckle-draggers," said the cane-wielder. "A gentleman travels with his own blood supply."

Barbara held Eugene's arms, one limp and the other cockeyed from the pain. "I need to get to Amberly," she said. "Come with me."

For its false pretensions to cultured humanity, Eugene wanted to put a stake in the cane-wielding vamp. He had no stake. He was rooted to the sand, crashing, physically and psychically.

He had failed, all the while believing he was winning. Duped as CWS took Amberly, without a fight from her beloved, her protector, her man, and made her into a monster.

No. A captive.

A captive monster.

What did that even mean?!

Eugene was exhausted. Earlier that day he had received a plea for help, from a faraway land, a place that had been calling to him for years now. That plea was his lifesaver now. He needed refuge, to heal his heart and restore the connection to his ancestral slayer instincts.

And he needed to lead the resistance. That was clear now. Eugene's instincts promised him this faraway land was the place to begin.

He asked Barbara the worst question in the world, one that would haunt him. "Will you be alright?" *With a vamp.*

Barbara said she would. With a vamp.

He gave the stage and his cursed beloved wide berth as he shuffled off the beach, so addled he couldn't find the Melaleuca booth. A gift for the mustachioed Mexican guy, he could keep the product and get a great jump building his slayer network.

Eugene wondered if any airlines offered traction on their

overseas flights. Lufthansa maybe?

Florence climbs over the lip of the stage, grabs the suicide bomber by his vest and flings him into the crowd. There is a huge sound and white light and I'm on my back, immersed in the sound of a heart monitor gone flatline.

But alive. I'm on my feet before Florence, the Avett Brothers, stage hands, cameramen and reporters. The crowd nearest the stage lies in pieces or in misery, covered in blood, clothes and skin shredded. Those beyond the blast perimeter mill about, silent and dazed.

"Morbius!" someone cries, vampire or human, I cannot tell. "Save us!"

Thousands of people on this beach, and I can feel each and every one of them, loving me, hating me, judging me. Losing their minds.

As emergency personnel converge on the bombing victims, the crowd regains energy. A hairy man in a Euro-Speedo picks up a splinter of bombing detritus and jams it into a vampire's heart. A vampire who had been knocked to the sand rolls over as if to his lover in bed and bites a still-stunned human.

I run backstage as Trubadur comes out from behind a huge bank of speakers, which belong to the Foo Fighters (who last I saw were being attacked in their autograph booth by a gang of leather-jacketed vampires). It appears he was assaulted too, disheveled, shirt torn and blood-spattered, hat collapsed.

"This is why I didn't want you here," he says.

"What is happening?"

Trubadur satisfies himself I am unharmed. "There is a conservative faction who do not like the revolution we bring."

I point to the crowd. "They're calling me Morbius. Is it true?"

Trubadur wipes blood off his chin. The junkie, he must have found some poor stagehand as soon as I turned my back, drinking her when he was attacked. "That label means different things to different people." He pushes the dent out of his tall hat and takes a look inside, which seems to confirm what he was going to say. "Allow them to label you, and we jeopardize everything we want to accomplish."

He's right. I've been told who I am, forever. A good little girl.

A smart-ass hellion. An unmotivated student who needs to get back on the paved path and follow it to a solid future.

Finally—and all it took was being bit (twice!) and turned into a vampire—I realize exactly why I am here. What I am meant to accomplish.

And now these people in the crowd want to tell me who I am. Morbius. Queen of the vampires. They want to dress me up in someone else's clothes and set me onto another paved path.

"I won't let them. I know why I'm here. I have a vision. It's mine, and it has nothing to do with Morbius."

Trubadur's eyes fill with love for me. "I wasn't ready for you to leave the house and be seen," he says. "But I see it now. It's time."

There's a groan from behind the speakers. Trubadur doesn't want me to but I investigate and there's Bono, blood oozing from his throat.

"You bit him! Cornelius!"

"Trubadur," he corrects me.

"Sweetie," says Bono. He props himself up, leans against the speakers. "I'm okay."

"Go on, Stela," says Trubadur—then he blinks, twitches like Porkie putting the death-shake on a squeaky toy. "Amberly." He points me back onto the stage. "Go out there and make your own destiny."

"Stelllaaa," Bono does a decent Brando. He too waves me on. "Give them the bumps."

Returning to the stage, surveying the scene, this must have been what the Troy beach looked like from Achilles' tent on the hill. A slaughter in process, the humans desperate for a hero.

I may not be that hero, and I will never choose a side. But I was put here to lead. The videos were just a start, just a whisper to the world. I have now found my voice.

"Vampires! Enough!"

My voice rolls over the crowd like a gunshot echo through a cowboy canyon. The thrashing, writhing frenzy becomes still.

"Who are we?!" I demand. "Are we the same failed fools who have been murdering each other since time began? Are we the same God-damned *fools*?!"

My voice is huge, it's bigger than my throat, my chest, my

head, it's the voice of the great and powerful Oz, it's Martin Luther King, it's rock'n'roll, it's amplified before it hits the microphone. Oh my God—this is what it's like to be Bono.

"We have the chance to remake the world! Right here and right now! Humans and vampires alike will try to stop us. We saw them here tonight, the drone in the sky and the suicide bomber on stage, afraid to let the world *change*! Profiteers who make a fortune from war and chaos!"

The people find their voices and call out to me, and to each other, blessings, support and commitment.

"These are holdouts from the old regime who fear change, who fear our revolution! They claim to represent us, but they are protecting no one but themselves! They are desperate! They encourage us to tear each other apart, so they can hang onto their money and their power!"

The crowd seethes.

"So we have to decide, right here and right now: Will we let them rule our world?"

The crowd answers: "NO!!"

"Will we let them war-monger? Will we let them use our religion, our national and political allegiances, and our historical connections against us?"

"*NO!*"

"Then I ask you to join me now, you here today. And *you*," I speak to the cameras, all in a cluster, risen from the suicide blast. I can see each and every one of you out there, hungry for a better world. "*You* who would be here if you could. You who read the news with horror, or who no longer read the news, in jaded surrender. Today I ask you to join me, to join each other, to seize the chance, the one chance we will ever have, to bury our stakes and sheath our fangs."

The crowd's euphoric release lifts me, carries me, crackles inside me and erupts from me in a scream of pure joy.

"Now, today and from this day forward, vampires and humans alike, we take our stand. We turn our backs on the hate and the division, and we stake our claim!"

The roar that rises from the sand cleanses the blood that was spilled, and joins the roar of a hundred million souls around the world, ready for the change.

A new drone zooms skyward, piloted by a man standing on a boulder. It launches a missile, fiery orange in the early night, impacting with a fireworks blast and sparkling shrapnel rain, the remains of the drone that attacked us falling to pieces on the sand. People cheer and parade souvenirs along the beach.

Offstage stand Trubadur and Bono, arm in arm, nodding their approval.

"A perfect symbol of the New World," I tell the crowd, pointing to the sky. "The old guard comes down, and a new bird takes flight." Okay, that's a little hokey, but they love it. "Take what you've seen here, what you feel right now, take it back to your towns, your cities, your homes!" I swear I can feel every heartbeat on this beach, in sync with my own.

"We love you, Morbius!" someone cries out.

This time that name is greeted with nothing but cheers.

And so maybe I am Morbius. But I'll guarantee there has never been a Morbius like me.

"And I love you all! May we have the courage to stand strong and see this through! And may God bless us all!"

The Avett Brothers carry their fallen brother off the stage. Florence must have revived and slipped away. The dead and wounded from the suicide blast and a thousand other altercations are being stretchered off and tended to.

"Let's all give a special thanks to the real heroes here, our first responders!"

The crowd claps for them.

I make eye contact with the lead singer from the Foo Fighters, the one who used to be in Nirvana. He is shaken, two of his mates are bloody, but they are on their feet and accepting apologies from the vampire gang that assaulted them. He gives me a thumbs-up.

"And now," I ask the crowd, "who's ready to get back to the party? Who's ready for the Foo Fighters?"

The crowd cheers and begins clapping, rhythmic and accelerating.

The Foo Fighters guy frowns angrily at me and points at all their equipment still sitting backstage.

"My bad," I tell the crowd. "Make that Foo Fighters in an hour." That earns me my first boos as Morbius.

STRONG AND SUPPLE

Jaelle Skudza sat facing Victor, in chairs in the middle of the yoga room.

"I'm going to need you to open your mind to what I propose."

"I told you," said Victor. "I'm not going to waste any more time on your Om and Lotus."

Jaelle spread her arms, voice rising. "Are we sitting cross-legged on the floor with our eyes closed? No. I am compromising. For the good of the world. I am asking you to do the same."

The Gypsy neuroscientist had phoned him at midnight, a few hours after he left Darla. They had carped at each other for most of the brief call, continuing in person. The only thing they implicitly agreed upon was an inability to sleep. Victor was going crazy without a clue where to find Amberly or Barbara (or Eugene). And Jaelle desperately wanted to start over. But that was going to require an apology, and Victor was intent on extracting one.

Now it was two a.m. and his defenses were sagging.

The Gypsy's skin was smooth, stretched thin over a deep rippling pool. Her eyes were the gateway to that pool, lights shimmering in the depths. He wanted no part of that.

"Why are you suddenly willing to work with me?"

"Because I have no choice," she said. "Because survival demands it. Because I have a way to change even the vampire brain."

"I like my brain the way it is."

"Do you? You enjoy being unwilling to accept any input that doesn't fit a rigid, predator's paradigm?"

"It beats the way it was before."

"I am sure a world free from guilt is blissful. But do you miss *thinking*?"

"Thinking? It was worrying."

"You have the rare opportunity to couple the intelligence God gave you, with the decisiveness vampirism created for you." Jaelle leaned back in the chair. "To have a mind like mine."

"That is some sales pitch."

"You see vampires' weaknesses. *I* see the neural walls vampirism has erected to protect you."

This observation somehow evaded those defenses, which belatedly demanded he jump up and storm out before he was compromised by emotion.

Jaelle saw it. "I can make it so those defenses are no longer necessary. I can open your mind so it can *work* again. With confidence. It doesn't have to be either-or."

Victor stared at the big coffin-like box. "I'm not getting in there."

"I won't close the lid until you're comfortable."

"You're going to close the lid?! No."

"It is good for you we are doing this while everyone else is home sleeping. How embarrassing."

"I'd rather sit in Lotus and Om than get in that thing."

The little woman splashed her fingers in the isolation tank water. "Take off your clothes and get in there."

"I have to take off my *clothes*?"

"Do you want to be dragged under and drown?"

That didn't help.

Wearing tight swim trunks and goggles, Victor lay in the water, warmed just above his 93-degree body temperature, so that he only felt it if he moved. "I float."

Jaelle snorted. "Of course you do."

He opened his eyes; yes, she was looking at his fat.

She saw him notice. "We add salinity for buoyancy."

He closed his eyes. "So how does this work?"

"For you, there is no work. You simply lay there. Let your mind wander. Sleep if you like. Dream. The neural interface will record everything."

He wore Jaelle's modified virtual reality helmet with the hard shell removed, now more like a swim cap, thickened by a layer of firm gelatin embedded with electro-sensors reading and transmitting a three-dimensional picture of his neural activity.

Jaelle went to her control board where the active connections of his mind were represented colorfully and graphically. "Close your eyes and tell me what you're thinking right now."

"That I hate you."

"You hate the Roma."

"I don't even know what that means. No, it's just you."

"Good, good."

"Your skullcap smells like a bunch of blue webbing."

"That is not a smell. It is a sight."

"I see smells."

"And you hear them, too."

Victor opened his eyes but couldn't see her.

"Your auditory cortex is firing non-stop," said Jaelle, "and in synchrony with your visual cortex. I've never seen anything like it. The mapping options to your human cortical regions are practically unlimited. I'm going to close the lid, but you'll be able to hear me and talk to me, no problem. There. It's good, you are in your own world now, everything you see and hear and smell will be of your own making. We will build connections between the human and vampire regions, inputs and feedback loops. The brain is 'plastic,' an unfortunate term chosen by neuroscientists that fails to evoke the intended sense of the brain's flexibility, its re-route-ability. We are going to build a whole new web of connections in your human region. Of course those neurons have been enlisted for other duties by your vampirism, so you may see a drop-off in some abilities …."

Amberly was back in her room. In fact, she had launched a home-based business and was sitting before a bank of computer screens that had displaced her bed. The setup had the feeling of permanence and gave Victor such a relief. Barbara was all smiles and painting, her easel now in the corner of Amberly's bedroom. The rest of the house hardly seemed to exist.

To Victor's consternation, Amberly had rounded off her fangs.

She didn't plan to bite on a regular basis, only when she went out partying with friends. He was worried those nubbins wouldn't effectively draw blood, creating embarrassing situations for her. He wished she had come to him for advice—Dentist Mulvane could have set her up with very attractive falsies.

Her call center—that's what it was, Victor wasn't sure what all the computers were for, because she just took calls, from Facebook, RAND Corp, Citigroup, all looking for consultation on the XFP system. Victor was griping that X was dead and a thief and it should be called the VFP, V for Victor, and Amberly on the phone kept shushing him. Then the roof flew off their house.

"Victor, return to us!" a woman called from outside. It was a realtor. Without the roof, Victor could look down and see her standing on the lawn, pounding in a For Sale sign.

"Stop that!" Who gave this realtor permission to sell their house? Not Barbara, she was happy now.

"Have him return slowly," a man's voice cautioned. Victor ignored him. "He's coming out of a dream."

Barbara was gone. He went to the easel—she had painted a flimsy garden stake so realistically that it appeared to be pounded into the canvas.

Amberly screamed. The tornado that had ripped off their roof was carrying her away.

Victor's limbs were sluggish and his throat constricted. "*Amberly.*"

The floor of her room melted in the sunlight, turned to quicksand. He sank fast, legs dangling over an abyss where the living room should be—

"Wake up!"

Victor abruptly sat up and sloshed water out of the isolation tank. Jaelle sat at a terminal eyeballing him.

The dream came back to him. He pulled off the skullcap. "What time is it?"

"A little after two p.m.," said Michael, leaving his programming chair.

Victor reconstructed his last conscious memories while a full contingent of technicians and programmers stole glances at him from their workstations. "I was in there for *ten* hours?"

"The good news?" said Michael. "You're nowhere near Rip Van Winkle."

Victor climbed out of the tank. His body felt terrible, uncoordinated, as if still traveling through the dream quicksand. "And the bad news?"

Michael handed him a towel. "You were in there for a day and a half."

"I was not." As he said it, Victor had a sense of a whole life lived in a magical, off-kilter world. "What? Really?"

"We accomplished a lot," said Jaelle.

"Jaelle hasn't left her chair since you got in the tank," said Michael.

"My daughter needs me!" said Victor. "You said you already had my brain figured out! Why did it take you that long to read it?"

Jaelle exchanged a glance with Michael. All ears were tuned to their conversation. "I wasn't reading your mind. I was rewiring it."

"How could you do that?" *I don't feel any different. Do I?*

Jaelle smirked at Michael. "That he wants to know *how*, and not 'how dare you,' is a promising sign."

Victor slammed his palm on the iso tank lid. "Talk to me!"

Jaelle clucked and turned her attention to her monitor. "Your vampirism still shares the stage. I suppose that is good. Get dressed. We will take a walk."

"Don't give in to the peer pressure to put on a bunch of clothes," said Michael, checking him out. "It's summer time, for crying out loud."

Victor tightened his gut and retreated to the former tanning center's dressing room. He almost fell over putting on his pants, kept upright by the cramped walls. He wasn't dizzy, just weak, as if he had been an astronaut at zero gravity for a year.

Jaelle waited for him in the hall and they walked outside. "It was your wife who convinced me we could accelerate what I had hoped to achieve through meditation."

"You met Barbara?"

"She thinks very highly of you."

"Very highly, extremely lowly. We have no middle ground."

"A perfect relationship. No advancement occurs at equilibrium."

"Isn't that what you wanted to do to me? Find the middle ground?"

"Not at all. I need a sugar hit." Jaelle pointed him to a yogurt shop. "You can pick your own toppings, and have as many as you want. That really lights up my amygdala."

"They charge you by weight," Victor pointed out.

"Good thing they don't charge by enjoyment." They filled their cups, Jaelle clucking happily. She bought his yogurt and they continued their walk, the heat immediately working on their desserts.

"I am hungry enough to eat yogurt," said Victor. He took a big bite, tripped on a small upheaval of a sidewalk slab, stumbled and dropped his cup. "Oh come on." He picked up the cup, not enough to salvage. He held his spoon and looked at Jaelle's.

"I am not swapping saliva with a vampire. Go back and get another."

He pouted as they continued their stroll. "I need blood. It feels like a month since I moved a muscle."

Jaelle gave him a knowing look. "I told you there may be deficits created by the neural rerouting."

"You made me clumsy?"

"Did vampirism improve your physical abilities? Of course it did. That was likely what has been sacrificed. Last in, first out, as they say." She savored a big, toppings-enhanced bite. "Don't worry. It will be worth it."

"You want to hook me back up to your vampire finder. First I need to find my daughter."

"Mm." This was not a yum-sound for the yogurt. "A lot happened while you were under. Your daughter is fine, despite an attempt by her enemies."

Victor stopped. His heart hammered. "What happened?"

Jaelle kept walking, forcing him to do the same. They continued into a residential neighborhood. "You can read about it online. Your daughter is most definitely Morbius. And now we are in trouble."

"Jaelle, where is she?"

"It happened in Cancun. But I'm sure she is elsewhere now."

She took another big bite. "Humans are the ones in trouble. There was another drone strike this morning. Amsterdam. Killed two more of our biggest contributors. In the name of counter-terrorism. And yesterday the vampires announced a shadow government." She picked out a gummy bear and a cookie dough bite and chewed them with relish. "A world-wide *politburo* to offer 'guidance' on national laws. Their first 'suggestion' was to make it illegal to slay vampires. One of your congressmen has already introduced a bill to make it U.S. law."

"I don't care about a vampire politburo," said Victor. "Who attacked Amberly? Was it a vampire? Was it a suicide bomber?"

"Don't worry about her. Morbius takes care of herself."

Victor took her cup of yogurt and threw it over a hedge row.

Jaelle scowled through the shrubbery at her ruined dessert. "You are still stupid."

"I want my daughter!"

Jaelle crossed her arms. "Go."

She watched him make ungainly strides in the direction of the command center.

"If I did my job, you will be back."

ROMANIA IN THE MODERN DAY

A pretty young woman manned the battery-operated elevator that whined and jerked down the salt mine shaft in Transylvania's layered hills.

She blushed continuously. "How do you—" She swallowed to moisten her throat. "How do you find our country?"

"My ancestors are from Romania. In fact, one of them is still living." Eugene's shoulders drooped and his head sagged back so that he stared up through the wire mesh elevator ceiling. "And he is a vampire. Because of him I need to kill myself and the love of my life in order to fulfill what I guess you could call my Romanian destiny."

"So, you feel at home?"

He held the pose, looking at the shrunken square of gloomy sky. "Not at the moment."

She took a deep, prolonged breath and urged him to do the same. "The cave air is good for you, for your …" She searched for the word, touching her chest. "Breaths."

For the past two days, Eugene's mind had been incapacitated with uncertainty, indecision, anguish, denial. He had gotten lost repeatedly on the way here. That included driving from his apartment to the Houston airport. He sucked air and the salt burned his nasal passages. "Feels great," he lied.

The young woman smiled. "It is great to be in your pyramid."

"It's not a *pyr*—" Eugene checked himself; he would chalk it up to a translational limitation. He gave her a curt nod. "It's good to have you on the team."

Keeping one hand on the elevator operation handle, she crouched and retrieved from her backpack a piece of paper. The style of the border and printing suggested a certificate, in Romanian. It was in the shape of a triangle. She offered it with a pen. "Will you autograph?"

"No."

She was crushed.

"Okay."

Delighted, she gave her bony back for his signature. The pen poked her repeatedly as he signed his name and wrote an admonition:

Pyramids can't grow a bigger base, but a money tree can branch out.

The elevator came to rest and Eugene climbed over the safety arm. A small tunnel led into a hangar-like cavern, the ceiling 80 feet at its highest, wide enough to park 747s side by side, with slightly undulating, worn-smooth floors and curved walls patterned like the marbles from Granny Foreman's Chinese checkers game.

To his right was a chapel; to his left a ropes course and zip line. Ahead, a bearded young man with unruly hair very much like Eugene's, standing on recessed narrow-gauge rails. He waited until Eugene was almost on him before snapping to attention, hand to his forehead in salute.

"*Buna ziua*," said the young man.

Good day. A YouTube video taught Eugene that one on the flight over. "And also to you."

"Vlad Trestian, at your service. Heir to the greatest slayer of them all, Vlad Dracula the Impaler!"

"For God sakes, man, Dracula was a vampire."

"He was the *Impaler*, you see? Regardless, I am proud to be at the top of your Romanian pyramid."

Eugene went off. "Can you build a *pyramid* from the top-down?! Think about it, Vlad! From this point forward, please refer to this as a *multi-level marketing organization*."

Vlad bowed. "It is a pleasure to meet the great Eugene Maistru."

"Maistru is my evil ancestor. I go by Foreman."

"Foreman is the last name of Morbius."

Eugene wanted to scream. "Eugene then! Just Eugene. Where are the slayers?"

"We are currently practicing casket seek-and-find in the tunnels."

Eugene liked using classic code names. "I am interested to see your team in action."

"Please. Follow me."

With the young woman from the elevator they traversed the cavern until the rail line branched and led them down a still-sizeable corridor. Yellowed electric lights with exposed cords illuminated charcoal-colored walls streaked with pink, smooth to the eye, grainy to touch. They passed intersecting corridors, some lit, others dark. An occasional battle cry and terrified scream drifted to them.

"Should we tell them we're coming?" said Eugene. "I do not want to get shot."

Vlad gave him an uncomprehending look. Again the language barrier.

They veered down a small tunnel with a low ceiling. Eugene clipped salt stalactites with his head; something grabbed his arm. He spun out of his longcoat in a crouch, crossbow leveled.

His coat hung snagged on a ceramic plaque. The plaque came off the wall with his coat. About to chuck the small crusty square to the floor, Eugene pocketed it on impulse.

Vlad clucked at his torn sleeve. "We do have insurance. But our deductible is very high."

They left the last light behind and Vlad turned on an infrared flashlight that did little to guide them. He scanned the walls, finding occasional glowing arrows leading down ever-tighter tunnels that sucked the moisture from Eugene's tongue.

"The slayers don't get flashlights," said Vlad. "We want them to become accustomed to operating in the dark."

"Why?" said Eugene.

"Shh." Vlad held the flashlight under his chin; it made his short beard glow cherry red and cast a thicket of shadows on his face. There were grunting sounds nearby. "It sounds like they found a casket. Shall we see how they're doing?"

He pushed open a wood door. It creaked. He put the light back on his face and whispered, "Nice touch, eh?"

The room was pitch black. Eugene only had a sense of movement to go along with the grunting, the squeal of pulled nails and the clatter and thud of what he guessed was a coffin lid.

Someone chirped a nervous challenge to their arrival. Eugene didn't need to understand Romanian to translate, *Who's there?* I'm going to get shot, he thought.

Vlad turned on the light, a ceiling-mounted halogen bulb. Crowbars, hammers and stakes thunked to the powdered salt floor and three slayers yelped and covered their eyes like mole people thrown into the sun.

"What are you doing?" Vlad yelled at them. "Finish the job!"

The slayers bumped shoulders and heads reaching for the fallen tools. A string-bean woman was first to come up with a stake and held it in striking position over whatever lay inside the coffin. A tall paunchy man grabbed a hammer, swung and smashed her fingers. "Aiyee!" she howled, holding her damaged hand.

The third slayer took up the stake, held it in place and turned his face away. The hammer-wielding slayer tappy-tapped the stake until the point was set, then lengthened his swings until the stake was fully driven.

"Bravo!" Vlad clapped and his young woman assistant enthusiastically joined the applause. "Job well done!"

The slayers blinked and bowed, chests swelling with pride and heaving in search of oxygen.

Vlad turned to Eugene. "Are you pleased?"

"Tell me this is a joke," said Eugene.

Vlad cocked his head. "Do you joke about vampires where you come from?"

"Never," said Eugene. "Assemble your slayers in the main room. We begin our real training in 15 minutes."

"I have 20 slayers practicing their hammering skills," said Vlad, eyes darting toward the woman's limp, bruised hand. "Can they finish?"

"No."

Eugene stood on a ping-pong table and looked down on 30 or so slayers. Some wore miners' helmets. Most were still squinting in the gloomy cavern. A few had donned sunglasses. They were predominantly men, ranging from early teens to late in life.

"Hello?" A gentleman in a Turkish fez raised his hand. "Does this mean we are ready?"

"Hello," said Eugene. "It does not. It is just the opposite. It means I am going to lose my deposit on that Learjet. Because the Romanian team is not going to make me any money. Because you will all be dead."

Confused glances were exchanged. A teenage boy began to sob.

"Contrary to what Vlad has told you and what you must have seen on a late-night thriller-chiller film festival, vampires do not live in the dark and sleep in caskets, waiting patiently for your stakes. They are wide awake in the sunlight, infiltrating your governments and screwing your wives and daughters! They are fast and strong and thirsty for your blood!"

An elderly slayer man thrust a stake in the air. "Let us go and get them!"

"No!" said Eugene as everyone pushed and shoved to get to the elevator. They shuffled back to the ping-pong table. "Okay. First of all, let's give it up for Vlad for choosing this location. It's hidden, it's fortified—it's the perfect training facility."

Vlad hung his head. "It was Jaelle Skudza's idea."

For a non-slayer, Jaelle was highly regarded by the slayer community. Eugene might have known she had a hand in this training center. He had awoken from his coma after the Castle Chenonceaux slaying to a thank-you card from Jaelle for his efforts to eradicate the vamps tormenting Gypsies in southern France. He wanted to offer her a discounted buy-in to his Provence real estate investment trust, but of course being a Gypsy, she would be unable to provide the permanent address required by the IRS. Too bad, that REIT had done extremely well.

"Second, we're going to get in shape. You can't slay if you can't breathe. I understand the air down here is healthy. That's good, because you're going to be sucking buckets of it.

"Third, I have a credit card courtesy the Mohammed bin Rashid Al Maktoum foundation." He held it aloft and received some oohs and aahs. "I am going to bang it for all it's worth to buy you the simplest and most effective crossbows on the market, the Kalashnikov of crossbows, and an assortment of concealable, quick access, ready-grip Teflon-coated battle stakes.

And then you are going to drill, drill, drill, until you can shoot the eye of a newt from 20 yards after a duck-and-tumble maneuver, and quick-stake your opponent in hand-to-hand close-quarters combat.

"Fourth—"

"Excuse me, hello?" said a thin middle-aged woman.

"Hello," said Eugene.

"Can we also have a long, beautiful slayer coat like yours?"

Eugene opened his coat like a flasher. "This is a superb garment. It's breathable and yet weather-resistant. It discreetly conceals your weaponry and has pockets for nail clippers, tweezers and what-not." He was not pleased about the torn sleeve. "But no. Clothing is not authorized in our multi-level marketing compensation agreement."

The woman threw up her hands and wailed, digging her long nails into her palms, drawing blood. "To be slayer, we must *look* like slayer!"

That made sense. "Alright then. I'll up-front the expense and deduct it from your first Slay-Dividend. Miss …" He looked to Vlad's assistant.

She held up a notepad and pen. "I will collect all the slayers' measurements."

She was good.

"Fourth," Eugene continued, "we will be uploading to each of your smartphones my Slayer Fundamentals course. Normally this retails for $99.95 plus a $10 monthly user license. I'm waiving everything but the up-front $99.95."

Everyone cheered. Some high-fived each other.

"Fifth, all training sessions will be conducted in squads. Each squad will be organized so that it is headed by an upstream MLMO team member. That way each squad leader has a vested interest in the development of his or her squad."

The thin middle-aged woman who coveted his coat took a break from sucking on her bleeding palms to ask, "Hello? What's an 'upstream MLMO'?"

"Hello again. It's the person who recruited you into this multi-level direct-to-consumer marketing organization."

He was receiving an awful lot of blank stares. Eugene squeezed his crossbow stock until it complained. "The *pyramid.*

Each squad will be run by the highest person in the *pyramid*."

"Ah, yes." Lots of nodding.

"Lastly," said Eugene, "I'm in need of a Buddhist meditation and grief coping expert. I understand from talking to Vlad on the phone that there is a man named Zenlen in this, ah, pyramid. Zenlen, can you please raise your hand."

No hand raised. Vlad, sitting on a pile of salt and looking demoralized, spoke. "He is in Târgu Mureş. He said the mine was warping his Ohm frequency."

Târgu Mureş. Of course. History had come full circle. In the birthplace of the eternal conflict between good and evil, he would learn the serenity necessary to bring the Morbius bloodline to its final resting place.

"Is there a TV and DVD player on site?"

"The cinema only plays reel-to-reel," said the bright young assistant. "But I have a DVD machine at my house 26 kilometers from here."

"Good." From his satchel Eugene pulled a DVD box-set. "This is the Insanity workout. You have 30 days to get into the best shape of your lives."

"I will go retrieve my 52-inch flat-panel television set and Sony DVD player," said the talented young woman. Then her face contorted into abject grief. "Is it Blu-Ray? I do not have a Blu-Ray player."

"It is not Blu-Ray," said Eugene.

She was elated. "I will have them back here within the hour."

"I will ride up with you," said Eugene. "Everyone, I'm very encouraged with the talent I see here before me. I'd like you all to arrange yourselves in squads of no more than seven slayers. Vlad, if you could coordinate that?"

Vlad looked re-energized to have been delegated such an important job.

"When your weaponry is delivered, I shall return," Eugene announced like MacArthur to the Philippinos.

Three hundred kilometers away on the other side of the Carpathians, Larry Cocachello tipped their guide and sent him on his way.

"You are sure you can find your way back?" said the guide.

Larry couldn't blame him for asking. From the moment their guide picked them up at the Bucharest airport and every moment in between until this moment standing north of the city in a hillside forest, it had been a shitshow.

David Copperfield, well who would have thought that he might be a little out of sorts in the legendary land of vampires? Larry knew it would be bad, and so did David, and so it was. God bless the poor soul he wanted to come, to help destroy Victor. But it was like caring for a junkie monkey.

Then there was Teddy, final surviving member of Project Well Done. He had fallen into catatonia upon liftoff in Houston. Larry had to take him by the hand to get him from point A to B. He had to put a fork in Teddy's hand, and food on that fork. He had to ask him if he had been drinking enough water, and if he had to pee.

The Lufthansa flight attendants had warmed to the task. They had not become warm, but they had been very helpful. South of Greenland, a tall blonde massaged Teddy's legs to ward off blood clots, and over the North Sea another tall blonde stimulated his eyelids to preempt jet lag.

Finally when they entered this Romanian hillside forest, Teddy had come alive.

This was worse. Turned out Teddy had joined a millenarian cult called Roots that believed humans needed to return to their birthplace (caves) and wait out God's vengeance upon the vampires (a soon-to-be unleashed bloodborne virus). He had viewed the text from Larry—

Hey u wanna find Victor's Heel in a Romanian cave?

—as The Sign. The catatonia must have been an emergency mental reconciliation to his final moments above ground. Now he was Rambo meets Gandhi, militantly ready to sit in a cave and wait for the vampires to drink themselves to death.

"Get!" Larry ordered away the guide. After all, he had a hunter's sense of direction. One time, he had swerved to avoid a rafter of out-of-season wild turkeys, his pickup tumbling and barrel rolling for a hundred yards. Two hours later when he came to and crawled from the upside-down vehicle head bleeding and concussed, with the sun at high noon, he had instinctively oriented and started toward the boar blind he had constructed three weeks prior and five miles away. He was there before nightfall, over the roughest hill country Texas had to offer. He could find his way back to Bucharest.

And he didn't trust Nico, the guide—he had found Larry, rather than vice-versa. After reading the sixteenth century and Robert Louis Stevenson diary posts, Larry had a chilling intuition this cave held the secret to destroying Victor. And then an email had hit his Yahoo inbox, from Nico the Romanian tour guide. The type of email that should have been relegated to spam.

"Looking for an authentic Romanian adventure? Wondering what the Morbius hoopla is all about? We are the certified authorized guide to the Infamous Cave! Mystical paintings and Mythical beasts? Could the legends be true? Come and decide for yourself! Include airport transfer, hotel night, transportation to and from The Cave, headlamps, and one in-cave snack." (*As described in the diary of Ugenosz Maistru.)*

"But a guided cave tour is part of the package you paid for," Nico now protested. "And mythical beast repellent."

"You heard the man," Teddy barked at Nico. "We got this! Now get!"

As Nico picked his way down the hillside, David quailed. "Is the cave adequately marked?"

"We're fine," Larry assured his hunchbacked companion. David was nearing another nervous fit. Larry unshouldered his backpack and took a seat on a boulder a couple yards from the cave entrance. "Let's have something to eat before we continue."

On the leg from Dulles to Frankfurt, David had been fidgety. By the time they were on-board the Fokker 100 for their flight to Bucharest, he was seeing spiders on Larry's face. The second time, Larry caught David's hand before he could kill the "spider."

While Teddy stood like a statue in the corner of their Bucharest hotel room, Larry had Yelp'd a vampire with papers from the World Health Organization certifying a clean bill of health and a recent prophylactic shot, to bite David. It went down behind an iron fence in the overgrown driveway of a deserted house adjacent to their hotel.

David had immediately calmed down. He was a blood bitch

junkie, one of the saddest hallmarks of the age of vampires. Larry hated the bloodsuckers all the more, and blamed Victor the very most.

David was now 14 hours without a bite and getting jittery again. His Lucky polo shirt stuck to his sweaty hunchback so that his collar was askew. Cursing the warped state of the world, Larry adjusted David's collar and dusted the young man's back with the talcum powder Larry relied on reduce long-hike chafing.

"Let's recall why we're here," Larry drawled. He pointed to the root-covered opening that Nico had needed hours to find, despite working from what he claimed was an authentic copy of the original "Skender's map" referenced in Ugenosz Maistru's diary. "That cave holds the secret to the end of Victor."

David nodded spastically. Teddy mimed cocking a pump-action shotgun.

"So when we go in there, we're going to focus on one thing and one thing only: why we're here."

"That will keep the Hellspawn away, right?" said David.

"The *Litmus* will decide," said Teddy, referencing the cult-issued divining stick, garter-belted low on his shin, that supposedly wobbled in the presence of subterranean evil. "Only the *Litmus* knows whether the Hellspawn will remain deep in its sulfurous lair, or join the bloodbath above!"

Larry took David by the chin to reclaim his attention. "When I'm hunting, I don't think about what my target wants to do. I focus on what *I* want to do. Do you understand that? It makes all the difference."

"It makes all the difference." David's pores excreted oily sweat that gave off a just-turned cauliflower scent. "All the difference."

"Are you going Rain Man on me?"

"No!"

"Who are you?"

"The Magic Man!"

"Who's the Foreman?" Teddy asked himself. "Me!"

Larry pressed his thumbs against David's jaw hinges. David seemed to like that. "And who am I?"

David smiled. "Mellow Cocachello."

"And what can we do together?"

David stood. "Everything. Bitch."

A hint of the old David. Time to capitalize on it. "Let's go spelunk."

They walked to the cave entrance, a vertical slit with a bulge in the middle.

"Looks like a shaggy twat," said Teddy. From his satchel he produced a cigar box. "The perfect place to scatter Berry's ashes."

Larry did a double-take. "How did you get Jay's ashes?"

"It's charcoal ash from my grill," said Teddy.

David chortled.

"Dude!" Teddy shouted at him. "Show some respect!"

David sobbed and sank to his knees.

Larry pulled him to his feet. "Get it together, Magic Man." He helped David shed his backpack. For all the hassle, Larry drew motivation from his former accounting direct report. As with the world, underneath all the evil deposited by the vampires, the real, human, healthy David waited for the opportunity to emerge.

Teddy put the cigar box back in his satchel. "We'll hold a ceremony. Below."

Larry navigated the lip and used roots crisscrossing the entrance to rappel down the steep incline. His headlamp picked up the cave floor and he let go of the roots, sliding the last few feet to level ground. Teddy tumbled down and took him out. He started to chew Teddy's ass but was drowned out by David's hysterical worry. After much cajoling, he convinced David they were not under Hellspawn attack, and to join them.

Their headlamps worked exceptionally poorly, as if they drew power not from batteries but the sun.

"I can't see the *Litmus*," Teddy fretted.

"Shh," Larry shushed him.

"Here?" Teddy whispered loudly.

"What?" Larry hissed.

"Is this a good place for Berry's ashes?"

"Jesus H. Crackers, how would I know?"

"I'll wait."

They all three stood there. Disgusted with himself for hoping David or Teddy would go first, Larry shuffled forward.

His headlamp flickered. He tapped it and the elastic headband slingshotted it right off his head. He finally found it by the dull beam of Teddy's headlamp. But it was dead.

"There's a fire up ahead," said Teddy. "Fellow Rooters!" He ran off.

"Teddy!" David started after him, hesitated, and then turned and ran for the entrance.

Larry caught him and towed him deeper into the cave. He pulled out the Governor, a dual-action handgun, shotgun shells to disable an adversary and bullets to end its misery. "*Teddy*," he hissed. "*Slow down*."

The light from Teddy's headlamp grew dimmer.

Larry hustled David forward. They came upon Teddy, standing in front of a red glowing wall.

The glow resolved into a forest scene. A 14-point buck offered a ball of fire to a naked woman.

"Now what do you make of that?" Larry couldn't take his eyes off the scene, which appeared to play out before their eyes. The buck, the woman, the fireball, they were crudely drawn and vibrantly animated.

"Shape-shifter," Teddy interpreted. "He's bringing his woman the blood diamond he stole from a camp of evil South African black market gem brokers."

"That's why I suck at art appreciation," said Larry. "I don't see that at all."

"Can we go?" said David.

"Not until we find what we're looking for." Larry had to tuck the Governor back into his pants and tow them both, David digging in his heels, Teddy mesmerized.

Larry's eyes adjusted enough so that the two weak headlamps showed the way ahead. After 20 yards or so they came upon another eerie, glowing scene.

An audience of yellow faces laughed as a king tossed the big buck into a fire.

"King of the blood diamond brokers," said Teddy. "Taking his revenge. And how the Japs love the deer roast. They probably haven't eaten meat in a month."

Larry frowned at him.

"Back then Japan was an island," Teddy explained. "Nothing could make it across the sea but some grains of rice."

David shivered. "I think the deer is the Devil."

Teddy slapped him upside the head. "Dipshit! What kind of punishment is that—the Devil *loves* fire! That's where he *lives*!"

"Oh yeah," said David. "Now can we go?"

"This feels like the right place to scatter Jay's ashes," said Teddy. "A pile of ashes will add realism to the painting."

For Larry this was not a painting but an obscenity occurring as they watched, viewed through a wormhole, already far too real.

"I think I'll wait to get deeper," Teddy decided

"Larry, do we have to keep going?" David whined.

"I don't know." Tendrils of thin air worked their way down his throat. Larry wanted to spit even as he kept swallowing.

"Why do I feel like the perfect place to start our new Roots civilization is just around the bend?" said Teddy. He hurried forward.

"He's very intuitive," said David. He followed the ex-foreman. Larry was now trailing, falling behind, having difficulty making his feet go.

Teddy and David oohed and aahed over the next scene. Larry grew weak in the knees looking at it, sweat as ill as the air beading on his forehead.

A creature wore the buck's skin. It was using hoof-hands to mold a woman from clay. A vampire woman, with a crown. A happy audience watched.

"I told you!" Teddy crowed. "The hero is a shape-shifter!"

"And talented," said David.

Against the urge to flee, Larry moved closer, desperate to glean a clue to Victor's demise. The figures bled and ran together, blending hideously, the color of serpent underbelly, dirty mohair and oxygen-depleted blood.

Now he saw it. "The clay vampire woman is Morbius. Amberly Thetherson."

David peered into the scene. "Does that mean *Victor* is the shape-shifting deer-man?"

"Sculptor of evil," Larry confirmed. It all made perfect sense. "The cave is telling us that to destroy Morbius, one must first destroy her creator. But how?"

There came a growl, low and slow like an outboard trolling

motor just below the waterline. Behind them. Between them and the entrance.

One time, in the pine forests north of Houston, Larry had been cut off from safety by a huge boar. Such an animal could not be distracted or decoyed. Such a beast wasn't content to drive the hunter away—it *was* the hunter. Escape was only possible *through* the beast.

Which in this case was a lion with a snake for a tail and a goat head grafted on its back. *Just like the boar*, Larry told himself, and drew the Governor.

David screamed and made a run for it. The corridor was narrow but high-ceilinged—he parkour'd off the cave wall and soared over the beast. Larry was thrilled to see David still possessed that athleticism.

The tail snake snagged David's foot and dropped him hard to the floor. The goat bleated fire and the lion turned on David. Larry squeezed past them and ran.

Fight overcame flight and he skidded to a stop. Teddy slammed into him. The former foreman outweighed him by 100 pounds. Larry saw bright lights, even though the cave remained dark.

He couldn't have been out for more than a moment because charcoal ash still floated in the air. Teddy was unconscious. The lion roared and Larry was again in full flight through the corridor, up the slope and out the root-crossed opening.

He tripped and fell hard descending the forested hill. Pain replaced enough of the fear, so he could again consider David. It was late in the afternoon and mist moved through the trees. Finally, he convinced himself to return to the cave.

He found David squeezing out through the roots. He was bone-white but smiling, in a touched-by-an-angel way. Larry hugged him, and then struggled to keep up as David glided down the slope.

"David, what about Teddy?"

"No," said David.

"Does that mean the monster got him?"

"The chimera," said David. "Yes."

"Teddy is dead."

"No." David paused his descent, the beatific smile gone. "He was being, sort of, mated, with."

"Oh. Geez Louise."

David brightened again. "But I do know how to get Vic."

"How?"

"The chimera showed me."

Eugene drove his Dacia Dokker rental minivan across the Mureș river, near a meadow that looked to have been devastated by a tornado, defoliated and littered with debris, nothing standing except a mammoth stage, left unmolested in the way that tornadoes and rock concerts roll.

Târgu Mureș sprawled across the plain below Transylvania's layered hills. Traffic was heavy through a colorless Communist-era industrial and commercial district and into downtown, where the buildings added centuries and an infinite amount of style.

The Plaza V Executive hotel was something else, post-Commie, Euro-techno. "Buna ziua," he greeted the pretty front desk clerk. "Checking into your hotel, please."

"Buna ziua," she returned the greeting. "You have a reservation?" She spoke careful, nearly accent-free English.

"Nein."

"Nine reservations?"

"Sorry, no. One. Foreman. Eugene." He handed her his passport and credit card. "I see you had a big concert outside town."

"I am sorry?"

"I saw the damage outside town. Music fans are animals. Not country-western fans, of course. I hope it was a rapper, for the hotel's sake. Rock'n'rollers are campers."

"I am sorry?"

He tried a different tack. "Who played?"

The clerk cocked her head. "You have been living in a cave?"

Language barriers! Oh for the day when he could implant a Google translator in his earhole and voicebox. "Do you know where I can find Jaelle Skudza?"

The clerk paled. "This Roma is not welcome here in Romania."

"The Roma have been persecuted long enough, madam!"

"No-no, only this particular Roma. I propose you will not

seek for her."

Of course—Jaelle was discriminated against because she was a *slayer*. Eugene clenched his jaw. Vampires had the upper hand. They were masters of public relations. His MLMO slayer armies couldn't come on line soon enough.

"Plus," said the clerk, "I think she is in America."

"Tell me," said Eugene, "does your hotel qualify me for Hilton Honors points?"

"No."

"Is there a free continental breakfast?"

"Of course. The wi-fi too is free."

"I don't do unsecured networks."

"Here is your room key. You have a message." The clerk handed him a slip of paper that said *See you at seven in the sauna!*

"Who is this from?"

"The giver of the message did not indicate."

"Who gave the message?"

"Yes."

"The giver."

"Of course."

"Can I see your teeth, please?" Eugene caught the clerk by the lapel and performed a falsie check. He was forced to conclude she was human.

"Sir," said a second clerk coming to the aid of her shaken coworker, "our policy is for you to please keep your hands off of us." She saw the butt of his crossbow. "Our parliament is expected to ratify the resolution from the Unity Council. Soon it will be illegal to slay vampires. And to carry crossbows in the hotel."

Guests loitering in the lobby gravitated toward the scene. Eugene stalked through them, hand on his crossbow. "If cockroaches could talk, don't you think they'd recommend a law banning roach motels?! Wake up, Romania!"

The stairwell handrails were glowing neon tubes and the purple neon room numbers were at floor-level, in a nearly undecipherable font. Inside his room Eugene holstered his key in the wall slot to activate the electricity, and then pulled out the little plaque from the mine. At the sink he scrubbed away caked salt grime, revealing words that gave him an inexplicable thrill.

Kárpáti Mining
Alapított 1568

He also washed the salt from his face. His skin had never had such a healthy glow.

According to the address given him by slayer Vlad Trestian, Zenlen could be found on the other side of the busy main drag. Eugene dashed mid-block across the northbound traffic to a long center island, pretty with trees, benches, roses and statues. As he waited for a gap in the southbound flow, a distant building caught his eye, squatting beyond rooftops adorned with colorful Baroque ornamentation and the onion domes of Orthodox churches: the blunt line of a medieval fortress bastion. Eugene stared too long—he had missed his traffic gap. He walked down the center island to cross at the light.

Inside a handsome pale yellow building Eugene poked his head into one empty office after another before climbing a narrow creaky staircase to the 2nd floor, formerly a ballroom now furnished with rent-a-desks, half of them occupied with men staring at laptops. A young couple played ping-pong and four young men played intense, silent foosball. At least one of the foosball players and a drably-dressed desk denizen were vampires.

"I'm looking for Zenlen."

The people at the desks seemed relieved for an excuse to look away from their work. The ping-pong and foosball players remained focused on their games, although the vampire player now kept an eye on Eugene.

He approached a bald bespectacled man at the nearest desk. "Is Zenlen here?"

The man shrugged his shoulders.

"He doesn't speak English," said the next desk dweller, fiftyish, in a suit with vest, wispy combed-across hair. "Who are you looking for? Oh, do you mean Lenny?"

A few others giggled. Eugene pointed a finger pistol at the two vampires and pulled his finger trigger.

"We don't want trouble here," said Vested Suit.

"How much does it cost to rent space here?"

"One hundred lei per month."

Eugene nodded at Vested Suit's computer screen. "Good deal if it includes the porno subscription."

Vested Suit colored and closed the browser.

"Trouble," said Eugene "finds those who fear it the most." He should let Zenlen accrue the Slay Dividend in order to send motivational waves up and down the local MLMO network. But one must never let an opportunity pass un-seized and so he brought his crossbow to bear and shot the foosball vamp in the heart. The unevolved creature howled and fell dead onto the game table. Its putrid death dust floated into the sunlight beaming down from the high dormer windows.

The other vamp leaped up and ran out the door at the far end of the room. The humans booed Eugene, gave him the thumbs-down sign.

Vested Suit stood, angry. "If we gain the reputation of being racists, no one will invest in Târgu Mureș!"

"As long as there is blood to drink," said Eugene, "you will receive plenty of 'investment.'"

"Sssssssss," the rent-a-deskers hissed him.

"Zenlen?" said Eugene.

"I'll only tell you to get you to leave," said Vested Suit. "This time every day, Lenny is at the fortress."

A few blocks' walk brought Eugene to a chaotic intersection in front of the fortress. Road construction and a wedding at the nearby Orthodox church tangled traffic and made a cop in the middle of the street testy. After a heated discussion with a motorist intent on driving his BMW past the construction barricade, the cop rapped the Beemer's hood with his nightstick and ordered the driver back the way he had come.

Eugene regarded the fortress, atop a slight rise. Fat cream-colored bastions anchored the corners, connected by brick walls. Bastions and walls were featureless but for vertical archers' slits.

This medieval leftover seemed invisible to everyone else. Motorists did not gawk, no tourists walked through the gate. The wedding party had spilled out of the church and now milled about laughing and posing by their street-parked cars, without a glance at what loomed above them. The bride flirted amongst the groomsmen, hands busy keeping her skirts off the ground and eyes flashing with life, while the groom talked to some old people, one eye always for his bride.

Eugene had never imagined his own wedding. He wished he hadn't seen this one; the romantic image of his self-sacrificial destiny now withered compared to the romance he and Amberly would never experience.

The policeman blew his whistle in Eugene's ear. "Mişcare!"

He stood in the middle of the street. The whistle snapped him back to cold, honest reality: Vampires had slaughtered romance. There would nevermore be any to find, until slayers fulfilled their obligation.

He passed through the fortress gate. There were actually two walls, ten yards apart. Forty feet above him a man with wraparound salt-n-pepper hair-and-beard sat cross-legged atop the inner wall.

"I'm looking for Zenlen," Eugene called up.

The man startled to the sound and toppled backward. He uncrossed his legs and clawed at the tile roof, saving himself. Upright once again, he took a settling breath, swished his arms like a belly-dancer and settled back into cross-legged meditation.

Inside the nearest bastion was a staircase that provided access to a walkway 10 feet below the top of the wall. At an inside corner where wall met bastion, Eugene belted his overcoat behind him and climbed to the parapet. It was 18 inches wide. He ran at the bearded man, leaped, spun a 360 and landed in a Matrix-style crouch stance.

The man didn't flinch.

"Zenlen, I presume."

The man drew a long breath through his nose, held it, and clapped in front of his own face. It startled him. "God damn it!"

"Your control was impressive," said Eugene.

"I was just about to move into the 5th dimension!"

"If indeed you are Zenlen, that is what I am here to learn. You see—"

"Zen Len, is that what they called me?" The man gripped his thigh in sudden agony. "Thanks to you I am now aware that my leg is cramping!"

"You are welcome." Eugene removed his coat, his shoulder-to-hip crossbow holster, his bandolier of bolts, his engineer boots and the calf-harnessed stakes, his Trotsky cap and his leather cravat throat wrap, and sat cross-legged. He was extremely flexible, easily achieving Lotus.

Zen Len peeked. His face colored and he squeezed his eyes shut while massaging his thigh and surreptitiously tugging his foot into a tighter position. "Ommmmmmmm."

"Ommmmm," said Eugene.

"Whaaaat aaarrre yooooou doooing?" said Zen Len.

"Searrrching forrrr peeeeace. To saaaave the worllllld, I neeeed to killlll mysellllf. And my girllllfriend."

"Ommm—" Zen Len cut the Om short, irritated. "Fine. First you will need to cleanse yourself."

"I enema periodically."

Zen Len wrinkled his nose. "Of all worldly possessions."

"I will get my lawyer started unwinding all my businesses. But I intend—make that *need*—to keep slaying in the meantime. May I keep my crossbow?"

"No," Zen Len said sharply. "Then, you will need to take a spiritual journey."

"Can we do that here, now?"

"Seven years in Tibet."

Eugene opened his eyes to look at his watch. "I can do a week."

"There is no shortcut to Nirvana," said Zen Len.

Eugene stewed. "Let's make a deal. I'll let you in on a couple of my slaying secrets for a few of your tips and tricks."

"No!"

"I'm in turmoil, Zenlen!"

"That is not my problem. And it's just Len! Or Kensho Len. I'm having it legally changed."

Eugene breathed through his nose. "Mind if I just sit here with you for a time? I do feel the peacefulness."

"Actually I do," said Kensho Len. "I purposefully chose this position midway between the bastions that housed the locksmith and coopers' guilds. There is something mystical about imagining the *key* to a perfectly built *barrel*. I am currently feeling an imbalance. You are blocking the cooper vibes."

"Oh I am so sorry!" Eugene started putting everything back on. "I should have mentioned—I am Eugene Foreman, head of the International Slayer Multi-Level Marketing Organization! And I am going to recommend the Mohammed bin Rashid Al Maktoum Foundation audits your up- and downstream distribution channels before making any payouts!"

"Do it! I'm squeaky clean!"

"Don't come crying to me when some low-level vamp takes you down!"

"Don't let my aura hit you on the ass on the way out!"

Eugene stalked across the parapet to the bastion and parkour'd down to the walkway. He felt worse than ever. Not centered, not ready for the sacrifice his destiny required. He hurried down the bastion stairs—and was sent flying into the stone wall.

The vampire that stood over him, Eugene barely recognized. Yet he *knew* the vamp in his every fiber. Eugene couldn't believe he hadn't felt it before.

"The CWS."

"You can call me Trubadur." No longer a Southern gentleman, the former Civil War Soldier wore a tunic, blousy trousers and a tall felt hat. He posture was erect, his hair had gone from white to brown, and his fangs were perfect. "Or Grandpa."

Eugene struggled to his feet. "You lost the right to our family name when you laid with a bloodsucking scumbag."

Trubadur kicked him in the chest, bouncing him off the wall again. "Do *not* talk about Nadia. I loved her. And I never intended to get bit." He broke Eugene's crossbow over his knee and stabbed the bolt into Eugene's shoulder. "But it was the best mistake I ever made. I have to admit that this slow, not-so-graceful aging as the Morbius carrier has been trying at times. But now that I have my Morbius—and now that I get to *bite*—life couldn't be better."

"Life? Since when does dead flesh animated by Satan's dark magic qualify as being alive?" The bolt was buried too deep to pull out. Eugene's quick-dry undergarments wicked away his cold sweat as he struggled not to scream. "I should have known you were a lying vamp from the start, sending me to Germany to find my origin."

"You have 'kick me' stamped on your forehead, son." Trubadur kicked Eugene in the nuts. "You're an embarrassment to the Maistru legacy, you really are. But it was important for you to hear from someone who truly understands Victor Thetherson's evil nature."

"Of course he's evil," Eugene grunted. "He's a vamp."

"Speaking of which, do the flames of *l'amour* still burn hot for your little sweetheart?"

"Where is Amberly?"

"Pursuing world domination." Trubadur hauled Eugene to his feet. "Indirectly." He chuckled. "Interesting how the Morbius curse works. She truly believes vampires and humans can live together." Using the crossbow harness as a carrying strap he hauled Eugene up the bastion stairs.

"That's not the curse." Eugene thumped along the stone steps. "That's Amberly. I'll set her straight. Or I'll kill her."

Trubadur snarled and rammed Eugene headfirst into the wall, compressing his vertebrae. "You're talking about my daughter, you little shit."

"Your daughter?"

Maybe it was the concussion. Maybe it was history lingering in the mortar between the stones or imprinted in the mining plaque in his pocket. But now it was a different vampire toting Eugene up the boot-polished steps and onto the rampart walkway. A bigger vampire, primal and powerful and intent on his destruction. Eugene recognized the end of the line as the vampire lifted him overhead, and he could only think of his children.

"Stela!" Eugene cried out.

The vampire stared wide-eyed up into his face. "What did you say?"

"Stay away from my family, Canterpark!"

The vampire looked confused and distressed. His arms wobbled.

And now Eugene was looking through his own eyes; the moment had passed. He pressed the Spider-Man-style trigger on his wrist and shot a pencil stake into Trubadur's eye. The vampire screamed and dropped Eugene over the side just as Kensho Len dove from above. Eugene caught the lip of an archer's notch and hung on as he slammed into the wall. Kensho Len and Trubadur hurtled past.

Left arm nearly useless, Eugene struggled mightily before gaining the walkway. He looked down at the strip of grass between the walls. Only Kensho Len lay there, head turned at a real bad angle.

The Plaza V Executive hotel spa was down on level "-1". The spa was lit by red and purple neon tubes jumbled like spaghetti on the ceiling. There were two whirlpool hot tubs, a massage room and a dry sauna, which sounded like just the ticket. When Eugene entered, naked but for a do-rag head wrap and a weeping shoulder bandage, the other six patrons left. He laid down groaning, letting the heat cauterize his wounds and burn the vampire stink from his flesh. The clock struck seven.

"I don't like seeing you injured," said his favorite voice. "But it does feel wonderfully familiar."

Eugene sat up too fast. His concussed skull turned his stomach inside-out and he staggered forward to puke into the coals.

"You poor dear."

He swatted away Amberly's hand and in his dizzy hastiness fell to the wood plank floor and burned his ass. He stood. Amberly offered him a towel. He shook his head.

"I show you everything I am. And you hide your true nature."

Amberly blushed, grinning. "You didn't show me *that*."

"Don't joke! We had a romance for the ages! Now the troubadours of tomorrow will have to sing of how I retrieved my double-pointed stake and sui-slayed you."

Amberly wore a sexy sun dress. She bit her lip in alluring fashion and drew a little blood. "From what I know about the Morbius bloodline, and from what I see now, you have all the weapon you need."

Eugene fumbled for a reply. He grabbed a towel and wrapped it around his waist. "If that is what it takes! You don't think I will?!"

"I know you would, honey." Amberly's eyes softened and she took a small step toward him. One small step was all it took to push his heart into his throat. "I wish you would have given in to me at Mt. Rushmore," she said. "Before things became complicated."

His legs were weak. He had to sit before he fell, shamefully vulnerable before the vampire. Eugene blamed the concussion, the smell of sour turnips from the vomit baking on the coals, and the couple pints of blood lost before the local doc patched him up. "I am super glad I didn't."

"Eugene." Amberly sat some distance down the bench. "The world isn't monochromatic the way we thought. Black and white used to make sense. But as we mature we see such a richer palette."

"Can't. I'm colorblind."

"And that's a good thing, sweetie. When we get past the surface differences and see the *individual*, while recognizing the additional strengths that vampires bring to this world—"

"Vermin don't have individuality."

Amberly slammed the bench. "Would you grow up?"

His first glimpse of the vampire steel in her.

She moved closer. The sauna's intense heat brought pink to her luminescent cheeks. "I never knew how miserable I was. You saw it, Eugene. It's the reason I acted out in school and drove my parents crazy. It's why I took up with a rebel like you." She winked. "I didn't realize it, but my angst was growing every day as I shuffled along with the rest of the world, in those gigantic ruts that society plows for us. Our free will was gone; the ruling elite had already decided our destination."

"You're referring to extermination at the hands of the vampire."

She humored him with a tight smile. "I'm talking about eternal conflict. Conflict not as a means to a better place, but as the goal itself. Christian versus Islam, Left versus Right, Nation versus Nation. My father versus you. Never-ending, and never resolving anything. We're born into the armies of cannon fodder, our lives destroyed at birth and the world stuck in its dark place."

"If there is so much evil in the world that the conflict must be eternal, then so be it."

"It's a *lie*, Eugene." Amberly had him in her eyes, her cheeks, the purr softening her voice and her every single movement. He loved to watch her talk.

Had loved it.

"All these people in conflict, they aren't evil," she told him. "Their decisions might be, but it's because they were misled. From now on, *we* are going to lead them. People won't be allowed to make those evil decisions."

"I'm not concerned with *people*."

"Eugene, I'm so excited about the future. I want you to be excited. I want you with me." She moved closer. "Things have changed, honey. Vampires are leading and the people yearn to follow. I've seen it. You're not going to be allowed to slay us anymore."

Eugene gritted his teeth. "Please don't say 'us.'"

"I love you, Eugene. I always will, with all my heart." She looked at the door. "This place, Târgu Mureş, it's special for us. You can feel it, too. I'm not surprised to find us here together."

The concussion, the extreme heat, his baked vomit, it was all getting to him, dulling his judgment and opening him to her manipulations. "Leave me alone."

She caught him as he staggered for the door and forced him against the hot wood wall. Eugene knew his skin was burning but he couldn't resist her. He struggled not to look into her eyes.

Her face was inches from his, her breath on his throat. She touched his chest and God help him, it felt good. "We can unite the world, Eugene. You and I. Let's end our conflict. Let us be that example."

Her nose pressed against him, her face, her lips. His backside was on fire, his front twice so.

"Love me, Eugene."

"No. No. No!" He screamed at himself, to push her away and run, run, run, and now he was skidding through the spa's main room and up the stairs into the lobby, bleeding, burned, naked, sending people scurrying as he continued taking the stairs flight after flight.

On the seventh floor, he turned around and started to head back for the sauna, before remembering he had tucked his room key in the do-rag head wrap.

THERE WILL BE BLOOD, IN THE WATER

It had been quite a while since Victor was eyesore and stiff-necked. Or introspective enough to realize it.

He wasn't sure he even could have been stiff and sore as a vampire, prior to his time in the isolation tank. For certain-sure, pre-tank vampire Victor wouldn't have spent hours sitting and researching at the computer.

On the party boat across the Galveston Channel, he declined the call to play musical chairs for tequila shots. The game was disturbing considering the clientele: young children and African gangsters, tourists and vampires who belonged in the Houston police department's now-discontinued pit. Depravity and violence had become mainstream such that the party boat's human parents embraced their kids' curiosity with vampires swilling tequila, cursing like sailors and salivating over the blood they would be drinking at the Comity Club on the Ocean Star Offshore Drilling Rig and Museum.

Refreshing his dormant programming skills, Victor earlier had asked his computer to scan web content and put together a story about Morbius, about Amberly, about the *StakeOurClaim* movement. Thanks to the share-and-bare-all mentality that had made such a success out of Victor's predictive modeling software—stolen and christened the Xtensive Feedback Predictor by the now-deceased vampire X—the story his author-bot pulled together was long and detailed. Victor now knew that Amberly had held a rally in Transylvania two nights ago and was holding one in Mumbai tonight with Bollywood heartthrob Priyanka Chopra, who planned to be turned on stage, and rogue Bangladeshi vampire Wingdingland, who was receiving a ceremonial staking (in his slippery heart, not his Heel) to symbolize society's cleansing through vampire-human unity and sacrifice.

He also knew that a certain high-ranking vampire had taken residence on this former oil rig off the Galveston coast. The "Comity Club" kept popping up in the story. Converted from museum to vampire-human good-time meeting joint, it exemplified the new borderless world. Personal accounts of time spent in the Club led Victor to two theories: erasing borders erases inhibitions, and there will always be someone to draw new lines.

Watching the party boaters confirmed both.

A skinny bucktoothed African gangster vampire demanded of an Iowan mother, "Have your son bite me!" He picked up the 10-year-old and offered his throat.

The woman tucked the front end of her reverse mullet behind her ear and smiled nervously. "But he's not a vampire."

"We are all Placido today," said one of the gangster's buddies through a cheekful of khat.

"Go ahead, Milt," said the boy's father, tequila spilled on his plaid short-sleeve shirt. "I'd do it, too, but my TMJ is acting up."

The boy was all for it. It took him a moment to get the angle right, then he put a big bite on the African gangster vampire.

Who screamed in pain and dropped the boy and threw an errant kick at his head, to gales of laughter from his gangster buddies and good-natured chuckling from the boy's parents.

The gangster vampire hopped about looking at the blood on his fingers from the wound on his neck, regaining his malevolent good humor while the boy took high fives from partygoers and licked around his lips. His face suddenly screwed up and he ran to the railing next to Victor and vomited over the side.

This gave new life to the bitten vampire. "You have to learn to hold your blood, boy! Let me show you how it's done."

He grabbed the boy's mother and sank his fangs deep in her throat, to cheers from the partygoers and ill clapping from her husband. From under his Astros baseball cap and behind his sunglasses, Victor saw a glow from the gangster vampire's left retina. He similarly catalogued the other vampires' Heels, keeping his mouth shut and working out the computer-kink between his shoulder blades.

They were a raucous disembarking crowd funneled into single-file behavior through a tight doorway and down narrow corrugated stairs into the bowels of the out-of-service rig, a low-ceilinged room with a disco-lit parquet floor where vampires and humans danced together.

Sitting sloppy cross-legged against the far wall was a vampire who could not have stood up without banging his head on a girder or putting it through a sound-absorbent tile. Victor had enjoyed Dikembe Mutombo as a basketball player. Now his L4 lumbar glowed like a pinhole-light through his bellybutton and the cottony disco-resplendent tribal kimono. That button begged for one of Eugene's crossbow bolts.

Victor made his way past pairs, trios, knots, and stragglers. He did not glide, he bumped shoulders and stepped on toes, receiving looks, yelps and curses. This vampire den was no place for apologies—the predominant emotion was giddiness, convertible to rage. Better to say nothing and keep moving.

Casinos and vampire dens, great places for humans to get free booze. Victor's belly brushed an elbow and sloshed a martini glass. He felt no need to apologize for his lack of coordination. *That would be like apologizing for being here. Or for being, period. That would be stupid.*

He realized he was no longer seeing himself through others' eyes, whether as fat schlep or dangerous intimidator. He could only describe his new self-conception as an *achievement-in-process*. Neither did he see himself as if in a mirror, didn't watch his own grimace or snarl, hunched shuffle or cocksure stride. He was no longer a localized entity to be measured, but a *distributed*, electric being with psychic arms acting upon those around him and stretching into the future where his accomplishments waited.

This was something beyond that brief moment of glory long ago when, as a college senior, he had recovered from Legionnaire's disease, discovered mousse and landed dates. His mindset now had nothing to do with pride in his physical form.

And it was more than the confidence he had gained from vampirism, which had protected him behind a forcefield that allowed him freedom to think and act unilaterally upon the world.

Victor was beyond confidence. He was liberated.

A smooth-skinned vampire in a skin-tight mock-naval uniform blocked his way. "Welcome to the Comity Club." He took Victor's hand and rotated it to see his unmarked wrist. "First timer? Or an inveterate 'auditor'? We do have a few humans who get their kicks, but truly don't want to be pierced." He nodded at Victor's mouth, bared his own fangs with a sly grin. "But we haven't had a vampire yet who could resist a bite. Fucking insatiable, aren't we?"

"A thirst for life."

"Well said." The faux-naval vampire produced a needle gun. "That's why we need to inoculate you, big fella. We promise our clientele they'll walk out the same species they walked in."

Victor stopped the gun before it pierced him. "My bite is already neutered."

"This is a policy without exception." The vampire's eyes widened as he truly looked at Victor. "You're X-Ray. Victor Thetherson."

"X-Ray? I like that."

It was chilly below decks, despite space heaters along the walls. Victor hated the feel of a ballcap, but enjoyed the heat capture. The brim impaired his "vision"—his Sight worked best with all five senses unimpeded. But he had wanted anonymity.

Now his identity was on everyone's lips and the room temperature jumped a few degrees. He tossed the Astros cap and sunglasses and winked at the faux-naval vampire. "We'll call you First Mate Femoral Artery."

The vampire's breath caught in his throat. "Fuck you," he managed to say.

"Make that the *right* femoral artery," Victor said loudly and pointed.

The vampire retreated, covering his right upper thigh with the vaccine gun. "What the fuck are you doing here?"

"Looking for my daughter."

The gangster vampires from the party boat quailed when Victor's eyes went to their Heels. The effect was See-No, Speak-No, Hear-No Evil comical, vampires covering, bending and contorting to protect their weaknesses.

He approached the vampire Dikembe Mutombo. Nestled beside him in an iron collar on a chain leash was a poor, foul, moaning creature with a leopard pelt on its back and a leather breastplate. Deferentially addressing Mutombo was a dumpy, blinking human in an ill-fitting suit.

"We are eternally grateful for your donation, Mr. Mutombo," said Dumpy Blinker. "This school will make a huge difference for the Congolese children."

"We are lucky to live in one of the world's few moments of *positive* revolution," said the former NBA legend vampire. "We can't miss the opportunity to teach new ways to the next generation." He nodded at Victor. "Even as the terrorists work to keep us perpetually at war."

Victor was wary of attack from the chieftain's bodyguards and hangers-on. "War or subjugation," he said. "Those are the choices."

"There is a third way, my friend," said Dumpy Blinker. "Education."

"Only if our teachers aren't vampires."

"That's extremely offensive," said Dumpy Blinker. "If you must persist with your prejudices, sir, I insist you keep them private!"

"Victor Thetherson is a paradox," said vampire Dikembe. "A vampire who kills vampires; and the one who gave us the greatest vampire of all."

"I didn't give you my daughter. But if you help me get her back, I promise to kill fewer of you."

Dumpy Blinker went bug-eyed. "With your permission, Mr. Mutombo?" He shook his finger at Victor. "Your narrow definition of 'humanity' is exactly the reason our African-American brothers suffered for 300 years in this country. But we have learned from that mistake, and I promise you we won't allow vampires to suffer outside the definition of humanity for another 300 years!"

"Even as a vampire," said Victor to Mutombo, "you have to take exception to that comparison."

"Finally, a chance to debate a *vampire bigot*." Dumpy Blinker peered at Victor as representative and ambassador of that species. "Tell me why you are so unwilling to live side by side with our 'pointed' brothers and sisters."

"Because I hate them." This was no less true for him in this rewired, post-isolation tank state. Being in the presence of his former basketball favorite clenched Victor's heart to a fist.

"You can't say that!" Dumpy Blinker pleaded with him. "Mr. Mutombo is a philanthropist!"

"Fine." Victor pushed Dumpy Blinker aside and addressed the vampire Mutombo. "Help me bring Amberly home and I'll put you on my Do Not Slay list."

"She is no longer your daughter. She is our Morbius." Vampire Dikembe's lightly-bloodshot eyes bulged with reverence. "She belongs to us all, vampire and human alike."

The fist that was Victor's heart beat against his ribs. "She is still my daughter. And you know that not every vampire is so enamored with her. I want you to spread the word, Dikembe. To Adamo Abele and his faction. Hands off Amberly." His eyes flickered to Mutombo's Heel. "Or else."

The Congolese-American vampire fastened the bellybutton-level hook of his kimono with impossibly-long fingers, and wagged one of them at Victor. "Uh-uh-uh. I have made a living defending my valuables."

His flunkies roared with laughter, high-fiving each other and wagging their fingers at Victor. Dumpy Blinker joined in, his stubby finger twitching like Porkie the Morkie's cropped tail.

"This *house* is valuable!" The faux-naval vampire incited the room. "This club represents the new world we're creating! And we refuse to let anyone come into our house and smack talk!"

Fight or flight? Victor considered both and decided on something different. "The way I heard it, Dikembe, you were dunked on in the Congo, to the tune of 20 mill."

Mutombo bared his lion-like fangs. He had been swindled on a gold purchase by a Congolese warlord, and then revealed his vampirism by drinking the warlord dry.

"And then you flagrantly fouled him," Victor complete the analogy.

The former NBA star vampire scratched the leather tummy of his foul, chained wretch, which seemed to soothe them both. "You forgot to mention," Mutombo wagged his finger again, "that gold scam was the kind that *humans* have been getting away with forever. That is why I embrace the vampire. Bantu, Hutu, Tutsi, communist, capitalist, Christian, animist, Muslim, we do not care. Justice is all we seek."

"Justice does require a judge. That would be the vampire, correct?"

Mutombo smiled. "Play by the rules. That is not too much to ask."

A woman emerged from a doorway behind him. Tall, blond hair plastered to her square severe face, dressed like a Wagnerian warrior nurse, mouth contorted in what might look like a smile from afar. She put her hand on Mutombo's shoulder and he put his hand up her kilt. "Amberly has a new daddy now," she talked like a poorly trained robot. "Trubadur Maistru."

Victor stepped closer, and the poor pelted creature growled. "What do you know about her?"

The Aryan Warrior Nurse grabbed Mutombo's face and kissed him violently. She pounded his chest while sucking his face. When she broke the seal, he laughed and her lips bled. "I am the one who was to be Morbius!" she labored through the statement. "Your little bitch stole it from me!"

"Watch your mouth," said Victor.

"Trubadur wants a pawn." She looked like a vampire but Victor couldn't see a Heel. And she was not afraid of him. "He will spank her if she misbehaves." She kicked the pathetic chained creature until its growls turned to mewls. "And she *will* misbehave."

At the thought of the ancient vampire freak touching Amberly, vampire rage consumed Victor. "Help me find her and you can play Morbius to your heart's content."

She ground her backside into Mutombo's lap. The ex-NBA superstar vampire's smile became a wince. "Only one person I hate more than your daughter," she said. "Her father." She shoved her throat in Mutombo's mouth. He took a pained, half-hearted nibble. She stood up and wiped away slobber. "I know *your* Achilles' heel."

Victor found a smile. "You are obviously very sexy. But you're not my type."

She wagged her finger à la Mutombo. "Not *that* Heel."

Victor was tackled from behind and driven to the steel-and-sawdust floor. Vampire fangs bit at the back of his neck, scraping his skin through a mouthful of his polo collar. Victor thrashed at the vampire fastened to his back. Its jaws tore away his collar, twill strips embedded like cheap floss between fang and incisor.

"Idiot!" seethed the Aryan Warrior Nurse. "You can bite him *anywhere*!"

A slim stake buried itself in her chest.

"Hilda!" Mutombo bellowed. He tried to jump to his feet, but his long-abused knees refused and he tumbled atop his wretched pet.

The Warrior Nurse gaped at the shooter. "I am *not* a vampire!"

"Too bad," said the slayer, in his sixties and dressed like a frogman. He stabbed a stake in the khat-mouthed vampire from the party boat, ducked a chair thrown at his head and fired another projectile-stake from a pistol that looked like a flare gun, under his arm, ultra-cool and perhaps killing his second human of the afternoon. "Guilt by association."

Victor's assailant was the bucktoothed gangster vampire who had bit the Midwest mother. He was lanky and stupid-strong, free of Victor's floss-collar and biting at his hand.

The frogman slayer leaped on a cowboy vampire's back and staked his chest. "I'm here for you, my love!"

The wretched chained creature came to life. She hopped on Mutombo's back, double-wrapped her chain around his neck, levered her feet between his shoulder blades and leaned back like a water skier, strangling him.

Bucktooth was distracted. Victor slugged him in the throat, grabbed his ear and yanked his head to the side.

"Vampire, I see your Heel!"

As intended, the announcement claimed everyone's attention. Victor stabbed two fingers into the gangster vampire's eye. Through bulging eyes Mutombo watched his henchman howl and die, right before the wretch's chain cut through his last layer of sinew and found bone.

Mutombo's head lolled lifelessly and the chained wretch fell to the floor. Her slayer frogman hero shot an intervening gangster vampire and brought the old lady to her feet.

She kissed him. "Another meat-eater falls at the hand of Edna Campbell, pescetarian, former member of the balless bunch of dilettantes named PETA, avenger of Slayer Sven Millefond—and soon-to-be-lover of Bad-Ass Burton!"

Edna placed her leopard pelt like a death shroud over Mutombo. Turned out she was not wearing a leather breastplate, but rather was naked. She rummaged Mutombo's pockets under the pelt and came away with a key, which Bad-Ass Burton the frogman slayer used to unlock her collar.

"Freedom!" he proclaimed for Edna. He bent her backward—the sound of her spine cracking was gruesome—and kissed her manfully.

They parted with a lip-smacking crackle. "Apologies," said Edna. "I've been on a hunger-strike since Dikembe bagged me. Edna's a little dehydrated."

Burton swept her into his frogman arms, checked his diver's watch, and sang to her. "I do believe it's time for us to fly!" When a flapper vampire woman sought to prevent it, Burton shot her with his stake gun.

The vampire woman took it in the chest and laughed.

"Solar plexus," said Victor. Burton's elderly hand was a little shaky—to be fair, the bulky pistol looked heavy, and Edna was in his other arm—and his next stake *thunked* into the flapper vampire's rib.

It was nearly as good as a kill. The flapper vampire cowered and limped for shelter; vampires left, right and center shrank from Victor's roving eyes. A path cleared to the exit.

At the door Burton surveyed the room. "I'd say two kills for certain-sure and possibly another three." He looked to Edna. "To get credit on my slayer pyramid account, I might need an affidavit from you on the numbers, honey."

Victor's last image of the rig room was the shrouded Dikembe Mutombo vampire jumping to his feet, striking his head on a steel beam and going down arms a-flailing on top of Dumpy Blinker.

They hustled up the staircase and onto the platform. "The sticky mines are set to blow in three minutes," said Bad-Ass Burton.

"My hero," said Edna, rubbing her leathery body on his rubbery suit.

They climbed into an inflatable dinghy tethered to the rig.

"You are the most competent—no, I take that back," said Victor. "The *only* competent slayer I have ever seen." A shuttle boat full of vampires and their collaborating human donors motored past them, oblivious to their dinghy and eager to join the rig party. "There might still be hope."

Water crackled in Victor's ear as Jaelle's lead programmer Michael fitted the modified virtual reality helmet on his head. He was melancholy after his time in the isolation tank. He had sprouted fur and run through the streets, jumped the fence at a petting zoo and killed an alpaca, for sport. He had flown, out of the tight alley between the old commercial buildings next to the Opposite-Striped Zebra where Nikki had maneuvered to be his first bite, and soared into downtown, past the spire of the new Bizco skyscraper and his gaping former coworkers. Dreamtime had ended in bed next to Barbara, looking into each other's eyes, touching each other, closer and closer.

"Let's find us some vampires, shall we?" said Jaelle.

"Sure."

Jaelle paused Michael's helmet fitting. "It is okay to take time to recover. You were in the tank for 33 hours."

He would have guessed a week. He was *settled.* As the melancholy receded, Victor had never been so at peace. And so ready to do some damage. "I'm good. I have a particular vampire in mind."

"If we knew in advance who you're looking for," said Michael, "I could have searched the Net based on driver's records, reported sightings, facial recognition." He was subdued today, as were the other programmers and drone pilots in the room. They fed off Jaelle's tension. She viewed this as their final attempt, with no confidence in success. Talking warmed Michael up. "We might have been able to find your vampire."

"We have enough fine candidates," said Jaelle. She stared at Victor. "You are sure you are ready for this?"

He settled into the chair, enjoying the cool gel skullcap. "Yes."

"I'm getting a good vibe," said Michael. He leered at his coworkers, warning them he couldn't help himself. "Of course I always get a good vibe from this big glass of sweet tea."

Victor stared into Michael's sweat-wet armpit as the programmer fiddled with the helmet's interface with the chair, which in turn connected to the local servers and ultimately to a million cameras and a squadron of drones worldwide. "Likewise."

The programmers and pilots chortled. "We need Victor to focus, Michael," one of them chastised. "You can seduce him after."

Michael sighed. "Unfortunately, that's not the vibe I'm getting." He looked past his armpit at Victor. "Unless?"

"No."

Michael hummed. "Guess that means the suggestive patterns I inserted into your iso-dreams didn't work."

Jaelle stood on an exercise step borrowed from the adjoining yoga studio. She had a fistful of Victor's shirt and distaste on her face. "Take your time. Breathe. Take breaks. Do not put too much pressure on yourself." Her tightening grip on his shirt suggested otherwise. "We are still learning."

"Let's kill some vamps."

She stared into his eyes, uncertain about what she was seeing, before stepping down and hovering over the pilots' consoles.

"Thumbs-up when you're ready." Michael hugged him and went to his computer station. He saw Victor's thumb. "Hold onto your butts, here we go."

Victor's first view was bird's eye looking down on their city block. He sensed a vampire on the sidewalk in front of the yoga studio and Low-T clinic—and now he was panning the nearest traffic camera toward the "hot spot."

"Woman in short shorts and a tight pink shirt in front of this building."

"She takes turns with another vamp keeping an eye on Jaelle," said Michael. "We don't want them getting too suspicious about what we're doing in here, so we have Jaelle regularly teach meditation classes. And we don't slay them."

"He found that traffic cam on his own," said one of the programmers, voicing amazement that coursed through the room. "And he oriented it himself."

Victor had an idea of other "eyes" available to him, and went looking for them.

After a virtual dive through a downtown rooftop, he was in an art museum watching a well-dressed vampire admire a Monet, Heel pulsing through the fat rolls at the base of his neck.

Now he was back outside flying above the metro area. Victor grew rollercoaster giddy-queasy to find four vampires together in a Humvee, the vehicle spewing orange clouds from the four Heels calling to him; he tracked them down the interstate, from above and via a cop car camera, before peeling off.

He craned his neck back and expanded the breadth of his gaze, looking for a higher eye in the sky.

And now he was zooming in on the Baja peninsula, the southernmost bulge on the eastern coast, the water striped sky blue and turquoise meeting a ribbon of beach and rugged dunes with a dusty village between them, bleached ramshackle buildings and colorful festival tents, maybe 50 pickups, jeeps and SUVs clustered around a marina hosting a flotilla of fishing and diving boats. On by far the biggest, a sport yacht with a long prow, sat a vampire in a white fedora sipping on a blood straw attached to a flunky donor's forearm.

His appendix was ready to burst. At least in Victor's estimation.

"Adamo Abellllleee, time for you to die."

"You found him?"

Jaelle's incredulity was cut off by the *shoosh* launch of a Hellfire missile over the high-fidelity speakers of the drone pilot's monitor. The missile smashed through the tinted windows of the yacht's bridge and blew the craft into two pieces, bow and stern each pointing skyward. A fireball blew out of the stern's conning tower, blasting the bow, bursting the decking in a shower of fiberglass, launching Abele and his tethered donor onto the dock.

"Whoa-whoa-whoa," said the drone pilot. "I swear I was waiting for authorization to take the shot."

The blood donor lay crumpled on the dock. Abele struggled to his feet and ran for shore.

"I have a lock on the runner," said the drone pilot. "Permission to—"

Shoosh the second missile dive-bombed and came in low off the bay. It impaled Abele and carried him into the dive shop.

A compressed-air tank screamed skyward, preparatory to a flash that overloaded the Predator's camera, the scrambled video clearing just in time for the shockwave to buffet the drone.

It stabilized and flew in for a close look at the carnage.

Bodies were in pieces, aflame, lifeless, on the beach and in the water and atop flaming tents and shacks.

"Holy shit," said Michael.

"Victor," said Jaelle. "Any read on Abele?"

"He's dead."

There was a pause, and then clapping, one by one until everyone joined the applause.

"Fuckin-a *right*," said one of the programmers. "It fucking *works*!"

The room erupted in cheers, hugs, high-fives. Jaelle went to Victor.

"You did it. That was incredible. Beyond my dreams." Restrained but elated, she took one of his limp hands. "Your Sight, it doesn't just allow you to find their weaknesses. You can find *them*."

He took off the helmet and loomed over her. He accepted an awkward hug against his belly and then moved past her. "I need air."

"The tide has turned," Jaelle announced. "That is the blow we needed to bolster our friends, and discourage our enemies."

Victor took the air for 20 miles across town with the Charger's windows rolled down. He pulled into the Darla's driveway, got out and leaned against the car, and tried to understand his feelings about what had just happened.

The Charger's electronically-enhanced engine, his aura, something brought Darla to the door.

She read his distress and hurried to the curb. "What happened?"

Victor squeezed her hand. "How are you? How is Kimberly?"

"You know. Why don't you come in."

Victor walked with her to the stoop. "I'm sorry to do this to you. Showing up like this."

She pulled him across the threshold. "At this point? After all the times you've come to me, and left me? I've come to the conclusion you and I don't really control our relationship." She held his hand down the hallway. "Are you hungry?" She made herself laugh. "I should clarify. All I can offer is something from the fridge."

"I'm fine." They moved into the living room and sat close together on the couch. "I just killed a lot of people."

Darla's worry fit easily into the recently formed lines around her eyes and mouth. "Tell me."

He was exhausted, no energy to relive the horror. "The slayers, Dr. Linciome's people, this Romanian neuroscientist Jaelle, they have a way for me to tap into a drone network, to use my Sight to find the evolved vampires. And kill them."

She stroked his temple with fingertips longer than their chewed nails.

"I found the vampire I was looking for. The drone strike, it wasn't pinpoint. We destroyed the whole area. I killed a lot of vampires. And humans." Victor leaned his face into her hand and closed his eyes. "It was unbelievable."

"It's okay," Darla said, not convincingly. Victor burrowed his forehead deeper into her palm and then her collarbone. He put his hands on her and hugged her as hard as he dared.

"Never again," he said. "I'll never do that again."

"I'm sorry." Her body stiffened; she was preparing to tell him something painful. "Did you hear about Mel Parish?" she referred to Bizco's chief of construction. Tears ran down her cheeks. "He was killed at his home. They say it was a CIA counterterrorism team, for God's sake." She smoothed his shirt against his shoulder to occupy her shaking hands. "They said he was part of a cell trying to take down the government. Another Bizco employee was attacked and killed at the same time, in our lobby. There was a melee, people trying to get out of the building. A lot of people were injured, three of our employees seriously. Everyone has been asked to work from home until further notice."

Mel Parish. Victor couldn't come to grips with the loss of the gruff, burly leader. He felt responsible.

Darla wiped away her tears and settled her breathing. "Now I have a team of accountants 'working from home.' You can guess how that's going to go." Her attempt to find dark humor only made her look more miserable. "Kimberly was handling things poorly, before. I don't know if I'll ever be able to get her to leave the house again. I don't know if I want her to."

"You and Kimberly, Barbara and Amberly, you're all depending on me. I'm failing you if I walk away from Jaelle and her drones."

Darla saw him tunneling down a path of self-defensive anger. She always knew. "It's okay. Everything going on, it's bigger than you and me. What the vampires are doing, killing people like Mel, calling them terrorists—no one seems to understand how wrong it is. Everyone is so desperate for something *different*. They're willing to try anything. You've done everything you can. It's not your job, it's not possible, to change people's minds about vampires. Your job is to bring Amberly home." She kissed his cheek. "I know you'll do it. You brought Kimberly back to me."

She kissed him softly. He kissed her back, and the contact was wonderful. He had been floating for years, unattached, untouched. He wanted to be anchored, to be in contact. He put his hands on her hip, her waist, her ribs.

"Victor, why are you here with me?"

The dream in the isolation tank had finally unveiled his future—the lack of a future with Barbara. "I love her. I don't think I've ever lied to you about that." In the dream, he had experienced the sweetest moment with Barbara—and awoke with the aching certainty that she was a lover he had lost long ago, who could only come to him, haunt him, in his dreams. "But it's not going to happen with her. I don't want to pretend any longer."

Distress shrank Darla's body, drew it away from him, made it rigid and small. Her touch became supportive, platonic. "You can't give up. Just because it's hard, and with everything happening—"

"I'm not giving up." He rested her hand against his chest, fingers open and pressed flat against him. His pectoral muscles had softened and Victor couldn't care less. "I agree with what you said about our relationship, that it seems to be out of our hands. It's just as true with Barbara. I keep getting pushed away from her. I keep getting drawn to you," he said. "I love you,

Darla. And I'm ready to stop fighting it. I want to be with you."

"You want to be with me." She sobbed and laughed. "I suppose I'm so stupid to love to hear you say that. But I don't care."

They hugged as the sun set and the house went dark and their bodies finally relaxed.

"I need to go back to the house." Porkie the Morkie had no doubt overstayed his welcome with the neighbors. "You'll be alright here tonight?"

"Of course."

"I will be back tomorrow."

Darla walked him past the stairway, speaking quietly. "I'll tell Kimberly. I don't know how she's going to see this, you and me. I hate to throw something else at her."

"Well, we could—"

"But I'm going to," said Darla. "We'll figure it out as we go."

"Okay." Victor kissed her and left.

With his finger on the garage door button, the Charger's headlights picked up a shadow where his front door should have been. Any chance he had left it open? Victor couldn't remember the last time he had gone out the front door.

His heart thudded in his chest. He contemplated reversing out of the driveway and parking down the street, hopping the backyard fence and crawling in through an upstairs window. But his headlights had already announced his arrival. He triggered the garage door.

A shaved-head tattooed vampire met him in the garage. Victor came around the front of his car—they collided and Victor slammed him against the Tony Horton poster. "Why are you in my house?"

"It's a shame, all that room going to waste." The vampire spoke with difficulty, his English poor to begin with, and the heel of Victor's palm jamming his head against a steel-frame storage rack. The poster ripped. "Since your women keep moving out."

Victor didn't sense a Heel. He looked for something sharp to ram through the vampire's chest.

"Adamo Abele sent me," said the vampire, with the same accent, Italian. His front teeth were all chiseled to points. "He has your wife."

"Barbara? *What?*"

The vampire stopped struggling, demonstrating submissiveness. Victor backed off.

"You were understandably upset to learn you signed off on killing your daughter," said the thuggish Italian vampire. "So you killed Dikembe Mutombo and blew up the Galveston club. That's a violation of your agreement with Mr. Abele. Mr. Abele wants to remind you how evil Morbius is, and provide you some additional incentive to avoid further violations—"

Victor body-slammed the vampire to the cement floor. "I just *killed* Abele! On the Baja," he added to overcome the vampire's doubts. "I blew him up! I blew everyone up! Where was she?! Where is Barbara?"

The vampire's head had ricocheted off the floor, causing him to bite through his tongue. "You killed Mr. Abele? Where? On his yacht? My family was with him!"

Victor rammed the vampire headfirst into the Charger's front bumper. Fiberglass and the vampire's neck both cracked. The unimproved Italian vampire stared at Victor wild-eyed and head askew. Victor hauled him onto an exercise mat, grabbed a 10-pound dumbbell and hammered it through the vampire's teeth.

"You think I give a fuck about *your* family? What about my wife? Where is she?!"

The vampire was trying to indicate a lack of knowledge on that subject when Victor punched the dumbbell through his face.

"Hi," Molly Pierce his neighbor called as she came up the driveway with Porkie the Morkie on a leash. "I saw your garage door open, and Porkie was *so* excited to come home. Oh. Uh, is everything okay?" She came around the Charger and put her hands to her mouth.

Victor left the gory dumbbell racked in the vampire's skull. "They have Barbara." He stared dumbly at Porkie sniffing at the already-rotting corpse.

Molly darted in to grab Porkie. The Morkie growled far above his pay grade, ready to defend his found spoils. Molly scooped him up and pulled Victor by the arm out to the driveway. "Is Barbara okay?"

"I'm going to have to ask you to take care of Porkie for

another couple days or so."

BRIDGE NUMBER NINE

A crowd boiled on the Pont Neuf, at the right temperature for the momentous occasion. In a temporary hut slapped together where the bridge crossed the tip of the Île de la Cité, Joshua Linger, second in command at the NSA and vampire Doyon, gave final instruction to the new French vampire proconsul.

"You must demonstrate to them that you are ready to assume—"

"I was born ready!" Eric Parascand's hair complemented his bronze skin. Somehow his fangs countered the cruelty of his bloodless lips. His suit was like butter. "The centuries melt away at this moment. It was only yesterday I was starving in the Argonne, hunted by peasant and nobleman alike. And now the world is ours!"

"Balance, *mon ami*." Linger eyed the unevolved she-vampire responsible for the press conference media system and the human male who coordinated logistics. Neither reacted. "Strike that delicate equipoise between democratic ceremony and the reassurance one receives from a competent autocrat."

"José, please."

"Joshua, *s'il vous plaît*."

Parascand showed fang, really his most reassuring expression. "We have trained for this moment. *You* have put us in position to succeed. Trust me to make my contribution."

Over the P.A. system they heard the emcee's introduction of Parascand. He pulled back his upper lip for Linger's inspection. "Do I have anyone in my teeth?"

They enjoyed a good laugh. Parascand kissed Linger on each cheek, ruffled the logistics coordinator's hair, ignored the unevolved she-vamp and strode out of the hut, wading into the crowd on his way to a stage midpoint on the bridge's northern span.

Sales pitches of varying degrees of legitimacy had been made on the Neuf for hundreds of years. Linger had watched Napoleon enthrall the masses from nearly the same point above the Seine. History was looping back on itself, restarting another new age. Napoleon could have only dreamed of the power they were going to wield.

Of course, Napoleon never had to deal with worldwide broadcasts of difficult-to-justify smartphone videos of his peeps doing awful things to others. But bad press had always existed, in an arms race with censorship. Right now, Linger and the NSA had pulled ahead; the little emperor would have appreciated the media blackout at Linger's fingertips, courtesy a drone over the bridge that could emit encoded infrared rays to disable smartphone video functionality.

Parascand mounted the platform and stepped to the microphone. He paused and Paris held its breath.

"Good evening," he said in English, doing a great Bela Lugosi.

Scattered laughter. It really should have been a better ice breaker. Linger worried.

Not Parascand. He resumed in French. "I am blessed to stand in front of you today. In front of you, and with you. With you all, human and vampire alike."

"Bullsheet!" A vampire leaped atop the concrete sidewall and screamed at Parascand in accented English. "The *beautiful* vampires, you mean!" Linger tried not to judge but in all honesty this vampire was very homely. "Yes, you *stand*—on our *throats!*"

"Nonsense." Parascand was smooth. Charles Valery had been his official superior, but like many of the evolved, Parascand was not moneyed, not landed, and resentful of Valery and his conservative brethren's desire to protect their wealth at all costs. Parascand had in fact always taken his cues from Linger. "I am all about protecting the delicate throat of the common man."

The urbane, bronzed Parascand was the right vampire for this job. Governments worldwide were publishing non-binding resolutions in support of the principles advocated by Amberly

Foreman, seeking vampire leadership to resolve historical conflicts. Creating proconsul positions was the next step, to provide "advice and consent" to national governments in coordination with the proconsuls from other regions. Parascand loved to attend meetings.

"Bullsheet!" said the vampire protestor. "You rule for yourselves, not for us!"

Parascand played to the rest of the crowd. "Watch your step, my friend. The manure is piling up around you!"

Again there were fewer laughs than such fine repartee warranted.

"I accept this proconsul appointment, graciously and humbly. Today we begin the difficult, but ultimately rewarding, process of joining hands with other countries." The day was muggy, the billowed clouds letting through only the softest light, putting the prettiest face on Paris's monochromatic bone-colored stone. It made Parascand's skin look spray-tanned. "Today we move to end the conflicts draining our time, our treasuries, our lives—"

"Thief!" The crowd was predominantly human, sprinkled with vampires in proportion to the general population. This human had come prepared with his own portable P.A. system, with speakers matching those put in place by the Parisian government, strung along the bridge's two spans. Linger wished he had brought his soundwave jamming technology.

"You are using the same words as Amberly Foreman!" said the man. The crowd screamed her name, their roar sweeping past Linger's hut into the throngs on the island and dopplering across the opposite expanse, terminating as a low moist growl in the crowd pushing onto the bridge from the Left Bank.

"But the words mean something *different* to you!" cried the man. "You are stealing her words! You are stealing our revolution!"

"My good fellow, there is no revolution." It seemed that Parascand still believed he had the crowd on his side. He walked to the end of the small stage, beyond the buffer created by a row of standards bearing the new pan-national proconsul emblem, designed (gratis at the V-8's request) by a prestigious Swiss advertising firm. "The little American girl has merely appointed herself spokesmodel for the *evolution* we have been preparing for centuries."

"*Viva la* Morbius!" someone cried out.

"We are all Placido!" said another.

"This guy sucks!" yelled a man in front of the stage. He splashed Parascand with his water bottle.

The proconsul vampire picked the man up by his throat. A vampire from the crowd flew through the air and slammed onto Parascand's back. Parascand threw the water bottle man off the bridge and clawed at the vampire, dislodging him. A vampire woman leaped on stage and attacked Parascand high while humans dove for his legs.

"Holy shit," said Linger to no one in particular, although the logistics coordinator and sound system vampire acknowledged the sentiment. A ferocious fight was occurring on the stage. "Good thing they don't know his Heel."

The crowd surged forward, buffeting their hut, howling for Amberly, Morbius, revolution. No dissenters were apparent.

P.A.-borne screams pierced the air—human, vampire, Parascand's. A vampire climbed a light pole to show the crowd their proconsul's dismembered arm.

So much for the Heel concept, thought Linger.

Blood was in the air. Humans and vampires alike cavorted on the stage, brandishing parts of Parascand, high-fiving each other, waving *#StakeOurClaim* signs. Not for the reason he had anticipated, and a bit belatedly, Linger disabled smartphone video technology on the Pont Neuf.

The human and she-vamp displayed impulses just shy of decisions. Linger took the initiative and jumped into the crowd-flow, angling his way out, the correct method to survive a riptide. Eventually he made it onto the island, where many were trying to reach the overloaded Pont Neuf.

As Linger hustled in the direction of Notre Dame at the other end of the island, he received many suspicious and downright murderous looks, along with a text message marked urgent from Mao Fe Te who had been overseeing a similar proconsul installment ceremony in Hong Kong.

In fact, urgent texts were flooding in from their Middle East- and Asia-based agents. Linger didn't have the stomach to read them.

JUST VISITING

The house was the surviving remnant of his family, a remnant they had been ready to forsake and sell. The house seemed to resent that; Victor smelled mold, "smelled" in his vampire way, an image of flat waves like low whale calls rising off a glistening membrane. As with any smell, over the course of a few days the constant mold-call became mundane and then inaudible, invisible, forgotten.

Victor read everything he could find on vampire history and vampire current events, and meditated. He had gone back to the Low-T center, but the doors were locked. When Jaelle understood he would never again tap into her drone network, she had shut the program down and returned to Romania.

But meditation was in his soul now, and so he did it on his own, sitting on the floor in the living room on a thin cushion for two hours every day. He thought about nothing, and everything came to him. Everything he had read, everything he had ever done, said or known, like puzzle pieces with flexible contours reassembling into different pictures—predictions of what he expected to occur. He had become a version of his predictive modeling program, the one stolen by the vampire X and christened the XFP.

Two revelations had also come to him, one of them ironically, coincidentally about the XFP system; the other regarding Eugene. Victor had spent the morning devising a stone that would kill them both.

Never had his mind worked like this. Calm, focused, driven.

Meanwhile, his body had degraded. Still vampire-enhanced, but nowhere near what he had been enjoying.

And he didn't miss it. The mind Jaelle had given him—*uncovered* for him, because after all, nothing had been inserted into his skull nor, to the best of his knowledge, removed—was a problem solver. Victor wouldn't trade one neural connection for a buff bod.

This was it, finally. Victor's mind had been cleared of the self-consciousness that had derailed his creativity, and relieved of the addiction to domination that had him always running through a tunnel. The air was fresher now, and the landscape limitless.

Too bad his problems were intractable. Vampires were ascendant—they had basically already won. Jaelle's VR drone interface when harnessed to his Sight was a potent counterforce, perhaps even a path to human salvation. But the cost was too great.

Turning his back on Jaelle's machine wasn't an intellectual, principled decision. He became physically sick even thinking about donning that helmet. It was a form of post-traumatic stress syndrome, he was convinced. He trembled picturing the innocent people on that Mexican beach, ended by his weapon.

Victor imagined Barbara among them and lost it.

In his despair he mourned for Amberly. He had failed his daughter, failed to protect her from one villain (Trubadur Maistru) after another (Eugene). So what if he could slay every other vampire alive. What then? Even if Tripp found a cure for evolved vamps, Victor had arrived at a terrible certainty that the Morbius bloodline was different, and incurable.

Granted, the Morbius curse was transferable, via the bite. All he needed to do was convince Amberly to give up the greatest power the world had ever known.

One she seemed to be enjoying immensely. The crowds she attracted were rockstar-worthy, without planning or publicity, just sudden social media wildfire. Victor watched videos—smartphone slap-togethers and slick productions posted to her YouTube channel. She was incredible.

His daughter was a leader.

Victor needed to stop thinking of Amberly as his daughter. She was the empress of vampires; and Victor suffered from an intense loathing every time he watched her. That was the natural effect of the bloodline that had entwined itself in his fiber.

The garage door started up and a vehicle eased in.

He was an idiot for not changing the code, not quite the brain he believed himself to be.

He was also not quite the ass-kicker he used to be. Victor texted Eugene:

Come to the house! Vamps!

Before he reached the mud room, Victor heard-smelled-sensed her. He was close to fainting as he opened the door and saw Barbara get out of her car. He made it down the two steps and leaned heavily against his Charger's hood. "Barb."

She was bawling as she marched past him. He reached for her.

"I'm only here for Amberly."

He pursued her. "I was afraid you were killed in the drone strike in Mexico."

"Almost was."

"Barb, wait."

He brought her to a stop, assisted by her wracking sobs. She had lost weight. A gash ran into her hairline, closed with butterfly strips. She favored one side.

"Can I hug you?"

She accepted, passively.

"I didn't know where you were, and then I heard you were—that you were gone. I tried to book a flight, but I'm on a no-fly list. I received a call from the State Department telling me not to go down there." The words spilled out while all he wanted to do was hold her and listen to her tell him what happened.

Barbara collected herself. "I'm here to see our daughter."

"She's not here."

"She's upstairs."

Not wanting to upset her, worried she had suffered worse trauma than was apparent, he accompanied her to Amberly's room. They found her sleeping.

Barbara fell on Amberly in a sobbing embrace. Victor got as far as the foot of the bed. He couldn't bring himself any closer. It was all he could do not to step back when Amberly raised her head and showed her fangs.

"I was trying to sleep," she complained.

"Your mother was almost killed. We have been unbelievably worried about you."

"It's okay," Barbara soothed. "You must be exhausted."

"How did you get up here?" said Victor.

"I came in the front door and just walked past you. You were deep in meditation."

"That's not good."

Amberly grinned. "I climbed in through my window."

He looked at her window and was taken back to a time not that long ago, when Amberly was so very much younger.

Amberly went there, too. "I was a lot better at it than you." She pushed her mother's hand away from her neck.

"You're gaunt," said Victor.

"Thank you," said Amberly.

"That's not a compliment," said Victor.

"Sure it is. I'm a woman."

"I would love it if someone called me gaunt," said Barbara.

Amberly's face dissolved from smiling to tearful despair.

Barbara tenderly brushed her hair from her face. "What is it?"

She couldn't speak through the sadness.

"Why do you think?" said Victor. "She's Morbius."

Barbara shot him a reproachful look.

"Why did you have to be a vampire?" Amberly sobbed. "Why didn't you let Tripp cure you? Then this wouldn't have happened to me!"

"Oh, my baby," said Barbara. Amberly swatted away her attempted comfort. "It's okay now, you're home. We'll figure it out."

"You can't figure this out!"

No, you cannot, thought Victor. He remembered his text to Eugene. As quickly and unobtrusively as possible he slipped out his phone and texted:

False alarm, don't come.

His stomach knotted. The internet was thick with vitriol for Eugene. Slayers accused him of being as cowardly as his ancestor, unwilling to sacrifice himself to slay Morbius. Accused him of sleeping with her.

Eugene had posted a video message to the world, vowing to give his own life, to "sui-slay" Morbius.

"I have people *killing* each other because of me," Amberly wailed. "Do you know what that feels like? I want to *help* people. Everything I'm doing is to help us live together, and it all just turns to *shit*."

"Honey, that's not true—"

"They are *killing* each other, Mom. Is that okay with you?"

"Of course not."

"It's my fault! Don't you think that *hurts*? How am I supposed to live with myself?!"

"You just have to, you have to figure it out—"

"Figure it out? That's your advice? Oh, God, you are such a great help. You are *such* a good mother."

Barbara moaned, wounded. Amberly threw herself into her pillow and yanked the covers up. "Get out."

"Honey—"

"I just want to *sleep*. That's why I'm here. Can you at least let me do that?"

"Barb." Victor waited at the door.

She didn't want to leave Amberly's side, wanted to talk to her and try to help. She rested her hand on Amberly's blanketed shoulder for a moment and then hurried past him out of the room.

"We love you, Amberly," Victor managed, with her vampirism cloaked under the blankets.

"No you *don't*. Get *out*."

Barbara was collapsed on the front room couch. Victor put his arm around her and finally she moved into him, leaned on him, and for some time he held her while she wept.

"We've failed her," Barbara whispered. "We failed our daughter. Our only daughter."

"I know."

This wasn't what Barbara wanted to hear. "Are you okay with it?"

"Of course not."

"You don't seem upset. You didn't even *touch* her. She needs to know you love her."

"I do love her. But I have a little problem." Victor worked to temper his tone. "She's a vampire."

"So are you!"

"Yes, but I'm cursed—or blessed, depending on one's perspective, with the ability to see their weak spots. And the desire to exploit them."

"She's your daughter!"

"Barb." She had scooted away from him. "That's why Trubadur Maistru chose Amberly to be Morbius. Because he knows I won't hurt her."

"And you won't."

"Of course not."

"Why are you even thinking of it?"

"I'm not *thinking* about it; I'm trying to *discuss* it." He calmed down. "Trubadur also chose her because of Eugene."

She grabbed a tissue from the end table. "Because he knows Eugene won't slay her."

Victor nodded. "Except this time he's wrong."

"No he's *not*."

"Eugene is insane. How long have I been trying to tell you that?" He was hungry for a *You were right*.

"*You're* wrong. He loves Amberly with everything he's got."

"And that's the way he'll sacrifice himself."

Barbara gaped in horror. Fresh tears rolled. "How can you sit here and say that?"

"I've been doing a lot of thinking—"

"Oh, really."

Victor tightened his lips as much as his fangs allowed and breathed deeply through his nose. He couldn't blame her: she didn't know about his mental improvements. "I know I haven't given you reason to put your faith in me."

"Can I ask you something?" She shifted to face him. "Did you see Darla while I was gone?"

Powerful mental processes did not equate to a truth serum. "No."

She slowly nodded, perhaps believing him.

Victor paused long enough to give the topic respectful closure. "The only way to save Amberly is for her to bite someone."

"Does Amberly understand that?"

"I'm sure Trubadur told her."

"Why does she want to be a vampire?"

"She wants to be Morbius. That's a different thing."

"It's killing her! You saw her up there."

He tried resting his hand on her knee. "I'm worried about you, too."

She let it stay. "I went to that vampire gathering in Cancun to find her. It didn't go well. I was kidnapped by Adamo Abele. To force you to fulfill your promise to kill Amberly."

Victor choked down a retort. He was smart enough to let the criticism slide, but not strong enough to forget about it, and so it added to a pile that would hopefully decompose before the weight demanded relief. "I am very sorry you had to go through that. Did he hurt you?"

"No. And that took some doing. There was more than one vampire—one in particular, actually, who wanted to bite me."

"I can't blame him."

Barbara stared into his soul. "Have you ever bitten Darla?"

"No." Victor had absolutely no doubt that lying was the right answer, and he sold it.

She sagged into the couch. "Why would vampires want her dead? Is it because humans love her?"

"I think it comes down to money. Abele and his crowd have a lot to lose."

They sat quietly.

"Can't Tripp cure her? It worked on you." Barbara was exhausted, Victor felt her slipping toward a breakdown.

"I guess I'm a lower-order vampire."

"I mean it. Why won't it work on her? Why can't he figure it out?"

"He's trying. And then we'd still have to get Amberly to agree to take it."

"Shoot her with a tranquilizer dart," said Barbara.

It had been so long since he was genuinely amused, his smile threatened to jump to laughter.

And then he had a light-bulb of an idea. He needed to go see Tripp.

Barbara's eyes were heavy. She let her head rest on his shoulder, and fell asleep.

Victor tried to meditate, to keep his mind from traveling upstairs. Against his will, rage seeped in, far beyond his normal revulsion for vampires. He wanted to go upstairs and end the Morbius bloodline.

No no no.

He took Barbara's hand from her lap and squeezed it. She squeezed him back and burrowed deeper, drawing her knees up. Victor found comfort there, if not tranquility. He was able to stay put and let the hours tick away. Let his women rest.

Night came. Amberly came downstairs.

She read his face. Did she feel the same hatred for him?

For my Sight. He wasn't his Sight, and she wasn't Morbius. They were each afflicted; he needed to think of these invaders as separate from the hosts.

Barbara startled to her feet. "Are you going out? Are you sure you're ready? You should lay low for a while."

"I actually feel pretty good." Amberly did look refreshed.

"Well I feel awful," said Barbara. "How long will you be out? I'll make sure your sheets are fresh. I'll go shopping. Make a list of what you want. I'd have you text me but I lost my phone."

"Mom, I have to go." Amberly headed for the door.

"No. No, no. You need to stay here." Barbara hurried after her. "Why would you go? Where are you staying?"

"I have so much to accomplish." Amberly looked at her father. "Vampirism isn't a way to impress people and get promoted. Not for me. It's the opportunity to do something wonderful for the world."

Victor wanted to shake her. "Your vampirism is the worst thing that ever happened to this world."

"Victor!" Barbara raised her hand to slap him, then instead maneuvered to keep them separated.

"Because you're selfish." Amberly's face had transformed, beautiful and terrible, the face that captured a billion souls, with something vicious for her father. "We're lifting everyone above that attitude so that we can finally work together."

Victor held her gaze. "I see your Heel."

Amberly trembled, eyes filling with tears. "You are evil." She tore away from Barbara's grasp and left the house. A car waited for her at the curb. She was gone.

Victor held up his hands to preempt Barbara's rage. "I want her to know she's vulnerable, so she takes some precautions."

"That's bullshit." She hovered at the door, clearly considering following Amberly's lead. "You don't say that to your daughter."

I don't believe she'll ever be that again. "Please don't go," he asked her. "Please stay here and rest some more. I need to go see Tripp. Just for a bit. I'll bring dinner back." He didn't dare touch her but managed to get the front door closed and locked. "We can figure this out. Together."

He didn't push for agreement or wait for an argument, grabbing his keys and heading for the Charger.

The Rice campus at night was well-lit and deserted. Fear of sexual assault, fear of the vampire—today's students preferred to have their encounters in structured situations of their choosing. Victor had read that campus alcohol use was in steep decline. It made for an eerie walk from the parking lot to the Longevity Labs.

Landscaping had replaced the drone-demolished front of the building. The Labs' footprint was smaller, its face finer, more glass and lithe steel. There was no receptionist, just a speaker and keypad. Victor thumbed the call button.

"Can I help you?" It was Iulia.

For crying out loud. Is she with him everywhere? "Victor. For Tripp."

No reply. A pause, maybe ten seconds. A buzzer sounded and the door clicked open.

He found them together in a small office. Tripp rose and gave him a hug. "Buddy, how are you? You're looking less *GQ*."

He meant fatter. "Just another of my many manifestations."

"I like it. You look good, honestly."

Victor dipped his head to Iulia. "Your rectal Heel is glowing beautifully tonight."

"Oh come on," Tripp complained.

Iulia collected her e-pad and phone and made for the door. "Exactly the boorish behavior I expected from the vampire everyone hates." She banged against a chair to avoid contact with him.

"I'm sorry, baby," Tripp called after her.

A door slammed down the hall.

"Must you?" said Tripp.

Victor grimaced. "Does she have to follow you *everywhere*?"

Tripp plopped into a chair. "She funds this lab, you dick."

"How?"

"The NIH. She's researching unique vampire immunities that could be adapted for humans."

"How noble. How does she tolerate *your* search for the cure?"

"She doesn't. She wants me to focus on longevity. Her goal is to convince me a cure is unnecessary."

Victor said nothing, eyebrows raised.

"*Another* one of her goals is to get repeatedly in my pants," Tripp defended her motives. "She's always been hot for me. Vampirism just gave her the confidence to pursue it."

"One's passions and motivations can change as a vampire."

"Human or vampire, I know when a chick grooves on me, you jerk. And I have to say, being with a vampire is—"

"That's fine to keep to yourself."

"If you recall," Tripp needled, "I had to listen to your tales of vampire conquest."

"I came to talk about the evolved cure."

Tripp's face clouded. "Nothing good to report."

"Are you truly still interested?"

"*Yes.*" Tripp crossed his arms and scowled. "Where did this calm, thoughtful you come from?"

"You don't like any of my personas, do you?"

"I was kidding." Tripp was wounded. "Maybe I trust our relationship enough to kid you. And tell you the truth."

Victor was brusque. "We don't have time to worry about the state of our relationship."

"Relationships with the people I love are the only reason why I'm fighting for the world."

Victor got to the reason for his visit. "Have you considered analyzing the prophylactic they were using at the Comity Club?"

"Comedy club? I have no idea what you're talking about."

"Comity," Victor enunciated. "On a Galveston oil rig there was a club where vampires and humans could safely interact. Vampires had to receive a shot that supposedly neutralized their ability to pass along their curse."

Intrigued, Tripp searched the internet. "Ah, that's the place that was sabotaged. 'A modern social club for exciting, safe meetings between humans and vampires,'" he quoted. "It says they have clubs due to open soon in Dubai and Rio." He clicked around. “Nothing about the prophylactic. No, wait.” He frowned as he read. “There’s a slayer site accusing the National Institutes of Health of funding the clubs and legitimizing vampirism with their ‘vampire rubber.’” He unleashed a flurry of keystrokes. “I have access to the NIH collaboration network. Let’s see what they’re saying.”

“I can spare you the gossip and misinformation,” said Iulia, in the doorway. “The social clubs are mine, with a few investors. I created the prophylactic.”

Always outsized in his expressions and actions, Tripp shook his head like he had a bee in his ear. “You invented this rubber? Why?”

“To bring us together.”

“You and me?”

Iulia gave him a wan smile. “I was thinking more broadly. But yes.”

Tripp loosened his string tie and pulled his collar down to reveal a number of bite bruises in various stages of healing. “Without this *rubber*, your vampirism is communicable?”

“My curse is the only one that isn’t.” Victor all but called Tripp a fool.

Tripp’s arms hung limp. “Vic, I think you need to excuse us.”

Victor wasn’t leaving until the pot was sufficiently stirred. He addressed Iulia. “This prophylactic worked on evolved vamps, didn’t it?”

Reluctantly, with hatred for him, she nodded.

Tripp’s eyes bulged and his hands flew up as he gaped at Iulia. “That’s what I’ve been *killing* myself for!”

Iulia moved close to Tripp while taking pains to keep her distance from Victor. “Of course I know that. And of course I cannot share it with you.”

“You *have* to.”

“So you can destroy me?”

“Nothing would be destroyed.”

“*Everything*,” said Iulia. “I only was able to create this prophylactic because of the boldness vampirism gave me.”

“You were brilliant before.”

“It’s not the same. It’s the difference between *possessing* intelligence and *using* it. I wouldn’t have had the *idea* much less the bravery to start the social clubs."

"You mean Dikembe Mutombo's gangster hole?" said Victor.

"That was a lesson learned," she snarled at him, but even as a vampire she was too cute and bouncy to menace. "And the beginning of the end of the old guard." She appealed to Tripp. "You *know* I don't approve of what Linger and his government friends are doing. But those days are almost over. With Amberly we have the chance to bring vampires and humans even closer together."

"That will only end badly for humans," said Victor.

Iulia pulled Tripp tight as he struggled with what he was hearing. "You and I are the perfect example. Do you think it can work between us?"

Tripp searched her eyes. "I do."

"And the prophylactic makes it even better."

"It's a vampire Trojan horse," said Victor.

Tripp turned on him. "That's a little hypocritical. Barb seems to groove on you just fine as a vampire."

"I told you," Victor said, enjoying the moment. "I'm one of a kind."

"Well that's for sure."

"She needs to share her research with you."

Iulia gave him her darkest look. "You are evil."

"You have to understand where Vic's coming from," said Tripp. "His daughter—"

"She is the best thing that has ever happened to this world," said Iulia. "You would destroy that?"

Victor focused on Tripp. "We all know where I'm coming from. How about you?"

Tripp appealed to Iulia. "There is *basic* research knowledge to be gained here. And shouldn't we have this option? Shouldn't someone who is a vampire have the choice?"

"Oh, there would be no choice. Sooner or later, it would be forced."

"Vampires control government. Everyone is nuts for Amberly. No one is looking to force a cure."

"A *cure*." Iulia choked on the word. "What do you cure, but a disease?" Tears ran down her cheeks. "Is that what you think I am?"

Victor moved closer to Iulia and whispered, “You should see yourself through my eyes.”

She recoiled. “Get out of my lab!”

“You need to go, bud.” Tripp steered him out of the office. “But thanks a lot for giving us a topic for discussion.”

BUSINESS LUNCH

Trubadur hadn't been in Romania since the Communists ruined it. After centuries of efforts to bring together Slavs, Hungarians, and the original Romanized peoples, Romanians had finally shed ethnic conflict, united in their distrust of their government and one another.

The colossal People's Palace was the perfect emblem of this new Romania: built to last forever by the dictator Ceausescu, rich with potential but empty of the trust necessary to bring Romanians together, untapped, gone to waste.

The perfect home for the world's shadow vampire government.

A guide employed by the mayor's office met Trubadur at a non-public entrance on the behemoth's north side. A pregnant cat slunk away down a corridor lit by bulbs hanging from wiring strung and stapled along the ceiling. The electrical wires branched through transoms above doors leading to large offices and meeting rooms. Some doors were open, revealing imposing desks, tables, ornate lamps and wood-carved chairs. Closed doors were secured by string fastening door to jam by gobs of wax.

In passing Trubadur pulled off the strings.

"Why do you unseal them?" the guide fretted in Romanian. He tried to re-secure a door but the wax crumbled. "Now they will need to inspect every room in this wing for fingerprints and communicable diseases."

"Why?" Trubadur's Romanian was unevolved, peppered with Turkic words which had been cleansed from the language after the Ottomans' fall. He clipped his sentences short to avoid arousing suspicion. Damned to a perpetual Communist hangover, Romanians searched for deeper historical causes of their failures. The Maistru name was synonymous with original sin.

"That is the procedure recommended by the original architects. They have disappeared, but we must assume there was a reason."

"To make Ceausescu happy," said Trubadur. "That was always the reason."

The guide was old enough to have lived through those dark times. He had only scorn for Trubadur—vampire or no, he obviously too young to have earned an opinion. "To make someone else happy, that has always been Romania's destiny." He waved at the stairwell door. "Fifth floor."

"It's a new world of mutual happiness, my friend." Trubadur pulled a wad of lei from his wool trousers. "Goods, services or blood—you should demand fair payment."

With a grunt the elderly man ignored the money and walked away. His voice echoed in the outsized hallway. "If I have to, I'm happy to."

With an eye patch, feeble lighting and a marble uniformity of the steps, he took his time ascending, spitefully "un-sealing" the door to each floor.

On the fifth floor the door was propped open. Joshua Linger waited for him in the hallway. He took in Trubadur's unusual appearance, from the tall hat to the long wool embroidered coat to the high leather boots. "I heard you chuckling on your slow, slow way up. You must be looking forward to this."

"I am so excited to finally meet the great Catalan vampire, José Linaré."

"I go by Joshua Linger. Unlike humans, we have lived our history, and so we are wise enough to eliminate the relics of our past failures." Linger's smile suggested he viewed Trubadur as just such a relic.

The Doyon was in a sport coat and turtleneck. Was he protecting his Heel? Or was it a decoy—not the smartest move, one could survive a slaying attack to the throat, but not comfortably. Trubadur had a hunch that Linger's soft spot was indeed under that ribbed cashmere. His hunches were usually spot-on thanks to his brief time possessing the Sight, even if it never really worked for him like it had for Nadia.

"Humans are doomed to repeat the mistakes of their past," said Trubadur. "Not because they don't know their history, but because they are slaves to their nature. As are we."

Linger shook his head. "Did your tour take you to our operations in the west wing?"

"Why would I want to tour this abomination squatting on the graves of Wallachian neighborhoods?"

Linger smirked. "Wallachia? Maybe you are a slave to your past, Cornelius."

"Trubadur."

Linger grinned. "One can't be considered a slave if one embraces the arrangement, I suppose. Well, Trubadur Maistru, as evidence of our *new* nature, more than 70 countries have contributed staff—we have 500-plus vampires and humans here, coordinating with nearly every national legislature to enable the passage of vampire-friendly laws. *That* is the mark of a people looking to the *future*."

"You can't even keep your V-8 vampires singing from the same hymnal."

"At least you and I are singing the same tune." Linger motioned for them to proceed down the hall. "You are correct, we still have relics within our leadership who have a lot to lose with progress."

"Like Charles Valery and Adamo Abele."

"You took care of Valery, and we handled Abele."

"Victor Thetherson killed Abele."

"You're mistaken. It was a drone strike."

"But not yours."

"Fog of war," said Linger. "Who can say? Our movement has much to gain by claiming credit." The U.S. government had done just that. Yesterday's press release trumpeted Abele's killing as retaliation for the attack on Amberly and the Vampalooza, as well as proof of the government's war against all terrorists, human and vampire alike. "We also have much to gain with Morbius coming to prominence at such a fortuitous time."

Trubadur stopped walking. "It's no coincidence."

"Regardless. The point is that we have the opportunity—"

"I am tired of your lack of respect!" said Trubadur. "I

sacrificed. The greatest sacrifice a man and a father could ever make, to give Morbius to the world. I suffered for centuries, waiting for you and the rest of your selfish, squabbling ilk to figure it out!"

Linger acknowledged Trubadur's accusation with a dip of his head. "Your sacrifice and patience are acknowledged. We thank you for your service."

"My *service*," Trubadur mocked the insufficiency of the word.

"We would also like the opportunity to reward you. For helping us keep sweet young Morbius's eyes on the ultimate prize."

Trubadur cocked his head so that his single eye had full view of the vampire Doyon. He knew how desperately Linger and the V-8 council craved power, and how badly they needed Amberly to achieve it. He was glad they saw him as the kingmaker, the power behind the throne.

"Assuming you still have any sway with her."

"She's practically my daughter."

"I understand she is Victor Thetherson's daughter. It's creepy that you want to father another man's daughter." Linger stroked his chin. "Is there a term for that? Pedopaterphilia?"

"Don't you dare slander my *legacy*." Trubadur's blood-frenzy sprang to his hands, throat, and mind. Centuries of blood-drinking suppression made for an ongoing dam-break of near-psychotic reactions.

Linger remained condescendingly calm. "My apologies. It's just that we rarely see you with her these days."

It was true. Where was Amberly this week? Beijing? God damn that headstrong girl! Trubadur removed his hat and gazed inside. It was hard to see in there with one eye. "She can conduct pep rallies on her own."

"It's more like the Arab Spring." Linger darkened. "Yes, the girl is fulfilling a portion of her legacy, convincing humans to accept us. She drew a crowd of 150,000 in Tokyo. It finally prompted the Japanese government to support our bill of rights. It also resulted in the slaughter of our chosen proconsuls in three countries. She seems to believe in democratic rule. The mob will trample her—and you—with the rest of us."

Trubadur believed he remained inscrutable. Having only one

eye helped. "You would have me do what?"

"Guide. Lead." Linger smirked. "Be a father figure. However you like to think of it." He invited Trubadur into the next room. "And then be rewarded."

Seven vampires waited in a formal salon furnished in early Romanian, the style of a people on the Western edge of the Eastern floor-sitters; there were chairs, but they did not invite, no cushions and no contours. Some vampires stood, some tried to look comfortable on straight-backed, flat-seated wood chairs.

"Everyone," said Linger, "may I introduce the vampire who brought us Morbius—"

"You!" Titathia Babas's nine-year-old girl eyes bulged. "The slayer who aided Morbius during the Transylvania Terror!"

"Tita," Linger warned.

"Guilty as charged," said Trubadur. He stared up at giant, angry Boris Dostonov. "The two of us slayed a lot of vampires back in the day."

"He is proud!" Boris advanced as Trubadur retreated around a skinny high-backed chair.

"That was *before* he became a vampire," Linger clarified.

"Slayed a few more since then," Trubadur corrected him. "*Mostly* unevolved." He bumped into Katanze Utz and snagged his overcoat's embroidery on fishhook fangs. They scuffled until Trubadur was forced to doff the coat, for the moment hung from Katanze's teeth. The little crossbow slung at Trubadur's side was revealed, generating gasps and howls.

"For Christ's sake," said Linger.

"I have no insight on *him*," said Trubadur. "But speaking of 'sight,' I can't say whether this is from my brief time possessing that power or by osmosis while my beloved Nadia wielded it, but I seem to have a sixth sense for your soft spots."

This put pause to the constricting noose of vampires around him.

"Nadia!" Tita hopped onto a chair with Vlad Țepeș' face carved in the teak back. Trubadur realized the room was vampire-themed; made him look again at the painting over the fireplace. It was Mortimer Canterpark. A glamour painting in Trubadur's estimation. "Nadia was his Morbius bitch!" Tita screeched. "She pointed out our Achilles' heels and he pulled the trigger!"

"Now he has his new pretender to the throne of Morbius," said Ari Ben-Begin.

"That little bitch Amberly," growled Boris.

Trubadur maintained his calm. He nodded at Dostonov's midsection, a little below eye level. "Liver, no?"

Boris roared and turned sideways. "For me to know!"

"She *is* Morbius," Tita insisted. "Morbius is a trick from God to destroy us!"

"Everyone," said Linger. "Call Amberly what you will. But there is no disputing the fact she is a vampire loved by humans. And so we have much to gain by capitalizing on her gift."

"Which means working through me," said Trubadur.

"I want to party with that girl," said Kelly Kale. She had risen through the ranks quickly. One couldn't rise as Kelly had—coming to Australia as an exiled British convict and then in 230 short years becoming the most powerful vampire on the continent—living to party. But that seemed to be the case.

"Blond bimbos who don't know enough not to consort with someone who would lead a *democratic* uprising to overthrow us," said Mao Fe Te, turning his back on Kelly, "must stay quiet."

"I must take a hammer to your ugly head, mate!" Kelly had to be restrained. "When I get through with you—"

"He'll look like this guy." Trubadur pointed at Katanze, who had a clump of red-and-black thread stuck between his protruding snaggle teeth.

"How dare you insult one of the eight remaining rulers of the world?" thundered Moanmar Saladat.

For Trubadur, this vampire in his flowing robes and headdress was every Turk who had tried and failed to subjugate the Wallachian people. "You'll be fortunate if you're allowed to rule whatever desert shithole you call home."

Now Ari Ben-Begin's blood was way up. "The *real* Morbius will have a special place in his chamber of horrors for you, pretender."

Just another Turk in Trubadur's eyes. "Morbius is always female, you idiot. Don't sell your camel, that's my advice to you."

“Oh Lord,” said Linger.

“Knock-knock,” announced a man in bellhop uniform, entering the parlor. “Lunch is here.”

“Not now!” said Ari.

The cluster of humans shuffling into the room hit the brakes, bumping into each other. Dressed in white tunics and pajama pants, fear all over their faces, the first through the door shoved the trailers to compel them to reverse course.

“Please come in,” said Linger. “We could use something to take the edge off.”

The humans, eight of them, pushed, shoved and jockeyed to be furthest from the vampires. The bellhop gave a sharp command in Romanian and they stood still. He did a quick headcount. “Please accept my apology,” he stammered. “I didn’t bring enough for everyone.”

Moanmar Saladat was apoplectic. “Linger! You expect us to break bread with this apostate?”

One of the humans fainted. The bellhop waved smelling salts under his nose.

“So much for Turkish hospitality,” said Trubadur.

Titathia walked angrily to the humans, selected a tall towheaded young man, waited for the bellhop to cut him from the herd, and led him to the carved Țepeș chair. The young man appeared relieved to have drawn the cute little girl. How much could she drink?

“We will eat *you*, traitor,” Tita told Trubadur. She jumped onto the back of the chair, yanked her lunch’s head back and tore into his throat, chomped it like a cob of corn. Blood and gore flew.

“That’s enough from all of you,” said Linger. “Trubadur is our guest. He is guardian to Morbius. I brought him here to coordinate our approach.”

“And isn’t our approach to *lead*?” Mao drooled at the sight and sound of Tita’s feeding. “This Morbius, she *empowers* the people.” Inwardly curved teeth, heavy accent, mouthful of saliva, all combined to make him almost unintelligible. “A well-run state requires all power to rest with the *leaders*.”

“Why do we even debate approaches?” Ari’s hands rhythmically clenched as if milking a cow. He was somewhat distracted by lunch cooling their heels. “We have no proof she is

Morbius."

"There is no *approach*," said Trubadur. "And there is no debate. Amberly will follow the path destiny has already paved." He plucked his coat off the floor and made for the door. The humans shuffled as one away from him, herding themselves into a corner. "And I will be at her side, enjoying every moment. It remains to be seen what role you will play." He tipped his tall hat to Linger "I stand ready to receive your supplications."

His guide waited down the hall at the stairwell exit, smoking. Stomach growling, Trubadur hurried away from the sounds of banquet-style feeding. Kelly Kale's voice caught him. "Maistru!"

The guide paused in mid-drag, unable to decide which vampire better deserved his gaping stare: the root of all Romanian evil or the blond bombshell Aussie vampire. Trubadur left him coughing out a mouthful of smoke.

"A moment for a vampire bimbo?" Kelly interlaced her fingers with his and led him down the hall and into the balcony seating of a huge concert hall with a magnificent chandelier and red velvet chairs and walls. She steered him to lean on the back of a seat and stood between his legs.

Trubadur's heart accelerated. "You're missing lunch."

"I'll clean up the leftovers. Boris never finishes his meal. Nervous stomach." She stroked his cheek; Tru couldn't say what sort of appetite he was dealing with.

"Believe it or not," said Kelly, "Linger isn't the only one in our group who believes that Amberly is Morbius. And understands her true power."

"Believe it or not, I don't really care."

"Because Morbius is going to do her thing, with or without the Doyon and his fabled Group of 8, hm?" She lifted her hair as if to pin it up, then let it fall gloriously about her shoulders. Kelly Kale smelled divine, intoxicating. "I believe we need Morbius. I believe that without her, we're through."

"Of course. It is prophesied."

"Not in the Doyon's eyes." She had a restless body, sliding around the inside of his legs. "He believes Amberly has fulfilled her purpose. He believes that at this point, she serves us best as a martyr."

He gripped her arms. "Even if he was insane enough to try,

she's Morbius! She can't be killed."

Kelly made no effort to break his grip. "She can be slain, by sacrifice. Few of us are as old as you, mate, but we all know the legend. Of course Linger saw Abele fail, so he doesn't have complete faith she can be eliminated. But he's betting that Claudius can make her close enough."

"Claudius." Trubadur's chin sagged. "I should have had Eugene slay him."

Kelly laughed. "Your boy-toy slayer would have been pulled to pieces."

She was right. Claudius had holed up for centuries in a cave on Crete like some sort of pouting minotaur, receiving sacrificial homages from around the world. Trubadur believed it was the impending appearance of Morbius that had brought him into the light.

There was a tickling at his wounded eye. Kelly was fiddling with his patch.

"Is there a hole?" Her finger probed under the leather and jabbed the tender healing orb.

"Ahg!" Trubadur batted away her hand and it went to his crotch. She nibbled at his Adam's apple. Her lips were silky soft, warm and moist.

"Let's find a spare room, love." She brought his hand to her breast and applied pressure to his crotch. "We have a few hundred here to choose from. Maybe we'll find some old Communist bones to fuck amongst." Her body was moving under his hand, against his stomach and thighs. "Would that turn you on?"

It would. But Trubadur had what might or might not be an irrational fear of sex. He broke it off. "It's the monk's life for me, I'm afraid."

Kelly moved hard into him; he thought he was about to have his monastic vow broken. "Then what do you say we take your guide back to my place and drink him like a fine wine? We can talk about what to do about Claudius."

He kissed her. "It's a date."

LITTLE RED RIDING HOOD

Midnight as Victor tucked himself in. The air conditioning was off; he was naturally cold enough as it was—a source of friction with Barbara, who was hot-blooded. Now he was clammy under the covers, fully clothed, sweating but still too cold-blooded to remove the blanket.

Plus, he needed to hide the gun.

Post on *StakeOurClaim.com*
by Amberly Foreman
tags: XFP, drones, unity

Hi everyone! What a journey we are on together! I am so pleased with how far we've come, and excited about what awaits us.

Across the world, countries have passed laws prohibiting discrimination against vampires—including staking! Can you believe staking was ever considered okay? What century is this? All I can say is, it's about time!

At the same time, we the people have rejected attempts by certain power-hungry vampires to take advantage of the situation. Yes, we need vampires in positions of authority—it's the only way we're going to end all the hatred and war ripping our beautiful world apart! But a small group of vampires don't get to decide who has that authority—we the people do! I'm excited to lead that democratic effort to elect our leaders of tomorrow!

Unfortunately, those power-mad vampires are harming our chance at harmony by using drone strikes against citizens. Now it's true that the citizens they're shooting are in favor of slaying vampires. That's awful!! But that doesn't give our government the right to kill them!

Listen to this, I have learned their awful secret: The government has a backdoor into the Xtreme Feedback Predictor system, the "XFP" software used by some of the world's biggest businesses and government departments. Vampires in the NSA are using the XFP to predict the movements and location of anti-vampire people across the U.S. and the world.

If you are one of the companies or government departments using the XFP, for the safety of your employees you must disable and uninstall that software! Only then can we restore the privacy we all have the right to expect.

That's a good first step. But we all need to demand that our government stops using lethal force against us! As a symbolic protest, a twist on the classic sit-in, I will be checking out. Please understand that it wounds me deeply to step away from the Stake Our Claim movement at such a crucial moment in our transformation. But it's necessary. Starting today, I am withdrawing from public life.

I will not return until our government renounces this violence!

It will also be good to get away from that crazy Trubadur Maistru or Colonel Sanders or whatever he's calling himself these days. I'll hate him forever for kidnapping me. I'm glad it's true that you can always go home again!

In the meantime, keep up the great revolution! I love you all!

Tears dribbled down Eugene's cheeks as he drove to his final destination. The tears interfered with his driving. Anticipating this emotional reaction and unable to afford any such physical handicaps, he had pre-dehydrated himself. His tears should run dry by the time he was ready to sui-slay Amberly.

The Morbius. The vampire messiah, the root of all evil. His destiny, the ultimate fate and terminus of the Maistru bloodline—to end the Morbius curse. Eugene looked at the double stake lying in the passenger seat. If only it wasn't Amberly's breast he needed to pierce.

Four hundred years ago Eugene's ancestor, Trubadur Maistru, had failed this duty. Spectacularly. Look where that had led. Vampires on the cusp of world domination, humans on the brink of extermination. Trubadur Maistru himself the second-most-evil being on the planet.

Second after Amberly.

His beloved.

The last tears plopped onto the front of his thin Hanes t-shirt. Threadbare cotton that would part like spaghetti strands before the point of the stake.

Eugene had never been so scared, and so committed. The world hung in the balance.

Blog Post on NewSucks.com

We'll begin this post by saying: We're pro-world peace!

We've had nefarious folks reading between the lines of previous posts and alleging an anti-vampire slant, and from there drawing the ergo-ipso-facto conclusion we hate peace. Wrong! You'll never find a blog (or the bloggers behind it) more committed to peace. Or to keeping the meat sacks they reside in puncture-free.

Big event just announced this morning: a Peoplooza scheduled for the National Mall in D.C. next week. Anonymous organizers bill it "Freedom's Last Stand." What next, a graphic of Little Big Horn as their official emblem? The federal government has pre-labeled it a terrorist training camp and has warned that its armed sky-eyes will be hovering. And so, hesitant to be branded anti-peace (by a predator missile), we the media dedicated to frontline coverage of these turbulent vampire times, are seriously debating skipping it.

Meanwhile, rumor has it Amberly Foreman and her team have accomplished something fantastic in their quest to end war. Some are speculating on a Russian pull-back from the Ukraine. Others are claiming to know that it's something much bigger: an Arab-Israeli peace agreement. If true, and assuming it's more convincing and eternal than even the 1970s Camp David accord between Egypt and Israel, well, that's peace we can all applaud.

In all seriousness: That's a vampire we can get behind.

Eugene parked and walked the last block. He waved to a neighbor who had surely seen it all in this house, as his legs carried him to the backyard. Like a pirate Eugene clenched the stake in his teeth and climbed the ivy-covered trellis. He gagged and spit out the stake and climbed down to retrieve it. Like a contestant on a Nickelodeon gameshow he pinned the stake under his chin and resumed climbing to the bedroom window.

Blog Post on politicsasunusual.com

Well, the days of crony politics are over. One heard the death knell in the screams of four of the vampires appointed to the newly-created inter-national policy coordinator positions. A lucky few heard that fatal tolling and gracefully withdrew of their own volition.

Now the people will decide. A new voting app has been downloaded 500 million times and rapidly counting. Rumor has it the app's inaugural use will be voting for Amberly Foreman as consul.

"Consul" is a title that harks back to the more or less democratic days of Rome when two of them were elected to oversee the republic. The consuls would govern in alternating months. So far there has been no discussion of Amberly Foreman sharing power.

Sources tell us the inter-national vampire policy coordinator roles—"proconsuls"—will now also be elected, rather than appointed.

This system has been created to facilitate vampire guarantees of world peace. We understand each nation will elect vampires to various strategic positions, "praetors" responsible for actual enforcement, to fulfill the will of the people.

We are weary of constant warfare! the people have cried. Vampires present a way forward. They have promised not to meddle in national affairs, beyond keeping us from being at each other's throats.

The rise to power of the vampires has been lightning fast. This political blitzkrieg would not have occurred without Amberly Foreman. She has enraptured the world, a vampire paradoxically promising a bloodless revolution.

She has also just announced she is temporarily withdrawing from the movement. Does the vampire juggernaut have enough momentum now to carry on without her?

A figure at the window. Victor had made it easy on his intruder, the window ajar. It slid open and the unlawful entrant crept to his bedside.

Victor clicked on Amberly's lamp. "Here to finish me off?"

"Ahg!" Eugene shook the double-pointed stake at the heavens, cursing the fates, the moment, Victor.

"A happy ending for Mr. Victor?" said Victor.

"The Sight picked the perfect dufus," Eugene raged. "You couldn't get laid and die if your daughter's life depended on it! Which it did!"

"You're the reason she's Morbius!" Victor roared. "Your insane ancestor picked Amberly because he knew you wouldn't slay her!"

"But I'm going to!"

"Oh no you're not." Victor couldn't remember if this was the type of pistol that needed to be cocked. "I knew you'd figure out

Amberly was home."

Eugene clapped the knuckles that gripped the stake to his forehead. "That was *your* post on Stake Our Claim, pretending to be Amberly! I knew it sucked too badly to be hers!"

"I wrote it at your level."

"You lured me here to kill you," said Eugene.

"To kill *you*."

"You want me to sui-slay the both of us."

Victor seethed. "No, I want to prevent you from doing that to Amberly."

"It is my destiny."

"There's a cure on the way," said Victor. "They had a breakthrough."

"If only that was the way the Morbius curse is fated to meet its end."

"We make our own fate, you idiot."

"If I show up at Amberly's real bedside with this stake, and it turns out she's cured, great. The two of us will live happily ever after."

"That's not on the list of possible futures," said Victor.

"We make our own futures."

Victor clicked off the safety. "Promise that you won't hurt Amberly."

Eugene shook his head without taking his eyes off Victor. "Sorry. That mistake has been made once. I won't let the Maistru name down again."

Victor whipped off the blanket. The pistol was leveled at Eugene. "I was hoping you'd say that."

Eugene laughed. "What vampire has to use a gun? You are the worst vampire ever."

The slayer's smug face caused Victor's finger to squeeze the trigger, just shy of firing. "Only because I can't stand the thought of touching you."

Eugene shuddered. "Good, because the thought of your breath on my neck gives me the willies." He pointed the stake at Victor. "Morbius is the anti-Christ. Do you think the anti-Christ can be disabled with a hypodermic vial of cure juice? Do you?!" He became emotional. "I love Amberly!"

"Shut up!"

"I love her," Eugene screamed. "And I'm going to push this stake into both of our breasts!"

The pistol bucked in Victor's hand as if it was firing. "Shut your mouth, or I'll shut it for you!"

"Any time, fat boy!"

"Ahg!" Victor leaped out of bed and flung the gun away and tackled Eugene. They grappled on the floor, rolling about, snarling and grunting. Victor strained for Eugene's throat while trying to block his head punches. Eugene somehow got his feet in Victor's gut and sent him flying upside down and slamming into the wall. Victor landed on his head and Eugene grabbed the chair from Amberly's vanity and raised it over his head.

"No!" said Barbara charging into the room. "What are you two *doing*?"

Eugene returned the chair to the vanity. "Your ex is a putz."

Victor sat on the floor, head swimming. "He's lucky I traded brawn for brains, or you would have found him dead and dry."

"Someone needs to tell your putz ex he got screwed on that trade."

"That's enough," said Barbara.

Eugene bowed to her. "I'm very glad to see you not undead, Miz T. I knew I shouldn't have left you with that vampire."

"You what?" said Victor. "You left her with a *vampire*?"

"It wasn't Eugene's fault at all," said Barbara.

"If fatboy had told me you were in trouble, I would have come back and rescued you."

"Thank you, Eugene. I know you would have."

"Weasel dick," Victor steamed. "Tell Miz T what you plan to do to Amberly."

Eugene retrieved the double-pointed stake. "Suicide-slay her."

"No you are not."

"I'm sorry." Eugene looked Barbara in the eye. "I have to."

"There's a gun on the bed," said Victor. "Let's shoot him together."

Barbara put her hands on Eugene's cheeks. "Let's find Amberly together. She needs our help."

Eugene took Barbara's shoulders. His eyes reddened, tear ducts firing blanks. "There is only one way we can help her now."

Barbara squeezed his cheeks. "No."

Victor had the pistol. "Look out, Barb."

She shook her head. "We're not killing each other. Eugene, go. We love you. Amberly loves you, and you love her. We'll find a way." She stayed between the gun and Eugene as he crawled out the window. "I trust you."

Eugene was gone. Barbara turned back to Victor. He put the pistol on safety and was trying to figure out how to unload it.

"Biggest mistake of our lives, Barb."

Blog Post on StakeOurClaim.com

Hi everyone! Amberly Foreman here—the real Amberly this time ☺! Sorry for the confusion. While I agree with most of what our "guest" blogger said in the post from earlier today, that wasn't me!!

And I'm not going anywhere!! I wouldn't leave you all, not at such an important time for people and vampires all over the world.

We have some big votes coming up! Hopefully you've all downloaded your voting app by now. If not, what are you waiting for?!

These will be the most important elections of our lives. The first vote will happen at the rally in D.C. this weekend. I'm looking forward to seeing everyone—please make the trip if you can! This is a crucial moment to show our solidarity and love for each other.

See you soon!

GAINFUL EMPLOYMENT

In the temPermanent conference room, Larry, Florence and David came together. This was the first time all three unemployed accountants were in the temp agency office together.

"Brings back memories at Texahoma, doesn't it?" said David.

Florence glared at him. "Working for Vic? Is that what you want to remember, you dumb lump?"

When David slumped, his hunchback really popped. "I was thinking about the happy hours."

Florence shook her head. "You really couldn't afford to lose your looks."

Larry evaluated Florence with extreme circumspection. He had seen a picture of her as a young woman back when Victor's infatuation was fixed, before her disastrous years as a New Zealand sheep rancher's wife. Larry believed he had seen goodness in young Flo's face.

Was that why he was willing to help her steal Victor's curse? Because he trusted some dried-out seed of goodness dormant deep beneath her awful crust to germinate and bring beauty to the world?

Not really. Larry just hated Victor so. The Thethersons were losers. Larry couldn't explain why he had humiliated himself and the Cocachello family by taking a job under Vic. And how could Victor have been a manager in the first place? His boss Jay Hansen, God rest his soul, never seemed able to figure that out. The fates had tormented them both with the loser.

And then the fates had granted Victor this power, this unearned power of the vampire. The cave in Romania made it clear Victor was the source of the vampire evil taking over the world, and that stopping him was their only hope.

And he bit my mother!

Florence could become Satan's second coming and Larry wouldn't regret helping her at Victor's expense.

Florence had developed a facial tic, jutting her jaw and sliding it back and forth. She paced and worked her jaw, sinew quivering in her turkey neck. "What a got-damn pair you two must have been in Rome."

"Romania," David corrected.

"That's right." Larry wanted to pat David on the head, so proud of him. "Different than Rome."

"I know that," Flo snarled. "So is that why you dragged me in here? To see pictures of the two of you holding hands in front of the Vat—, the, uh …."

Larry was sure she was about to say *Vatican*. "Dracula's castle?" he offered. "Sort of." He snapped his fingers until David gave up his phone. He called up the photo she needed to see.

Tap-tap at the door. The temPermanent accounting placement manager poked her head in. "Good morning. How are my favorite accountants doing this morning?"

"Good," said David.

"Good," said the tP manager. "Lots of exciting opportunities out there."

"So excite me already and find me a got-damn job," said Florence.

"Well, I want to," said the placement manager. "I would love to see you permanently placed." She crossed her arms. "But it's a partnership. This time in our office is meant for you to bolster your marketing potential. Have you all spent time today updating your LinkedIn profile?"

"My what?" said Florence.

"Or filling in the white spaces on your resume to complete a colorful picture?"

"I'm going to sue your racist ass if you don't get me a job," said Florence.

The placement manager was black. "I hope you're not saying I'm discriminating against you because you're white."

"Because I'm a vampire, dipshit."

The temp manager grew agitated. “Are you equating being a vampire to being black?”

“I’m equating being a vampire to being able-bodied amongst the handicapped. And to being fucking *thirsty*.”

The temp lady nodded, and left the room.

“I’m not a vampire,” David called after her.

“Believe me, she knows.” Florence scowled at Larry trying to show her a picture on David’s phone. “Shit. I thought you might have forgotten about your butt-buddy travel slideshow.”

“Here.” David took back his phone, established a connection to the temp agency’s wi-fi, and brought the picture up on the room’s projector screen:

David in the Romanian cave smiling and making the peace sign.

“Our little spelunker,” said Florence. “You have the hunchback for it.”

“Check out the painting,” said Larry.

On the cave wall behind David painted in cool blue was a scene with two vampires. One grinning in triumph, blood dripping from its fangs, sporting a glowing, all-seeing eye. The other with a sad face and bleeding neck, the ghost of a now-lost third eye faintly visible on its forehead.

Florence pointed at the lower right corner of David’s picture. “Is that a snake?”

“Yes,” said David. “That was its tail. The rest of him was a lion and a goat. It wasn’t as scary as it sounds.” The color left his face. “Actually it was. But it was nice to me.”

“What’s that say?” Florence peered at faint blue words on the cave wall over David’s shoulder. “Enlarge and enhance upper left quadrant.”

David zoomed on his phone with thumb and finger. “I can enlarge but I can’t enhance.”

Florence sounded out the words. “Munus studiose tuenda?”

“It’s Latin,” said Larry. “It means, ‘Protect your presents because others will try to steal them.’”

“Scroll down,” said Florence. Scrawled in yellowy-red like a naughty child’s crayon on the wall was the translation in English. “Jealously guard the gift,” Florence read with a cackle. “Your new snake-lion-goat friend realized he better not take any chances on the translation with you numbnuts."

"The cave showed us that Vic is the source of all evil," said Larry.

"Is he now," said Florence.

"The only way to stop him is for you to bite him."

"Amen to that," said Florence.

"But then," David was troubled, "you have to use the, the Eye thing, to find the Achilles' heels of—"

"Got it covered," Florence snapped at him.

"—the *bad* vampires," David finished weakly.

Florence worked her jaw, tongue pushing against wrinkled lips. "Now we have to figure out how to get my fangs in Victor's neck."

"I could pop him with a trank dart," said Larry. "I could dial in the dosage so that he'll be awake, but not able to move."

Florence scowled. "You'll probably kill him before I can bite him."

"You should do it while he's meditating," said David.

"'You should bite him while he's taking a dump,'" Florence mimicked him in a dunce voice.

David frowned at the slight. "At the Low-T center. Dr. Linciome says Vic loves it. He said it improved Vic's brain. He wants me to do it, too."

"What are you babbling about?" said Florence.

"Doesn't surprise me that Vic's got low T," said Larry.

"He doesn't," said David. "Well maybe. I don't know. But there's a meditation tank and they hook up his brain to some kind of machine. Dr. Linciome is doing it too, as part of his rehab. He says it's amazing. I want to do it. For my brain."

"Good for you," Florence mocked. "I don't give a rat's rotten ass about you. When does Vic go there?"

"I don't know. Dr. Linciome says he's not sure how long the meditation tank will be there, so I should get in as soon as possible."

Florence yanked open the conference room door and yelled, "Wendy, get in here!"

Wendy the temPermanent accounting placement manager peeked over her computer, locked eyes with Florence, took a deep breath and small steps and joined them. "What can I do for you?"

"Get hunchback or weasel face a job at some Low-T center."

"It's a yoga studio, too," said David. "They used to have tan—"

"I don't give a good got-damn," said Florence.

"Well," Wendy hedged. "I'll have to check to see if they're a client."

"Did I ask you to *check* anything?" said Florence. "I told you to *do* it. I don't care if it's cleaning the shitter. You get one of these two douches a job there. Today." She took a handful of Wendy's suit jacket. "Or I will fucking eat you."

Looking miserable, not even bothering to straighten her jacket, Wendy surveyed her candidates. "I'll probably have better luck with the hunchback."

"David," said David. He asked Florence, "Do you want me to get you in the meditation tank, too?"

Florence glared at him.

"She wants you to tell her when Vic comes in," Larry explained to David. "Excuse me," he called to Wendy who was hurrying back to her desk. "See if that Low-T place has any accounting jobs."

It would be nice to get a discount.

LAYING DOWN THE LAW

In our underground bunker of sorts, Trubadur and I can't hear the noise of the hundreds of thousands of people down the street on the National Mall, waiting for me to speak to them.

"How can this be the National Aquarium?" asks Trubadur.

"It's such an awful aquarium, I knew we could talk quietly here." It's subterranean, on a side street not too far from the Capitol, gloomy like a cave, with run-of-the-mill tropical fish looking miserable behind thick old Plexiglas. We occasionally come across another person. The place is such a dark labyrinth that we can have a private talk.

"Closing this fish hole can be your first act as consul." Trubadur's eye has mostly healed, his new eye both whiter and a more intense auburn than the other. And maybe a little bigger? He is tall and broad-shouldered with beautiful shoulder-length hair. This is what Eugene could look like as a vampire.

Tru has the look. But he doesn't get it.

"I'm not a ruler. I won't be making laws. I'm here to end war." I give him a smile. "Don't you think that's enough?"

"Of course." Tru leans against one of the fat claustrophobia-contributing pillars. "I think about how life could have been back in Romania when I was young. If we didn't have to worry about the machinations of the emperor in Vienna and every power-hungry Magyar noble. The constant Slav invasions. The fucking Ottomans." He dazzles me with a smile. "What you're talking about is a great start. But once we have people feeling safe, they will look to us for guidance."

I spread my arms and deliver one of my favorite lines. "Be fruitful and multiply."

"Ha. That's good. But throughout history when opportunities are missed—"

"Trubadur. Honey. *This* is the opportunity. Not for *me*; for everyone. Human and vampire. For the South Koreans not to live in fear of the North. For the Ukrainians not to live in fear of the Russians. For *everyone* in the Middle East not to arm themselves against their neighbors or their brothers who follow different versions of Islam."

"My you've boned up."

I hear a patronizing tone.

"And all those peacemaking efforts are a blessing," says Tru. "But then we—"

"We."

"—we need to plan our next—"

"Our."

"Hmm?" says Tru.

"You use 'we' and 'our' a lot."

"Of course."

"Of course? Why?"

"We're a team, father and daughter—"

"I have a father."

"Ha! You know what I mean."

I shake my head.

"Partners then. You're the beautiful face for the movement—"

"Figurehead, you mean?"

"Not at all." He takes my hand. "You are Morbius, my love. The one and only. But you're 17 years old. You haven't seen what I have."

"How much suffering do I need to see to know ending war is the greatest gift the world can receive?"

"The fun doesn't end after Christmas morning," says Trubadur with all the passion that runs in the family. I'm a fan of that kind of intensity, believe me. But he's no Eugene. There's a touch of crazy in Trubadur's eyes. "It's how you *use* your gifts."

"I like your analogy. It will be up to the *people* to decide how to use my gift."

Behind Trubadur the cutest clown fish stares at us through the glass, big eyes and a little smile on his fish lips.

"It's *your* gift," says Tru. "The gift *I* gave you. I picked you for this, Amberly, so we could lead together."

"And I want you involved. Run for one of the proconsul positions. Eastern Europe maybe?"

"I won't be appointed into some lesser role—"

"Elected, not appointed."

"God *damn* it." Tru flings the nearest crowd-control stanchion against the aquarium glass. The clown fish puffs in fear. I've heard that shortens their lives. "You're not listening to me!"

"I hear you fine." An aquarium attendant comes hustling around the corner. He gets a look at Trubadur in full vampire mode and leaves us.

"You need me, Amberly. You have no idea. You aren't safe—you are destroying plans laid down for centuries by incredibly powerful vampires."

"I'm aware. I've spent the past month meeting with vampires around the world, getting ready for this day. All of them are aware they're risking their lives to join my movement."

In Romania, behind the V-8's back I met with the team coordinating anti-discrimination laws across the world. (The *V-8*! How hilarious is that? At least there actually are eight of them now.) In Cairo I had the pleasure to meet the special forces teams who will be "convincing" the Middle East it's time for peace.

Tears fall down my cheeks thinking about their bravery. "I know all about the vampires who hate what I stand for."

"Linger will destroy you unless he believes you and I are together."

The power lust in his eyes—both of them, old and new—it sickens me. "Why wouldn't we be together? Why wouldn't you support me?"

"I *created* you, you dumb little—"

"Bitch?"

Blood travels up and down his face. I can hear it and for a moment I want it, I want to bite him and drink him to death. But of course that's not a great idea.

Trubadur picks up the stanchion he threw, still hooked to velvet ropes. I think he's going to put it back, but then he swings it like a lumberjack against the aquarium. Fortunately, that Plexiglas is more durable than the stanchion—the disk base clanks to the floor, leaving Tru holding the metal tube. He throws it aside with an anguished roar.

"I love you. You know that." His voice is low and husky. "But if you're not with me, I can't promise anything."

I check my phone's crowd cam, looking out from the stage I'll soon be standing on, the exact spot where Martin Luther King addressed a nation desperate for peace.

MLK would be proud of me.

It's time for me to go.

"I appreciate the gift you gave me, Tru. Now it's time for me to use it the way it was intended. I hope you'll consider being a candidate for proconsul or one of the national praetor positions."

He stares at the floor, hands clenched. "Claudius will come for you."

A shiver prickles my back. I've heard about him. "Then I only hope I can accomplish my destiny first."

A couple steps and I'm around the pillar, around the next corner and away from him.

Trubadur's howl reaches me at the service elevator.

"I never should have picked you!"

Iulia walked out of a Caribou Coffee on the edge of the National Mall. Squeezed into a rowdy, partying sea of humanity. *Humanity*: she included vampires in that term, the same way she considered women part of mankind. Two very different species, one often at the other's throat, dynamic and thrilling as a team.

"I'll send you the updated business plan tomorrow," she said in passable Greek, in parting to the handsome venture capitalist being carried in a different direction by the crowd. He would be investing in her Comity Club on Cyprus, modeled after her first disastrous but ultimately successful club in the old Galveston Channel oil rig.

Iulia stepped into the street and felt the pull immediately. *Amberly*. Iulia felt her, in her heart and in her gut, soothing and intoxicating all at once. Everyone felt it, Iulia saw this in vampire and human faces alike; a need to be close to Amberly.

And an excitement for the future. *That* most of all. Iulia had always been motivated to learn, to discover, to create. But an aching loneliness had always occupied a significant corner of her mind. If she had happened to enter that corner, gray and stretching to the end of her time, she would fall into despair, sometimes for days.

She wasn't alone; this lack of hope suffused her generation. They recognized it in each other, in Bucharest, in Beijing, in Houston. Desperation for meaning and purpose.

And look how their faces had changed! The beauty Iulia saw now in the women and men embracing and singing and craning for a view of the stage where Amberly would address them, it moved her. She met the smiling, open face of a young human woman in a wheelchair and gave her a hug. For Iulia and those around them, this symbolized everything Amberly had given them.

"Would you like me to help you get closer to the stage?"

The young woman almost demurred, then grinned. "Sure."

"Let's do it."

The sea of humanity (broadly speaking, of course!) parted for the wheelchair and they cruised right to the very front. Iulia felt a tinge of guilt, then decided that any other able-bodied person could have done the same if they had only reached out to this sweet girl. Her next thought was that she should take her handicapped mother more places.

In passing they received a good look at the Peoplooza.

Consumed by the Rally, the Peoplooza was nothing but a small irritant whose dreams of accretion would surely be frustrated. Perhaps 500 humans (containing very little humanity!) huddled together holding signs:

Vampires Are Not Human!

The Stakes Have Never Been Higher!

Cure What Ails Us!

Their chants were swamped by the volume of the surrounding hundreds of thousands. The 'Ploozers looked lost and worried. Skirmishes occurred on their borders, but otherwise they were ignored, tolerated, an anachronism providing dark amusement for the partying masses.

U2 was doing a set. How long since they had been a warm-up? That would be before many here were born. This delirious mob was young, few north of 40 years old. This was a generational movement. Iulia wished she could have persuaded Tripp to come.

Tripp, Tripp, what an incredible, edible man! Iulia had been nuts for him from the start, their first genetics class together at Rice. He was too much for her then, so quick-witted and effortlessly confident. She had convinced herself she hated him, him and his type.

But of course there was no Tripp type. He was an original. Iulia loved the way his limbs joined his body, his jaw, his silly Western accent and clothes. This she could admit only after becoming a vampire. The "curse," as the Peoplooza people would call it, had relaxed her. It had opened her eyes, or rather turned them away from her constant self-examination. When she was finally able to gaze upon this wild, passionate man, Iulia knew she had loved him from the first.

And Tripp had finally been allowed to see all of her. The day she realized he loved her, too—Iulia became short of breath remembering the feeling. It was a dream come true.

One more dream granted by vampirism.

And all the proof she needed to know that bringing vampires and humans together was her calling. Amberly would open eyes, and Iulia would give them gathering places to see each other. To touch each other, in the intensely transcendent way humans and vampires connected.

U2 was done. Iulia and her handicap sticker named Janice were below the stage runway projecting from the rotunda stairs into the crowd. People hugged the two of them and hugged each other. Bono's last words couldn't be heard for the deafening roar as Amberly appeared.

She rose upon a circular dais—had they bored into and hollowed out the rotunda steps? In a tailored blue metallic jumpsuit, Amberly stood as goddess on a pedestal. She thrust her hands and raised her face to the sky, and everyone howled with her.

"Feel it!" Amberly screamed, and the world screamed with her.

A tight formation of menacing drones flew 20 feet above her head and continued over the crowd. One hundred yards out, the drones banked straight up and hovered, a missile under each wing, humming above the humans of the Peoplooza.

"Don't worry," said Amberly to the 'Ploozers. "They will not harm you!" She lowered the pitch below fevered. "But can you tell us," she cried out to the 'Ploozers, "why it's alright to kill us?"

Iulia had to cover her ears for the sonic rage, an octave higher than anything before.

"I will not stand," shouted Amberly, "for our government's illegal killing of our citizens!" The crowd largely went along with this. "But I cannot *take*," she seethed, "vampires treated like monsters!"

There was unanimous deafening agreement.

"So you," she pointed at the 'Ploozers, "the ignorant and the evil, you who would pound a *stake*," her voice cracked and Iulia saw raw anguish, "in my *breast*—look up and see that you are *known*!"

The 'Ploozers, that self-appointed pearl of humanity, was crushed by the surrounding crowd, compressed to a defensive nugget, 500 people occupying 20 square feet of lawn churned to dirt, flailing for their lives.

"No!" Amberly's voice was a savage knife, severing the vigilantes' justification. "We give you one final chance! We ask for *nothing* from you but the right to live our lives!"

A drone dropped from the formation, free-falling to within a few feet of the 'Ploozers' heads, scorching them with its landing jets and propelling them to grovel in the dirt.

"We will have peace!" Amberly cried, and the assembled thundered:

"*Peace!*"

"But we know that not everyone is ready—ready to give up war." She paused and the National Mall fell remarkably quiet.

"And so," her voice echoed in the stillness, echoed through the ether by live feed to the hundreds of millions amassed at rallies around the world at all hours of day and night, "we are willing to *pry* the weapons from your hands and *grind* them to dust!"

Iulia imagined the world shuddering in its flight around the sun, gaining a moment of time that would be relived and invested and reaped by billions and generations to come.

"Today," said Amberly, turning the world's volume from 11 down to 5. "Today ..." She took them all the way to 1, at the sound and sight of the emotion that ruled her. "We achieved something *no* one thought possible. Today …"

Was there ever such simultaneous, world-wide anticipation?

"We brought peace, to a place where *everyone* has faith, and no one had a future."

Humans and vampires began to weep.

"Today, peace was made in the Middle East. Peace—not just between Israel and the Palestinians—"

It was hard to breathe, hard to find air that had not been sucked into a collective gasp, hard to process what remained.

"But peace between Jews and Arabs."

The cheering had to build gradually as the air was shared and hugs were exchanged.

"Today is the first day of the Peace." Amberly absorbed and encouraged the ecstasy drenching the Mall. She nodded, each bob of her head deepening, lengthening. "But a word to those who prefer to remain at war: Our Peace did not come without bloodshed."

The joint Hamas-Fatah strike force gathered in an anteroom in a tunnel under the West Bank settlement of Negelem. Their leader who went by the nom de guerre Badr al Gadr had just received the message they were waiting for.

"The rockets are airborne," he told his team, eight of Palestine's most experienced fighters. Six from Hamas and two from Fatah, because the latter hadn't been able to get their shit together, as usual. When at the last second the Fatah leadership decided to convene a committee that would be chosen by election to select their final two fighters, Hamas had tabbed two more of its men and headed into the tunnel.

His soldiers pulled down their facemasks while al-Gadr wiped the dry erase board clean of the Israeli settlement mock-up. Al-Gadr had used the drawing to walk the team one last time through their attack on the settlers.

"Let us take advantage of the chaos of the moment."

"God willing, we will weaken the resolve of the occupiers," said Abu Khoanis, a veteran of Beirut.

"Katyushas willing," al-Gadr referred to the shells that would now be landing in Israel proper. They didn't have the accuracy to target the Negelem settlers, they would surely blow up just as many of their own. But the rockets would be sufficiently disruptive to give al-Gadr's strike force time to kill a few and abduct a couple more before the Israeli soldiers arrived.

Those soldiers might not respond promptly anyway. These settlers were disobeying the Israeli government by building outside the boundaries that had been "zoned" for settlement. But while the Israeli government might not rush to their aid, neither would they punish the settlers for their disobedience. That was up to al-Gadr and his men.

The settlement occupied a rocky, barren slope. The tunnel opened behind a boulder. Al-Gadr's team had joked about how this would be another "Jesus moment" for the Jews.

As they walked briskly through the tunnel, al-Gadr kept hearing sounds of pursuit. Facemasks played tricks on the ears. One thing he had learned as a leader of men, one never looked back.

Abu Khoanis, bringing up the rear, turned as the first vampire slammed into him. A second vampire flew through the air and tackled two more of al-Gadr's men. A third vampire, scuttling upside down along the ceiling using wire bundles and pipes for purchase, flanked the guerrillas, dropping to the floor and throwing al-Gadr against the wall.

Back to back, four Palestinian guerrillas dropped to a knee and opened fire with an assortment of Russian, Chinese and American semi-automatic rifles. Slugs embedded in the three vampires' bulletproof vests and tore through their arms, legs, throats, faces. Blood and gore spattered the walls, and the vampires fell.

Al-Gadr was only semi-conscious and three of his team were dead, throats shredded. The youngest guerrilla, Akbar Zinne, not yet 17, had emptied a clip into the vamps and now calmly, coolly reloaded. "The desperate Israelis, they need to recruit monsters to win their war."

One of his comrades pulled up his facemask, sweating. "They were behind us. They were coming from Palestinian territory."

"Some would say," came a deep voice from that same direction, "that it is monsters who wage war. So what does that make those who end it?"

This vampire filled the tunnel, which to be fair was tight. In a khaki t-shirt and combat pants, he was armed with a big curved knife, or perhaps it was a short sword. He threw it to one of his vampire comrades who neatly caught it and stabbed it into the chest of a Fatah fighter.

The remaining guerrillas opened fire. The big lightly-dressed vampire was hit multiple times but barely slowed. He picked up a Hamas fighter by the head and swung him like a club, smiting al-Gadr's men. His fellow vampires leaped on the fallen guerrillas, silencing screams, feeding noisily.

With a final swing and twist, the big vampire was left holding the head of the Hamas fighter while the body flew down the tunnel. The remaining Fatah guerrilla ran after that body and continued on toward the settlement entrance.

Now there was only Badr al-Gadr's ragged breathing. He looked up at the big vampire. A bullet hole in its forehead was already healing.

"So I see we Palestinians are once again on the wrong side of history," said al-Gadr.

The giant, evolved vampire loomed above him. Al-Gadr received his fighter's head in his lap.

"Only an ignorant few," said the vampire in Arabic with a Jordanian accent. "Most in the Arab world are weary and ready to lay down their arms."

Al-Gadr glared. "Maybe Fatah and the West Bank. You don't speak for a single Gazan."

"I was shown to this tunnel by al-Hamza."

Al-Gadr's stomach twisted at the mention of one of Hamas' senior members and (formerly) a passionate veteran of the resistance. Behind al-Gadr's back, al-Hamza had sold out. Behind his back, al-Gadr pulled the safety ring from his grenade and slid it across the floor into the pack of feeding vampires. "Then he will rot in hell with the rest of you."

The big vampire picked up one of his unevolved associates and tossed him on the grenade. The explosion shattered eardrums in the confined space, but the vampire's body largely absorbed the blast.

Al-Gadr watched in horror as the bomb-ravaged vampire got to his feet and began shrugging off what should have been mortal damage.

The vampire leader cleaned his face of his unevolved soldier's flesh and gore. "Here and across the Middle East, there are still a few holdouts who prefer eternal conflict. Today we send them a message."

Al-Gadr slumped against the wall. He had seen one of the American vampire girl's speeches on YouTube. Now her words—her essence—finally resonated. This vampire was right. For al-Gadr's children and their children for generations to come, it was time to seize the chance for an end to the heritage of mourning.

"God is good. I am ready. I will be your message-bearer."

The big vampire retrieved the knife from the guerilla's chest, knelt down before al-Gadr and jerked a thumb at the carnage behind him. "This pretty much says it all." He slit the Palestinian's throat, took a few fortifying swallows, and led his team after the remaining guerrilla.

They emerged from behind the boulder into the heat. The settlement's children had been herded near the synagogue for protection while another 20 or so settlers surrounded the Palestinian guerilla. He was unarmed, while the settlers displayed two assault rifles, a knife, handheld farm tools and extreme displeasure. They cheered the arrival of the small vampire squad.

A broad-shouldered kibbutznik kept the rifle trained on the guerilla while extending his hand to the huge evolved vampire. "Yisrael Chenow. Thank you for flushing out the terrorists. I am embarrassed we didn't know about their tunnel."

The evolved vampire who went by Balthazar ignored him and continued into the settler circle where he overpowered the Palestinian. In their brief struggle he bit him in the shoulder and the hand and then on his face. He mauled the Palestinian as a bear would. The surrounding settlers blanched.

"Well," said Chenow the settler's brawny spokesman, waiting for Balthazar to wrap it up. "We are grateful for your assistance."

Blood-drenched Balthazar rose. "We are here to end your conflict."

"If anyone can convince the Arabs our claim is righteous," said Chenow, "it is you."

"We are also the only ones who can convince the Jews to respect boundaries."

A woman settler spread her arms. "Israel's ancient boundaries stretch east farther than the eye can see even from the hilltop."

"Allow me to demonstrate otherwise." The hulking Balthazar twisted the woman's wrist until both he and her arm were behind her back, and chomped on her neck. He broke her spine in his jaws and shook her limp body like a terrier to a rabbit.

The cries of the youngsters were drowned out by the discharge of the settlers' assault rifles. They couldn't match the vampires' firepower. Four by four they fell, first to fang and then by their own weapons, now wielded by the vampires.

From the synagogue, from the nascent fields, from the unfinished dwellings, more settlers came at the vampires, to the same end. Soon only the oldest, slowest and very young remained.

Balthazar's voice reverberated across the rugged hillside strewn with bodies. "Your government has abandoned you." He had to pause, breathing hard from the exertion. "The age of peace has arrived. If you abandon this settlement, we will allow those remaining to live. Even a vampire has a stomach. Ours are full." He approached a stooped man of 70-plus years. "But if you insist, we can make room."

"Murderers!" a preteen girl screamed.

One of the unevolved vampires laughed. "How can this be murder? We're vampires!"

Balthazar scanned the shocked faces of the remaining settlers. When no one spoke, he roared in frustration and savagely bit the stooped old man.

"Enough!" cried a boy of maybe 13, taking a half-step forward. He appealed to those who remained. "It's time for peace! Remember what Amberly says: The only future is together!" He turned to the vampire leader. "If we leave, will we be safe from attack by the Arabs?"

"You have our word," said Balthazar.

The boy saw his fellow Jews begin to nod. Tension left his young shoulders. "Well then, Mr. Vampire. You have a deal."

One of the unevolved vampires tackled the boy and bit him too wickedly for survival.

Balthazar growled. Out of the settlers' sight, he would end that vampire's life with one of the stakes he carried for these discipline issues. The unevolved; it was hard not to hate them.

"Apologies," he said to the traumatized settlers as he pulled the vampire off the boy.

"You said you would protect us!" said the young girl who had called them murderers.

"From the Arabs," Balthazar qualified.

"*You* look Arab!"

"Ah," said Balthazar, "there's the key. I am an Arab and a Muslim. But first and foremost, I am a vampire."

Word of mouth and repeated social media blasts meant nearly everyone had the app. Whether they were at the rallies in D.C. and around the world, or watching live feeds, or sleeping in their beds, the voting app now sprang to life and sounded an alert.

"To ensure integrity in the process," said the young man who had taken over for Amberly at the microphone, "voting will last five minutes. Five minutes, people!" He had a light British accent, an open handsome face, and was comfortable at the mic. "That's not much!"

The crowd laughed.

"A five-minute political season? How refreshing is that?" He nodded through the applause. "We only have time to run ten attack ads!" The young man enjoyed the mock booing. "Kidding! Now, our favorite young lady vampire would do a much better job than I conducting this vote, but since Amberly is the *candidate*, she didn't think it would be appropriate."

Iulia texted Tripp:

Wish you were here. Are you voting? Don't cancel out my vote! ☺

"Really, truly," said the young emcee, tight jeans and button shirt, cuffs rolled up, groomed five o'clock shadow, hair trimmed and slicked, "this vote makes official what we've all been asking for. What we all want and what our governments have refused to give us!"

Working, Tripp responded. He wasn't happy (to put it mildly) that she refused to give him access to her research, to the secret behind the prophylactic. In Iulia's opinion, the prophylactic was the secret behind the future peace between their species. If the vampire community thought the "rubber" was a step toward a cure—which would validate the specie-ist claim that vampirism was a disease—then Iulia's Comity Clubs (and Iulia herself) would be in jeopardy.

She had explained that to Tripp. He understood. But he was still a specie-ist himself, and believed it his duty to create a "cure" for the evolved. Iulia knew that in time as the clubs strengthened the vampire-human bond and as their own relationship deepened, his heart would change.

"This position," said the emcee, "the position of consul, will be as big or as little as *we* want. It can be as short as six months, or last as long as a young vampire can live! It's all up to *us*! Next Saturday, eight regions around the world will elect proconsuls reporting to the consul position. The Saturday after that, each nation will elect its praetor, reporting to the regional proconsuls. Through the praetors, proconsuls, and consul, vampires all, we will ensure the Peace is kept among countries, sects, and tribes. And that's *it*, everybody! That's all you'll get from these public servant vampires. Just *peace*!"

The world thundered its desperation for an end to conflict.

"Just peace. And isn't that enough? Isn't that everything?"

Iulia crouched and pressed one ear against Janice's backrest, plugged her other ear with a finger, and thus avoided losing some hearing as she texted Tripp.

Magical what's happening here. I want to come home and tell you about it.

She sent him a Snapchat of the ecstatic crowd.

The emcee checked his phone. "Sorry, I ran long. Now you only have two minutes to vote." He played it up. "Kidding again. I did in fact take more time than I was allotted, but you will not lose a second of your precious voting time. So everyone, please open your ClaimStake app, and in five, four, three, two, one—*now*, simply vote 'yes' or 'no' on electing Amberly Foreman to the new consul position. People of planet Earth, cast your vote!"

Iulia voted for Amberly as a text from Tripp came in. Her euphoria melted.

Better you don't come here for a while. I think I need some time to sort it all out. Bigger forces at work than our relationship, I guess. Sorry.

Balthazar the Arab vampire leader of the Middle East Peacemaker team gave a thumbs-up to the bulldozer driver as he finished leveling the unauthorized settlement. Higher on the hillside smoke curled from the rubble of the collapsed tunnel. He checked his ClaimStake app and saw Amberly had won the consul position with 92% of the worldwide vote. Good.

He whistled to his lounging team. Time to prepare for their next punitive mission, against the so-called Islamic State. He was a lucky leader—truly his vampire commandos could not get enough carnage. He wasted not a breath on rah-rah motivational speeches.

Balthazar figured they would have the Middle East and North Africa cleaned up by November. Then he was hoping to be assigned to discipline government officials around the world who hadn't fully bought into Amberly Foreman's vision.

There were twice as many people in the Low-T Center's repurposed tanning room as when Victor had entered the meditation tank ten hours ago.

He spoke to Jaelle Skudza, one of the newly arrived. "We had an agreement." Which was, he would not have to see her when he came for his thrice-weekly sessions.

The Romanian gypsy neuroscientist folded her arms. "This is the first of two vows we will violate today, vampire."

She was ruining the peaceful buzz he always enjoyed after a meditation session.

Winnie patted the dentist's chair with the modified VR helmet. "We have a way for you to use your gift without fear of collateral damage."

"No chance," said Victor.

"No drones," said Winnie.

Victor accepted a towel from Michael who nodded at his fatter gut. "I won't stand for my crushes getting soft," said Michael, who was on the extremely soft side. He scored a few chuckles.

"What is it this time?" Victor called from behind the privacy screen Michael held for him while he stripped off his swimsuit.

"Terminator robots?"

"Close," said Winnie with a wink for Jaelle.

Pants on, Victor came out from behind Michael's screen. "I'll never be part of something like that again."

"God bless you for that." Winnie's appearance and movements were strikingly better since starting sessions in the meditation tank hooked to Jaelle's machine. "That's what sets you apart from far too many vampires. And humans."

"Mm-hm," said Victor. "But?"

Winnie smiled. "I know you want to use your Sight."

"I am."

"Not to maximum effect."

Victor sighed as he buttoned his shirt. "We're going in circles."

"We have a more interesting course for you to drive." Winnie arched an eyebrow and deadpanned, "You *were* using a race car metaphor?"

Amidst irritation at being cheated out of a euphoric ending to his meditation session, Victor was grateful for the return of Winnie's fluid wit.

He put on his shoes. "What I'm doing is wondering why I'm not in D.C. protecting Amberly."

Jaelle stood behind the row of software engineers at their terminals. "What if we could take you there now?"

Victor paused at the door. "I would wonder about the strings attached."

"Fewer than the ones dangling from Amberly's promised world." Winnie's good humor had evaporated. "This is no longer a war for humanity. We've lost. I appreciate your refusal to accept innocent casualties, I really do. But I can't accept a world ruled by vampires. I don't know the reconciliation between those two positions."

They stared at each other.

"Okay," said Victor.

Jaelle was marching on him. "If you don't at least try—"

"I said okay." Victor tossed his wet swimsuit to the floor and sat in the chair. "Hook me up already."

Twenty-two members of the Transylvanian multi-level

marketing slayer organization walked onto the D.C. National Mall. They wore khaki jumpsuits. Their helmets were lined with neural interactive sensors and outfitted with GoPro cameras and microphones.

They were armed with state-of-the-art electronic crossbows. They were pelted with fruits and plastic water bottles and small smooth river stones.

"Stay in formation," commanded Vlad Trestian, upstream on the pyramid. "No one fires or retaliates until we get authorization from the queen bee."

No one in the crowd moved aside to let them pass.

"Excuse me, pardon me."

Most of the Romanian slayers spoke some English. Threading their way through the crowd made it difficult to stay together. Their ultimate destination was the island of Peoplooza people, 80 yards away. Vlad reached the beleaguered anti-vampire protestors with five of his slayers.

A woman in a trenchcoat stepped forward, eyes bulging at the crossbows. "Are you crazy?"

"We are here to protect you," said Vlad.

"You're going to get us annihilated!"

"Don't worry. We are a highly trained strike force."

The woman nodded at the sky without being too conspicuous. "So are the pilots running those drones."

Vlad raised his eyes. "We have the greatest pilot on our side."

"God? Oh great."

"I refer to—"

Vlad received a crackle and then Jaelle's voice in his ear. He raised his hand in apology and spoke into his mic. "We are deployed and ready."

A man stepped forward from the hostile surrounding sea and punched Vlad in the nose. The Transylvanian slayer's lights blinked out. When they came back on, he was sitting on the chewed-up lawn.

"Vlad," Jaelle was saying. "Are you there?"

"Still here."

"Good. Let's get you slaying."

A pure musical note entered both his ears and met in the middle as a lightshow, changing the world for Vlad and twenty of his slayers. (One had lost her helmet when a park ranger tackled, disarmed and arrested her.) The slayers seemed to grow a foot taller, able to survey the entire mall. Certain individuals in the sea of humanity now stood out like phosphorescent fish.

Vlad walked forward. Angry people buffeted him; the man who had punched him screamed at him to back off. Vlad only had eyes for a vampire in a backward-turned ball cap and two-piece matching jogging suit, bobbing to get a better look at Amberly on the stage.

"I need to know the Achilles' Heel," said Vlad.

"Surprisingly enough," came a man's American southern drawl in his ear, "he *is* evolved. Femoral artery, upper right thigh."

"Hello!" Vlad barked. The vampire turned to him at the apex of a bob and Vlad sent a crossbow bolt into the prescribed spot.

"Holy moly," said the voice in his ear. "Perfect shot!"

The vampire's back arched, propelling him further in the air. He landed with a thud. People pushed and stumbled away from his death. Vlad went in search of his next victim.

Victor saw a huge swath of the crowd, everyone who was within eyesight of the 21-strong slaying force. He saw what the helmet-wearing slayers saw, he heard what they heard. And he felt the crowd—felt what *they* were feeling, fear of slayers and excitement for Amberly and pent-up energy to finally *do* something.

An evolved vampire came in fast. "Hispanic in a tight stocking cap and black short-sleeve shirt—his Heel is two inches above right hip bone."

Thwack! One of the slayers nailed him. These Romanians could shoot!

A slayer shouted something unintelligible.

"In English, please," said Victor.

"I have one! Hurry!"

A tall vampire in a conservative plaid dress shirt and khakis advanced on a slayer, mayhem in his bespectacled eyes. "Dead center on the breastbone," said Victor.

Thunk. A different slayer shot a human woman, dead center on the breastbone.

"Not her!"

The woman fell and Victor's heart sank. Vampires kept appearing and slayers kept begging for guidance.

"Young man in tight dirty white t-shirt!" said a slayer.

"Clavicle," said Victor.

"What?" said the heavily-accented slayer.

"Collar bone, left side, just above—"

Fft. A bolt drilled the vamp's Heel, perfectly placed.

"Here-here-here," a slayer screamed.

Sweat poured down Victor's back. "You must describe the vamp! I'm seeing *everything*, I can't tell who's talking!"

"Dracula-looking motherfucker!"

Oh that guy. "Not evolved, oddly enough."

A bolt pierced the vampire's heart and he died wailing.

Victor heard Amberly's voice over the event's sound system, calling for a stop to the slaying.

"Rugby shirt is human!" Victor warned of an enraged attacker wielding the jagged broken neck of a crème soda bottle.

"What is 'rugby'?" asked a slayer in rough English.

"Orange and black stripes!"

The slayer neatly knocked the rugby man out with the stock of his crossbow.

Vampires and humans alike attacked the courageous band of Transylvanians. Savage collisions took two more slayers off-line. Victor barked out Heels when a description was provided, and added a description of the intended victim if he sensed any uncertainty.

The pace quickened, the slayers in danger of being overwhelmed. Victor saw everything, but neither he nor the slayers could talk fast enough, the language barrier making it doubly difficult.

"Perky little brunette in cute sun dress!" Vlad called for the Heel of a vampire woman chewing his ass in a foreign language.

It was Iulia.

"She's Romanian!" Vlad the slayer exclaimed. "Heel!"

There was a pause at the other end. "Unevolved," said the man in his ear, so dispiritedly that it flattened his southern drawl. "Heart."

The Romanian vampire woman knocked Vlad to the ground and charged another slayer who was drawing a bead on a bearded vamp.

The man in Vlad's ear was wrong. It wasn't the heart. She wasn't unevolved. Her Heel was the bottom tip of her spine, her tail bone, the coccyx. Vlad could see it! Glowing, beckoning. He pulled the trigger on his crossbow—he had never felt so comfortable with the weapon; his aim had never been so true. The bolt nailed the vampire in her cute little backside and he saw her Heel explode in a shower of sparks.

"No!" the man in his head roared.

He was not just in Vlad's *ear*, but in his *head.*

And Vlad was in his. It was *his* eyes that saw that vamp's Heel.

And that one—Vlad spotted a vampire with a throbbing yellow ear. From his hip he shot the creature right in the sweet spot, dropping him in a tumbling rolling wipeout.

"We can see them!" Vlad yelled in Romanian to his compatriots. "We don't have to *hear* him—we can *see* their Heels!"

Sirens screamed and so did the crowd, thousands around them fleeing or attacking. The Peoplooza clutch broke apart—some ran to escape, some fought off crazed assailants, and a few wielded stakes and looked for vampires. Cops with nightsticks waded into the melee and found their marks. Amberly's voice carved the air from the surrounding loudspeakers, begging the slayers to lay down their weapons.

Chaos reigned. Vampires realized something was horribly wrong, their hidden Heels exposed. They ran. Vlad's slaying team were hounds in pursuit, yapping excitedly as they fired on the run, hitting their marks. The center of the Mall was vacated in an expanding circle, vampire corpses revealed like beached, poisoned fish.

Vlad ran after a weightlifter vampire who used a human as a shield. As he closed for the kill, Vlad caught a glimpse of a glow on the vamp's musclebound back.

And then the glow was gone.

Knock-knock.

Victor was vaguely aware of someone poking his head into their control room—the janitor wondering if they needed their wastebaskets emptied. Jaelle ordered him out.

Curlicues of warm garbage filled Victor's nose.

Violently he was slammed from the chair to the floor, the VR helmet raking his skin as it ripped off his head.

He lay dazed under Michael, who was just as stunned.

Florence picked the programmer up and tossed him a second time, to the other side of the room. She leaped on Victor. He caught her with her fangs straining for his throat.

She was in too tight, she was too strong, Victor had lost strength and Florence was in frenzy. Sirens and bells sounded in his head, her lips on his throat, sucking his skin into her mouth.

Winnie wrapped her in a bear hug and she head-butted his face, breaking his nose and his grip. She overpowered Victor on her way to his throat.

"Heel?" someone shouted.

"Heart!" said Victor. "She's—"

A stake came so far through Florence's chest that it pierced Victor's ear. He yelped and shoved her away.

Michael stood over him panting and unsteady. "That bitch is *what*?"

Victor sat up and watched Florence die. "Unevolved." Sadness twisted in his chest. He prayed not to see any final glimpse of the Florence who had infatuated him all these years. He held her hand as best he could while her fingers clawed for something her eyes struggled to see.

And then with a gasp everything sagged and she was gone.

David in a janitor jumper dashed out the door. "Grab him," said Victor.

Two engineers could be heard overtaking David and dragging him back to the room.

Victor retrieved the helmet and sat in the chair.

"Don't bother," said Jaelle. "It's over." She pointed to a big screen on the wall, a drone's-eye view of the National Mall.

Smoke rose from blackened holes in the lawn, craters scabbed with bodies.

"The feds ended it," said Jaelle.

Victor slid out of the chair to his knees, fighting the need to be sick.

In Romanian Jaelle gave a command to one of the programmers, who relayed it in Romanian to the surviving slayers. She covered her face in her hands.

David was transfixed by Florence's decomposition. Victor drove him against the wall. He dug a finger into David's throat, probing for the underlying bloodstream. "Was she trying to steal my Sight?"

David nodded.

"Was Larry involved?"

David nodded.

"People died today because of Florence and Larry. And you." Anger sank his finger deeper into David's throat. "I don't want to see either of you, ever again. You got it? I will suck you dry, David. I will kill you both. Will you tell Larry?"

David nodded.

Carnage. It's fucking carnage.

Bryan, our emcee and my personal political consultant, tries to get me below the dais into the tunnel, and I nearly literally take his head off. I am not leaving! People are *dead*, a lot of people, vampires and humans, slain, bitten and blown to fucking bits by our government's drones.

A woman in a wheelchair lies dying on the grass. Her useless legs were blown off by a drone-launched missile. No paramedics are coming to the rescue, they are a bit busy, and I can't stop the life that gushes out of her. I think I recognize the vampire girl lying slain beside her, it's hard to say, her face is so soft and empty. I turn away from the blood and the smell of death and the screams of the near-dead, to keep from losing my mind.

What am I supposed to do? What should have I done differently?

I've awakened so much passion. The same way passion came to life in me. The time for change has to be *now*. I know it, I feel it. Billions of us feel the same.

But millions are against us. Ruled by fear. Desperate for the status quo. Unable to change, to adapt, to evolve.

That's the kiss of death! History proves it—those who don't evolve, from the Neanderthals to the dodos, they die. But it doesn't happen quickly, does it? Not without a war.

War. That's what I'm here to end. Instead, I started one.

And it's terrible. It's killing me.

I sit on the edge of the dais, knees drawn to my chin, trying not to see, eyes open and thoughts begging to go somewhere else.

Eugene stands below me, looking up. In a trenchcoat with his hand on the trigger of the crossbow slung over his shoulder. Not his mini, this weapon is full-size with a bolt like a spear.

"Are you here to do it?" I ask.

He looks exhausted. There's blood on his coat, his shirt, his face, his hands. Eugene looks spent and struggling in a way I've never seen. Has he finally seen enough death?

"Are you here for me?" I ask again.

"Amberly, did you see what happened here?"

"Are you fucking kidding me? I saw everything! I *caused* everything!" I'm screaming down on him, on my feet, ready to jump on him and see how it turns out.

His face is white, making the blood spatters stand out, even if I couldn't smell every drop, I'm sick on it, no, drunk on it, too much, the world doesn't know when to fucking *stop*, when it's had enough. How do I teach it? Blood is life, blood sustains us, human and vampire alike, we share our most precious resource.

Eugene swipes the blood across his cheek. "I don't know how to avoid what's coming."

"Which is what?"

"My destiny."

"You God-damned dummy. You think you're some kind of Romeo. But I'm not your fucking Juliet." I stab my finger at the field of death. "I fucking *hate* this! But it doesn't matter. We're changing the world, Eugene."

His hand slides off the stock of his crossbow and falls to his side. "This was the beginning of the end, my love."

The rage building within me is swamped by those two words.

My love.

Eugene, I ache *to be with you.*

"Don't ever use that word again," I tell him. "You don't have what it takes to love me."

He stares up at me as he backs away from the dais. "That's the question, isn't it?" Without leaving my eyes, he raises his hand and flags an Uber car trolling the Mall's perimeter. "Do I or don't I? Either way it's a tragedy."

The Uber driver slaloms through the killing field and straddles the sidewalk. Eugene opens the back door. They haggle over the price. Eugene won't accept a peak rate. They reach compromise and my Romeo leaves me.

GOODBYE, HOUSTON

Twilight soothed the city as Victor pushed out the door of the Low-T Center. The heat stopped boiling refinery fumes to release redbud and silverbell perfume, fulfilling the Southern evening's perfect promise.

"You are stupid to go out." Jaelle peered from the doorway as if into a rainstorm. She was increasingly preoccupied with the government's retaliation. "By morning we will have the hard site fully stocked and ready for you."

"For Barbara, too."

She grimaced and waved at the outside world. "If you get yourself killed or taken, we are done."

"Do your job and get everyone to the site. I'll be there."

Thanks to Jaelle, he felt exposed walking the two blocks to his Charger. Would he hear the drone's missile and have a split-second to react? Did he still have split-second reflexes? How much durability did his curse provide? Good questions. He tried not to break into a run.

Any idea of getting his thoughts in order on the drive to the Longevity Labs was lost to the ill turmoil in his gut. Tripp buzzed him in and Victor trudged down the hall with no plan.

Tripp was in his office leafing through a stack of papers. "Viccy babe. What's up?"

Did you hear about the Rally? It turned into a war. The government bombed the place. A lot of people died.

"I killed your girlfriend."

Tripp's head twitched. A frown disappeared, reappeared.

"Iulia was there, in the crowd. I was on the machine, Jaelle's virtual slaying—"

"She's dead?" The bottom fell out of Tripp's voice. "Iulia's dead? I texted her." He reached for his phone for proof, pawed away papers covering it. "I have a text from her. Vic, why are you saying this?"

"I'm sorry." Victor moved into the room as Tripp stood and wobbled sideways, bumping into the desk. "I helped the slayer see her Heel. I didn't mean to. I'm sorry."

"You're *what*?" Tripp threw himself forward and threw a punch that caught Victor on the temple. "You hated her!" He bulled Victor backward, splintering the door jam and crashing into the hall. "You targeted her!" Tripp fought to get on top.

"I didn't know she was there," said Victor as they struggled. "God-dammit *stop*."

Tripp's knee crushed his arm and he got punched hard in the face. Victor went limp, a ploy and a plea, and Tripp pulled his next punch to Victor's ear, filling his head with the echoes of a well-struck gong. Tripp lurched to his feet and thudded against the wall.

Victor waited until the gonging subsided and his jaw regained coordination. "A lot of people died. It's the start of a war. Iulia was in it. And I am sorry. I wouldn't do that to you."

"Shut up. Get out of here. I hate you, Vic," Tripp's voice cracked. "I fucking hate you." He shuffled into his office and closed the door.

Victor sat in the hall. "You need to get to her place," he spoke through the door. "Before the police, or whoever." Struggling to his feet, he felt like his old fat self. But his mind was clicking. "We need the cure."

"Fuck off!"

"You're the only one who can do it."

"And cure who? Who, Vic?"

Victor's forehead touched the door. "Hopefully a lot of people."

Tripp was sobbing as Victor headed for his car.

He didn't take the chance of calling Darla. He used his cellphone hardly at all now—there was a popular street sign meme, the silhouette of a man talking on a phone with the silhouette of a missile coming for his head.

There was no time for this visit, and seeing him was the probably last thing she needed. Victor went anyway.

He heard Darla pad down the hall and was enveloped by her warm aura even with the door between them. Whether she similarly felt him or was insufficiently security-conscious, Darla opened the door without question. Her eyes settled into his and she sagged against the door.

"I don't have to come in."

"Sure you do." She stood aside and followed him down the hall, into the living room. "I've been thinking about you. And Amberly."

"I'm worried for her, to say the least," said Victor. "How is Kimberly?"

"She's different. She's at a meeting right now, planning for a conflict-free world." Darla tried irony, looking shell-shocked. "They have all these ideas, 'initiatives' to make the world a better place. I just want her to go to school and get a job. They're planning to go to the Middle East to help them rebuild, now that the Arab-Israeli war is over."

"After what happened today in Washington," said Victor, "war is just getting going. And I'm going to be hard to reach for a while. You need to convince Kimberly to lay low."

"I'll keep trying," she said without confidence. "You look wiped out."

He was lightheaded, and let her guide him to the sofa. "I'm probably a quart low." He should have bitten David.

They sat with their hips touching, her hands tucked between her knees. "I've been thinking about our relationship. How Jay set us up to hate each other. God rest his soul."

Victor doubted God had access to Jay Hansen's soul.

"But nothing could stop us from liking each other, could it?" said Darla. "I think about the trip to Germany, at the Verrstagg office. And all the times since then we've tried to make it work."

Victor pressed his leg against hers, but forced his hands to stay put.

"I've always said that your vampirism doesn't define you," said Darla. "That it's *you* I see. And love."

"I have always appreciated that."

"But I think what I was actually doing was pretending your

vampirism isn't a *part* of you. It kept us apart." She started unbuttoning her shirt. "It kept me from sharing everything with you."

"Darla, no."

"I want that with you, Victor." She lowered her shirt past her shoulders. "I've thought about this. I want you to bite me."

"No, no, no."

She was in his arms, a kiss for a moment and then her face pressed to his shoulder and her throat at his lips.

"Take me, Victor. Drink me in."

Her skin was soft and delicate and wonderful. He had been so thirsty, but now a different need consumed him. As his mouth opened against her throat, Victor realized it was a mistake.

He pulled her into a tight hug and willed his body to retreat from the brink.

"If I did that," he whispered to her, "it would be the end of me."

He held her, touched her bare back and shirt-wrapped waist as much as he dared, and then pulled away and squeezed her hands.

She wiped away tears. "I should have let you bite me in Germany."

Victor smiled. "I care for you so much. It's terrible for me to keep coming back here to say goodbye."

Her eyes sparkled. "I'm just so scared one of these times you're going to mean it."

He kissed her and left her one last time.

Or so he intended.

Barbara cried as they drove northwest out of Houston toward the hardened site where Victor would be protected from drone strikes while he commanded a death-dealing slayer pyramid.

"Porkie will be fine."

She sniffled and sobbed. "I know. Maybe that's why. I don't want him to forget about me."

"He will not. No way."

"Or Amberly."

He drove the Charger, hyper-sensitive to any sign of a tail. He constantly checked the sky.

"I know you need to do this," said Barbara. "I'm all for it. But in the meantime, we're failing our daughter."

He handed her his phone and told her the passcode. "Scroll all the way over," he directed, "to the Find Amberly app."

Barbara looked from the phone to Victor and back.

"Open it." Victor spared glances as she brought up a GPS map with a red dot. "Where is she?"

"New York." Barbara drilled down until the dot rested on a warehouse in southwest Manhattan, close to the river. "How does this work?"

"I put a tracer in her pocketbook. It's a key part of my predictive modeling program, the one X stole. Tiny unobtrusive tags. The program uses them to aggregate data over long periods of time in order to predict movements and locations. They work for simple tracking, too."

Barbara was impressed. "You also have a Find Eugene app." She launched it.

"I put a tracer in his stupid ugly boot."

"He's in Kuala Lumpur."

Victor just scowled.

"So you can predict where Amberly will be?"

"Not without a lot more data. She's not leading a predictable life. But we can keep an eye on her. Try to keep her safe." By that he meant 'kill Eugene if his dot approaches hers.'

They drove for a while. "Barbara, I'm thirsty."

She offered him a drink of her tea.

"I need blood."

"We should have stopped at Larry's house."

When he had told her about Florence's fatal attempt to bite him and steal his curse, Barbara had been savagely happy to hear Florence was dead, a little disturbingly so. Now she wanted him to take vengeance on Larry and David, too.

"I couldn't bite that crusty sonofabitch."

"Then you should bite his mother."

Victor looked at her a couple times and enjoyed seeing she was serious. "I already did."

Her eyebrows rose. "Well, then. We'll stop at the next truckstop and find you a willing victim."

He kept his eyes on the road. "How come you never asked me to bite you?"

"Ha! That's for your little tramps."

Victor took the opportunity to enjoy her while she stared straight ahead. Shapely knees showing below her hemline, flat stomach providing nice posture, hair again reaching her shoulders after she had chopped it off. She turned him on. He would have liked to taste her blood.

She knew he was getting an eyeful. "That's not the way a man and a woman love each other."

"But you kind of like the rough stuff."

"*That's* all good."

Victor smiled.

She checked Amberly's red dot and set his phone on the center console. "You need to put this app on my iPad."

"Welcome to my humble home," said the short balding man with eager eyes as they all stepped off the bus that had ferried them from the armory parking lot in nearby Bastrop. And it was humble: two small stories, old, well-kept.

"We are very thankful for your hospitality," said Jaelle. "Dr. Linciome wishes he could be here to thank you in person."

"You tell Winnie to get his head back on straight," said their host. Dr. Linciome was again in the hospital after Florence's abuse, the doctors dealing with bleeding on his brain. "It kills me not to go see him. But I don't think I should call any attention to our friendship right now."

Victor introduced himself and Barbara.

"Doug Sessler. Pleased to meet you." He redirected Jaelle's team as they hauled equipment from the back of the bus, away from the house to an unpainted wood barn. Sessler held the creaky door and gave Jaelle and Barbara a hand navigating the raised floor jam. The barn was unbearably hot.

Michael and another programmer hauling the meditation tank struggled to get under a metal rod hung with bridles and blankets.

"First rule to survive the zombie apocalypse," said Sessler, squeezing past everyone to the far corner. "Misdirection. Of course my bunker was for the government, not zombies." He pulled up a trap door and revealed a staircase. "The barn retains some heat rising from the equipment."

The bunker was pleasantly cool, spacious, enough head room to take the edge off any claustrophobia. The main room already looked like a command center with computers and monitors displaying live video feeds. "I'm part of a network responsible for monitoring hotspots all over the world," said Sessler. He paused, hands on hips. "I'm not sure how to integrate your equipment."

Michael grunted and sweated his end of the tank down the tight steep stairs. "Worry not. System integration is what we're all about." He set it down with a groan. "In fact, I volunteer to start that integration immediately while the rest of you unload the bus." The other programmers looked for things to throw at him.

"Let me show you the sleeping arrangements." Sessler had four bedrooms, each with three sets of double-stacked bunkbeds. "We're equipped to handle a small army. Speaking of which," he said to Jaelle. "I need to check on our security team. They said they'd be here by now."

"We don't have much time," said Jaelle. "We need to hurry."

"Understood."

"And once we close that door, it stays closed," said Jaelle. "Until it's over."

Sessler bounced on his toes, full of nervous energy. "I'll be right back."

Jaelle's team followed him—including a chagrined Michael—leaving her with Victor and Barbara.

"How long are we here?" said Barbara.

Jaelle was brusque. "For the duration."

Barbara was polite, but not deferential. "And how long is that?"

"Until they're dead," said Jaelle. "Or we are. That will be up to your husband."

"We're divorced," said Barbara.

"Now Jaelle is going to get ideas," said Victor. He received no smiles. "I'm going to help the guys."

While Barbara chose a bedroom and began to unpack, Jaelle followed Victor up into the barn. "Your woman understands? Once that door is closed, we won't take the chance to open it. People coming and going, that's how we are discovered."

"Barbara understands."

"What is she going to do with herself?"

"Worry, mostly."

"She should not be here."

"Give her a job. Barb is good at anything."

"If she *asks*, I will."

"Don't worry, she will."

Jaelle blew a gasket. "We are against the wall!" As the programmers passed by with a load of equipment, she pushed Victor into a horse stall. "You will have no time for her!"

"I won't take the chance of leaving Barbara out there. Exposed. She's been through too much."

"Bah. We all have. We have all lost—"

"Jaelle. I know this woman. We're lucky to have her here." Victor marveled at a nascent sense of humor tickling his mind. "To keep Michael's hands off me, if nothing else."

Michael winked in passing. Jaelle knotted her hands in fists. "Do you understand," she said in a low, well-articulated rasp, "how many lives we are going to lose?"

Victor sobered.

"I lost six men and women in Washington," said Jaelle. "Four were killed. Two are in prison. Maybe they wish they were dead."

"I understand—"

"No you do not. You sit in your chair and play your video game—"

"It's a little more committed than a video game."

Jaelle slapped him. "We offended your sensibilities with the drones. Because you don't want to be responsible for killing innocent people. But now *our* people are dying. And you *are* responsible."

Victor kept his chin available to her hand. "Our people are soldiers, not civilians. That's the difference."

"Our people are *right*," Jaelle seethed. "*That* is the difference. You are sacrificing the wisest and the bravest to save stupid sheep." Her expression was beyond disdain, worse than disgust. "If your woman interferes with our task, I will make an exception to open the door."

YOU CAN'T GO HOME AGAIN

I went home, again. Just being in the neighborhood calmed me.

Our house was empty. Six newspapers lay in the driveway. My people say my father is responsible for the slaying that started with the rally in D.C. and has been happening ever since at a terrible rate. They're searching for him—not too eagerly, it seems to me; what vampires want to try their luck against X-Ray the All-Seeing Eye? In any event, they're saying he went into hiding. Mom must be with him.

My parents turned against me. And in an instant the world turned with them, from loving me to trying to ruin everything I've worked for.

Are we incapable of salvation? Are we innately self-destructive? At the moment when peace is finally at hand, are we wired to freak out and destroy it all? I refuse to believe that. I refuse to give up.

Believe it or not, I was sitting on our front steps and heard Porkie barking three doors down in the Pierces' backyard. I jumped their fence and took him and drove him here, to Trubadur's house in Acres Homes.

I receive a text from Tripp.

Hey, lil Thethy, how are you? Thinking about you. Missing Iulia so much. Slain at your rally. She thought the world of you. Funeral Thursday. Can you come? You would take away some sadness.

Porkie scratches the back door.

"It's too dangerous out there, sweetie. You have to go potty? I need to put you on the leash so I don't lose you." I can't even tell if the fence is in one piece behind all that junk.

The doorbell rings. Hm.

"Hold on, honey." Porkie's so skinny and small, the leash lying on the floor serves as an anchor.

On my doorstep is a beautiful tanned blond vampire; legs, boobs and hair.

"Oh my," she says. "You are striking."

"Thank you. You want to come in?" I nod at the Cabriolet parked top-down at the curb. "I can't promise your car is safe."

"I'll need to grab a bite before I leave, anyway. I appreciate volunteers for dinner. Kelly Kale, by the way."

"Amberly." We shake hands. "But I guess you know that. Tru must have guessed I'd be here."

"Right you are." Kelly has a nice Aussie accent.

"Our last conversation didn't end well. Is that why he sent you?"

"He's worried about you," says Kelly. "But I'm here of my own volition. Perky pup."

Porkie the perky Morkie drags the leash, stumpy tail wagging. At Kelly's foot he pees on the floor.

"Saves us a trip outside," says Kelly. "A little sunny for my taste." She makes herself comfortable on the couch. "So how are you, dear?"

"Fine."

"Really? You don't look well. You've got bitty bags under your eyes. And you've lost weight since I saw you on the telly in D.C." Kelly removes her light half-sweater, showing off sleek tanned arms. "Come sit with me. And your little nipper, too."

I try to sit against the arm but she pulls me next to her.

"I think you could use some contact, yes?"

"I'm fine." I blink back tears that come out of nowhere. Her body is warmer than I would have thought, and she smells divine.

"Things are rough right now." She drags her fingernail across my forehead, sending tingles across my face. "Terrorists just killed a great number of innocents in Paris and Buenos Aires. And I hear something seems to be happening in Los Angeles as we speak."

All this affects me terribly. "I don't understand the hatred."

"It exists. Always has." Kelly kisses my forehead. It feels good to relax into her. "We've been waiting patiently. It's time to strike back."

"The government is already doing that. It isn't helping."

"Drone strikes are just popping heads off weeds, luv. You know how well that works. We have a deep-rooted problem. With humans."

"No. There are so many who get it." I shift to face her. Kelly gently rubs my stomach, she knows where it hurts. "So many people want peace. You've seen the crowds."

"At some point they'll turn on us, too." She gives me a sweet kiss on the cheek. "We can live together. We need to. But we're not equal. You know that. Look at you." She runs her hands over my shoulders and down my arms, sliding closer. "You're a knockout, outside and in. Everyone grooves on you. Everyone wants to touch you." She kisses my cheek. "So let me touch you."

It feels nice.

"You've led us to this point, all by yourself," she says. "Now let us help. Let us share the burden. I know it's hard. The decisions are very, very hard." She kisses my cheeks, my nose, my chin. "We have truly exceptional vampires ready to help you take the next step. Let's put them in as proconsuls, and we can send a coordinated message to the humans."

I stop her hand as it goes to my chest. "The proconsuls need to be elected."

"So elect ours. If you provide a list, they'll win."

"I can't." This is *no* on two levels: Kelly is trying to overpower me. Porkie growls at her. "Not when everyone is so excited about what we're doing. For the first time, they're empowered. I won't ruin that."

"If we don't act, there will be nothing left to rule."

I stand. "I don't want to rule."

"I know." Kelly looks at Porkie growling at her. I pick him up and she moves in close. She puts her hand on Porkie, trembling in my arms. "You're not cut out for it, sweets. That's okay. We're here for you. Once we establish order, we'll have the peace we've all been yearning for."

There is something in her that she doesn't want to show me.

It's dark and ugly.

"Good fella," she says to Porkie, scratching his back while he pees on my chest. "A lot rides on this election. Everyone's future." She walks to the door. "Yours, too."

She leaves and I take Porkie outside and sit on the stoop and hug my knees until I get myself under control.

I send my first text since Trubadur kidnapped me.

I remember Iulia. She was wonderful. I am so sorry. I would love to come to the funeral. Don't tell anyone yet, ok? And could I ask you to move it back two days to Saturday?

Porkie's a good boy, he stays close to the house. That bitch Kelly was right, it's too sunny.

We go back inside. "Okay, honey." I take a deep breath and relax my body some more. "I have to take you back to the Pierces now. They love you so much, don't they?" I kiss him up. "Mama's got more work to do."

WHEN DOTS COLLIDE

Opening his eyes after time in the tank, the air always had form and substance. Victor saw currents drawn into mouths and eddying from noses. It was a sense of smell; on the swirls of air, Victor tasted the room's ambient emotion. Right now, it was sharp with raw desperation.

Barbara waited beside the tank. "The black dot is coming to Houston."

Eugene was the black dot.

Victor rose in a whoosh of salted water looking for a towel. "We need to leave."

"Ha," said Jaelle. "No chance."

"We're leaving," said Barbara. "Our daughter is in danger."

"*You* can leave any time," said Jaelle to Barbara. "For *you*, I'll make an exception." She turned back to the monitor she was studying with Michael. "Don't you know? Your daughter in danger is what we're all working for."

Victor grabbed Barbara before she could attack. "Go get ready."

"I'm packed. I'm waiting for you."

Jaelle turned on them. "The government is searching for us non-stop. We are perfectly hidden. Today is the biggest of our lives. The vampires are orchestrating the election from Iulia's funeral—"

"Amberly is orchestrating it," said Barbara. "We need to be there."

"*Every* vampire will be there." Jaelle unleashed a stream of Romanian invective following Victor into his bedroom. "They're all coming. This is when Linger and his cabal will make their move. This is when we slay them all!"

He stripped off wet trunks in front of Jaelle and the programmers who had followed her. "That will be a good distraction for Eugene." Barbara had a change of his clothes laid out, the rest in his suitcase. "We'll get a few final slayings out of him, before I kill him."

Jaelle gasped. "You're going to kill the greatest slayer in the world?"

"He's going to kill Amberly!" Barbara screamed at her.

"*Bun*!" Jaelle screamed back. "Good! That is his destiny!"

"We're leaving." Victor moved Jaelle aside when she wouldn't budge.

Michael filled the doorway. "I can't let you leave, handsome."

Victor bared his fangs.

Michael quailed and Victor punched him the nose.

Michael staggered back and fell on his backside.

Two engineers rushed Victor and slammed him against the wall. He snarled and knocked one to the floor.

The other, he overwhelmed and bit. And drank.

"Whoa, whoa, whoa!" Sessler tried to pry them apart and Victor elbowed him in the throat. He drank some more.

Jaelle was pale. When he raised his head she pointed at the stairs. "Go."

Barbara was already there with their suitcases. Victor took Sessler's keys from his pocket, squeezed past Barbara, and pounded on the trap door. "Open it!"

"Open the door," Jaelle instructed the security guards over walkie-talkie. "Let them go."

As the door was unlocked, Michael groaned. "Why does Paul get *bit* and I get *hit*?"

The three-man security detail were burly military types, well-armed. They hadn't left the barn for two weeks, charged with ensuring no one entered or left, and now appeared crestfallen having to stand down.

Barbara threaded her arm through his as they hurried for Sessler's pickup. "You are a stud."

Eugene sat on the roof of the Bane Lake Park recreation center. He watched the crowd build and workers prepare for the vamp chick's funeral. And the election. He rubbed the tapers of the double-pointed stake.

His chest was still tender from the near-sui-slay of Victor. The thought of putting the stake point back in that same half-healed hole made him queasy.

Workers inspected the stage where Amberly would praise Iulia and her "comity" clubs as everything good in the world, and damn slayers as the root of all evil. The stage was close to the lake, facing the recreation center, allowing the crowd to array stadium-style on the hillside.

Eugene's plan was to unfold the glider wings, soar down the hill and tackle Amberly off the back of the stage, impaling each other upon impact. He had a steel plate harnessed tightly to his back to ensure the stake would push clear through the both of them.

It was possible no one would even notice, with the battle royale that would be raging. Vampires were turning out in droves, to see Consul Amberly, show solidarity amidst all the slaying, and be present for the simultaneous worldwide election of her proconsuls. Balthazar and his vampire strike force were providing security. And the V-8 vampires were coming to hijack the process.

This wasn't standard event security. No one worried about snipers or suicide bombers; Morbius was durable. There were at least 30 other slayers and civvies on the steep roof with Eugene. One had already tumbled off, ambulance sirens wailing shortly after. Everyone should be prepared to hear that sound all day long.

Jaelle had anti-drone drones in the sky. Eugene expected casualties from all the flaming drones plummeting to earth. Ten different multi-level marketing slayer teams were converging to deal death at Bane Lake Park. These were just the slayers Eugene was aware of. The number of people signing up for service was mind-blowing. It brought tears to Eugene's eyes.

In the past two weeks he had been in Gaza, Nairobi, Lahore, Kuala Lumpur, and Hiroshima, outfitting and training. Men, women and youngsters alike hungered for glory. And the money was good. A mid-level manager with thirty downstream slayers could expect to make ten grand on a good weekend. The Gates and Mohammed bin Rashid Al Maktoum Foundations were generous. Eugene himself of course was now rich. Wealth that his heir would enjoy.

"Are you okay?" asked Burton. He was one of five roof-mounted slayers wearing glider wings—chaff to draw the vampires' fire before Eugene sailed in to end the Morbius line.

"I'm crying for a number of reasons," said Eugene. Partly it was the Chula hot sauce daubed under his eyes to keep his contacts moist after a sleepless night.

"It's very understandable, young fella," said Burton.

"You're probably going to die, too," said Eugene. "Hope you kissed your loved ones goodbye."

"I did a lot more than that, let me assure you." Burton trained his binoculars on Edna, sitting in a lawn chair on the outskirts of the gathering, on a platform at the top of a kids' zip line. "This soldier knows how to prepare for battle."

"Amen," said Eugene. They fist-bumped.

"Boy, sure is hot up here," said one of the other glider-slayers some time later, when the hillside was packed and a flotilla of boats had anchored in the lake. He clawed at his hoodie sweatshirt, held fast in place by the glider harness.

"Slide over here, I'll help you out of that," said Burton.

"No-no." The slayer wasn't comfortable with any maneuvering on the steep roof.

Eugene, in his Trotskyite cap, black canvas overcoat, black pants, and tall black boots, just chuckled. The sun at 11 a.m. beat down on the south-facing asphalt-shingle roof, bringing the ambient temperature to 105°. His wicking UnderArmour underwear was doing its job.

"Son," said Burton to the miserable sweating glider-slayer. "Compared to the discomfort they tell me I waited in for hours on end with every SEAL mission I was ever on? This is nothing."

"What do you mean, 'they told you'?" said the slayer.

"How the hell would I know how miserable it was?" said Burton. "I was focused on my mission."

Eugene took a bite of ostrich jerky. "I'm glad the world got its money's worth out of you." He had grown to appreciate the crusty old SEAL slayer.

A man stepped up to the microphone. Surveying the scene, he choked up, taking a couple attempts before he could speak. "Welcome, everyone."

Eugene pulled out binoculars. He recognized him—Victor's friend, Tripp.

"Amberly suggested moving Iulia's funeral to today to accommodate more people," said Tripp. "I told her I hoped there would be a big enough turnout to do justice to Iulia's life." He looked at the bank of video cameras in the media pit in front of the stage, simulcasting to the world. "This is close." He nodded through the applause.

A Sikorsky troop transport helicopter swept over the trees and drop-landed on the beach behind the stage, scattering attendees. A small group of vamp men and women disembarked, among them a vamp giant and a little vamp girl. The V-8. They congregated at the rear corner of the stage.

"Balthazar." Looking through his binoculars, Burton pointed at a big paramilitary vamp eyeballing the V-8 and giving orders over a walkie-talkie. "He killed my men in Istanbul." From inside his shirt he pulled out a chain heavy with dog tags. "This is for you, boys."

Eugene tucked the double-pointed stake through the leather loop on his belt. "Don your helmets!"

Burton and the other glider-slayers did so.

"We lost Iulia," said Tripp. "At the rally in Washington D.C. To a slayer's stake."

There was booing, and scattered cheers.

"All I can tell you is …." Tripp choked up. He nodded at calls of encouragement. "The world lost a beautiful woman."

"A beautiful *vampire*," a woman yelled, spurring a cacophony of conflicting opinions.

"Iulia would have been floored to see you all here today," Tripp talked over the noisy crowd. "And she is leaping straight up to Heaven, to know a certain someone is here to celebrate her life. Ladies and gentlemen, human and vampire, I'm pleased to introduce Amberly Foreman."

Amidst a predominantly enthusiastic response, a guy shouted repeatedly, "Vampires rot in hell!"

Eugene was chanting along; and then Amberly took the stage

and he fell in love all over again.

No time for that! He had already made his peace. There was nothing left to debate or reconcile. How could theirs be a romance to last 'til the end of time if one of them was an evil vamp?

He took Burton's binoculars and panned the crowd. A sizeable minority had their hands megaphoned to their mouths, amplifying their angry disapproval. Eugene watched one of them get bit by a rough-dressed vampire woman.

Yes, most of the people booing were slayers. But not exclusively. The times, they were a-changing.

"What the hell?" Burton tapped on the shell of his modified virtual reality helmet. "Cent-com, come in. Cent-com. Victor. Victor?" He wore an expression Eugene didn't like and said, "There's no one there." Burton's butt slipped on the roof and he barely caught himself. As if his butt crack was suddenly pouring sweat. "Jesus H. Christ. We're on our own."

Victor and Barbara hadn't wasted time on the short detour to Bastrop to retrieve the Charger. Now Bane Lake Park was beyond capacity, vehicles jamming the lot and backed up for half a mile, and Doug Sessler's F-350 was a bitch to park. Victor drove across the road and parked in an adjoining field, and they hoofed it.

As they neared the road Victor had to steady Barbara as she faltered. "What's going on?"

She looked at the stubble field. "This is where Jay Hansen died."

"How do you know?"

"I killed him."

"What?"

"Jay attacked me. He and Florence lured me out here. I thought they were going to help me find Amberly. He had Florence try to bite me. He was trying to get back at you."

"Holy shit, Barb." He lowered his voice amidst others walking toward the park. "How did you do it?"

She was trembling. "He wrecked his car right here. He was probably going to die anyway. But I helped him along."

Victor hugged her and a passerby-couple cheered their inter-species love. "Well that is incredible," he whispered. "I'm going to ask you to marry me as soon as all this is over."

She looked at him. "Why wait?"

Victor kissed her. "Barbara, will you re-marry me?"

"I will." They joined the flow heading for the park. "If we get Amberly back."

"That's a prerequisite?"

"I think it probably is," she said.

The rec center was crowded, mostly the elderly taking refuge from the heat. A loudspeaker carried Amberly's voice.

"Today's vote is the biggest in our history," she was saying. "Not just in America, but around the world. Today we decide our future: Either we continue down the path of Peace, or we return to the war, bloodshed, and fear that has torn us apart for millennia."

"She's an incredible public speaker," said Barbara.

"Really impressive," said Victor.

Amberly's voice switched from radio to concert hall as they exited the back side of the rec center. "The world has become more uncertain the past two weeks. The world has become more violent." She stood on a stage at the bottom of the hill, gesturing grandly. Her voice was strident, emotional. "But we must not let that violence sway us. We can't let fear guide our votes!

"And we can't wait for *them*." She jabbed her finger at a cluster of vampires, set apart by pale skin and costume dress, uniforms, ruffles and hats, huddling under a small slice of shade provided by the stage awning. "We can't rely on the so-called V-8. Because then they will *rule* us. If we want to create Peace, it's up to *us*. Not the government! Not so-called leaders! You and me! The people!"

Victor and Barbara threaded their way down the hill. People who had been sitting on lawn chairs and blankets rose to their feet, cheering distractedly while working the voting app on their phones. It made their progress toward the stage easier.

Vampires were everywhere. Maybe a quarter of the crowd. They were evolved, from around the world.

Heels glowed and grated on Victor.

"You're squeezing my hand too tight," said Barbara.

A short, meaty vampire hopped and yelled in a Scottish

brogue, “Peace! We want fookin’ peace!”

He banged into Barbara.

Victor slugged him in the side, just missing his kidney-bean shaped Heel.

The vampire came raging at him, but then realized who Victor was and how close he had just come to dying.

The vampire snarled, “Traitor,” and slipped away.

Barbara spoke in Victor’s ear. “Our daughter. We’re here for Amberly, and nothing else.”

“It starts with the vote today for *your* candidates,” said Amberly. “Not for the slate put forward by Joshua Linger and his friends.” At the edge of the stage she called to the crowd, voice quavering. “And it starts by taking a stand *right now* against the slayers among us!”

Heads rose from their phones. Across the hillside, slayers donned Jaelle’s VR helmets.

“Uh-oh,” said Victor.

“We have a choice,” Amberly shouted. “We can live in a world where we rely on *others* to protect us, and decide where we can go, and who we can see, and what we can do. Or we can protect *ourselves*!” Her voice cracked. “This is the moment we decide! Right *now*! Are we brave enough to *fight* for our families, for our loved ones, for ourselves? Are we going to let these terrorists ruin our lives?”

The response—*No!*—was mixed with slayer team leaders ordering the attack, followed closely by the muffled thump of stakes and bodies colliding.

“This is a war for our freedom!” Amberly screamed. Victor heard her desperation for a beautiful world. “End it! End the terror! Fight for our future!”

Vampires with stakes in their bodies pummeled slayers. They beat slayers with their own helmets and ripped-off limbs. They bit and drank and killed.

Victor retrieved a stray crossbow-fired stake and rammed it into a vampire’s back-of-the-neck Heel, saving a young slayer woman.

Barbara checked the red and black dots on her phone, then turned to look at the rec center roof. “*Now*, Victor. We have to get to Amberly *now*.”

Blood and screams filled the air. Slayers came in droves from the grove of trees, bravely charging blind to the vampires' Heels, firing crossbows and praying for a lucky shot. Victor agonized while Barbara had his arm, forcing him toward the stage.

"Victor!" The Romanian screech hurt his ears. Jaelle was hurrying down the slope with Michael, who lugged an oversized backpack and helmet.

A vampire cut them off. Jaelle raised a stake two-handed and charged.

The vampire blocked her strike and went for her throat, but Victor tackled him and bit his neck. Jaelle tossed him the stake and Victor impaled the armpit Heel, reeking up his senses like a radioactive decaying peach.

Jaelle kicked the vampire in the face while Michael heaved the pack onto Victor's back. "We brought the gizmo."

Victor put his arms through the straps and buckled it in place. Barbara was nowhere to be seen. The machine weighed a hundred pounds, ran hot, and sounded like a jet building for takeoff. He donned the helmet.

The world reset with a jolt across his eyebrows, a rush of sound and a sweeping serenity of vision. He saw the hillside, from above and below, from all angles at once. He smelled (the only word to describe the sweet music resonating behind his eyes) the fear keening through the park. It came from the vampires.

Joyous cries erupted from the slayers, suddenly Sighted.

Jasmine's father Marcos had nearly succumbed to a vampire. Now he drove a stake in his assailant's right lung, his Heel, dead center. He leaped to his feet looking costume-fit, saluted Victor and ran toward more combat.

Amberly stood at the mic, crying. "No. No. Stop."

Victor became disoriented by the sensation of seeing himself—Larry stood before him in a slayer's VR helmet, gripping a stake. Behind him was his mother.

"I hate you," said Larry. "You ruined my life."

"Because I stopped letting you ruin mine." Victor clubbed him alongside the head, knocking Larry off his feet and the helmet off his head, ending the virtual mirror. "I told David I would kill you if I saw you. I meant it." He overpowered him and went for his throat.

"Victor, please, please don't!" Mrs. Cocachello labored to pull him off her son. "Don't hurt him."

Victor shoved her away. "Too late."

"It's *not,*" she beseeched. "It's never too late."

Victor was shocked at how her voice didn't make his skin crawl. He glared at her, but nothing about her face was maddening. Facelift? Extreme makeover? No, it was deeper.

Mrs. Cocachello helped Larry to his feet. "I promise you," she said, "if you spare my son, this is the last you'll see of us."

Larry bent to pick up his stake. His mother slapped his hand and then his face. "You will *listen.*" She pulled him by his shirt, navigating passage through the melee. "Our feud is *over.*" She gave Victor a look he had never seen. Respect. "I've had a change of heart. Thanks to your bite—"

Larry put his hand over her mouth. "Please don't say that."

She patted his hand and led him away.

Amberly screamed and Victor turned to the stage.

Three paramilitary vampires shot him at close range. He went down, unable to breathe, going into shock.

Eugene and Burton watched a monstrous vampire utterly destroy a five-man slayer team. People ran for their lives—for all the horror already unleashed, this was another level of fear. Confronted by this fanged beast, a husband and wife slaying team froze, each wetting themselves, darkening their shorts and running down their legs. The vampire impaled them simultaneously with long black stakes.

"He has a tail," said Eugene. He hadn't known that about Claudius. He broke a sweat and his hands shook.

"The bigger they are," Burton said unconvincingly, mumbling the rest.

Claudius leaped across the hillside and landed in front of a woman. Barbara Thetherson. She was half his size. Claudius put her kicking and screaming under his arm and strode for the stage, destroying victims as he went.

"We go *now,*" Eugene commanded the glider slayers.

This moment had been coming for so long, but now it came too fast. He desperately ran through a checklist—rent paid up, cable cancelled, *Coming Soon: New Management* message on his multi-level marketing websites, *You're Welcome* banner on his slayer site.

His will—everything to Amberly; Barbara as her survivor on the condition she never remarry Victor; otherwise everything to the Little Sisters of the Poor.

Was that even a real organization?

Too late, should have thought of that before. Now he was running down the roof and leaping, wings unfolded, following the glider slayers already flying into the fray.

The wings lifted him onto a breeze that carried toward the lake. Eugene nosed the glider into a hard dive.

One glider slayer appeared to have broken himself on impact. Automatic weapons barked as Balthazar's commando unit shot another two out of the air while dragging Victor's carcass toward the waiting V-8.

Good, thought Eugene, another loose end snipped cleanly off.

Burton flew at Claudius and narrowly missed being staked. The former SEAL slayer was an athlete; he banked hard right, shot one commando and struck another feet-first, straddling and staking him.

Claudius dropped Barbara and hurled a wicked stake, the speed and mass such that an impact crater opened in Burton's chest.

Edna wailed.

Eugene struck Amberly like a 165-lb. bird of prey and carried her off the back of the stage, just like he drew it up.

They locked eyes before slamming into the beach.

Amberly dug a trench in the sand and Eugene tumbled into the water. He threw off the glider pack and unholstered the double-pointed stake.

She was stunned; she looked seriously injured, her beautiful body twisted. Eugene's heart broke.

He needed to do this quickly.

He pinned her arms to her sides with his knees. She raised her head—he was relieved. He didn't want her to die crippled.

"My love," she said.

Her gaze was the one that had won his heart. He put one point to that heart and the other to hers. "You knew it would come to this, didn't you?"

Tears filled her eyes. "Why does it have to be this way?"

The stake moved into them and they both gasped. "Never mourn destiny's decisions," he told her.

Amberly's eyes were so wide. "Sweetheart. Why do men always think their destiny is violence?"

Eugene held her shoulders, bringing them closer together. He struggled to talk. "It's the way of the world."

She closed her eyes, tears spilling. "You're right. I witnessed it. I'm ready to go with you."

Eugene screamed his last and pulled her to him—

Wham! he was knocked flying across the sand. The vampire commando Balthazar rolled through the tackle and leveled his assault rifle. A stake bounced off his thick-skinned neck and another smashed the lens of his Ray-Bans. Eugene brought his mini-crossbow to bear and shot him up his nose hole. Two slayers tackled Balthazar, or at least tried to.

Victor came to. Weird dreams! His soul had left his body to soar over Bane Lake Park. He had seen Barbara in the arms of a horned, tailed demon. There had been no Heavenly light for his soul to fly to, only the flames of Hell burning like scattered forest fires below.

Of course, those fires were Heels and his soul's eye was Jaelle's virtual reality. He still wore the helmet.

Slayers ran past the stage toward the lake, allowing Victor to see the scene with many eyes. Eyes that could once again *see*; Victor watched Jasmine's father Marcos put a bolt in the mastoid process Heel of a burly commando vampire, head bristling with stakes as he toppled to the sand beside Eugene.

On the stage waited the demon vampire, dressed in animal skins, wild-hair, nocturnal eyes. Barbara struggled under its boot. "Kill him, Victor!" she cried. But no Heel was visible. Tripp lay stunned a few feet away.

"The All-Seeing Eye." The demon leered at Victor and stepped harder on Barbara, making her scream in rage and agony. "I see it on your forehead."

Victor struggled to his feet. "Probably just an irritation zit from this helmet." His body buzzed trying to repair the damage from the bullets. The stage was too high, he didn't trust himself to make the jump, so he went around to the stairs. "Take your hoof off my wife."

The demon laughed. "Come to me, Seer. I am the Indestructible One. But I bet you are not."

"I'm willing to find out." Victor charged low; the demon caught him by the throat and threw him off the back of the stage.

Victor crashed-landed into a mob scene, bowling over slayers and vampires all converging on Amberly's distress. He caught a glimpse of her, blood on her front as she was tended to by a vampire.

The demon landed on him. The force was stunning, driving Victor so hard to the sand that his only sensation was black pain filling him head to toe.

Eugene fired a stake-bolt that Claudius caught and whipped back at him. Eugene dodged it with a nifty tuck and roll. "Heel, Vic!"

Claudius laughed. He crushed Victor's head between his palms, buckling the helmet. "I am the super-man. I am the devourer of slayers." With Barbara screaming from the stage and Tripp struggling to hold her back, Jasmine's father Marcos charged. The devil-vamp dropped Victor to grab and bite the spandex-clad slayer, drinking him dry in a gruesome instant.

The vampire helping me takes a stake in the gut and howls in his death throes. I am numb. I watch Kelly Kale stab her finger through the throat of a cute little girl vampire while strangling a snaggle-toothed Asian vampire between her thighs. A slayer has his head ripped off by another of the V-8, Moanmar Saladat, who in turn is staked through the top of his skull by Trubadur, who screams, "Die, Turk!" He screams this again when he ducks a bite and stakes the V-8 vampire Ari Ben-Begin.

The love of my life Eugene runs with slaying stakes in each hand at Claudius and leaps like Neo in the Matrix. He is impaled by the demon vamp. I close my eyes.

The world has collapsed around me and I am unmoved. I was wrong about humans and vampires alike. We are all killers. There can never be peace. I brought us together, only to hasten each other's murders, and I am so ashamed. I put up no struggle when sweet-smelling gore-splattered Kelly Kale kisses my mouth and carries me in her arms into the water.

How many times could Victor die and return? This time, Jaelle's crippled VR had sent him to Hell on a nightmarish river of blood. He pried the helmet off and stood.

The demon-vamp backhanded him. Barbara met him where he landed, and the demon came at them. Tripp moved in front of them with a slaying crossbow. His knees shook.

The little old Romanian Jaelle Skudza jumped on the demon's back. He peeled her off and sank his fangs in her throat. She died cackling.

The demon cast her aside and swatted away Tripp's weapon.

Jaelle sat up. She was still cackling, albeit in some pain.

The demon turned his glowing eyes on her and then grabbed his throat. He struggled unsuccessfully to swallow. His wild hair wilted and his tail tucked between his legs. He went to his knees and said something like "Bolundulie guggleflest" through yellow foam pouring from his mouth.

"The old Warren G. Harding gambit," said Jaelle. She removed the synthetic neck wrap, dripping with poison.

"A classic," said Eugene, lying in the sand on his side so as not to disturb the stake sticking through his hip. He smacked the hand of a slayer who tried to remove it.

Barbara and Tripp helped Victor to his feet. They skirted the demon vampire's last writhings to reach Eugene's side.

"Amberly," said Eugene.

A small outboard motor fired up a few yards offshore and the little dinghy headed toward a 50-foot cabin cruiser on the lake. A beautiful blond was at the tiller. Trubadur Maistru stood in the bow.

Eugene's feet kicked up sand as he grabbed his glider pack and the double-pointed stake, dodged Victor and ran past the stage, screaming in pain.

Tripp stripped off his shirt, shucked his boots, peeled off tight jeans—which meant he was naked. He ran into the lake until it was deep enough to swim, like a naked Michael Phelps, arms slicing and feet frothing and white ass mooning.

Victor could not swim. "Shit." He took off after Eugene,

Barbara running with him.

The hillside was out of a Civil War battlefield, bodies at terrible angles, missing limbs, utterly abandoned by Life, some decomposing. They found Winnie Linciome standing over the old slayer Edna, on her knees beside Bad-Ass Burton, deceased, a stake buried in a gaping chest wound. He wore a glider.

"Winnie," said Victor, panting. "Ma'am."

"He was a good man," said Edna.

"We're sorry for your loss," said Barbara.

"He was a helluva man," said Edna a little louder, scratching the corpse's buzzcut like he might have liked when he was alive. "That includes being a *helluva* lover."

"I'm sure he was," said Victor.

"Why?!" Edna wailed with fists thrust toward the heavens.

"We really need that jetpack," Victor told Winnie.

"Come here, dear," said Winnie, grim-lipped. "Let me comfort you." He pulled Edna to her feet and was embraced and groped. Victor and Barbara worked the glider free and Victor donned it, buckling it as he ran up the hill. He was gasping for breath by the time he pushed through the rec center door.

"Skinny slayer with a jet pack?" he asked the roomful of wounded, shell-shocked survivors and their attending paramedics. A man with a bandaged neck pointed at the front door.

A ladder lay on top of the shrubs. Victor manhandled it against the gutter and climbed.

The roof was stupid-steep. Sweat wet his hands and nervous legs jittered the ladder as he transferred to the roof and crawled up. He came over the peak as Eugene flew away.

The glider pack had two handles, one with a button. Victor depressed it. A fan whirred and propelled him laterally along the peak.

"Oh f-f-f-f-" He skidded on his knees and bounced on his chest and somehow regained his feet in time to turn, careen down the roof, and launch flying toward the lake.

He streaked through the air 15 feet above and parallel to the slope. Victor screamed and craned his neck up. He buzzed the stage, the onlookers on the beach, Barbara swimming away from shore, and then finally Tripp, arms looking leaden and near to drowning.

The getaway dinghy was tethered to the cruiser; Eugene was landing on the deck. Victor's fan was too small, he too heavy; he splash-landed 20 yards short.

Eugene streaked toward the cruiser, inches above the water, banking straight up at the last second to stall the glider and drop cat-like on the deck.

Trubadur ran out of the cabin and tackled him against the bulkhead, cracking the glider and dislodging Claudius's stake from his hip.

Trubadur fought to bite him. "Is it wrong to suck on your great-great-whatever's neck?"

Eugene stabbed him repeatedly with the stake until Trubadur collapsed.

"Yes." He shucked the broken glider on his way to kicking open the cabin door.

Kelly Kale was bent over Amberly, who was lying on the couch. Kale turned to him, blood on her lips. Amberly's throat bore the vampire's bloody marks.

"Oh, thank God," said Eugene.

"No," cried Amberly, distracting Kale as Eugene charged with the double-pointed stake. Kale instinctively shielded her former Heel, her womb.

The stake pierced her chest.

Eugene kept his legs churning, picking her up and into the wall. His end of the stake impaled his heart and slammed into the steel plate harnessed tightly to his back, which served as a hammer that drove the stake fully through this latest and final incarnation of Morbius, pinning them both to the wall.

Amberly screamed and tried to pull them apart. Eugene put a death grip on Kelly Kale, the Morbius, who tried weakly to push him away. They would not be separated.

"I'm so glad," Eugene whispered. "Honey, you're set. I left you all my MLMOs."

"What?" Amberly was desperate, crying. "What, baby?"

Eugene's brow furrowed. "Pyramids."

Trubadur staggered into the cabin. "Morbius." He ran to the gruesome coupling and thrust his throat upon Kale's mouth.

"Bite me, Kelly! Bite me, God damn you!"

Amberly smashed his head with a cheesy but sturdy lighthouse lamp, and then used it to pulverize Kelly Kale's face until the light in her eyes winked out.

Trubadur lay moaning on the floor.

"Eugene." Amberly held his face. "Eugene, my love, please don't leave me." She kissed his beautiful cheeks. "It's done, Morbius is dead, you did your job. Sweetie, please *please* stay here with me."

Eugene's eyes opened. He struggled to turn his head to look at her. "I've known you're special, since I saw you with your skirt hiked up to show me some leg."

Amberly sobbed. "You're my hero."

"You're mine," he whispered and drew his final breath. "Take the cure, okay?"

His knees went soft and he slid off the stake. Amberly guided his body to the floor.

"No no no," she cried.

He was gone.

Her fault. All of it.

Eugene, and so many others. She couldn't live with herself. Everyone had trusted her, and it had all been a lie. She couldn't live after causing so much death. She went to Kelly Kale's skewered body and put the point of the stake in her own bloody wound, in the entry Eugene had so wisely started. She leaned into it.

Trubadur pulled her away and crushed her in his embrace, bent her back and exposed her throat. "*Draga tatei*. Sweet, sweet Stela. This is our destiny."

Barbara caught Victor at the cabin cruiser. He was a terrible swimmer. He pushed her up into the tethered dinghy and likewise she helped haul him out of the water. From there they climbed the boarding ladder onto the cruiser's deck. Victor wrenched free a thin aluminum tube from the fractured frame of Eugene's glider. Blood droplets on the deck chilled their hearts and led them into the cabin.

"This is our destiny," Trubadur was saying, Amberly in his arms.

Barbara rushed him screaming, "Pervert!"

Trubadur caught her by the throat and lifted her off the floor.

His Heel throbbed—that's the word that occurred to Victor—between his legs.

Victor put his all into the slaying strike and planted the pipe deep into Trubadur Maistru's groin.

The ancient vampire gave the pipe a couple tugs. He had a moment of clarity and looked Victor in the eye.

"What a raw deal," said Trubadur.

"Tell me about it," said Victor.

Both hands on the pipe, Trubadur fell over and died.

PULLING FANGS

Absolutely the most beautiful Houston day of the year when they received the call from Tripp.

The cure is ready.

Victor, Barbara and Amberly packed their bags and left Doug Sessler's hardened site for the last time.

Slaying had slowed to a trickle over the two months since Iulia's funeral. Vampires were turning themselves in, the unevolved to be cured on the spot. The evolved had to take a number, receiving Temporary Blood-Drinker cards to ward off eager slayers.

Slayers were wise to ask; the anti-slaying laws had been repealed, but one could still face a civil suit for offing a card-carrying vampire.

Amberly had such a card in her purse. Victor and Barbara didn't trust a piece of paper to protect her. Sentiment had turned against vampires, and Amberly in particular. Every screen, big and little, played grisly scenes from Bane Lake Park and the rally in D.C., from other gatherings, from bars and dark alleys and homes, footage of vampires in their heyday feasting on humans. Each new video inspired outrage and more videos.

Humans had been silent victims. Now, the fear was gone and the shame dissolved in the worldwide social media mutual support group.

Vampires were branded evil, and Amberly their evil queen. Victor and Barbara had initially welcomed interviews (always from "an undisclosed location") as a means to get the word out: Their daughter was a victim of the true devilish force, Trubadur Maistru. They painted him as the real Morbius and Amberly as his innocent pawn.

The interviewers also asked about Eugene. Victor always pointed out the blood relation to Trubadur. Barbara always described Eugene as a hero.

In the broadcasts, the Thethersons always stressed that Amberly was no longer Morbius; the interviewers always noted that Amberly remained a vampire. So Victor and Barbara now refused all requests.

Every few days, Victor made the trip to Bastrop to meet Nurse Marcella, always bearing bags of blood. Amberly had no appetite; she was sustained by IV infusion.

The opportunity to be immersed in Jaelle's VR-Sighted slaying was a blessing for Victor. An escape from his worries for the future. And he wouldn't admit it, but even worrying about Amberly was a relief; it pushed down the fears for his own future.

Tripp met them at the Longevity Labs entrance. He hugged Barbara for some time. Victor tried to usher Amberly past them, but Tripp grabbed his arm and hugged him fiercely.

"Little Thethy." Tripp held out his hands to Amberly. She relented and was hugged. "It is so good to see you," he said.

She shook her head and tried to pull away, but there was no resisting Tripp's bear hug.

"I love you Amberly, you know that? The cure, I made that for you, you know *that*? Not for anyone else. All for you. The past few months, all for you."

The vampirism or the mourning for Eugene, one or both, had exhausted her ability to cry. She pressed her face into Tripp's chest and hugged him back.

"The least I could do after my swimming exhibition." Tripp ruefully mocked himself, looking to exorcise the bitter memory. "They had to rescue me in a pedal-paddle boat."

Amberly stood on tiptoe to kiss his cheek. "I know you're always here for me."

"Welcome to our last two bloodsuckers!" Jaelle called from a doorway down the hall. "Finally, we pull your fangs."

"She wasn't on my invite list," Tripp apologized, shooting Jaelle a dirty look. "Winnie's plus-one." He kept his arm around Amberly on their way to the treatment room.

"This place looks better than ever," said Barbara.

"Iulia made most of this possible," said Tripp. "And now emergency resources have been pouring in. Three other labs assisted me with the development of the cure."

Barbara touched his back. "Did Iulia's research help?"

"Made all the difference."

"She was really wonderful," said Amberly.

Life in her voice was music to Victor's ears.

"You would have been beautiful together," she said.

"Thank you, darling." Tripp led them past Jaelle into the treatment room where Winnie waited.

"Jaelle, you hard-ass Gypsy queen," said Winnie. "If Victor wasn't so in love with your meditation tank, you would be his final victim."

She crossed her arms. "My hatred for the vampire is the only reason we are all alive here today."

Winnie winked. "We can thank every one of us in this room. We also need to give thanks to one who cannot be here. Amberly, I am so very sorry. Eugene was a great young man."

Victor waited out what he thought was an unreasonable length of time for hugs and condolences. "So you're confident this will work?"

Tripp gave Amberly a last squeeze and went to his computer. "It worked on our ten guinea pigs."

"Evolved vampires who were less than willing to be cured," Winnie clarified. "Two of them from the so-called V-8. Boris Dostonov and Katanze Utz. Katanze tried to hari-kari his own Heel. We found him with a samurai sword in his back. Severed his spine before he could hit the kidney."

"Meanwhile," said Tripp, "big bad Boris was trying to kill one of our other potential guineas, Joshua Linger. Feds, the state, Houston, everyone was hunting for them. NSA got there first." He took Amberly's hand and sat her in a recliner equipped for the procedure and pushed a buzzer on the wall. "They gave us Boris."

"What about Linger?" said Barbara.

"I have a reliable contact at the NSA," said Winnie. "One of the few on our side who survived the purge. They have no intention of letting him go. Or curing him."

"I'm not comfortable with that," said Barbara.

"They're holding him in suburban D.C.," said Victor. "Thanks to Jaelle's VR, I've been monitoring the light of his Heel. I would describe it as flickering."

"They say he was actually begging for a cure," said Winnie.

"I agree with you, Barbara," said Jaelle. "They should slay him."

Nurse Marcella entered the room. "Well looky here," she greeted Victor. "Back for one last treatment." She gave Barbara a brief hands-free hug. The sight of Amberly made her stop. "Oh dear, there you are. Even more lovely in person."

Amberly acknowledged the compliment with a polite smile.

"It's an honor to help you," said Nurse Marcella. Victor couldn't have coached her any better. Amberly was in such a dark place; they were thankful the three of them had been holed up together in Sessler's bunker. They didn't trust her to be alone.

"To finish the testimonial," said Tripp. "Dostonov, Utz and the eight other little guinea pigs are under constant monitoring. It's been a week. I can tell you with six-sigma confidence, they are cured."

"That's as good as it gets in our profession," said Winnie.

"So don't be worried," Tripp told Amberly, who was grimacing as Marcella put in her IV. "You will be human again."

"Maybe that's what worries her." Victor stood back from the group. He was sweating, cold and clammy. "Everyone here assumes we can't wait. You assume we feel the same way about this as you do. Or maybe you just don't care."

Barbara stayed at Amberly's side, listening to him.

"It isn't *bloodlust* that defines us," said Victor. "Has that ever been an issue for either of us?" Barbara came to stand with him. "You don't understand how this so-called curse made us feel," he said. "I've never felt this confident. I've never been this at-ease with myself. I've never been this focused or energized."

"Surely you can attribute some of that to the meditation tank," said Winnie. "Don't you at least think it will help you maintain that state of mind?"

"I don't know. I don't know—do you?"

"Not 99%-plus," Winnie admitted.

Victor scoffed. "Not even close."

"Vic," said Tripp. "What choice do you have?"

"None. Which makes it worse."

"Don't lie to yourself," said Jaelle. "Yes, it *is* about the bloodlust. It is about the power. It is about our *fear*. The vampire isn't here for himself, for his own benefit. He is here to rule us."

Barbara backed Victor further from the group before he could react. She put her fingertips on his throat and spoke for his ears only. "If it's you and me you're worried about—"

"Of course it is."

"I'm not." She gazed into his eyes. "Not at all. We went so far south for so long. I didn't know you anymore. And then maybe it was your vampirism that brought me back. But that wasn't you, either. Not completely. I couldn't have lived with that, either." She moved in tighter. "What I see now, what's in your eyes and coming out your pores? That's you. That's the man I fell in love with. And it's not the fangs. It's all Victor."

He put his hands on her waist, anchoring them together. "I'm happy to hear that."

She touched thumb and forefinger to his skinny fangs. "Some pointy enamel is all you're going to lose."

He wished he were that confident. He prayed she was right.

Barbara stretched on tip-toe to his ear and squeezed his cock. "And we have a lot to gain."

He kissed her and drew blood on her lips, one last time. They returned to the others.

The treatment had begun for Amberly. She lay back in the recliner with the gene therapy cure flowing into her veins, eyes closed, face dissolved in misery.

He had suspected they might need to move from Houston. But there was nowhere in the world Amberly wouldn't be recognized. They planned to dye her hair, shorten it, restyle it. They considered a nose job, even offered to throw in lips; Amberly had always complained hers were too thin.

In the end, she went for none of it. She decided it would be worse if she were caught trying to hide.

Post-treatment, they remained sequestered at the Labs for monitoring and protection. Early in the second week, Amberly slipped out. Victor and Barbara fretted—she had refused to talk about how she was feeling, spending practically all her time sleeping, depressed.

She had returned that night with plans to start a foundation for peace. Two of her friends' families who had lost loved ones in the brief, bloody war—including Jasmine's widowed mother—had already pledged a portion of their life insurance proceeds to the new foundation.

"Some people hate me," Amberly had reported matter-of-factly after they retrieved Porkie the Morkie and returned home. "Most of them don't. People my age want to help. They're excited to make this happen."

Barbara had kissed her while they were both kissed by Porkie. "That is wonderful. I hope you'll still apply for college."

"If it makes sense," Amberly had said. "I'm going to call it the Eugene Foreman Peace Foundation."

"Really terrible name," said Victor. "Honestly. Nothing against him. He just had a terrible name."

Amberly had made a face at him and carried Porkie up to her room.

It was now three minutes later, and Barbara was kissing him. "I'm really excited about your cure." She touched him. "I'm glad to see you are, too."

Victor had been five times to a meditation iso-tank that Winnie had set up in rented space. The scientist and Jaelle planned a worldwide chain of rehab clinics centered on the device.

His mind felt good. It felt right. Victor was encouraged. He was cautiously excited about the future.

But he was more than a little nervous about sex. "What if I die?"

Barbara closed the bedroom door and kissed him onto the bed, pulling off his and her shirts. "I'll die if we don't."

"If I have to do this to save your life," Victor mumbled with her nipple in his mouth.

She pulled down his pants and slapped his cock.

"Ow! Fuck, Barb. We don't need the rough stuff now."

"Says who?" She nuzzled his balls and then squeezed them.

"Agh!" Victor clamped his hand over his mouth. "You crazy bitch! Do you want Amberly to hear us?"

She looked up from tonguing his cock. “What, we want her living here forever?”

The End

ALSO BY HARRIS GRAY

The Vampire Vic Trilogy
Vampire Vic
Vampire Vic^2 Morbius Reborn

The Imperfect Compromise – Hillary and Trump: One Year to Share the Presidency and Remake the Election System

Java Man

ABOUT THE AUTHORS

Harris Gray recently published *The Imperfect Compromise*, the popular voter's guide to the 2016 presidential election that hit #3 on Amazon's political fiction list. They have been collaborating since Allan moved to Castle Rock, Colorado and found author heaven, aka Crowfoot Valley Coffee. Jason has since added the Crowbar, which is like discovering that Heaven serves a nice selection of premium craft beers. The authors are currently fictionalizing Jason's days in a grunge-era Seattle band.

The website: harrisgray.com
The marketplace: amazon.com/Harris-Gray
The tweets: twitter.com/harrisandgray
The posts: facebook.com/HarrisGrayAuthor
The sharing: plus.google.com/u/3/102066651638902173967
The community: www.goodreads.com/harrisgray

www.ingramcontent.com/pod-product-compliance
Lightning Source LLC
Chambersburg PA
CBHW061307170626
46817CB00001B/83

* 9 7 8 0 9 8 8 8 9 5 7 9 9 *